Killing Ground

BY GERALD SEYMOUR

Harry's Game
The Glory Boys
Kingfisher
The Harrison Affair
The Contract
Archangel
In Honor Bound★
Field of Blood
A Song in the Morning
An eye for an eye
Condition Black★
The Journeyman Tailor★
The Fighting Man★
The Running Target★
The Heart of Danger★
Killing Ground★

★Published by HarperPaperbacks

GERALD SEYMOUR

Killing Ground

HarperPaperbacks
A Division of HarperCollinsPublishers

HarperPaperbacks
A Division of HarperCollins*Publishers*
10 East 53rd Street, New York, N.Y. 10022-5299

A hardcover edition of this book was published in Great Britain
in 1997 by Bantam Press, a division of Transworld Publishers Ltd.

ISBN 0-06-101195-9

Printed in the United States of America

First HarperPaperbacks printing: April 1997

Library of Congress Cataloging-in-Publication Data

Seymour, Gerald.
  Killing ground / Gerald Seymour.
    p. cm.
  ISBN 0-06-101195-9 (hc)
  I. Title.
PR6069.E734K55 1997
823'.914—dc21   96-51178
                    CIP

Visit HarperPaperbacks on the World Wide Web at
http://www.harpercollins.com/paperbacks

97 98 99 00 CC 10 9 8 7 6 5 4 3 2 1

For Gillian, Nicholas and James

The extremely dangerous prospect of a homogenized mode of criminal organization, in which a point is reached where one can no longer distinguish between the methods of the Yakusa, the Chinese Triads and Cosa Nostra, would create a kind of global mafia, and I ask myself how it could possibly be opposed . . .

Judge Giovanni Falcone

(Judge Falcone, with his wife and three police bodyguards, was murdered on 23 May 1992 at Capaci, northwest Sicily, by La Costa Nostra.)

PROLOGUE

MORE WINE WAS POURED.

More salad was offered.

More frequent apologies for the late arrival of the Host were given.

It was a good wine that the Guest drank, and a good salad of sliced tomato and country mushrooms and fennel that the Guest speared with his fork, and good apologies for the unavoidable delay in the arrival of the Host. The suspicion of the Guest that was inherent in his nature, a rock in his life, was lulled. He drank, he reached a thin ribbed hand across the table toward the water bottle. He scooped pasta from the plate in front of him between his dried and narrow lips, then more tomato, and there was a moment when the sauce of the pasta and the juice of the tomato dribbled down from his mouth and onto his chin where the poorly shaved gray stubble caught the sauce and the juice. The Guest wiped hard at his chin with the napkin suspended from the collar of his silk shirt below a scrawny and emaciated throat. He felt at ease.

It was a fine apartment to which the Guest had been invited. The dining table of polished mahogany was in an alcove off the main living area. There was a shined floor of dark wood blocks below him. He had walked to the table from the living area across a thick woven carpet from Iran. He thought the pictures on the walls behind him and in the living area to be of quality and costly but they were too modern for his taste. At the entrance to the alcove, set on a wire pedestal, was a headless statue in stone of a naked woman, maybe Roman or maybe a Greek antiquity and the Guest would not have known the difference, but the shape of the plump lower stomach stirred old thoughts in the mind of the Guest and he leered at the statue that was a meter high and wondered if the missing face of the naked woman would have carried eyes that were inviting or coyly lowered. Opposite him, across the table from him, were two men that he did not know, except that they were the chosen men of his Host. It was hard for the Guest to see the faces of the men because behind them the curtain drapes were pulled back and the faces of the men were shadowed. The Guest could not see the detail of the faces but he could see beyond them the high buildings of the city that were misted from the low cloud that brought a light spitted rain onto the plate windows and that masked the high ground of the mountains of Pellegrino to his right and Castellacio ahead of him and Cuccio to his left. It was a mistake on the part of the Guest to have allowed himself to be sat at a table where he looked into the light, and a double mistake to have agreed to take a chair that put his back to the door of the main living area. And rare for the Guest, in the seventy-third year of his life, to have put aside the suspicion for which he was famed.

The Guest cleaned the last of the pasta sauce of cream with garlic and closely chopped ham with a piece of bread roll. He belched as was his habit when he had enjoyed food. He drank. He belched again as was his habit when he had enjoyed wine. He pushed the plate away. He coughed from deep in his throat and his face colored at the convulsion and the phlegm came from far down in his throat until it settled as spittle on his lips, and he wiped his mouth with the napkin. He was reassured, he could hear the indistinct and soft words of his grandson murmuring from the kitchen beyond the door of the main living area. He was reassured because his grandson was armed as was his driver who would be sitting alert inside the hallway of the apartment and watching the outer door.

One of the men opposite him, the younger man of the pair, perhaps because he had been a waiter in a restaurant or a *pizzeria* before the trust had been granted him, came around the table and expertly cleared away the pasta bowl and the salad plate, and then his companion's bowl and plate and then his own. Done with quiet discretion, while the older man of the pair questioned the Guest on the great events of past times. The questions were asked with respect and probed at the unveiling of years long gone. The Guest warmed to the questions and to the respect with which they were asked. A telephone rang in the living area. He had ever seen, as a child, Cesare Mori, Mussolini's man on the island? The older man ignored the telephone. Had he ever met, as a teenager, Don Calogero Vizzini who had made the deal with the American invaders on the island? The bell of the telephone was cut. Had he ever known, as a young Man of Honor, Salvo Giuliano, the bandit who had for four years evaded so many thousands of the army and *carabinieri*?

In short, guttural answers the Guest talked of Mori and Don Calo and Giuliano.

The younger man was back in the dining alcove and placed a plate of thin sliced veal strips in front of the Guest. The Host had rung, a few minutes more, very close, and his most sincere apologies. The Guest's glass was filled, wine not water. The Guest stretched back far in his memory . . .

Yes, once he had seen Mori drive through Agrigento, bad times, with an escort of the bastard Black Shirts, Fascist thugs. His lip curled in disgust . . .

Yes, several times he had been taken by his father to Villalba and he had stood outside the door of the room where his father had talked with Don Calogero Vizzini and he could tell his listeners that Don Calo was indeed an artist in the control of men. His eyes lit, as if he talked of genius . . .

Yes, twice he had been in the mountains above Montelepre to tell Giuliano what was required from him, but the man was a fool and the man was arrogant and the man outlived his use. He made so small a gesture, but the gesture was of his weathered and nicotine stained index finger running across the sunken width of his throat . . .

He had known them all. The Guest was of the old world. It was right that he and his memories should be treated with respect. It was usual, in the lifestyle of the Guest, that he should sleep in the afternoon, having concluded his business of the day in the morning. Perhaps because of the wine, perhaps because of the quality of the meal served to him, perhaps because of the flattery shown him when he was requested to dig into that well of memories, the Guest did not feel any sense of resentment that the business of the day would be postponed until the time when he would usually have slept. It was important business. Had it not been important business then the Guest would not have considered traveling with his driver and his grandson across the island from his temporary and loaned home in the hills close to Canicatti. It was important business because it involved the division of interests between himself, the Guest, and the man with whom he sought to make an understanding, the Host. It was important business because it was necessary for the future that hostilities of the past should be put aside.

The Guest gulped at the slices of veal. He did not seem to notice now that the pair of men opposite him merely toyed with their food, only sipped at their wine. He liked to talk of Giuliano, he was happy to find younger men who showed an interest in the former times and were not anxious only about the present, he enjoyed the chance to explain how a man had risen too fast for his own good which was anathema to the Guest who had clawed his way over a period of half a century to control of the southern part of the island. And he was relaxed, and he was shown true respect, and the wine flowed in the tired old veins of his body. He heard the shuffle of feet across the thick carpet.

The Guest broke the flow of his speech.

The Guest turned in his high backed chair as he sucked from his fork the last of the thin sliced veal.

The Guest saw his Host.

The smile of helplessness, the shrug from the wide shoulders indicating matters beyond a man's control, the gesture of the thickened hands of obsequious apology. He waved his fork, no need for apology. In truth, he almost regretted that the opportunity was gone to talk further of the bandit, Salvatore Giuliano, and the death of the bandit, the end of the bandit who had gone beyond the time when he was of use, so long ago. He had to tilt his head to follow the movement of his Host who came so quietly from the main living area and into the dining alcove. It was four years since he had last met in person with his Host. He thought the man a little shorter than he had remembered him and there was a paleness in the cheeks and upper lip and chin that a razor had smoothed as if it were a child's face. The smile lit the face. He laid down his fork. He took the hands in his, broad rough hands in his own thin rough hands. Their hands gripped, their fingers clasped, and he felt the raw strength of the hands as if they bonded in friendship. There were some who said, others who knew him, that his Host had cruel eyes, clear blue, but to the Guest those eyes seemed only to show respect. His *consigliere* had told him, before he had left Canicatti, near Agrigento early that morning, that his Host had a way of looking at people that struck fear into everybody, a light in his eyes which silenced everybody near him, and then he had called his *consigliere* an idiot shit, and now he saw that respect that he believed due to him. The Guest coughed again, belched again, and yawned, and his Host broke the grip of their hands and their cheeks brushed in friendship. They were equals. The Guest assumed that a similar meal would be taken with the family from Catania. They were equals because they each had control of territory and resources and men. The time of the single rule of Riina, the time of the killings and massacres, the time of fear, was over.

The hands of his Host rested on the Guest's bony shoulders, he could no longer see his face nor against the light from the window could he see the faces of the men across the table from him. He did not want to be on the road to Canicatti after darkness. He wanted the business done, the understanding sealed between equals. He felt the hands dig into the bones of his shoulders. The business to be done was both a matter of the division of interests, and also the guarantee of consultation between the family of Catania in the east and the family of Agrigento in the south and the family of his Host in the north and west. Business to be done, business to be sealed. The hands of his Host were off his shoulders. They were close to his ears, first stretched out so that the joints of the fingers cracked as they flexed, then clenched together and from the side of his vision he saw the whiteness of the knuckles as they clenched. He thought that both the family of Catania and the family of his Host needed his arsenal of experience. He thought they required the experience gained from a long lifetime. He was the day laborer's son who had never lost the common touch of the land and of poverty. He was needed. He belched. He was so relaxed. He started to twist in his chair to face his Host. He did not see the quick movement as his Host made the sign of the cross. He . . .

The fingers and thumbs of the hands of the Host were around the throat of the Guest.

The men across the table from the Guest were rising from their chairs.

Against the ears of the Guest were the cuffs of the Host's jacket, ordinary material.

The Guest saw the coarse skin of the back of the Host's hands. The hands were locked on his throat.

The Guest struggled fiercely. He lashed out with his legs, as if he were attempting to kick himself clear of the hold of the fingers and the weight of the hands and the pressure of the thumbs. The chair on which he had sat lurched backward. He was sliding on his back across the wood block floor of the dining alcove, but always the strength was in the hands around his throat. The croaked cry for help was deep in his chest and stifled while his eyes, staring and bulging, searched for the door of the main living area through which his grandson and his driver should burst with their guns, and they did not come . . . Not to know, in his kicking throes, that a stabbing knife had taken the life of his grandson in the apartment's kitchen, that his driver was gagged and trussed in the hall beside the outer door. Not to know that five men had come with his Host into the apartment . . .

The Guest fought for his life until the will to resist was lost in his old body.

He was on the carpet. He was choking for breath and a little of the pulp from the tomatoes of his salad ran from his lips onto the carpet, and the piss flow came on his upper thigh and into the cloth of his trousers. The face above him, another old face, but flabby and jowled, had the sweat of effort running on it, and there was laughter at the mouth of the face and there was cold light in the eyes of the face. One of the men from across the table held the Guest's sparse hair, the other of the men from across the table sat on his legs, both made it easier for the Host whose hands never loosened their hold and whose thumbs gouged down onto his windpipe.

It helped him not at all that as a child he had seen the Fascist Cesare Mori, that as a teenager he had met Don Calogero Vizzini, that as a young Man of Honor he had carried messages to the bandit Salvatore Giuliano . . . Nothing could help him. He seemed to hear the caution of his *consigliere* in the dawn in the hills above Canicatti . . . He tried to shout that his Host was a shit, cunt, bastard . . . He wished that he could warn the man who was his friend, the head of the family of Catania . . . He knew it could last for ten minutes, the strangulation of a man. He knew it because he had done it. The sweat beads fell down from his Host's face and onto his own, and into his own gasping mouth, and he thought he could taste the salt of the sweat. He did not try to cry for mercy. Those last moments, before consciousness slipped from him, he tried only to maintain his dignity. If he kept his dignity then he would have also the respect . . . the need for respect was so great. He saw the face above him, he heard the cackling of the laughter and the grunted effort. He was slipping . . . It was right that the old man from Canicatti should die at the hand of his equal. That was the mark of the respect in which he was held. He was gone . . .

All the men bent over the still figure on the carpet from Iran laughed and sweated and gasped to soak the air back into their lungs. It was a joke. It was to be laughed at, the way they had fallen on the floor and slid across the wood blocks like kids playing. And to be laughed at too was the way that the old goat's tongue had come half out of his throat, and his eyes half out of their sockets.

The rain beat on the windows of the apartment. The mist shrouded the mountains above Palermo.

The body of a rival was roped in the old way, the way used to throttle a goat, the way of the *incaprettamento,* so that when the stiffness of death gripped the body, it would already be small with the rope tied to the ankles and hooking them up toward the small of the Guest's spine and then reaching up to the back of the Guest's throat. No symbol, just convenience. It was convenient to use the old way because then it would be easier to lift the stiffened body into the boot of a car . . . The body of the Guest would leave the apartment via the service lift from the kitchen to the underground car park beneath the block, and the body of the grandson, and the driver who was tied and bound and gagged and who had the terror in his eyes because he loved life more than respect.

As the lift was called, as the men came from the kitchen to clean the furniture of the borrowed apartment of fingerprints and forensic evidence, and to wipe the vomited tomato dribble from the carpet, and to swab the urine from the marble flooring of the hallway, the Host breathed hard as if the effort required to strangle a man taxed his strength to its limit, and the words came in panted spurts as he repeated what should be done to his Guest's driver. His Guest had been offered, in life and death, respect. The grandson of his Guest was a necessary cadaver, a matter without emotion. The driver of his Guest, strapped and gagged tight faced a bad death, a bad death for a bad remark made seventeen months before by the driver, a bad remark in a bar about a Man of Honor, a bad remark that had been relayed and was long remembered.

Later, when the two bodies and the live prisoner were taken in a car and a van from the underground car park, the Host massaged the numbness from his hands.

Later, when the two bodies and the live prisoner were carried in the wet dusk from the vehicles to a small launch moored to a quayside west of the city, the Host tapped on a Casio calculator the figures and percentages and profit margins for a deal that would send 87 kilos of refined heroin to the United States of America.

Later, when the two bodies and the live prisoner were weighted with crab pots filled with stones and were slipped into the dark waters of the Golfo di Palermo, the Host satisfied himself that the apartment was cleansed of evidence and let himself out of the main door and locked it behind him.

He disappeared into the night that caught the city, was lost in it from view.

1

"DO WE HAVE TO HAVE THAT DAMN thing on?"

"God, you found a voice. Hey, that's excitement."

"All I'm saying—do we have to have the damn heater thing on?"

"Just when I was going to get wondering whether the Good Lord had done something violent with your tongue, knotted it—yes, I like to have the heater on."

It was the last day of March. They'd left the three lane highway far behind. They'd turned off the two lane highway long ago, and a bit after they'd cut through the town of Kingsbridge. When the guy driving had dumped the road map on his lap and told him to start the navigation bit, they'd left the last bit of decent track. The guy driving used the word "lane" for what they were on now, and the map called it "minor road." The lane, the minor road, seemed to him to coil round the fields that were behind the high hedges that had been brutalized the past autumn by cutting equipment and had not yet taken on the spring's foliage. The high hedges and the fields beyond seemed dead to him. They bent round the angles of the fields, they dropped with the flow of the lane into dips and climbed small summits, and when they reached the small summits he could see in the distance the gray blue of the sea and the white caps where the wind caught it. It was not raining now. It had rained most of the drive out of London, then started to ease when they were just short of Bristol, then stopped when they were east of Exeter. It was four hours since they had left London, and he was quiet because he was already fretting that the guy driving had made a mess of the equation of distance and speed and time. There was a certain time when he wanted to get there, to the end of this goddam track, and he didn't care to be early and he didn't care to be late.

He asked, sour, "What sort of place is this going to be?"

The man driving looked ahead. "How the hell should I know?"

"I was just asking."

"Listen, man, because I work out of London doesn't mean that I know every corner of the country—and the heater stays on."

There was no rain, and the narrow tarmacadam surface of the lane was dry, but there was wind. The wind that made white caps on the gray-blue sea ahead, tossed at the few trees that had survived the winter gales that came hard at the Devon coastline and blustered the flight of the gulls above. If they hadn't had the heater on, if they'd had the window of the Cherokee Jeep down, then he didn't reckon he'd have been cold. His way of sulking, making his protest, was to wipe with his shirtsleeve the condensation of the inside of the door window beside him and on the inside of the windscreen in front of him. He wiped hard, a small release for his stress, but as a way of clearing the condensation it was lousy work and the window beside him and the windscreen ahead of him were left smeared. He heard the guy who was driving hiss annoyance beside him. He bent his head and studied the map and won no help from it. His finger followed the thin red line of the lane across empty space toward the blue-printed mass of the sea and on the map there were names over the sea like Stoke Point and Bigbury Bay and Bolt Tail. He looked down at his watch. Shit. He looked back at the map and the page spread across his knee was harder to see because the evening was closing down, and the width of the Cherokee Jeep filled the lane and the cut dark hedges were high above the windows. Shit. Goddam it . . .

The brakes went on hard. He was jolted in his belt. It was his way, whenever he was riding as passenger in a vehicle that went to emergency stop, to drop his right hand to his belt, it was the instinct from long ago, but riding as passenger in a lane in the south of Devon in the west of England meant that his belt was empty, carried no holster. And his way also, and his instinct, at the moment of an emergency stop to swivel his head fast, the pony tail of his hair flying, to check the scope behind for fast reverse and the J procedure turn. He grinned, the first time anything of a smile had creased his mouth since they had left London, a rueful twitch of his lips, because he reckoned the guy driving would have seen his right hand drop to his belt and seen the swift glance of his eyes behind. They had come over the summit of a hill, then there had been a hard right turn, then there had been the cattle herd in the lane. The big lights of the Cherokee Jeep speared into the eyes of the lumbering and advancing cows. A small dog, seeming to run on its stomach, came out from under the cattle's hooves and it was leaping, barking, growling at the radiator grille of the Cherokee Jeep. Behind the dog, behind the cattle, down below them, were the lights of the community that was their destination and beyond the lights and stretching away, limitless, was the sea. The breath hissed in his throat. He wondered what time the letter post came round to a place like this, reached the community down at the end of the lane beside the sea—some time that day, but not early, was the best answer he'd been able to get before they'd left London. And he wondered what time a young woman finished teaching the second year—some time in the middle of the afternoon, but she might stay on to check that day's work and to prepare for the next day's classes, and he had to add on to "sometime in the middle of the afternoon" how long it would take a young woman to ride a low power scooter back home along the lanes from the town behind them. It was important, when the letter was delivered, when the young woman came home. He wanted to hit her, meet her, after the letter had been delivered, after she had reached home and read it, but not more than a few minutes after she had read it. It was important, the timing, and it was down to him, the plan . . . He was stressed. He reckoned he could have killed for a cigarette, and in front of him on the glove box was the "No Smoking" sticker which was standard these goddam days in any Drug Enforcement Administration vehicle, back in the States or overseas. The time to hit her, was critically important.

The cattle split in front of the Cherokee Jeep. Either side of the radiator and bonnet and then the side windows, the cattle, a mixed Fresian and Holstein herd, scrambled on the bank below the scalped hedges, slipped, blundered against the vehicle. The driver's side wing mirror was pressured back. A wet and slobbering tongue squelched against the glass of the window. The Cherokee Jeep shook from the weight of an animal against the body of the vehicle behind him. The lights shone on the face of the man who drove the cattle, unshaven, pinched in the wind, weathered. He could see the agitation of the man as his mouth with the gaps in his teeth flapped in silence, silence because of the noise of the goddam heater. Beside him, the hand was reaching for the gear stick.

"Where the hell are you going?"

"I'm going to back up."

"How many miles are you going to back up? Stay put."

"He's telling me to back up."

"Then tell him to go eat his own shit."

"You're kind of edgy, aren't you."

The face of the man driving the cattle was close to the windscreen. The mouth still flapped. There were three teeth missing, he reckoned, and he reckoned that there was a denture set back home at the farm for inserting when the day was done and the evening meal was on the kitchen table. He spited himself, turned the Cherokee Jeep's heater higher so that the blast of dry warm air and the roar of the motor drowned the man's protest. The perspiration ran on his forehead and in his groin and down the small of his back but he could not hear the protest of the man driving the cattle. The man was peering at them through the windscreen, squinting through narrow eyes at them.

"Like we're out of the zoo," Axel said.

And he should not have said that, no. Should not have said that because Dwight, the driver, was Afro-American. At Quantico, in an Ethics class, they would have gone ape. A remark such as his last might just have been enough to get a guy busted out of the Training Academy. Axel did not apologize, he seldom made apologies.

The man driving the cattle stared hard at them, at two guys in an American Cherokee Jeep, wrong side drive, peculiar numberplate, one white with a goddam pony tail of hair, one black as a dark night.

"I get the feeling we're noticed," Axel said in bitterness.

Daniel Bent, farmer, sixty-nine years of age, working the land of his father and his grandfather and his great grandfather, who had maintained the development of the twin Fresian and Holstein herds to championship status, cursed Axel Moen and Dwight Smythe. He cursed them richly, obscenities and blasphemies, because he saw the risk of one of his cows falling from the bank between the road and the hedge, plunging under the body of the four-wheel-drive and breaking a leg. He noticed, too fucking right, the bastards and recognized them for Americans, and wondered what was their business late in the day on the lane to the coast.

When the big vehicle, too big for these roads for sure, going at speed and ignoring the 30 mph limit, came past her, Fanny Carthew saw them. Mrs. Carthew, artist of sea views in oils, eighty-one years old, muttered the protest that in the moment afterward gave her a tremor of shame and would have shocked her fellow worshipers at the Baptist Hall in Kingsbridge if they had heard her utter such words. The cause of her protest— she had to heave at the leash on which she walked her venerable Pekinese dog right off the lane and into the nettles of the verge. She knew them to be Americans, the scowling white one with his hair ridiculously pulled back and the colored one who drove. She noticed them and wondered about the business that brought them down the lane that led nowhere.

Because the Jeep was slowing, moving as if with hesitation past the houses, Zachary Jones saw them. Zachary Jones, disabled building worker, fifty-three years old, short of a leg, amputated below the knee from a construction site fall, sat at the window of his cottage. He saw everything that moved in the collection of homes at the end of the lane that was too small to be called a village. With his binoculars he noted every coming and going, every visitor, every stranger. The binoculars' magnification flitted from the face of the white one to the face of the black one, and he thought they were arguing and thought they disputed their directions, and then down to the tail end registration plate. Zachary Jones had worked the building game in London, knew diplomatic plates, before coming home as an amputee to live with his spinster sister. He wondered what brought Americans from their embassy down to this God forgotten corner of nowhere.

Mrs. Daphne Farson saw them from behind her lace curtains, then lost them when her view was obscured by the sign in her front garden that advertised bed-and-breakfast accommodation. She knew Americans.

The retired clergyman, the occasional gardener, the crab fisherman, the retired librarian, the District Nurse, everyone who lived in that community at the end of the lane beside the sea shore, saw the big Cherokee Jeep edge down over the last of the tarmacadam, pause in the car park for summer visitors, reverse, turn, come back up the lane and stop just short of David and Flora Parsons' bungalow. All of them heard the engine stilled, saw the lights doused.

All eyes on the Cherokee Jeep and all eyes on the front door of David and Flora Parsons' bungalow. The waiting time . . . A small collective shiver of excitement held the community.

"You sure it's right?"

"It's what I was told, a white single story in a crap place," Axel said.

"We got here, so when you going to shift yourself?"

"She's not here."

"You know that? How do you know that?"

"Because her scooter's not parked in the driveway."

"Maybe she put it in the garage."

"Her father's car is in the garage, she leaves the scooter in the driveway, if it matters to you . . ."

"You haven't been within a thousand miles of here before, you've never met this woman before . . . How come you know that sort of detail, or am I getting bullshit?"

"I had it checked."

"You had it checked, down to whether she put a scooter into the garage or left it out in the driveway?"

"Checked." Axel said it sharply, dismissive, like it was obvious that such a detail would be checked. The headquarters in Exeter of the Devon and Cornwall police, through their liaison officer, had provided information on the progress of an airmail letter through the city's sorting service, information on the hours worked by a young woman teacher, information on the nighttime parking of a scooter. He believed in detail. He thought that with detail people more easily stayed alive.

It had been the idea of Axel Moen. It was the operational plan of Axel Moen. What he wanted most, right now, was to smoke a cigarette. He opened the door beside him, felt the cool of the air, the grip of the sharp wind coming up off the pebble beach, heard the rustle of waves on stones. He reached back and grabbed for a windcheater. He stepped down onto the grass beside the road. Ahead of him, behind a low fence and a trimmed hedge was the bungalow and the light was on over the door. He lit the cigarette, Lucky Strike, dragged on it, coughed and spat. He saw the shadowed bungalows and cottages, with their lights in the windows, stretching as a haphazard ribbon away up the lane to the bend round which the young woman would come on her scooter. It was the sort of place he knew. He wondered where the letter would be—in her room and on her bed or on her dressing table, on a stand in the hall, in the kitchen. He wondered whether she would tear the envelope open before she discarded her coat or her anorak, whether she would let it lie while she took herself to the bathroom for a wash or a pee. He heard Dwight Smythe open his door behind him, then slam it shut.

"This young woman, does she know you're coming?"

Axel shook his head.

"You just walking in there, no invite?"

Axel nodded his head, did not turn.

"You feel OK about that?"

Axel shrugged.

He watched the top of the lane, where it emerged from the bend. The woman with the dog stared down the lane at him, and he could make out the man in the window with the small binoculars aimed at him, and he saw the flicker of movement behind the curtains of the house that advertised bed-and-breakfast. It was as it would have been for a stranger driving on a lane on the Door Peninsula, the scrutiny and suspicion. Where the finger of the Door Peninsula cut out into Michigan Bay. And, going north from Egg Harbor and Fish Creek, from Jacksonport and Ephraim, they would have stared at a stranger coming in the dusk and followed him with binoculars and peered from behind curtains. Far in the distance, back beyond the bend in the lane, he heard the engine. It sounded to Axel Moen like the two-stroke power of a brush cutter or a small chainsaw. He dragged a last time on the cigarette and dropped what was left of it down onto the tarmacadam and tramped it with his boot and then kicked the mess of it toward the weeds. He saw the narrow wash of light from up the lane, back beyond the bend.

"You're a mafia man, right? Have to be a specialist in mafia if you're based down in Rome. What's—?

"Mafia's generic. Don't you work 'organized crime'?"

"You going to play smart-ass? Actually, if you want to know, I am personnel, I am accounts, I am administration. Because of people like me, arrogant shits get to run around and play their games. What's this young woman—?"

"Lima Charlie November, that's LCN, that's La Cosa Nostra. I work La Cosa Nostra, we don't call it 'mafia.' "

"Forgive me for breathing—I apologize. Best of my knowledge La Cosa Nostra, mafia, is Sicily, is Italy, is not quite adjacent to here."

"Why don't you just go wrap yourself round the heater?"

The scooter's light was a small beam, dully illuminating the bank and hedge at the top of the lane, then sweeping lower and catching the woman with the dog, then swerving and reflecting in the lenses of the binoculars in the window, then finding the moving curtain at the bungalow that advertised bed-and-breakfast. He saw the arm of the rider wave twice. The scooter came down the hill and was slowing. The brakes had a squeal to them, like a cat's howl when its tail is trapped. The scooter came to a stop in front of the bungalow where the light shone "welcome" above the porch. The engine was killed, the light was doused. He had not seen a photograph of her. He knew only the barest of her personal details from the file. No way that he could have had a decent picture of her in his mind, but when she was off the scooter and tugging the shape of the helmet from her head, when she shook her hair free, when she started to push the weight of the scooter into the driveway in front of the garage, when she walked under the light above the porch, she seemed to be smaller, slighter, than he had imagined. She turned a key in the latch, pushed the door open. The hall light flooded over an ordinary young woman, and he heard her call that she was back, an ordinary young woman's voice. The door closed behind her.

Dwight Smythe, above the sound of the heater, called from behind him, "So, when are you going to bust in, no invite?"

Axel walked back toward the Cherokee Jeep.

"So, when are you going to start to shake the ground under her feet?"

Axel swung himself into the passenger seat.

"So, do I go short of answers?"

Axel said quietly, "About a quarter of an hour for her to read a letter? Don't ask me!"

Dwight Smythe arched his eyebrows, spread the palms of his hands wide over the wheel. "Would I dream of asking, would I, what a young woman from down here has to do with DEA business, with organized crime, with La Cosa Nostra in Sicily ...?"

The professor had said, "If you take the hip and pelvis of Italy and think about it, and look at the map up there, well, that's the piece that's joined to Europe, and that's the bit that's high class tourism and finance ..."

When the rookies were not on Crime Simulation or Firearms Procedures or Physical Education or Legal classes or Defensive Tactics, when they were not crowded into the Casino School or the Engineering Research Facility or the Forensic Laboratory, then they sat in on Public Affairs. It was nine years since Dwight Smythe had listened to the professor at the Public Affairs lecture.

"Come on down and you've the thigh of Italy, which is agriculture and industry. Move on lower, and you have the knee joint, Rome—administration, bureaucracy, high life, the corruption of government. You following me? We go south, we have the shin—Naples, Sorrento—and it's going sour. There is a heel—Lecce. There is a foot—Cosenza. There is a toe—Reggio Calabria. The way I like to think of it, maybe that toe is bare inside sandals, or at most the protection is the canvas of a pair of sneakers. Sandals or sneakers, whichever, they're not the best gear for kicking a rock ..."

At Quantico, out in the Virginia forest off Interstate Route 95, FBI and Marine Corps territory, where the Drug Enforcement Administration recruit program is tolerated as are relations from the wrong side of the tracks, the professor was a legend. Any heat, any cold, the professor lectured Public Affairs in a three piece suit of Scottish tweed. The material of his suit had the same roughness as the wild beard splaying from his chin and cheeks. In the lecture room, with his maps and his pointer, he taught the recruits the rudimentaries of the countries that would fill their files, the societies they would interact with, the criminal conspiracies they would confront. And he did it well, which was why he was remembered.

"The Government of Italy, for a hundred years, has been stupid enough to kick with an unprotected toe against the rock that is Sicily. My advice, if you've set your mind on kicking rocks with a bare toe, is go and find one that's not granite or flint. Sicily is hard mineral, and the toe gets to be bloodied, bruised. That rock is a meeting point, where Africa comes to Europe, different cultures, different values. The rock, granite or flint, has been shaped by history. Sicily is where the conquerors liked to come. You name him, he's been there—Moors and Normans and Bourbons, and before them the Greeks and the Romans and the Carthaginians and the Vandals. Government in Rome is just seen as another freebooter, the latest, come to cream off more than his share."

The professor used a big lectern that took his weight as he leaned forward on it, and the voice came from deep in the whiskered beard, pebbles churning in a mixer.

"If you've toned your muscles, if you can swing a pickaxe, if you've journeyed to Sicily, then take a hack at a piece of ground. You may have to go looking awhile first to find ground that's not rock. Find it and hack—chance is you'll dig up an arrow head or a sword blade or the iron of a spear tip, or maybe a bayonet or a mortar round or a rifle's cartridge case—the weapons of repression and torture. Imagine you live there, when you hold whatever you've dug in your hand. When your history is one of dispossession, expropriation, incarceration, execution, then that sort of colors your personality, sort of shapes an attitude, each new conqueror molded the Sicilian view of life. The lesson dinned by history into the modern generations tells them trust is a luxury to be kept tight round the family, that the greatest virtue is silence, that you wait as long as it takes for the opportunity of revenge, then by God you dish it out. While Europe was civilizing itself a hundred years ago, down there on the rock, close to Africa, they were brigands and bandits. Not our problem, an Italian problem, until . . ."

Dwight Smythe remembered him now, like it was yesterday, and the recruits hadn't coughed, or sniggered, or fidgeted, but had sat rapt as if the old academic was telling them the reality of DEA work.

"For protection, the brigands and bandits formed a secret society. Rules, hierarchy, organization, discipline, but relevant only to Italy, running contraband cigarettes, fleecing an extortion racket dry, until—strange, I think, the way the little moments in our existence, the two cent moments have their day—until a Turkish gentleman named Musullulu got to share a prison cell in Italy with the Sicilian gangster Pietro Vernengo. They talked for two years. Those two years, in that cell, '78 and '79, it changed the face of society, they put you men in work. The drugs trade, the misery trade began in that cell, two men and their talk . . ."

So clear to Dwight Smythe, the Professor's words. Beside him Axel Moen sat quiet and still, eyes closed. Dwight knew the current statistics— a Federal Anti-Narcotics budget of $13.2 billion, of which the DEA took $757 million and said it was inadequate.

"The Turk talked heroin. The Turk could bring unprocessed morphine base into Sicily, via the Balkans. Good morphine base to make good heroin. In 1979, the Italians opened the cell door and Mr. Musullulu went his way, never been seen by a law enforcement agent since, and Signor Vernengo went back to Sicily and told the guys what was on offer. Don't ever think that because they didn't get grades at school the Sicilian peasants are dumb. For killing and conspiracy they are the best and the brightest, for moving money and for spreading the cloy of corruption they are the best and the brightest. They saw the window, they jumped through it. They had more heroin, more morphine base, coming onto that heap of rock than they knew what to do with, and they had the market. The market was the USA, they went international. The money flowed. They had dollar bills up their ears, mouths, nostrils, every orifice they owned. So you've heard of the Colombians and the Yakuza out of Japan and the Chinese Triads, but first on the scene was La Cosa Nostra of Sicily. The people I've just mentioned, the cartels and the Yakuza and the Triads, they're hard people but they've never been fool enough to mix it with the Sicilians. It's difficult to believe, but off that piece of rock stuck out between Europe and Africa come the big boys of organized crime, and what everyone's thrown at them just seems to bounce back. You see, gentlemen, ladies, down there it's a war of survival, as it has been through history, a bad place to be on the losing side, it's a war to the death . . ."

It's what the professor had said at a cold early morning session in the lecture hall at Quantico, with snow flaking against the windows, what Dwight Smythe recalled. He felt a sense of raw anger. The next week, nine years back, the professor had lectured on the marijuana crop out of Mexico, and the week after he had given over the hour session to the coca leaf production of Bolivia and Peru, and the final week of the course had been concerned with opium production in the triangle of Burma and Laos and Thailand. Dwight Smythe felt the raw sense of anger because the professor had seemed only a diversion from the main matter of the induction course. Sitting in the car beside the younger man with the blond pony tail of hair shafted down under the collar of his windcheater, Dwight Smythe knew reality. He was far from the office accounts that he managed on the fifth floor of the embassy, far from the duty rosters and leave charts he so meticulously prepared, far from the filing system he was proud of and the maintenance of the computer systems . . . He was with reality. The anger spat in him as he turned toward Axel Moen.

"What right do you have, what God given right do you have to play Christ with that kid, to involve her?"

As if he hadn't heard, as if the accusation were not important, Axel Moen, beside him, glanced down at his watch, like it was time to go to work.

"You're a mafia specialist—sorry, forgive me, I apologize, a La Cosa Nostra specialist—and you're not making, what I hear, a good job of winning. Aren't you ever fed to the teeth that you don't ever get to win?"

The chill air with the salt tang came into the cab of the Cherokee

Jeep, then the door slammed shut on Dwight Smythe. He watched the hunched shoulders of Axel Moen glide away, no sound against the throb of the heater, toward the little wrought iron gate and the path leading to the door of the bungalow over which the porch light shone. He watched the shoulders and the resolute stride through the gate and up the path and past the scooter parked in the driveway, and he thought of the preacher of his childhood talking of the Death Angel who came on the unsuspecting with destruction and darkness, and he thought it was wrong to involve an ordinary young woman, just wrong.

Wrong to break without warning, into a life.

"So sorry to trouble you, I hope it's not inconvenient . . ."

He could smile. When it was necessary, Axel Moen had a fine wide smile that cut his face. He smiled at the older man who stood in the lit doorway.

"My name's Axel Moen, I've come down from our embassy in London, it's to see Miss Charlotte Parsons. I surely hope it's not inconvenient . . ."

He could charm. When it was asked of him he could charm sufficient to bring down a barrier. He kept walking. There had been no gesture for him to enter the bungalow, no invitation, but he kept walking and David Parsons stepped aside. The frown was on the man's forehead, confusion.

"You're wondering, Mr. Parsons, at my name. It's Norwegian. There's a fair few of Norwegian stock where I come from, that's the northeastern corner of Wisconsin. They were farmers, they came over around a hundred years ago. I'd like to see your daughter, please, it's a private matter."

He could deflect. When it was important to him, Axel Moen knew how to batter aside the doubts and queries and seem to give an answer where a different question had been asked. The question would have been, what was his business? But the question was not put. It was a small hall, recently decorated but not by a professional, and he noted that the paper pattern did not match where the strips were joined, and the paint had run on the woodwork. He had a cold eye. It was a detached observer's eye. The eye of a man who gave nothing. He saw the small hall table with the telephone on it, and above the table was a framed photograph of the young woman in academic gown and with a mortarboard worn rakishly. The angle of the mortarboard and the cheekiness of the grin in the college graduation photograph rather pleased him, he had hoped to find an independent spirit. He towered over the man, he dominated him in the narrow width of the hallway. It was what he had to do and what he was good at, flashing a smile, breathing charm, and dominating. He was good, also, at making the fast judgment on the spine of a man, and he judged this one, pullover with the buttons undone and wearing yesterday's clean shirt and frayed carpet slippers, as a coward.

"She's having her tea."

"It won't take too many minutes," Axel said. He was good, as well, at playing the bully. The man backed away from him and shuffled toward the opened door at the end of the hall. There was a television on and a local news bulletin dealing with the day of a small place and a small town and small people. The man had no fight to stand his ground and ask the questions and demand the answers. The man went in through the door, into the kitchen area. Axel had broken into the sanctum of a family, fractured a mealtime, and he felt no guilt. The man muttered to his wife, at the stove, moving pans, that it was an American who had come to see Charley, and the wife had boldness and challenge in her gaze. Axel ignored the man and the man's wife. He stood at the entrance to the kitchen. The young woman was sitting at the table. She had a half slice of bread, margarine smeared on it, in her hand and halfway to her mouth. She quizzed him, a strong firm glance. She wore a full length denim skirt and a shapeless sweater with the sleeves stretched down over her wrists and no cosmetics and her hair was held up with a band so that it came from the back of her head as a pig's tail. She neither cowered like her father nor challenged like her mother, she met Axel's eye. In front of her, beside the plate with the bread slices and the mug of tea, was a torn open envelope and beside it were the two sheets of a handwritten letter.

"Miss Charlotte Parsons?"

"Yes."

"I'd be grateful if I could speak to you, a private matter."

"These are my parents."

"It would be easier in private, if you wouldn't mind . . ."

"Who are you?"

"I am Axel Moen, from the American embassy."

"I've no business with your embassy, private or not."

"It would be better, private."

She could have backed off then, but she did not. He pulled his shoulders back, consciously, to fill the kitchen doorway. He held her with his eyes. They talked on the courses about body language and eye to eye contact. The body language was domination and the eye contact was authority. She could have said that it was in front of her parents or not at all . . . She pushed her chair back, scraped it over the vinyl floor of mock terracotta tiles. She stood her full height, then as an afterthought she stuffed the half slice of bread and margarine into her mouth, then she swigged at her mug of tea, then she wiped the sleeve of her sweater across her lips. She was moving from the table.

Axel said, "You received a letter, Miss Parsons, please bring it with you."

She rocked, quick, fast. Her eyes blinked. She swayed, but she did as he asked her because he had the domination and authority. She picked up the letter and the torn open envelope and she walked past her mother and father, her own person. She went past him as if he did not exist, and her face was set. She led into the living room and snapped on the light in the standard lamp and cleared the morning paper off the sofa, waved for him to sit. She took the chair beside the fire. She held the letter and the envelope tight in her hands. He tried to judge her, to measure whether it was bravado, whether it was an inner toughness.

"Well?"

"You are Charlotte Eunice Parsons, teacher?"

"Yes."

"You are twenty-three years old?"

"How's that of interest to the American embassy?"

"I'm asking the questions, Miss Parsons. Please answer them."

"I am twenty-three years old. Do you need to know that I have a mole on my backside, and an appendix scar?"

"In the summer of 1992 you worked for eleven weeks as a home help and child-minder in Rome for the family of Giuseppe Ruggerio?"

"I don't see the importance—"

"Yes or no?"

"Yes."

"This afternoon you have received a letter from that family inviting you to return?"

"Who the hell are you?"

Out of the hip pocket of his trousers, he took the squashed wallet. He flipped it open, exposed the identification badge in gold-veneer metal of the Drug Enforcement Administration, thumb half covering the title of Special Agent, fingers masking the rampant eagle.

"My name is Axel Moen, DEA, I work out of Rome."

"You've come from Rome?"

"Don't interrupt me, Miss Parsons. I'm sorry, where can I smoke?"

"Sort your answer out. What on earth you are doing here, prying and poking? Come on."

But a small grin was on her face. She marched him back out into the hall, and grabbed a heavy coat off a hook, and then through a darkened dining room. She unlocked the doors, and let him into the garden. The kitchen lights washed half of the patio, but she led him beyond the light and onto the paving slabs outside a garden shed. She turned to face him, looked up at him, and the flash of the match caught her face.

"Prying and poking, so what the hell's your answer?"

"I work out of Rome—you should listen to what I say. I work in liaison with the Italian agencies. I work against the Sicilian based organization La Cosa Nostra. You were employed by Giuseppe and Angela Ruggerio to look after their son at the time their daughter was born. They have written you to say that two months ago they were 'blessed' with the birth of a second son, Mauro—just listen—and they have asked you to return to them to do the same work as four years ago. They live now in Palermo."

He threw down the cigarette, half smoked. His foot was moving to stamp on it, but she crouched and picked it up and handed it back to him. He stubbed out the cigarette on the ribbed sole of his shoe then placed the dead end in the match box.

"They live now in Palermo. How do I know? Giuseppe Ruggerio is sporadically under surveillance. There are not the resources, such is the scale of criminality in Sicily, for the surveillance to be full time. From time to time he is targeted. Tailed, wire tapped, mail watch, electronic stuff, it's routine. It's a trawl. The letter showed up. Angela Ruggerio posted it. The letter was intercepted, copied, resealed and went back into the postal service. In Rome I was shown the copy. The letter was tracked from Palermo to Milan, international sorting, Milan to London, London down here. We took that trouble to ensure the timing of my journey, so that I should get here after you received the letter, before you responded. This is my idea, Miss Parsons, I have initiated this. I want you to go to Palermo and take up that offer."

She laughed in his face. He didn't think the laugh was affectation.

"Ridiculous . . ."

"Go back to Palermo and work for Giuseppe and Angela Ruggerio."

"I've a job, I'm in full-time work. Before, that was just a fill-in between school and college. It's just, well, it's idiotic. It's a joke."

"I want you to accept the invitation and travel to Palermo."

Axel lit a second cigarette. The wind was on his face and cutting into the thin material of his windcheater. She was small now, huddled inside the shape of her coat and her arms were clamped across her chest as if to hold in the warmth.

"What do they call you, people who know you?"

"I get called Charley."

"Don't think, Charley, that I would have bothered to haul myself over here if this were not an important investigation, don't think I take kindly to wasted time. We get opportunities, maybe they come convenient, maybe they don't. Maybe we can handle the opportunities ourselves, maybe we need to pull in help from outside. We want you in the home of Giuseppe and Angela Ruggerio."

The bitterness hissed in her voice, and the contempt. "As a spy?"

"The opportunity we have, through you, is one of access."

"They treated me as one of their family."

"Giuseppe Ruggerio is a careful, clever bastard. You should take up that offer and work for Giuseppe and Angela Ruggerio."

"Go to hell. Bugger off and bloody get out of here."

He flicked the cigarette into the middle of the dark grass. He started to turn away.

"Please yourself, I don't beg. You care to live here, you care to spend the rest of your life living here, you care to cross over to the other side of the street when there's something you could do, please yourself. I thought that maybe you had some balls, pity is that I was wrong."

"You are, Mr. Axel bloody Moen, a total shit."

"Big words, but you're short of big action. You want to rot here then that's your problem. Don't talk about this conversation. If you talk about it you might be responsible for hurting people."

A small voice. She wouldn't be able to see his face, see the flicker of satisfaction. She asked, "Why do you need access to Peppino's and Angela's home?"

No sarcasm, and no laugh, and no bullshit, Axel said, "You get on board and you get told, so think on it. And think also on whether, for the rest of your life, you want to remember crossing over the road to avoid responsibility. Good night, Miss Parsons. When you've had a chance to think on it, I'll make the contact again. Don't worry, I can see myself out."

He walked away, back through the darkened dining room, and past the open door to the kitchen, and through the hall. He looked a last time at the photograph of Charley Parsons on the wall above the table with the telephone. He liked the cockiness and cheekiness in her graduation photograph. He let himself out through the front door.

Sometimes he used a driver, most times Mario Ruggerio drove himself. Whether he drove himself, or whether he rode with the driver, he used a mass produced, factory production line, saloon car. There was nothing flamboyant, nothing ostentatious, in the life of Mario Ruggerio, nothing to draw attention to him. That evening, if a car of the *carabinieri* or the *squadra mobile* or the *polizia stradale* or the *polizia municipale* or the *Guardia di Finanze* or the *Direzione Investigativa Anti-Mafia* had passed the Citroên BX that carried him as passenger, nothing would have seemed remarkable to the police officers of those agencies. He had been released from the Ucciardone prison, down by the city's docks, on 15 June 1960, and he had not been arrested since. He was now aged sixty-two. He was governed by twin obsessions and they were the seeking of power and the avoidance of capture. Without freedom there was no power. To maintain that precious freedom he traveled the city in a series of commonplace vehicles. To any of the police officers of those agencies, the sight of him at the traffic lights or at a pedestrian crossing would have been of an old man, tired by long life, being driven by a son or a nephew . . . but he was, and he knew it so well, to all of the police officers of all of those agencies, the most wanted man in the city, the most hunted man on the island, the most tracked man in the country, the most sought after man on the continent of Europe. He believed himself to have achieved the primary position on what the Ministry of the Interior called the Special Program of the Thirty Most Dangerous Criminals at Large. The police officers of those agencies would have seen, at the traffic lights or a pedestrian crossing, an old man who sat low in the passenger seat, a height of 5 feet 3 inches and a weight of a couple of pounds less than 13 stones, unstyled and short-cropped and gray-flecked hair, a low peasant's forehead, roving and cautious eyes, jowls at his throat and nicotine stained teeth, broad but bowed shoulders. They would not have known . . . Nor would they have seen the powerful thickset fingers with the nails cut back to the quick because the hands were held down between his knees. They might have seen his eyes, and if the police officers of the agencies had met those eyes, then Mario Ruggerio's head would have ducked in respect to their uniforms and their position, but they would not have seen his hands, clasping and unclasping, stretching and clenching. He moved his fingers and thumbs, worked the joints, because his hands were still bruised and aching from the effort of strangulation, and the rheumatism in his hands was always worse at the end of the wet months of the Sicilian winter.

There was a calmness in his expression as the driver brought him from their rendezvous point on the south side of Via Generale di Maria, along the Via Malaspina and across the Piazza Virgilio, but the expression of calmness was false. With the obsessions for power and freedom came neurosis. The neurosis was based on the fear of loss of power and loss of freedom, and the fear that was always with him was of betrayal. It was hard for Mario Ruggerio to trust any man, even the driver who had been with him seven years. The fear of loss of power and freedom governed the precautions that he took every day and every night of his life. He had the keys to sixteen apartments in the city, loaned to him indefinitely by "affiliates" who owed loyalty to him and him alone. The driver who had been with him for seven years was never given the address of an apartment block from which to pick him up, merely a street junction, and never given an address at which to drop him. When they came, that evening, past the decayed facade of the Villa Filippina and onto Via Balsamo, he coughed hard as if to signal for his driver to pull in to the curb.

He climbed awkwardly, heavily, out of the Citroën, and the driver passed him a small bag in which a kid might have kept sports clothes or stored school books, and then his cap of gray-check pattern. He stood among the debris on the pavement, among the filth and the paper wrappings, put on his cap, and he watched the car drive away. Always he satisfied himself that the car was gone before he moved from the drop point. The old eyes, bright and alert and clear blue, raked the road and searched the faces of drivers and checked the pedestrians. He knew the signs of surveillance . . . When he was satisfied, only when he was sure, he walked off down the Via Balsamo and across the wide Via Volturno where the street market was packing up for the evening, and he disappeared into the labyrinthine alleys of the Capo district of Palermo.

The most wanted man on the continent, in the country, on the island, in the city, walked alone and carried his own bag in the near darkness and around him radios played and women screamed and men shouted and children cried. He was worth—his own estimate and tapped out each week on his Casio calculator—something in excess of $245,000,000, and his calculator could tell him in the time that it took tired eyes to blink that the value of his worth was in excess of 637,000,000,000 Italian *lire*. The wealth of Mario Ruggerio, walking in the slum district of Capo, was held in government bonds, foreign currencies, blue-chip gilts on the European and New York stock markets, investment in multinational companies and in real-estate.

He pushed open a battered door.

He climbed an ill lit stairway. He found the key. He let himself into the room.

Only when he had drawn the thick curtains of the room did he switch on the light. The pain in his hands, bruised from strangulation, pitched at his mouth and he winced. He unpacked the small bag, his nightclothes, his shaving bag, his clean shirt and underwear and socks, and the framed photograph of the two children that he loved and the baby.

Carrying the suitcase, Giuseppe Ruggerio, known always to his family as Peppino, was first through the outer door and behind him was *piccolo* Mario heaving the children's bag and then Francesca with her soft toys, and farther behind him was Angela who tried to soothe baby Mauro's crying . . . the end of a four day break in the San Domenico Palace hotel of Taormina, five-star. Back home in Palermo, and the baby was hungry.

But the hunger of the baby was not high in the thoughts of Giuseppe Ruggerio. He had almost run, in spite of the weight of the suitcase, the last few steps from the elevator to the outer door of the apartment, and he had pulled hard on *piccolo* Mario's collar to propel the child backward as he had opened the door.

Inside, snapping on the lights, dumping the suitcase, his eyes roved over floors and walls—he saw the faint smear where the marble in the hallway had been wiped. On into the living area, more lights crashing on, checking the sofa and chairs where they would have sat, and on into the dining area and over the polished block floor and gazing at the smooth sheen of the mahogany table where they would have eaten. Pictures where they should have been, the statue where it should have been. Turning fast, into the kitchen, the fluorescent ceiling light hesitating and then shining, and the kitchen was as it had been left. Everything was as it should have been. A fast gasp of relief. He refused nothing that his brother asked of him, nothing . . . It had said on the radio that morning, on Radio Uno, in the hotel in Taormina, that the wife of a man from Agrigento had reported to the *carabinieri* that her husband was missing from home and her grandson and her husband's driver. The man from Agrigento with his grandson and his driver would have come to a meeting point in Palermo, and a *picciotto* of his brother would have met them there, then traveled in their car to the apartment in the complex of the Giardino Inglese, they would not have been able by cellular phone or digital phone or personal radio to communicate the ultimate destination. His brother was always careful.

"Peppino."

There was the shrill whine of her voice behind him. He turned. Angela stood in the living room. Angela held the baby, Mauro, and the face of the baby was red from crying. Angela, his wife of nine years, pointed down at the thick woven carpet from Iran.

"What is that?" The whine in her voice was from her accent that was Roman. "That was not here when we left."

Nothing to be seen where the carpet fabric was of magenta wool, but beyond the magenta was pure white, and the white was stained.

She accused, "Who has been here? Who has dirtied our carpet? The carpet cost you seventeen million *lire*. It is destroyed. Who has been here, Peppino?"

He smiled, sweetness and love. "I do not see anything."

She jabbed her finger. "Look, there . . . Did you give the key of our home to someone? Did you let someone use our home? Who? Did you?"

And her voice died. It was as if she had forgotten herself, forgotten her life and her place. As if she had forgotten that she no longer lived in Rome, forgotten she lived now in Palermo. The anger was gone from her face, and her shoulders crumpled. He had hoped so much that the short break, sandwiched between his journeys to Frankfurt and London would revive her after the difficult birth of baby Mauro. Peppino never cursed his brother, never. She was gone to the kitchen to warm food for baby Mauro. He bent over the carpet, over the stain, and from deep in the weave he lifted clear the dried seed of a tomato.

He went into the kitchen. She would not meet his eyes. Peppino had his hand on her shoulder and he stroked the soft hair on baby Mauro's head.

"When I am in London I will telephone to Charlotte. She will have received it. I will persuade her to come, I promise."

He tapped the numbers on the telephone in the Cherokee Jeep. He waited. He hadn't asked Dwight Smythe for permission to use the telephone, but then he hadn't spoken since he had come out of the bungalow, flopped back into the passenger seat and indicated they could move off. They were out of the lanes, had the speed going. Axel hadn't spoken because there was no requirement for him to talk through an operation with a guy who did accounts and personnel and office management, and if there was no requirement for him to talk, then he seldom did. He heard the phone lifted, the connection made.

"Bill, hi, Axel here. How's Rome? Raining, Jesus. This is not a secure line. I did the contact. She's OK, nothing special. First reaction was to chuck me out, second reaction was to think on it. She's predictable. She wanted to know more, but she's going to have to wait until she's thought harder. I'm going to call in at the local police HQ and work something out that'll help her thinking. I'll call you tomorrow . . . Sorry, come again . . . Hold on, Bill."

He reached forward. He snapped off the heater switch, quietened the cab.

"What were you saying, Bill? Maybe, maybe she could do it, maybe she couldn't, but she's all that's on offer. I'll see you, Bill."

He put the telephone back on the rest. He slouched his legs forward and worked his shoulders lower down on the seat back and closed his eyes.

Dwight said, staring ahead and following the road, "If I'd been her, I'd have thrown you out. You are a cold bastard."

"She called me a total shit. Your problem, her problem, I don't care too much what people call me."

"And you hooked her? Trampled in on her life?"

"Where I come from, north-west Wisconsin, there's good muskie fishing. You know the muskie?"

"We didn't fish round Albuquerque. There would have been trout up in the hills, but it wasn't for black kids in Albuquerque."

"Wear your chip with honor . . . The muskie is a big fine fish, but it's a killer and ugly as sin, it's hard and vicious on its fellows, it terrorizes a reed bank. Most anglers go out after muskie with lures, spoons and plugs. They get muskie, right, but not the daddies. The way for the big killers, the big uglies, is live bait. You get a little wall-eye, could be a small-mouth bass, latch it to a treble hook and sling it out under a float. When the little fish goes ape, when the float starts charging, that tells you that the big killer's close, the big ugly's on the scene. Put simply, the little fish gives you access to a specimen muskie."

Dwight Smythe said hoarsely, "That's rough on the little fish."

"If she goes then we'd try and wind her in when we get the shout, like when the float starts to charge we'd reel in the tackle," Axel said softly.

"You can live with that?"

"I just do a job."

There was a heavy lorry coming toward them, big, high lights, and Axel saw the driver's face and saw the gleam of sweat on Dwight Smythe's forehead, as if it were him that was being asked to travel to Palermo, live the lie, have the treble hook in his backbone.

"She'll go?"

"I should reckon so. Didn't seem to be much to keep her here. Yes, I reckon she'll go. She'll jump when she's pushed. If you don't mind, I'm kind of tired."

2

TRACY WAS FIGHTING VANESSA. Darren was sticking a pencil point into Vaughan's forearm. Lee was drawing with a felt tip pen over Joshua's writing pad. Dawn was tugging at Nicky's hair. A crash as Ron's chair tipped over backward, a scream from Ron as Ian dived back to his own chair and table . . .

And class 2B was regarded by the headmistress as the best disciplined and happiest class in the school, and class 2B had been singled out by the Inspectors three weeks before as a model. Tracy kicked Vanessa. Darren gouged the pencil point hard enough for it to draw Vaughan's blood. Lee had destroyed Joshua's careful work. Dawn had a fistful of Nicky's hair. Ian sat innocent as Ron bawled . . .

She could have belted each one of them, and lost her job. She could have smacked Tracy's hand, whacked Darren, twisted Lee's ear, thumped Ian, and that would have been the fast route to an Education Authority Sub-Committee (Disciplinary) Hearing. She imagined in the other classrooms, the other prefabricated blocks that sieved the drafts and leaked the rain, the teachers of classes 1A and 1B and 2A and 3A and 3B, and the headmistress on her rounds, and their surprise that class 2B was audibly and publicly in chaos. It was her second term at the school, her nineteenth week, and the first time that she had lost control of the thirty-eight children. She clapped her hands, and maybe there was rare anger in her voice, and maybe there was total contempt at her face, but the clapping and the anger and the contempt won her short respite. It had been a rotten, desperate night for Charley Parsons. No sleep, no rest. The kids knew her mind was far away. Kids always knew and exploited weakness. Five more minutes on her watch before the bell would go, before a quite bloody day was finished.

She had come in from outside the evening before and heard the front door close quietly after him. She had stood in the hall and heard the big engine of the four-wheel-drive pull away. She had gone back into the kitchen. Her mother, accusing: did she know that her tea was ruined? Her father, furtive: would she have time for the work to be done that night on class preparation?

Her mother: what was that about? Her father: who was he? "I can't tell you, so don't question me."

Her father: hadn't her own parents the right to know? Her mother: shouldn't her own parents be given an explanation when a total stranger barges into the house? "He said that if I talked about him, what he said to me, then I might be responsible for hurting people."

Her mother: didn't she know how offensive she sounded? Her father: had they scrimped and saved and sent her to college merely to learn rudeness? "He's a sort of policeman, a sort of detective. He works for something called the Drug Enforcement Administration."

Drugs? The shock spreading across her mother's face. What had she to do with drugs? The incredulity at her father's mouth and she had seen the shake of his hands. "I have nothing to do with drugs. I just can't talk about it. I have no connection with drugs. I can't tell you."

She had run out of the kitchen and across the hall and into her bedroom. She had flung herself down onto the duvet cover. She had held the bear that had been hers for twenty years. She had heard the worry in her mother's voice and the bluster in her father's voice. She hadn't had her ruined tea, nor had she done her preparatory work for the next day's class with 2B. Later, she had heard her mother's footfall outside her door and a light knocking and she had not replied, and much later she had heard them going to bed beyond the thin partition wall. A tossing and restless and hideous night, with the two images churning her mind. The twin images that denied her sleep were of the warmth and kindness of Giuseppe and Angela Ruggerio, and of the cold certainty of Axel Moen, they confronted her, the love shown her by Giuseppe and Angela Ruggerio, the matter of fact hostility of Axel Moen. She should not have given him the time of day, should have shown him the door. She thought she had betrayed the warmth and kindness, the love, of Giuseppe and Angela Ruggerio . . .

Her night had been unhappiness and confusion. Her day had been exhaustion and distraction.

It seemed God given, a moment of mercy, when the bell echoed through the low set prefabricated walls of the classroom. Perhaps the kids of 2B, the kickers and gougers and scribblers and bullies, felt the crisis and were afraid. They waited for her. Every day, at the end of classes, she swapped jokes and cheerful banter with the six-year-olds, not that day. She swept up the books and notes on her desk. She was first out through the door. It was her decision to go home, to apologize to her mother and father and to make believe that the tall American with the blond pony-tail of hair had never walked with her in the garden behind the bunga-low, never propositioned her, never talked of necessary "access." Her decision . . . She stopped beside a rubbish bin outside the classroom, reached deliberately into her bag, took out the letter of invitation and ripped it to small pieces. She dropped the torn scraps of paper, and the envelope into the bag. There was a mass of children around her as she walked toward the lean-to shed where her scooter was left for the day.

"Charlotte! Are you all right, Charlotte?"

The shrill voice bleated at her back. She turned. The headmistress faced her.

"All right? Yes, of course, I'm all right, Miss Samway."

"I just wondered . . . Charlotte, there are two men to see you. They're at the gate."

She looked over the running and shouting and charging horde of chil-dren going from the playground to the gate that led to the street. She looked between the heads and shoulders of the young mothers with cig-arettes at their lips, gum in their mouths, babies on their arms, bulging stomachs in tight jeans, who yapped about the night's TV. So much anger, fueled by the tiredness. She saw two men leaning against an old Sierra car, not the last model but the model before that, and the door which took the weight of their buttocks was a recent addition and not yet sprayed to match the rest of the bodywork that was scraped and rust flecked. They were not like anyone she knew. They wore old denims and T-shirts and one had a leather jacket over his shoulders and one wore a dirtied anorak. The hair of both men was cut short, and the one who was more slightly built had a silver ring piercing his right nostril, and the heav-ier one waved to her and she could see the tattoo between the wrist and knuckle of his hand.

"I don't know if they're friends of yours, Charlotte, but I don't want people like that hanging round my school."

She went to them. She stood her full height. The Headmistress behind her would be watching, and others on the staff, and the mothers would be watching. Little Miss Parsons, stuck up Miss Parsons, entertaining two low-life types who waited on the street for her. Something to talk about in the common room, and as they pushed the prams and led the kids back to the bloody little homes where the telly would blast all through the evening, and reading would involve the figures on scratch cards, and . . . God, she was just so bloody tired.

"Yes? You wanted to see me. I am Charlotte Parsons."

The one with the ring in his right nostril seemed to flick his fist open and in the palm of his hand was a police warrant card, and he said his name was Brent and muttered about "Task Force," and the one with the tattoo showed his card and said his name was Ken and the quiet words were "Drug Squad."

A frail voice. "What do you want?"

Brent said, "It's what you want, Miss Parsons. We were told you were looking for the grand tour."

Ken said, "We were told you needed a run round our patch, so you'd understand better the end of the importation road, that your particular interest was skag and rock."

Brent said, "But, Ken, we shouldn't go too fast for Miss Parsons, 'cos a nice girl like her wouldn't know that skag is heroin, now would she?"

Ken said, "Too right, Brent, and she wouldn't know that rock is crack cocaine. If you'd like to get in the back, Miss Parsons . . . Oh, don't go worrying, we squared it with the caretaker that he'll look after your scooter."

"Who sent you?"

Brent said, "Our inspector sent us."

Ken said, "The American gentleman . . ."

She shook. The trembling was in her arms, her fingers. The heaviness was in her legs, her feet. "And if I say that it's bugger-all to do with me?"

Brent said, "We were told that you might bluster a bit at first . . ."

Ken said, ". . . but after the bluster you'd be good as gold. Miss Parsons, I've been on Drug Squad a bit over four years. Brent's been on Task Force, drug importation team, for six years. All we get near is the creatures at the bottom of the pyramid. What we were told, sort of vague, you've the chance to hurt them right at the sharp end, nothing specific, but hurt the top of the pyramid. Now, if the bluster time's over could you get in, please?"

She did as she was told. She was good as gold, as Axel Moen had said she would be. She took the big step, and ducked down into the back of the old Sierra. Bloody man . . . The car was a fraud, clapped out exterior but a high performance tuned engine. Brent drove, and Ken was twisted round in the front seat so that he could talk to her. She thought she was tired, but as the car hammered on the lanes and then the fast road, she came to know the crow's-feet lines and the sack bulges at Ken's eyes. Something of a joke at first, about the tattoo only being a transfer that he could wash off each night, about a limit to the cause of duty, but old

Brent had gone the whole hog and had his nostril pierced for the god-dam job. They were not in the style of any policemen that she had met before. She thought a part of the smell came from the discarded polystyrene fast food plates that were dumped on the floor in the back, under her feet, and the rest of the smell came from the clothes they wore. They smoked hard, and didn't ask whether she minded them smoking. Ken said they weren't interested in cannabis, nor in solvents, nor in amphetamines, nor in the benzodiazapines like Temazepam and the barbiturates like sodium amytal. They worked the world of heroin that was skag, horse, smack, stuff, junk, and the world of crack cocaine that was rock, wash. She listened . . .

They came into the city of Plymouth, where Charley went for best shopping, for a dress for a friend's wedding, for Christmas presents and birthday gifts for her mother and father, and they talked her through the street cost of skag and rock. She listened . . .

They turned out of the city center and went north, climbing the long drag into the big housing estate. The name of the estate was familiar, from the local television, but she had never been there. Nothing urgent in the information they gave her, no passion, but the figures were beyond her comprehension. A worldwide trade in narcotics with a profit margin of 100 billion American dollars. Seizures and disruption of trafficking into UK the last year of £1.45 billion and what was seized and disrupted, on a good day, was one in five shipments and on a bad day was one in ten.

Ken said, "But they're the super glory figures, we don't operate at that level. We work down here in the gutter where the skag and the rock ends up. Down here a kilo of heroin, skag, goes for thirty grand, street price. Crack cocaine, rock, means £7,500 sterling, cheaper because of saturation. Out there in the big world they're talking thousands of kilos, tons—we're little people, we're talking kilos and grams." She listened . . .

Brent said, "You being a teacher, Miss Parsons, you'd be good at arithmetic. Ten grams doesn't give a big long high, ten minutes' worth for an habitual, but it costs, my sums, seventy five quid, and it's addictive, so you get to need a lot of grams, and that means you need a lot of cash, and you steal, fight, burgle, maybe kill, for the cash."

She saw tower blocks of homes, and terraces of homes, and she saw the children, like the ones that she taught, running in dog packs. She thought she saw a poverty and a despair . . . She saw an old man hurrying, limping, heavy on a stick, and his face was frightened and she wondered whether he had £75 sterling in his wallet. She saw an old woman scuttling with a shopping bag toward the dark entrance of a tower block, and she wondered whether the old woman had £75 sterling in her purse, or in the tin under her bed, or folded into her pension book and hidden, and she wondered how many old men and old women needed to be robbed to make a crack cocaine high that lasted ten minutes. She felt sick.

The light was going. Where the streetlights were broken, where the shadows clung, she saw ghost figures gathered. Brent cruised the car. Ken said, "See over there, Miss Parsons? See the tall kid. Most days he's there, he'll do about a hundred grams a week in rocks." Brent said, "He can do you skag as well, maybe some ecstasy. He's not special. He's one in a hundred, going on more. It's got hold of the place. Lift him, there's another ninety-nine." She saw the boy. He wore good Reeboks and Nike leisure wear and the cap on his head was the wrong way round. The contact she saw was short and sweet. Hands moved, money given over by the customer, goods given over to the customer. Brent said, "We're not even holding the line. The price is going down. It goes down when we're awash with it. The job of our young friend is to keep moving the rocks, getting new customers, creating demand. He's good in his market place." She listened . . .

Brent said, "I hope you're getting the picture, Miss Parsons. But I wouldn't want you to get the impression that this is C2 or C3 trade only. We could run you down to Plymstock or Roborough, up to Southway and round Goosewell. We can show you it anywhere."

"I want to go home, please."

Ken said, "No can do, sorry. The American gentleman said you should have the grand tour."

The unmarked police car slipped out of the estate. Charley looked a last time for the old people hurrying with their wallets and purses and their fear, for the kid with his Reebok shoes and Nike leisure suit, for the customers.

"Hi, Dwight, how was the vacation by the sea? How'd it go?"

"I'd rate him as cold shit."

His coat was flipped onto the hook of the stand, alongside the coat of the Country Chief.

"You'd better come in, you'd better talk."

He took a plastic cup and filled it with water from the dispenser. He walked across the deserted outer office and through the open door and into the Country Chief's office. It was a lowering dark evening outside, and there was rain in the heavy cloud that settled over the square. He was waved to a seat.

Dwight Smythe shrugged. "I reckon, Ray, I can cope with most sort of men. I failed with that bastard. Is he some sort of zealot? I thought Quantico was supposed to weed that sort. Right, he's rude, I can live with that. Right, he's aggressive, I can handle it. Where we part company, he elbows into a small and unsuspecting life, a young woman's life, and puts together a web to trap her, and does it cold. Me, I'm surplus to requirements, the chauffeur that's no longer needed."

"Did you read his file?"

"No."

"Do you know about him?"

"Not before I picked him up yesterday."

"Happy to make a judgment?"

"My assessment of him, yes, I feel comfortable with it."

"My opinion, Dwight, you're a lucky guy."

"How come, Ray, I'm a lucky guy?"

"A lucky guy, Dwight, because you have personnel and accounts and running this station to keep busy with." The eyes needled on Dwight Smythe. "You have fuck all of nothing to worry about."

"That is not fair."

"And true as hell. You, Dwight, are promotion material. You keep the leave charts regular, you keep wiping your ass, you keep the budget and expenses in blue, you keep your butt clean, you keep us all in surplus paper-clips, and you don't have to worry because that is promotion material. It's the road, Dwight, to the big office back home and the pile carpet, but it's not that joker's road."

"That is not fair, Ray, because without administration—"

"I have heard it before, I have practiced it. You are talking with the converted. When did you last carry a sidearm?"

"The way to fight organized crime is through the intellectual deployment of resources, not—"

"I've made that speech, Dwight. You think if I'd preached on body confrontation, nose-to-nose, I'd have climbed the goddam ladder? Grow up."

"I didn't expect to hear you, Ray, give out that sort of crap."

"Your consolation, what should make you feel good, the like of Axel Moen don't get to climb the goddam ladder. The ladder's for you and for me. It's you and me that like to collect the plaques for the wall, the photographs of the Director's handshake, the commendations and the bullshit."

"Sorry, I spoke." Dwight Smythe pushed himself up, drank the last of the water. He looked around him. The plaques recorded successful operations, the photographs witnessed the warmth of the Director meeting with a coming man, the commendations were polished print engraved on bronze. "And I don't recognize bullshit, Ray."

"You taking Melanie out tonight, something to eat?"

"Yes, why?"

"My advice, meant kind, call her, tell her to hold an hour so you can get your face into the computer, take a look at Axel Moen's file."

"For what?"

"Did he tell you his target?"

"He did not."

"Read his file so you get to know what sort of man gets put up against a way big target."

"Maybe in the morning . . ."

"Tonight, Dwight, read it."

It was an instruction. They prided themselves, the Country Chief and the four special agents and the clerical staff working on the fifth floor of the embassy, that they were a close team, that harsh words were rare, instructions came rarer. He walked out of the office. He went to his desk. He called Melanie and he told her he was held up and put her back an hour and asked her to call the curry house on the Edgware Road to hold the reservation for an hour. He checked with the file that was kept locked in the drawer of his desk for the entry code and the password key. He went into the NADDIS computer for the file on the man he called cold shit.

"We've just got the one at the moment. There was another one last month but it died. The other one died about three days before this one came in here," the nurse said. She was a big woman but with a gentle Irish voice. She spoke flatly as if she did not care to feel emotional involvement. "I couldn't tell you how long this one's going to hold on. Myself, I hope it's not too long. You see, she's damaged. She was damaged in the womb, pretty close to conception, she was damaged all the time through the pregnancy, she's damaged now. It's what happens when the mother is an addict. Her mother's nineteen years old, she's into mainlining with heroin, lovely girl, was and still is. The little one is seventeen days old and it's as if she's on heroin, same as Mum, same as if she was using Mum's syringe, Mum's tourniquet. This one's too far gone to be weaned off it, the damage is in the little one's system. That's why I say that I hope it's not too long . . ."

Charley stood by the door. She looked into the room, Children's Unit (Intensive Care). The baby seemed to shiver inside the glass case and the tubes hooked to its nose and mouth waved slowly with the movements. The nurse spoke as if they were alone, as if the mother, the "lovely girl," was not there. The mother sat beside the glass box. She wore a dressing gown, hospital issue. She stared blankly at the quivering baby. When Charley turned away, the nurse smiled at her, and said that it was decent of her to have bothered to come. That was an empty remark because the nurse did not know why Charley had come, did not know of the arrangement made by Brent and a hospital administrator. Charley hurried out. She thought she hated Axel Moen.

Brent and Ken were in the corridor. They led, she followed.

Out into the night air. Across a car park. There was a light over a door.

Brent knocked at the door. Ken rang the bell. They entered the hospital mortuary.

"This one's heroin but it could just as well have been cocaine. On average we get three a year. His father's a retired major in Tavistock, not that it matters who his father was, is," the pathology technician said. He was a young man with an angled nose on which were balanced heavy spectacles. He spoke as if the corpse, the retired major's son, was an item of no particular interest. "When they get started on it, heroin that is, they find the total relaxation from stress, from anxiety, must seem the way out of the problem, but . . . they step up the dosage, the withdrawal symptoms each time are harsher, more frequent. The dependency grows. This one, I heard, he broke into his parents' house and cleaned out his mother's jewelry case, all the heirloom stuff was worth one big fix. He would have been subject to tremors, muscle spasms, sweats. He would have loaded up in panic, but got the dose wrong. He would have been unconscious, then gone into coma. He ended up in here after a breathing failure. Of course, this is just a small city, we don't get that many."

Charley looked down at the corpse. She had never seen a dead body before. It was as if the skin had been waxed pale, and the body hair on the chest and in the arm pits and round the penis of the body seemed, to her, like a weed that had been poisoned. There was color in the bruised right arm, but the needle holes were dulled. She thought the body was of a young man of about her age and there seemed to be a peace about his expression. She didn't know, and she didn't ask, whether the people in the mortuary could have given his face the mask of peace, or whether the act of dying made the peace.

In the corridor outside the area where cadavers were stored in refrigerated bays, Ken was smoking a cigarette that was tucked into the palm of his hand, and Brent was unwrapping a boiled sweet.

They drove her back to the school.

They rang the doorbell for the caretaker who opened up for them.

Charley gunned the engine of her scooter. She sat astride the saddle. She arched her back, pinched her shoulder blades.

"Are you always as subtle as that? Squeezing my emotions. Winding me up, like a damn puppet."

Brent said, "Sorry, love, but it's what we were asked to do."

Ken said, "I don't know, of course, what it was for, sunshine, but it was what the American gentleman wanted."

She pulled the helmet down over her hair. Charley had seen reality, what she read in newspapers and what she watched on television, and she had not cared to know that it was reality in her own bloody backyard. She rode away into the night, and she cursed him and the tears ran on her face and were caught by the wind. On the road, in the lane, a car followed her and lit her back and never closed on her. In her mind was a jumble of images, unproven, of the island of Sicily and the city of Palermo. The lights of the car stayed in her mirror. Palermo . . .

No wind, no rain, no cloud. The island baked in spring sunshine. By early morning, the first warmth of the year suffocated the city. Over that city, which was pressed into a narrow seaboard between the Mediterranean and the mountains had settled a chemical mist of yellow hazed pollution from the vehicles jockeying on the Via della Liberta and the Via Marqueda and the Via Francesco Crispi and the Via Vittorio Emanuele and the Via Tukory. Invisible under that mist were the symbols of Low-intensity Warfare, the electronic signals, the microwave boosters, the pulses sent by telephone and radio transmissions, the pictures carried by covert surveillance cameras, the voices distorted by audio intercept bugs. Among the clutter of a modern society's legitimate communications, small fish in the big sea, were the messages, coded and masked, of a contemporary battlefield. Signals, pulses, tones, images, voices of men at war meandered under the foul tasting mist that clung above the roofs of Palermo.

When she came out of the common room, with the taste of instant coffee in her mouth, to bring in the children from mid-morning break, she saw him sitting in the parked car outside the gate. She thought of the housing estate and the despair and the poverty.

He did not trust the safety of any form of telephone communication.

Mario Ruggerio sat alone in the small room of the apartment on the first floor. The sounds, raucous, of the Capo district came to him through the opened window, through the closed shutters that filtered segments of sunlight into the room. The sunlight lay in shards across the table at which he worked and were reflected from a mirror and onto a side wall so that the brightness and the shadow latticed the picture of the agony of Christ. The crying of the hawkers, the shouting of people in anger and in mirth, the roar of the engines of Vespas and Lambrettas competed with the quiet of Radio Uno. Neither the noise from the alleyway below nor the voice and music close to him disturbed his concentration. Both the outside noise and the radio's voice and music were a necessary part of his security. In the Capo district of hardship and crime and wariness, a surveillance car and a surveillance team would be noticed and a quiet would fall over the alleyway. And if there was the arrest of a *super-latitanti*, a big man on the run, or if there was a swoop and roundup of suspects, then it would be carried on the radio and he would know. The outside noise and the radio's voice and music did not disturb him as he wrote the brief and cryptic messages with a fine point pen on the sheets of paper used for rolling cigarettes.

Education at school for Mario Ruggerio had lasted from the age of five years to nine years. No schoolmaster, nor schoolmistress, no academic, no lecturer, no professor had taught him the science of electronic communications, but he had no trust in the security of the telephone. There were those he had known who had believed they could talk through the landline system, and they sat now in the stifling heat of the cells at Ucciardone in the city of Palermo. There were others who had believed in the safety of the new analogue technology of the mobile telephone, and they rotted now behind the walls of Caltanisetta on the island or at Asinara prison on Sardinia. He had been urged the last year to believe in the total security of the most recent system, the digital network, promised that it could not be intercepted, and those men who had believed and promised now saw the sun and the sky for an hour a day through the net mesh above the exercise yard at Ucciardone or Caltanisetta or Asinara.

He laid the messages written on the cigarette papers across the table. He read them. He lit a small cigar. He coughed and spat phlegm into his handkerchief. He read the messages again and then gathered them into his ashtray. He was satisfied he had memorized the messages. He burned the papers on which they were written. The messages, now held in his memory, dealt with the matters concerning the movement of $8 million from a holding company in the Bahamas to a casino development in Slovenia, the switching of $4 million from a Vienna based account to a bank in Bratislava, the buying of a block of twenty-two apartments at a Corsican beach resort, the question of the life and death of a man in Catania, the problem of the persistent investigation by a magistrate in the Palazzo di Giustizia. Five messages, now burned, now memorized, would be passed, word of mouth, to five men in five bars over five coffees that morning.

His way was caution and suspicion. With caution and suspicion he maintained what was most precious, his freedom.

Later, when the sun was higher against the closed shutters, when he had smoked a second cigar, when he had listened to the radio news bulletin and heard the report that the Questura in Agrigento had made no progress in their search for a missing man and his grandson and his driver, he would slip in his anonymity onto the streets of the city and into five bars where his people waited for him. His people were the "cut-out" intermediaries who carried the messages, verbally, to construction magnates and politicians and the principals of the Masons or Rotary and bankers, and to the policemen that he owned, and to the churchmen that he had bought. All of those who received messages from Mario Ruggerio acted upon them immediately because he fueled their greed and fanned their fear . . .

Mario Ruggerio wondered, a fast thought because there was much in his mind, how were the children and the baby that he loved, and the thought brought a gentle smile to his face. The smile was still on his face as he walked down the alleyway in his gray wool jacket with his check cap worn forward.

When she came into the playground to halt the football game and round up the children with their lunchboxes, she saw him waiting and smoking in his car. She thought of the old man hurrying to his home on the estate.

From the balcony she watched him go. She held the baby. *Piccolo* Mario jumped excitedly on the balcony tiles and leaned across the pots of geraniums to see his father at the car below, and Francesca held her hand and cried quietly.

He turned from the car and he waved up at the bungalow, and Angela's answering gesture was a limp flap of her hand. She did not wait to see him into the car, nor to see him drive away through the main gates that would have been opened by the uniformed *portiere*. She left *piccolo* Mario on the balcony, she carried the baby and led Francesca back into the living area of the apartment, and past the statue that she thought disgusting and over the stain she could not remove in the carpet from Iran. She loathed Palermo. To Angela Ruggerio, the city was a prison. In Rome, if they still lived in Rome, she could have gone back to the university, but it was not acceptable in Palermo that a married woman should go alone to a university. In Rome she could have gone to a health gymnasium, but in Palermo it was not permitted that a married woman could go to a gymnasium without a friend for a chaperone and she did not have that friend. In Rome it would have been possible for her to have taken part-time work in a gallery or in a museum, but it was not possible in Palermo that a married woman of her class should go to work . . . She could not, in Palermo, paint the walls of the apartment, wield a roller brush, because, in Palermo, that would imply her husband could not afford to employ an artisan to do the work.

She loathed the city most when he left to go abroad. Then the money for household expenses was left in the drawer beside her bed, because, in Palermo, it was not usual for a married woman to have her own bank account, own credit cards, own resources. In Rome, during the good days in Rome, he would have talked with her the night before a business flight to London or Frankfurt or New York, but not now, because, in Palermo, it was not necessary for a married woman to know the detail of her husband's work.

She slumped down into the depth of the wide sofa. She flicked the pages of a magazine and read nothing . . . The boy shouted. *Piccolo* Mario yelled from the balcony that he had seen his uncle, really, and she must come. She pushed herself up from the sofa. She held the baby tight against her. She went onto the balcony. She looked down, across the car park, past the security gates, onto the pavement. She saw nobody, but *piccolo* Mario shouted that he had seen his uncle, yelled that his uncle had walked past the gates and looked for them and had waved, and she saw nobody that she knew. How many times did he come, the little old man with the bowed shoulders and the jowl at his throat and the gray jacket and the checked cap, and walk past the apartment in the Giardino Inglese and look up toward the flowers on their balcony, how often? She knew, of course, all that was said of *piccolo* Mario's uncle on the television, all that was written of Peppino's brother in the *Giornale di Sicilia* . . . She took the boy from the balcony. It was not right that the boy should talk of his uncle.

In four days they would be at the villa, they would be by the sea, where, if it were possible, she would be more lonely than in the city. She prayed, almost with fervor, that Charlotte would come.

When she rang the bell for the end of mid-afternoon break she saw him sitting with a magazine in his car. She thought of the old woman, in fear, going back to her one bedroom with the hidden tin of savings that made her vulnerable.

There were only two pictures on the walls of the room in the barracks at Monreale. There was the picture of his daughter and there was the photograph of Generale Carlos Alberto dalla Chiesa. The smiling ten-year-old girl and the militaristic portrait served to heighten Giovanni Crespo's sense of total isolation.

He dialed the number, he threw the switch that activated the scrambler.

Isolato, isolated, was a cruel word for the captain of *carabinieri.* His daughter was growing up in Bologna. He was isolated from her, saw her twice a year at best, three days at a time, and spoke briefly on the telephone each Sunday evening. That was isolation. But it was the general who had taught him the true meaning of the word *isolato.* The general, hero of the counter-terrorist campaign against the *Brigate Rosse,* prefect of Palermo, had been ridiculed, sneered at, whispered of, isolated and shot to death thirty-eight days after Giovanni Crespo had joined his staff as liaison officer. They were all isolated, all the condemned men, before the gunfire or the bomb. To stay alive, living and breathing and fucking and drinking, he thought it most necessary to recognize isolation.

His call was to an unlisted number in Rome, a quiet side street office on the Via Sardegna, to the desk of the DEA's Country Chief.

" 'Vanni here. Go secure, Bill."

He was asked to wait out. He heard the clicked interruption on the line. The voice was fainter, with metallic distortion. He was told he could speak.

"Just wanted to know how my friend was, whether my friend had optimism . . ."

He was told the young woman was "OK, nothing special." He was told she was "predictable" and that she had taken time "to think on it."

"You know, Bill, we don't even have a name for this. It is ridiculous, but we don't even have a name. So, we don't have a file, that's good, and we don't have computer space, that's better, but we should have a code name, do you not think?"

Giovanni Crespo, aged 42, captain of *carabinieri,* member of the specialist *Reparto Operativo Speciale* team tasked with securing the arrest of Mario Ruggerio, would never speak a confidence even on a line scrambled with state-of-the-art electronics. On the island he trusted no man. In his life he trusted only one man. He had taken the letter posted by Angela Ruggerio, sister-in-law of Mario Ruggerio, to Rome and to the one man he trusted. The detail of the matter was not shared with his own people, for lack of trust of his own people. He had taken the detail of the matter, the link, to his friend.

He was asked what he thought.

"Helen. Helen of Troy. Bill, when all else failed, in Italian we would say *uccello da richiamo,* I think your word is 'decoy,' yes? The decoy behind the walls. The way through the gate. Codename Helen, for when we talk, Bill. But, Bill, it is to be kept close."

It was authorized in Washington. Herb had authorized it. Yes, he knew Herb. He was told it should be kept closer than a choirboy's sphincter, and the Country Chief's laugh rang in his ear, pealing as if from inside a box of metal.

"Is that dirty talk, Bill? Hey, but, Bill, we keep this close. You call me when you have something, something on Codename: Helen. It's bad here at the moment, so quiet. There is nothing to touch, nothing to feel, nothing to see. When it is quiet then I have the anxiety. You tell him, he gives the Codename Helen a good kicking because I need her here, just tell him."

The one man that he trusted, that Giovanni Crespo would give his life to, was Axel Moen.

"Bill, he is moving, climbing. Did you see that a bad bastard from Agrigento went missing? Old-style, old-school, so conflict was inevitable. It is the *lupara bianca,* the disappearance. Between him and the top place, where he will try to be, is only the Catania man, that's what we hear. If he gets to the top place, our friend, then there is a time of maximum danger, perhaps for many people, when he would seek to prove himself. Bill, I have a big anxiety. The only way for our friend to prove himself is to kill . . ."

When she pushed her scooter out of the lean-to shed and buttoned her anorak and slipped on her helmet, she saw him look up and wipe the windscreen, and she saw him start to maneuver the car. She thought of the young mother, the addict, in Intensive Care.

They were the *ragazzi,* the kids, the boys. Though the magistrate called them, always, the *ragazzi,* three of them were aged over forty, and one was two years off a fiftieth birthday. The fifth, Pasquale, was the only one of the *ragazzi* still clinging to youth. The party, orange juice and a cake, was in the kitchen. The kitchen was for cooking and doubled as the communications room and rest area for them.

In the depths of the apartment, away from the closed door of the kitchen, a telephone rang.

It was as good a party as was possible on orange juice and chocolate cake. No alcohol. No alcohol was allowed on duty, nor for five hours before starting duty. Chocolate cake was permitted, and orange juice. The baby, Pasquale's first, had been born in the small hours of the morning and he had come straight from the hospital to start his duty. And they larked and fooled like kids and boys and there was spilled juice on the floor and broken cake on the table, and the birth of a baby and the pride of a father were celebrated. He had bought the cake himself, and the juice. If he had been a part of them, truly a member of the team, then they would have collected among themselves and bought the cake and the juice. He was too young, too recent, to have been wholly accepted, and his work was under continuous probationer assessment. It could have been that they resented his youth, there were some on the qualification course who said that the reflexes of a younger man were sharper than those of older men . . . He tried to be a part of the team.

The telephone no longer rang.

And those who had three children and four children and two children, and the *maresciallo* who was the oldest and had teenagers, competed with the horror stories of parenthood to bludgeon Pasquale. The black execution humor of his fellows played, mocking, around Pasquale's ears, the tales of the sleepless nights and the changing of shit filled diapers and vomited food and a swallowed ID card and the little hands that climbed a chair to produce the condom packet from the bathroom cupboard that was displayed to grandparents, and . . .

The laughter died. They heard, all of them, the footfall beyond the kitchen door.

All faced the door, like *ragazzi,* like kids and boys caught in a moment of guilt. He seemed with his eyes to apologize, as if he deeply regretted the intrusion into his own kitchen, into their communications room and rest room. They had started the party, opened the orange juice, cut the cake, because he had told them he was not returning that evening to the Palazzo di Giustizia, now he shrugged in his self-effacing way and brushed the graying hair back off his forehead and muttered that he must return to his bunker office. He held his briefcase in his hand and his raincoat was draped on his shoulders.

There was the snap of the *maresciallo's* radio, to alert the military in the street.

Crumbs were brushed off a Beretta M-12S 9mm pistol, juice was shaken from the barrel of a Heckler & Koch MP-5 machine gun. The vests of kevlar plates, proof against small arms fire and light shrapnel, were heaved up from the floor beside the oven by Pasquale, one for each man.

There was the clatter of the weapons being armed.

Left in the kitchen, debris on the table, half drunk glasses of orange juice, half eaten slices of chocolate cake.

They went out of the apartment and toward the door. The woman who lived across the hallway scowled, and the bodyguards gave her the eye and the finger because she had twice written to newspapers to complain of the danger in which she was placed by living in proximity to Dr. Rocco Tardelli. They went fast down two flights of stairs, in front of him, beside him, behind him. He was a small figure, hemmed in between them, skipping to keep pace. They were not his servants, nor his messengers, nor his cooks, they would never be his true friends. They had not volunteered to protect his life, but been given the assignment.

Out on the street the soldiers shrieked their whistles for the traffic to halt at the far junctions. Two of them were out of the main lobby and into the cars and hacking the engines. Guns drawn, the *maresciallo* in front of him, Pasquale behind him, the magistrate was bustled to the open door of his armored Alfa. As if he were pitched inside, as if he were a parcel to be dispatched . . . The sirens blasted. The tires screamed. The Alfa and the chase car hit the first junction and swerved right, scattered the cars and scooters ahead. They were not the servants nor the cooks of Dr. Rocco Tardelli, nor were they his true friends, but each of them in their differing ways felt a fierce loyalty to the small man low on the backseat of the Alfa who struggled through his heavy horn-rimmed spectacles to read a file as the car bucked, braked, accelerated and weaved. The other teams, those assigned to other investigating magistrates, regarded them with pity. They were the escort of the magistrate who worked stubbornly and persistently toward the capture and conviction of Mario Emanuele Ruggerio. They were the *ragazzi* of a walking corpse.

A tremor of a voice from the back of the Alfa. "I understand you are to be congratulated, Pasquale. Is the baby well, is your wife well?"

His mind churning the procedures of "cover and evacuate" and "defensive of life only" shooting patterns and "fight or flight" mode, Pasquale muttered, "Very well, thank you, Dr. Tardelli."

"You will be leaving me?"

"No, Dr. Tardelli."

"Because you now have a baby?"

"Please, Dr. Tardelli, you distract me . . ."

When she pushed the scooter up the drive and parked it in front of the garage doors and took off her helmet and shrugged her hair free, she saw him slowing in his car. She thought of the baby of seventeen days, hooked to tubes, shivering in a glass box.

"Did you read the man's file?"

"I did."

"Did you like what you read?"

"Not particularly, if you need to know."

The Country Chief, Ray, stood at the partition wall that blocked off

Dwight Smythe's work area from the open plan office. He had been a guest observer the whole of the day at a symposium organized by the British Home Office to talk through international cooperation on organized crime—and the day had been crap, the papers read before lunch by a Russian and a Spaniard and the paper read after the buffet by a Brit from the National Criminal Intelligence Service had been shit. The papers had been a recitation of seizure statistics and arrest statistics and asset confiscation statistics, and he'd reckoned them garbage. The papers were garbage because they did not go to the core problem of taking out the men who mattered, the men who made it happen. Complacency was a crime in the Country Chief's Bible, and that day there had been more complacency on show than food on the buffet table. He envied Axel Moen, didn't reckon Axel Moen suffered too many symposiums.

"You want to go work in La Paz, Bolivia?"

"No."

"He did. You want to get yourself into firefights where they need body-bags afterwards?"

"No."

"He did. You want to lift a bad man in Miami, testify to a Grand Jury, find out then that there's a video of you going into court and that the Cali people, the cartel guys, have the video and have your face?"

"No."

"You want to wear a Smith & Wesson, you want to look over your shoulder, you want to go to Palermo?"

"No, no, no."

He could be affable, the Country Chief, Ray. He could tell a good story at the Christmas party. He could charm the asses off the inspection teams. He could make a sour minded man smile. He was affable when he cared to be. His voice had a crunch, trodden down frosted gravel.

"You don't want it, Dwight, so keep your bad mouthing to yourself."

"What I'm saying—"

"Don't."

"You goddam hear me, Ray. What I'm saying, we are professionals and we are trained and we are paid. The young woman that he's got his hooks into—hear me, because I didn't just take time on the computer for Moen's file, I went into current assessments of La Cosa Nostra, down in Sicily, that's a killing ground—the young woman is an innocent."

The Country Chief, a moment, softened. "Maybe, Dwight, you sell us all short, maybe we're all thinking like you. And maybe we should all clap our hands and sing our hymns and get on our knees and thank our God that He didn't give us the problem. Have you got the budget figures for last month? Trouble is, it's a good plan. Might not, but might just get to work. Bring the budget through, please."

When she looked from the window, she saw him lying back, eyes closed, in his car. She thought of the grief of a retired major and how he would writhe in self-guilt. She thought of the body on the trolley.

Anyone who knew her or worked with her would have described Mavis Finch as a difficult person. Her family was up north, she had no friends in London, there was no one who would have shouted her corner. Those who lived in the same block of two- and one-bedroom maisonettes in a south west suburb of the capital would have spoken, if asked, of Mavis Finch's complaint flow about the noise of their televisions, about their pets, about their litter, about late visitors. Those who worked with her in the bank in the Fulham Road would have spoken, if asked, of Mavis Finch's carping criticism of balance sheets produced late, of account errors, of extended lunch hours, of days taken for minor illness.

She was unloved and unliked by both neighbors and work colleagues. To the more charitable she was someone to be pitied, to the less charitable she was a vindictive bitch. But the life of this lonely thirty-seven-year-old woman, without a man or a child or a friend or a hobby, was governed by a rule book. The rule book laid down the volume of her neighbors' televisions, what pets could be kept, when their litter should be put out, up to what time visitors were permitted to come banging on doors . . .

It was because of the needle eye of Mavis Finch for the pages of her rule book that Detective Sergeant Harry Compton, SO6, took an early dinner in the hotel fronting onto Portman Square. Her rule book for conduct in the bank on the Fulham Road extended beyond matters of lateness, delays, mistakes, sickness. Regarded by her managers as best kept distant from customers, it had been the previous June a combination of holidays and pregnancies and sickness that had forced them to detail Mavis Finch to counter work. It was because she had been at the counter, mid-morning, nine months before that DS Compton, Fraud Squad, toyed with a cod mornay in the dining room of a five-star hotel. Probably, Mavis Finch, that long ago morning, would have been alone among the counter clerks in having read in full the texts of the Drugs Trafficking Act (1984), the Criminal Justice Acts (1988 and 1993) and the Drugs Trafficking Offenses Act (1994). The Acts, taken in totality, made it obligatory for a bank to disclose "suspicious and large transactions." Of course, that mid-morning, Mavis Finch reported the deposit of £28,000 in £50 notes because had she not reported it she would, herself, have been guilty of criminal conduct. She had taken the name, Giles Blake, the address, she had noted what she described in the spidery handwriting of her report as an "impatience" by the customer . . . Compton watched the target, sipped mineral water, listened.

And so typical, Compton thought, that the buggers at NCIS should have taken from June to March to evaluate the bank's disclosure before passing the detail to Fraud Squad. Bloody typical. To Harry Compton, the National Criminal Intelligence Service should more often get its hands out from under its butt.

He had, because time was precious and allocated fiercely to priorities, around five hours of desk time and an evening to decide whether to hold open a file on Giles Blake or whether to scrawl across the existing seven sheets that "no further action" was warranted.

The desk time had produced nothing tangible, no evidence of illegality, but Compton had a nose, nostrils, that sensed an incomplete picture. A nice house in Surrey for Mr. Blake, a nice wife and children for Mr. Blake, bank accounts and stocks and money in building societies for Mr. Blake. Too much that was "nice," and not enough to substantiate it. Compton had gone as a young detective from the Harrow station to Anti-Terrorist Branch, and found the surveillance of Irish "sleepers" in smoky and beer-stinking pubs to be a decent definition of boredom. He had sought and found stimulation, he had transferred to Fraud Squad. He liked to say, if he met up, increasingly rarely, with guys from Harrow or Anti-Terrorist, that SO6 was the steepest learning curve in the Metropolitan Police. He was studying, nights, business management and accountancy, and when he'd those qualifications he'd be going for law. But, the old nose still counted.

What had twitched the nose of Harry Compton, stung the nostrils, was the guest that Giles Blake had brought to dinner.

The tables were adjacent. They liked to boast, from top to bottom of SO6, that their surveillance procedures were the best, better than Anti-Terrorist, better than Flying Squad. The ethos was "proximity." They had to blend, they had to risk burning out. It was not sufficient merely to observe, long-range, they needed "proximity" to listen.

He'd heard, once on a course, a hot afternoon, central heating turned too high, head beginning to drop, a lecture line that had hit him. "The accountants are more dangerous than the killers—the killers are small time scumbags, the accountants threaten a whole society . . ." He had used up the five hours of his allocated desk time, he had started to burrow into his evening's surveillance time, tracked Giles Blake from his London office to Portman Square, to the hotel, to the reception desk, to the bar, to the restaurant. The guest had come to the restaurant, shaken hands, hugged, sat down.

"A good flight?"

"It's every day, every week, not in your papers here, a strike of the airline workers, just two hours—so we were late away. Nothing changes in Palermo."

His nose twitched, his nostrils smarted.

The light came on over the porch. Axel flicked the wiper switch and the windscreen was smeared clear. She came out of the door. The windscreen blurred with the rain. She hurried through the small gate and she was hunched small with her arms tight around her body as if that would keep her dry. At the car she rapped her fingers on the passenger window. He did not hurry himself. He tossed the *Time* magazine copy behind him and onto the backseat and then he pulled out the ashtray and stubbed the cigarette. The rain ran on her hair and her face and she hit the passenger window with her fist. He leaned across and unlocked the door, pushed it open.

She ducked into the car and was wiping the rain off her head and from her face. She turned to him, angry. There was a brightness in her eyes, but her face was wrecked because her mouth was screwed, good anger. It was useful for Axel Moen to see how she handled good anger.

"Thanks, thank you very much."

"What do you thank me for?"

"Thanks for making me stand out there, get bloody wet, while you read your magazine, smoke your cigarette—"

"Care for one?" He held the packet in front of her, Lucky Strike, out of the carton from duty-free at Fiumicino.

"It's a dirty habit . . . thanks for keeping me in the rain while you read and smoke, before you open the door—"

"So you got wet, how's that cause to thank me?"

"Are you stupid?"

"Sometimes, sometimes not."

"It was sarcasm. In thanking you for getting me wet, I was being sarcastic."

"I find it best, Charley, always, so there's not misunderstandings, to say what I mean."

He grinned. Axel grinned because her face had flushed red. He saw the color spreading across her face by the light above him. It was good anger and getting better. She had twisted to confront him. He thought she might have put on lipstick at the start of the day but it had wiped off and not been replaced, and there were no cosmetics round her eyes and they were bloodshot as if it were two nights she hadn't slept well. Her temper was scratched, a nail in wood that the saw blade hits. It was important for him to read her temper.

Forced calm, "All right, what I mean . . . We don't have it now, we used to have a terrier bitch. When the bitch was in season, on heat, then a big Labrador dog used to come and sit at the side gate. He used to sit there by the hour, big bloody stupid eyes. You know what, that dog sitting there, all night, and sort of crying, he got to be just a bore."

"I'm hearing you, Charley."

Enjoying herself. "The town where I went to college, it was an army town, a garrison camp. Soldiers used to sit in their cars, on their bikes, at the gate and watch us, the girls. We called them "lechies," understand, lechers. They didn't have old raincoats, they kept their Y-fronts on, they didn't flash us. They were pretty harmless, but they got to be boring."

"Did they?"

"You here in your car, last night, all night . . . today at school . . . here now . . . it's getting to be a bore. It is causing embarrassment. Danny Bent, he says you could have injured his stock. Fanny Carthew says you damn near ran her dog over. Zach Jones wants to know if we've called the police. Daphie Farson wants to know if you're a pervert."

"Maybe you should go tell them to fuck themselves."

"That is—"

She laughed. He thought she was trying to be shocked and failing, because she was laughing. It was useful for him to see her laugh. When she laughed she was pretty, quite pretty, not especially pretty. She wiped the laugh.

"Where I was taken last night, emotional blackmail, it was pathetic."

"Myself, I'd say it was patronizing."

"Treating me like a juvenile."

"Patronizing, but I doubt it did you harm."

"What do you want of me?"

"Same as I told you first time round. There is an opportunity for you to give me access to the home of Giuseppe and Angela Ruggerio. I need that access."

She stared hard at him. There were shadows on her face that caught the small lines at her eyes and at her mouth. He thought now that he stressed her. It was important to him to see her stressed. He waited on her. It was not for him to lead her.

She hesitated, then blurted, "If I refuse, won't go to Palermo . . . ?"

Axel gazed at the windscreen, at the running water, at the blur of the beach and the jetty and dark outline of the headland. "I lose that opportunity for access. I have one opportunity through you. OK, we thought it out, you get the invitation, you write back and say that you're sorry and can't make it, but that you've a friend. We supply the friend. The friend is the Customs and Excise investigation team, a policewoman, whatever . . . They're too careful over there, wouldn't buy it. You're the one with access, Charley, only you. If you refuse, I don't get the access. Don't think I want someone like you down there, but I haven't another option."

She turned away from him, twisted her back to him. She jerked the passenger door open. She pushed herself out of the car. She told him that she would think on it one more night, and where she would meet him the next day after school. She asked him if he liked walking. She bent suddenly, peered at him through the door, and it did not seem to matter to her that the rain beat on her head and her shoulders and her spine.

"What would happen to me, if . . . ?"

"It went sour on you? If they were just unhappy about you, they'd fire you, send you home. Charley, I try and say what I mean so there aren't misunderstandings. It's a shit place and they're shit people. If they'd serious cause to suspect you then they'd kill you and go home afterwards and eat their dinner. It wouldn't bother them, Charley, to kill you."

He watched her run toward the light above the porch of the bungalow.

3

Egregio Dottore e gentile
Signora.

She sat in the classroom. She took a mouthful of a sandwich from her lunchbox. She sipped at the can of Pepsi. She had brought in with her, in the rucksack that strapped onto the back of her scooter, the sheet of notepaper headed with the address of Gull View Cottage. In the mid-morning break she had gone to the rubbish containers on the far side of the playground and lifted the lids of two of them and tried, hopelessly, to identify which plastic bag had been in the bin outside her classroom. She had not found the plastic bag. It was a fine day, the cloud was broken, and the crocuses in the pots around the prefabricated classroom were already showing with the daffodils, and she thought that the spring season was a time of hope and optimism, and she wondered how the spring season was in Palermo … She tried to remember each phrase, sentence, of the letter written to her by Angela Ruggerio and then intercepted and copied and tracked.

> (Sorry, *dottore*, and sorry, *signora*, but that is going to be the limit of my Italian—I remember quite a lot of it, but if you'll excuse me the rest will be in English!!)
> Thank you very much for your kind invitation. And my warmest congratulations on the birth of Mauro, and of course I was very pleased to hear that Mario and Francesca were well.

It was so clear to her, the Roman summer of 1992. School finished, exams taken. The miserable response of her father, who had expected too much of her grades. Not good enough for university but sufficient to win her a place at a teachers' training college. It had been her mother who had seen the advertisement in the *Lady* magazine. Her mother had seen the advertisement in the magazine at the hairdresser, copied it and brought it home. An Italian family living in Rome sought a "nanny/mother's help" for the summer months. She and her mother had written the application and enclosed a photograph, and her father had warned that Italians pinched bottoms and were dirty, not to be trusted and thieves, and she and her mother had ignored him as they usually did. The four months of the Roman summer of 1992 had been, quite simply, the happiest months of her life.

> I was very surprised to get your letter, and you will un-
> derstand that I have had to think about it very hard. Be-
> cause of the situation today in England I found when I
> graduated as a teacher (!) that it was really hard to find
> work. I think I was very lucky, Dad certainly says so, to
> get this job that I now have.

The Roman summer of 1992 had been magic months for Charley. From the time that she had walked down the aircraft's steps, pushed her trolley through Customs and Immigration, seen Giuseppe and Angela Ruggerio, with Mario holding his father's hand and Angela carrying the baby Francesca, and seen their welcome smiles, she had felt a true liberation for the first time in her life. They had greeted her as if she were a part of them, right from the time that Peppino, as he insisted he should be called, had driven them away from the airport in his sleek BMW, and she had sat in the back with the small boy beside her and the baby girl on her lap, had treated her as a friend already by the time the car had swept into the basement car park of the apartment on the Collina Fleming. She had thought then that her father was ossified in his attitudes and boring, and she thought that her mother was complacent in her outlook and boring, and to be away from them, first time in her life, was true freedom. Most mornings of that June and July Peppino, with the beautiful suit and smile and lotion scent, was gone early to his office in the bank, something to do with the Vatican. And most mornings of those first weeks Charley had taken Mario down to the *piazza* for the private bus to the kindergarten of St. George's School, high on the Via Cassia. And most mornings of that June and July Angela, with beautiful blouses and skirts and coats, was out in the shops of the Via Corso or at her volunteer job in the Keats Museum at the Piazza Espagna. Most mornings, while the *domestica* made the beds and cleaned the bathrooms and put the washing in the machines and did the ironing and tidied the kitchen, Charley had sat on the wide balcony and played with the baby, Francesca, and marveled at the view above the pot flowers, watered each day by the old *portiere,* stretching from the dome of the basilica of St. Peter's across the heart of the city and away to the distant shadows of the mountains. It had been heaven. And more of heaven in the afternoons, the Italian classes in a room off the cool of a courtyard behind the Parliament building, and then the roaming walks through the *centro storico.* When she walked the narrow cobbled streets of the *centro storico* she had never taken a map with her, so that each church and old piazza, each gallery and hidden garden, each tucked away temple and frieze from antiquity, had seemed a discovery that was personal to her. It had been her freedom.

> I have considered very carefully your offer that I should come to Palermo to help look after Mario and Francesca and baby Mauro. I am happy in my present job, I have ambitions to move to a bigger school when I have gained more direct experience. If I resign my position then I believe it would be quite difficult, at this time, to find another school that would have me in the autumn.

That summer of 1992, for the months of August and September, Charley had gone with Angela Ruggerio and the children to a rented beach villa a kilometer along the coast from Civitavecchia. If he were not away on the bank's business Peppino came to the villa at weekends. Seven weeks of sun oil and sand and ice creams and lazy evening meals and a growing love of Angela and her children. The good clothes from the Via Corso boutiques were left behind. The time for T-shirts and jeans and bikinis, and the fourth day on the beach Charley had taken courage and unhooked the bikini top and felt a desperate blushing shyness at the whiteness and lain on her stomach on the towel while Angela had lain on her back beside her, and never worn the top again and known her own parents would have called her a slut. She had talked of poetry with Angela and known her own mother had never read Keats or Shelley or Wordsworth. She had talked of social sciences, Angela's degree course at the University of Rome that had specialized in local administration, and known that her own father had believed the world began and ended with the study of marine engineering. It was the time of her liberation. And it had ended . . . It had ended in tears in her small room at the apartment

53

when she had packed her bag, ended in tears as she had hugged them all and kissed them all at the departure gate, ended in tears as she had walked alone to the aircraft. Magic was not real, was illusory. She had come home from a Roman summer of liberation and freedom to the drab college that trained her to teach.

> *Basta,* enough of me waffling on. I think you are pro-
> viding me with another fantastic opportunity to travel—
> which I certainly cannot afford to do on what I am now
> paid!!—I don't know anything about Palermo except
> that it is a city very rich in history. I cannot imagine it,
> cannot see it in my mind, and yet already I am excited.

She did not lie often, but it was a lie when she wrote of her ignorance of the city and its images. She was taken, her recall, to the images on the television screen of the apartment on Collina Fleming. The killing of judge Giovanni Falcone had been twelve days before her arrival in Rome, that summer of 1992, but the killing of Judge Paolo Borsellino had been forty-five days after her arrival . . . She sat in the classroom, with her lunch-box and her emptied can of Pepsi and she remembered the images of the television . . . It was only afterwards, after she had seen the images, that she had understood the quiet in the capital that weekend afternoon as she had browsed her way from the Colosseum to the Partheneum, and the quiet on the bus that had dropped her by the Ponte Flaminio, and the quiet on the street as she had walked under the pine trees toward the apartment on Collina Fleming. She had called her greeting in the hall, and not been answered, and she had gone into the little sitting area where they had the portable television. Even the child, Mario, and the baby, Francesca, had been hushed. Peppino grim faced had sat in front of the television and stared at the screen, and the chin of Angela, beside him, quivered. So it was a lie for Charley to write that she had no image of Palermo. The image in bright color was of the front of a block of flats, demolished, and of a car that had held 50 kilos of explosives, disintegrated, and of the faces of Judge Borsellino and five bodyguards, destroyed. That was the image of Palermo, and there were more images for her to recall because the television broadcast, interrupting normal schedules, had then shown the scene of the killing, fifty-seven days earlier, of Judge Falcone and Judge Falcone's wife and Judge Falcone's three bodyguards. The images were of the demolished façade of an apartment block in Palermo and of a cratered highway with broken cars scattered among rubble at Capaci. Peppino and Angela had sat with their silence and Charley had watched, seen and slipped away to her bedroom as if she had feared she had intruded into a world that held no place for her, but it had all been far away from Rome and was not referred to again, far away in Palermo.

> I am happy to take the plunge. I will sort out the matter of a new job when I get back because this is much too good an opportunity for me to miss—I accept your invitation.
> I look forward to hearing your suggestions for my arrival date.
>
> *Distinti saluti,*
> Charley (Charlotte Parsons)

Outside the window the bell clamored the end of the lunch hour. She was twenty-three years old. She heard the screaming excited babble of the children charging back from the playground. Other than when she had gone to Rome four years earlier she had never been outside her country. Her hand trembled. She had agreed to take an opportunity for access. She read the letter back. She would spy on the family that had shown her love and kindness and affection.

"Come on, children. Settle down now. Leave her alone, Dean. Stop it. Writing books out, please. Yes, writing books, Tracy. Darren, don't do that. Has everyone got their writing book?"

She folded the letter. She had been told that if she gave serious cause for suspicion she would be killed and that then her killers would go home to eat their dinner.

To refuse protection in Palermo was to lose the love of life.

Under the yellow haze of car fumes that lay below the surrounding mountains and that was held in place by the light sea breeze, the city was a mosaic of guarded camps. Palermo was a place of armed men, of carefully sited strongpoints, as it had been throughout history. Soldiers with their NATO rifles, huddled inside bulletproof shelters, held the street corners of the blocks where magistrates and politicians lived. Police bodyguards in armor-reinforced cars, deafened by sirens, escorted those magistrates and politicians from one defended position to another, from home to work, from work to home. Thug-minders watched over the personal security of the men who figured high on the lists of Interpol's and Europol's most-wanted suspects and had Kalashnikov assault rifles secreted in their cars but close to hand. It was a city of tension and fear, a city where the industry of protection flourished. The industry offering protection, fortresses and safety was spread thick across the city. It covered the servants of the state and the principals of the alternate society, and right on up and right on down through every stratum of Palermo's society. If the magistrate or the politician was denied protection, was isolated, he was as a floor rag left out on a line to rot in the sun, he was dead. If the boss of a family running a district of Palermo ignored the necessary precautions of survival, then other pigs would come to snout out the food in his trough. The hotelier running the four star *albergo* must pay for protection or face his guests' cars vandalized, his food contaminated, his business ruined. He sought protection. The bar owner risked fire if he did not buy protection. A construction magnate risked the denial of contracts and bankruptcy if he did not buy protection. The street vendor must buy it or reckon to have his legs broken, and the street whore on the Via Principe di Villafranca, and the bag thief on the Via del Libertà, and the taxi driver on the rank at the Politeama, and the heroin peddler at the Stazione Centrale. The seeking of protection was a habit of existence, unremarked and unexceptional . . .

To decline protection in Palermo was to refuse to live.

His hands were less painful that day. He could hold the coffee cup with his fingers and not spill the treacle thick liquid. He thought that his hands were less painful because of the warmth of the spring sunshine on them as he had walked on the Via Marqueda to the bar.

In the bar, where the television played a satellite channel's transmissions of continuous music promotion videos, Mario Ruggerio met with a man and talked the strategy of killing.

If he had talked with a man who was close to him, close tied by blood or friendship, he would have said that the matter of killing was abhorrent to him. But there was no man who was sufficiently close to him, not even his youngest brother, in whom he would confide his most prized and inner thoughts. His aloneness, his suspicion of intimacy and sharing, were key attributes that he recognized in his capacity for personal survival. His dislike of the strategy, matter, of killing had little to do with any sense of squeamishness, even less with any hesitation over the morality of taking the life of another of God's creatures. It was to do with security, his freedom.

In the conversation, punctuated by long silences, over the single cup of coffee, down to the dregs of the ground beans and the two sugar spoonfuls, the name of the magistrate was never used.

It was difficult to kill without witnesses. It was hard to kill without leaving traces for the forensic scientists of the *carabinieri* and the *squadra mobile* and the *Direzione Investigativa Anti-Mafia* to analyze for evidence.

It was complicated to dispose of a cadaver, even if an oildrum of acid were used or the "heavy overcoat" of liquid concrete on a construction site, or if the body was food for the fishes. All of those who had planned and carried out the killing of Falcone and Borsellino were now in custody, rotting or convicted *in absentia,* and, like wayward children, they had scattered evidence around them. The old way of killing, his father's way, was the *lupara,* which was the short barreled shotgun with the spread of pellets but that left blood spatters on walls, streets, carpets, rugs and pavements. The Magnum handgun with exploding bullets was the favorite of the wild young *picciotti,* the head case kids, but that too left evidence, shell cases, fractured bullet fragments, blood running to the street drains and smeared through interiors. He preferred the way of strangulation, but that was so hard now on his hands that had the rheumatic pain in them.

They talked, without using the name of the magistrate, right under the television.

The killing of a man served two purposes for Mario Ruggerio. The killing of a man would send a message to his family and his colleagues, and the killing of a man removed an obstacle that confronted the smooth running of his affairs. The killing of the magistrate, discussed in staccato words under the beat of an electric guitar and the hammer of a drummer, would send a message and would remove an obstacle. It was his belief that La Cosa Nostra should strike only when it was threatened and the magistrate, in the opinion of Mario Ruggerio, now endangered him. The shotgun could not be used, nor the Magnum, nor the Kalashnikov fired from the waist on automatic, because it was not possible to be that close to the magistrate. He did not know the workings of bombs in cars or rubbish bins, nor the methods of a command wire or of an electronic firing pulse, but the man he talked with knew of those workings and methods.

He would have preferred a world of quiet, a world where the interest of the state waned. He wished for a world of coexistence. He could reel off, without consultation of notes, the names of judges and prosecutors and magistrates in the Palazzo di Giustizia who also yearned for such a world of coexistance but in that conversation, in the bar, he did not speak the name of the single magistrate whom he thought now to represent a threat against his precious freedom.

It was agreed that a bomb was the necessary method of attack. And further agreed that the movements of the magistrate would be more closely observed to find a pattern in his travel. And finally agreed that the matter of killing was a priority.

He slipped away from the bar, an old man in a gray jacket and a check cap on the pavement of the Via Marqueda who attracted no attention, who flexed the muscles of his hand in the Palermo sunshine.

The prisoner had been brought from his shared cell on the third floor of the block. The doctor was the "cut-out." The doctor had asked for the prisoner to be brought to the medical wing for routine examination. The doctor and his own staff had been used three times before by the magistrate. The magistrate would not have reckoned on the chances of the survival of the prisoner if it were known in the corridors and landings of Ucciardone jail that the man, on remand and charged with murder, had requested a meeting. The request for the meeting, a prisoner wishing to talk with Rocco Tardelli, had come in a letter, barely literate, hardly legible, delivered to the Palazzo di Giustizia. He thought the letter, perhaps, had been written by the prisoner's mother. Men died, some quietly through strangulation, some noisily through poisoning, some messily through bludgeon blows, in Ucciardone prison when they sought to collaborate. It was of critical importance, at this moment that it should not be known among the prison staff that a man had asked to see the magistrate who was known to have dedicated his life to the capture of Mario Ruggerio. When the prison staff who escorted the prisoner to the surgery had been dismissed and the prisoner signed for, he had been taken by two of the magistrate's own security detail, his head covered by a blanket that he should not be recognized by watchers peering from the cell windows high above, across the yard and to the room made available for the magistrate.

Tardelli thought him pathetic.

The cigarette that the prisoner smoked was not half finished and already the man looked longingly at the packet on the table. Tardelli did not smoke but he always carried a nearly full packet in his pocket when he came to Ucciardone. He pushed the packet toward the prisoner and smiled his invitation that the man should help himself again. A new cigarette was lit from an old cigarette and the hands of the prisoner shook.

Tardelli thought him wretched.

They sat in a bare room, on either side of a bare table, they were enclosed by bare walls. There was no window and the light came from a single fluorescent strip on the ceiling around which wafted the spurted smoke from the prisoner's cigarette. Since the message had come from his office at the Palazzo di Giustizia, the report of a letter without signature to request the interview, the message that had interrupted the celebration of orange juice and chocolate cake, Tardelli had spent the major part of two days studying the file of the prisoner. It was his way always to be meticulously prepared before he faced a prisoner.

The prisoner spoke the name of Mario Ruggerio.

He detested personal publicity, he left it to the more ambitious and the more scheming to give media interviews, but it was inevitable that Rocco Tardelli should be known as the magistrate who hunted Mario Ruggerio. Half a dozen times a year he was told that a prisoner had requested, in conditions of secrecy, to meet with him. Half a dozen times a year a prisoner groveled for the freedom of the *pentito* program, for the opportunity to trade information for liberty. Once a year, if he was lucky, Tardelli would hear information that carried forward his investigation, drew him closer to the man he hunted. They came and they squirmed and they crossed the Rubicon. They condemned themselves to death if they were identified, if they were located, when they broke the God-given law of Sicily, the law of *omertà,* which was the code of silence.

The *pentito* Contorno had broken the law of *omertà* and thirty of his relations by blood and by marriage had been butchered in a proxy attempt to halt the information flow he dribbled. There was a saying of the peasants on the island: "A man who is really a man never reveals anything even when he is being stabbed." The *pentito* Buscetta had turned away from the code of silence and thirty-seven of his relations had been murdered. Another saying of the peasants on the island: "A man who is deaf and blind and silent lives a hundred years in peace." The *pentito* Mannoia was now a terrified man, existing on Valium tablets, in crisis. He had heard a woman refer to her *pentito* brother as "a relative of my father." It was an earthquake in their lives when they gave up the silence. Each year one of the prisoners who sat at the bare table in the bare room, hemmed in by the bare walls of the bunker, was useful to the magistrate. Five a year were rubbish wretches.

It was a sparring game for Tardelli and the prisoner.

"Why do you wish to take advantage of the Award Legislation under the conditions of the Special Protection Program?"

The eyes of the prisoner were on the choked ashtray. He stammered, "I have decided to collaborate because La Cosa Nostra is only a gang of cowards and assassins."

He could be cruel. Rocco Tardelli, mild mannered and round shouldered, could be vicious.

"I believe it more probable that you seek to 'collaborate' because you face the sentence of *ergastolo.* You face the rest of your life in prison, here, in Ucciardone."

"I have rejected La Cosa Nostra."

"Perhaps you have only rejected the sentence of life in Ucciardone."

"I have information . . ."

"What is the information?"

"I have information on the location where Mario Ruggerio lives."

"Where does he live?"

The prisoner snorted, the furtive eyes lanched upward toward the magistrate. "When I have the guarantee of the Special Protection . . ."

"Then you go back to your cell, and you consider. You do not seek to bargain with me. Back and consider."

"I can tell you where is Mario Ruggerio."

"When you have told me, then we think on the Protection Program. Then I evaluate and make my recommendation to the Committee. You talk, or you go back to your cell. It is not for you to make conditions."

It was important for the magistrate, Rocco Tardelli, to set the rules from the first interview. A thousand men had been received into the Protection Program. The budget was exhausted, safe houses were filled, *carabiniere* and military barracks bulged with the *pentiti* and their families. Most were useless. Most bartered long sentences of imprisonment for stale information. To a dedicated investigator, as was Rocco Tardelli, it was distasteful to exchange freedom for tired news.

"But I have come to you . . ."

"And told me nothing. Consider your position."

Tardelli stood. The interview was concluded. Most of those he met, the true leaders of La Cosa Nostra, were men he treated with due respect. It puzzled him, frequently, that such gifted men should require criminality to buttress their yearning for dignity. Because they had lost their dignity, it was hard for him to offer a *pentito* due respect. The prisoner, the blanket again over his head, was escorted back to the medical area. The doctor would call for prison staff to return him to the shared cell on the third floor of the block. The magistrate gathered up his briefcase from the floor, his cigarette packet from the table, his coat from the hook on the door. With his guards, he hurried down the corridor.

The sunshine hit their faces.

"You see, my young friend, Pasquale, maker of babies, I have to make him suffer. He has made the first move, but he will have thought he can control me. I have to show him that he does not. He will have thought he can offer me information, step by step, a little at a time, as he demands further privileges. That is not acceptable. I have to be able to judge that he will tell me everything that he knows. I have to be patient . . ."

They paused at the car, the armored Alfa. The lights were flashed at the gate sentries. The engines roared. The gates swung open. The sidearms and the machine-pistols were cocked.

"Is he a jewel, Pasquale, or is he false gold?"

"Please don't talk to me, not when we are moving, please."

He tucked down into the darkened interior of the car. The young man, Pasquale, was in front of him, the *maresciallo* drove.

He leaned forward, he caught the back of the young man's seat. It was a compulsion for him, to share and to talk. There was no one for him to talk with but the *ragazzi*. He despised himself, but to talk at times was the craving of an addict.

"You know, if I was afraid, if I could not tolerate the fear any longer, I could send a signal. There are routes by which a signal could be sent. Certain people, in the Palace of Poison or in the Questura, even in the barracks of the *carabinieri,* would send a signal, pass a message. I have only to say, in confidence, that a prisoner asked for me. In confidence, I would give that prisoner's name. In confidence, binding such a person to secrecy, I could say that I have rejected the offer of information from that prisoner. It would be a signal that I was now afraid. The message would be passed on, it would be heard. It would be understood that I was no longer a threat. If, in confidence, I sent that signal, then I could again go to a restaurant, go to the cinema, go to the opera at the Politeama, go to the hairdresser . . ."

The young man, Pasquale, sat rigid in front of him.

The magistrate said sadly, "I have to believe that I can live with the fear."

"I hear we cocked your posh grub. You won't find me crying, Harry. Wife was out, so mine last night was sausage, oven chips and beans."

"Didn't do too bad, sir." Harry chuckled. "Managed five courses, two gins for aperitif, bottle of white and red, brandy to wash it down . . ."

"Did we screw you?"

The detective superintendent, it was his show, led the detective sergeant out of the senior partner's office and across the hall and out through the front door, down the steps and across to the pavement where the Transit van was parked. Harry stood back to allow his superior to hand over the cardboard packing case first to the constable at the rear doors. They paused, each of them, wrung their hands, pretty damn heavy the boxes were.

"I was beginning to get the taste for it. Quite a good restaurant, actually, for a hotel."

"Till we horned in. Come on, next load."

They went back into the building on Regent Street, looking straight ahead and ignoring the white-faced junior partners and the secretaries who had little handkerchiefs clasped in their hands as if to safeguard them from the Doomsday collapse of their world. It was inevitable, what had happened the previous evening, because of the shortage of manpower in SO6 and the constant juggling of priorities. Listening to Giles Blake's assessment of the immediate future of the gilts market, toying with the cod to make it last because they were slow on their food at the next table and hearing the announcement break into the canned nothing music. "Would Mr. Harry Compton please come to reception to take a telephone call? Mr. Harry Compton to reception, please." Getting a judge out of his club and back to chambers, phoning the wife and pleading excuses, going through the evidence dossier with the judge and asking for a Schedule 1 Production Order under the Police Criminal Evidence Act (1984). Getting the judge's signature on the order, asking him to put nib to paper a second time for the search warrant, and seeing his reluctance because it was a solicitor that they were going to jump when the office opened in the morning. Maybe that had been worth it, the study of distaste on the good old judge's face, because it was a solicitor, same clan and same tribe. Harry Compton had done the donkey's load of the investigation into the bent bastard whose hands were into clients' savings, the greedy bastard who was excavating trustee funds, the solicitor who had broken trust, but it was the detective superintendent's show and he'd made the call that had hauled the junior man off his expenses dinner. The panic reason was that the senior partner, information received, was going abroad and hadn't given his colleagues a coming-home date. Under a Schedule 1 Production Order and a search warrant the papers and archives were being packed away in cardboard boxes, down to the last sheet and the last file, loaded up and would be driven for close analysis to the SO6 office behind Holborn police station.

Harry Compton was dog-tired, out on his feet. He had finished with the judge at midnight, had the briefing with the team at thirty minutes after midnight, been home and slept three hours, been up and driven to the senior partner's home in Essex for a dawn knock and the clicking of handcuffs. He trudged up the stairs again for the next load of papers.

"Where did we get to?" The detective superintendent stopped on the landing and breathed hard.

"Last night? Sort of nowhere and somewhere. Chummy meets a guy, they have dinner, they talk financials through the evening. It was pretty unexceptional stuff. Anyway, the NCIS material on chummy was kind of vague, not much more than a single report of a medium cash deposit in a bank, £28,000, along with sharp-moving accounts with plenty of action in drops and withdrawals and not a lot to point to where the money comes from and where it's going, but not showing up as obvious illegal. That was the 'nowhere.'"

They were back in the senior partner's office. A small mountain of cardboard boxes remained to be shifted. And there was more to move in the secretary's office, and more from the junior partners' rooms, and then there was the whole of the bloody archive in the basement.

"Get a hernia from this. You're a cussed sod, Harry, always keep the best to last. What was the 'somewhere'?"

The detective sergeant grinned, welcomed the compliment. "Smooth as new paintwork. The guest, wearing his money on his back, Italian, very tasty . . . and he'd flown in from Palermo."

Each of them heaved up a box and headed for the door.

"You wouldn't be telling me, would you, Harry, that every businessman from Palermo is bloody mafia?"

Harry Compton winked. 'Course they are—if it was a grannie aged eighty from Palermo, a kid aged five from Palermo, I'd have 'em locked up for 'organized crime.' It has a sort of ring, doesn't it, Palermo?"

"We can run the name through."

"Don't have the name, had a phone call before I'd even got stuck into the sweets trolley. I'll get the name."

"But you'll work this bloody lot first, too right."

There were forty-seven boxes of papers from the offices, and there would be twenty-nine plastic bin sacks from the archives, and they'd need going through before he could get back to a hotel in Portman Square for a guest's name. It would all be a matter of priorities.

She passed him the letter, but the American made no move to take it. He turned to face her.

"Who else has read this letter?"

She bridled. "Nobody has."

"You are telling me, certain, nobody else has touched this letter."

"Of course they haven't."

She watched. He took a handkerchief from his pocket, shook it, then took the letter from her. The handkerchief protected the letter from the touch of his fingertips.

To Charley, holding the letter in a handkerchief seemed ridiculous. "Why?"

He said bleakly, "So that it doesn't look as if it's been shown round, so that my prints aren't on it."

"Would it be looked at that closely?"

"We do it my way, let's understand that from now."

He was impassive. He talked as if to an annoying child. He swung round, away from her, to read the letter held in the handkerchief. Bugger

63

him. Charley had thought it clever to give him a meeting point on the cliffs. The dusk had been falling when she had ridden her scooter to the car park, empty but for his hire-car, that served the coastal footpath. He had been where she had told him to be. There was a nest of cigarette ends by his feet, enough for him to have been there for hours, from long before she had told him to be there. It was a good place for the big seabirds, and the gulls and shags and guillemots were chorusing and floating in the wind and settling on the rocks below where the sea's charge broke. It was a favorite place, when home just suffocated her, to come to. It was where she came and sat and brooded when the clinging attentions of her mother and father swamped her. It was a place of peace and wildness. She had thought it clever to come to the cliffs, to sit on the bench of coarse wood planks. Here she would be in control. He passed the letter back to her, then pocketed the handkerchief, then flicked a cigarette from the Lucky Strike packet.

"Aren't you going to ask me why I decided—?"

"Not important to me."

"Whether it's excitement or duty, whether it's adventure or obligation—?"

"Doesn't matter to me."

She bit at her lip. She ran her tongue the length of her lip. She had sought control. The blood was running in her. "Well, sure as hell, it's not your courtesies. You are the rudest man—"

"If that's what you want to think, you should fax it to them in the morning."

She crumpled, and the control that she had sought slipped further. "But . . . but I don't have the fax number."

He said, as if he were tired, as if it were tedious, "The fax number was on their letter."

"But I tore it up, didn't I? I wasn't going, was I? I destroyed the letter, and then I changed my mind."

He should have asked why she had changed her mind. He didn't. He was reaching inside his windcheater and he took out the folded sheet of paper and opened it. From the photocopy of the letter sent to her he wrote the number and the international code on a notepad, tore off the sheet from the pad and handed it to her. There was a growl in his voice. She thought him so bloody cold. "Write it in your own hand on the back of the letter."

She did what she was told. He took the paper from his notebook back and tore it into small pieces. He threw the pieces into the air and they flaked away below them, carried on the wind gusts, down toward the big birds as they settled for the night. Away beyond Bolt Head, off Start Point, she saw the first flash of the lighthouse, the raking beam.

"Is it necessary to be like that, so careful?"

"Yes."

"That's what I have to learn?"

"It's best that you learn, fast, to be careful."

She shivered, the cold caught her. His windcheater had none of the quilted thickness of hers, but the cold did not catch him and he did not shiver. She felt dominated and small. Said with acid deliberateness, "Yes, Mr. Moen. Right, Mr. Moen. Three bloody bags full, Mr. Moen. I'll send the fax in the morning."

"Tell me about yourself."

"Excuse me, shouldn't you be doing the talking? Who, what, you are. Where I'm going. Why?"

He shook his head. "Who, what, I am doesn't concern you."

She snorted in fake derision. "Brilliant."

"It's about being careful."

She felt the cold, the wind on her back, night wind hacking at the strength of her anorak. "Where I'm going and why."

"In good time. About yourself."

She took a big breath. He watched her and his face was shadowed but she did not think that if a flashlight had been shone on his features, or the full beam of the lighthouse on Start Point, that she would have seen any damned encouragement. As if she was being manipulated, as if she was one of the marionettes that were stored in the cupboard behind her desk in 2B's classroom . . .

She blurted, "I'm Charlotte Eunice Parsons, everyone calls me 'Charley.' I'm pretty ordinary—"

"Don't talk yourself short, and don't look for compliments."

"Fat chance . . . I'm an only child. My parents are David and Flora Parsons. Dad was an engineering manager at the naval dockyard at Plymouth, it was his whole life—well, and me—until two years ago, when he was made redundant, the 'peace dividend.' We lived then in Yelverton, which is up on the edge of the moor, north of Plymouth. He didn't think he could afford to stay there, so they upped and moved. He packed in the bowls club and the tennis club, cinemas and shops, he's paranoid about being hard up, broke. He bought the bungalow, he took his place in a gossipy and inquisitive little society, mean minded. God knows why, my mother went along with it. Where they are now, they're boring and sad and empty. Do you think I'm being foul?"

"Doesn't matter what I think."

She gazed out at the sea, at the darkening mass of the water, at the white foam spurts on the rocks, at the distant light rotating from Start Point. She thought she spoke a truth, and that truth was important to Axel Moen.

"I can't afford to live away from home, all I've got went into that silly little bike. If I had a promotion, a better job, when I've more experience, then I could quit and go and live in my own place. Not yet. Their lives are boring, sad, empty, so they're looking for a star, and I fit the role. It's always been like that, but it's worse now. There's days I could scream—don't think I'm proud of being a right bitch—and there's nights I'm ashamed of myself. The trouble with being a star, you learn as a kid how to milk it, you get to play the little madam. Not before, but there are times now that I disgust myself. They wanted me to be quality at tennis, but I was ordinary and Dad couldn't see that. They wanted me top of the form at school, and when I wasn't, it was the teacher's fault, not because I was just another average kid. They wanted me to go to university, and when I didn't get the grades, then Dad said the examiners had made a mistake. What saved me, what sort of opened the window to me, was going to Rome and being with Giuseppe and Angela, they were really lovely, they were wonderful. But you want me to spy on them?"

"I want access, yes."

She peered ahead. He wouldn't have seen it. She gazed down the depth of the rock face to where a crag hung out as a limp finger. A falcon worried with its killing beak at the feathers under its wing. It was personal to her, the peregrine bird. Sometimes, when she came to this place, she saw it, sometimes she heard the crying call of the female. If it came, she would see it because she could recognize the fast movements of the bird in flight and its rigid profile when it perched on the finger of rock. The bird was her own, nothing to do with him. It flew. She lost the sight of the bird.

"I came back from Rome and went to training college. I suppose I was a spoiled little cow from home and a patronizing little cow from Rome. I didn't seem to find it necessary to make friends. All right, let's have it straight. I thought most of the other students were pretty trivial, and they thought I was pretty stuck-up, you know what that means? I didn't have a boyfriend, not one of the students, but there were a few sweaty sessions with one of the lecturers, one of those who always apologizes and cries afterwards and moans about his wife, but he used to give me good marks. Are you married?"

"No."

"Ever been married, Mr. Moen?"

"No."

"Why not?"

"Just stay with the story, Charley."

"Please yourself. I've only once ever done anything worth while in my life, what I thought was worth doing. You see, when you know how to milk it's the big temptation to stay on the gravy train—God, that's rotten mixed metaphors. When you can get what you want without trying you get complacent, you stop trying. Big deal, but I went last summer to Brightlingsea, it's a small dock on the east coast, other side of London. There was a protest there against the export of calves to Europe. They were shipping the calves across for fattening up and then slaughter. It's the veal trade. It's revolting. I was there for a month, bawling and hollering and trying to stop the lorries. Yes, I thought that was worth while. Are you from a city or from the country?"

"Northeast Wisconsin."

"Is that country?"

"Big country."

"So you wouldn't care about the animals, you'd say that farmers have to live, people have to eat, animals don't feel fear and pain."

"It's not important what I think."

"Christ. What else do you want to know? What color knickers I wear, when my period is? You're a bloody bundle of fun, Mr. Moen."

"I think I've heard enough."

She stood. Her hair was jostled on her face. The wind had risen and now that she no longer talked in his ear she had to shout against the roar of waves battering on rocks.

"Could we murder something, like a drink?"

He murmured, "I don't drink, not alcohol."

"My bloody luck, a bloody temperance nut. Hey, I'll drink, you watch. And while I drink you can tell me whether what I am going to do is worthwhile—or don't you have an opinion on that?"

Charley strode toward the car park. It was her big exit. She pounded up the path from the bench and the cliff face. She was going fast and ahead of him. Her foot, in the black darkness, tripped on a stone. She was falling . . . "Shit." She was stumbling and trying to hold her balance . . . "Bugger." He caught her, held her up, and she shook his hand off her arm and stormed on.

"Yes, Dr. Ruggerio . . . Of course, Dr. Ruggerio, of course I'll tell Charlotte that you rang, I'll tell her exactly what you said . . . It is difficult, Dr. Ruggerio, she has a very good position at the moment, but . . . Yes, Dr. Ruggerio, we're very gratified to know that you and your wife regard Charlotte so highly . . . Yes, she's a lovely young woman . . . We are, as you say, very proud of her . . . I know she's thinking very hard about your offer.

She's out at the moment, something connected with school work . . . Send a fax or telephone to Palermo, yes, I'll see she does that tomorrow . . . You're very kind, Dr. Ruggerio . . . Yes, yes, I'm sure she'd be very happy with you again . . . My wife, yes, I'll pass on your best wishes . . . So good to speak to you. Thank you. Goodnight."

He put down the telephone. David Parsons glanced once, briefly, at the graduation photograph of his Charlotte that hung in the place of honor in the hall. He went into the sitting room. Flora Parsons looked up from her needlework, the cover for a cushion.

"God, you're a coward."

"That's not called for."

"Eating out of his hand and he's soft-soaping you. Crawling to him."

"He sent you his best wishes . . ."

"The letter comes, then the American's here. Half the village wants to know who he is. Where's Charley now? I haven't an idea. Where is she? I'm frightened for her."

"As soon as she's back, I'll speak to her."

"You won't, you're a coward."

It was her bravado, and when she'd finished she had only a few coins left in her purse. Back to the bar, refusing his offer to buy the second round. A pint of Exmoor draft for herself, and a double malt whiskey for herself, and another cup of decaffeinated coffee for Axel Moen with milk in a plastic carton and sugar in a paper sachet.

While she'd drunk the first pint and the first double malt whiskey, while he'd sipped the first coffee, she'd told him about the timbered, low-ceilinged pub. She had given him the history—supposed to be a smugglers' den, and a hundred years earlier it was supposed to have been used as a lodging for a hanging judge in the Monmouth rebellion roundup, supposed to be . . .

He'd looked barely tolerant, just uninterested. He lit another cigarette. "OK, listen, please. What you saw when you had your drive round, pusher's territory, small time—"

She interrupted. "I wouldn't describe an addicted baby in spasm as 'small-time,' nor would I call an over-dosed corpse 'small time.' I'd—"

"Be quiet, and listen. What you saw was the symptom of a strategic problem. Too many law-enforcement people spend their time, the resources given them, chasing thieves and muggers and pushers because it looks good and they get to seem busy. But they're attacking the wrong end of the problem. Let me explain. Take a big company, let's talk of a mega-multinational. We'll take Exxon or General Motors or the Ford

Motor Company, they're the major three American corporations. The total of their turnover, last set of figures I saw, $330 billion—get that figure in your mind—but the man you see is the salesman from the General Motors or Ford showroom, or if it's Exxon he's the guy who takes your money at the filling station. For the salesman or the guy on the cash till you should read 'thieves and muggers and pushers.' Narco-trafficking, the last set of figures, runs directly alongside those of General Motors and the Ford Motor Company and Exxon, so we are talking serious money— You with me?—but organized crime is not only about narcotics, you can add in the profits from money washing, from arms trading, from illegal-immigrant rackets, loan sharking and kidnapping and hijacking, from extortion. What the whole thing comes to, worldwide, is figures too big to comprehend, but we try. The figure is $3 million billion. It leaves the top corporations for dead . . . Hang on in there."

She bolted at the beer. He sat opposite her. The cigarettes went from his mouth to the ashtray, were stubbed, were lit, were smoked. He talked quietly and she clung to his words, as if he'd opened a door to her that showed a sea without an horizon.

"Hanging, but it's from my fingernails."

She won a quick smile that did not last.

"The salesmen of General Motors and the Ford Motor Company don't count, nor the guy on the cash till at an Exxon filling station, they're about as important as the thieves and muggers and pushers. Where it matters is head office. Get in the elevator at head office, head on up past the accountants and lawyers and the marketing people and the public affairs people, keep going up in the elevator, up past the vice-presidents for sales and finance and internationals and image, research and development, keep on till it stops or hits the sky. You are, Charley, in the presence of the chief executive officer. He matters. What he decides affects folk. He is god. His level is strategic."

She felt miniscule, a pygmy. The whiskey glass was empty, just the dregs of the Exmoor draft left.

"There are mafias in Italy, in the United States, in Japan and Hong Kong, in Colombia and Brazil, in Russia. Each of those mafias has a chief executive officer, one man, because there's no space for a gang session in a mafia or in a corporation, who acts pretty much like the chief executive officer of General Motors, the Ford Motor Company or Exxon. He lays down guidelines, he plans for the future, he takes an overview, and if there are major problems, then he gets to roll up his sleeves and go hands-on into detail. I'll hit some differences. The mafia chief executive officer lives out of a hole in the ground, on the run, hasn't a thirty-story tower for staff, hasn't a floor of IBM computer gear. Your corporation guy, take away his support and his computer, he'd fall on his face . . . not his mafia opposite. The mafia chief exectuive officer lives with a wolf-pack. To survive he has to be feared. If he is thought to show weakness, he will be torn to pieces. He stays cunning and he stays ruthless. I'm getting there, Charley, nearly there . . ."

"Fingers are getting a bit tired, nails are starting to crack." She hoped to make him laugh, another bloody failure. She did not believe he had talked this through before, she did not think it was rehearsed. It was not, Charley's opinion, a familiar and patterned story. It made her warm, with the whiskey, to believe she was not carried along a rutted story track.

"There's a commonplace. The mafias in Italy and the United States, Japan and Hong Kong, Colombia and Brazil, in Russia, have a sincere respect for the mafia of Sicily, La Cosa Nostra. La Cosa Nostra, out of Palermo, out of desperate little towns hanging in poverty off the sides of mountains, is the role model of international crime. It's where it started, where it's bred, where it lives well. They call it, in Italy, *la piovra,* that's an octopus. The tentacles spread out all over Europe, into your country, all over the world, into my country. Hack one off and another grows. You have to get to the heart of the thing, kill the heart, and the heart is in those little towns and in Palermo."

She trembled. Her hands were splayed out on the table. She whispered, "What do you want of me?"

"You offer the possibility of access to the chief executive officer of La Cosa Nostra. It's why I came to find you."

4

SHE SAT ALONE ON THE CLIFF, HER place.

The Headmistress had said, "There were four hundred applicants for your job, eighty applications from inside the county. If we'd realized that there was the faintest possibility you would just walk out on us then you wouldn't have even won an interview, let alone a short-listing. Don't you feel a responsibility to the children? Don't you feel something for your colleagues here who made you so welcome? When you return from this little episode in idiocy, don't think that this job will be waiting for you, and I doubt that any other job in teaching will be opening its arms to you after the report I intend to attach to your record. You've failed me, and your colleagues, and your children . . ."

In the common room, mid-morning break, she had announced her departure, and she had seen the expressions on their faces, orchestrated by the reaction of the headmistress, change from astonishment to hostility. The sneer of the divorced head-of-year teacher who always looked at her with the ambition of getting his hands into her knickers. The angered resentment of the young man who taught 3A and ran the library and took scouts on weekends and whose eyes mooned after her in the common room every day. The rank envy of the teacher of 1A who had three children of her own and her husband had run and her life was dictated by minders and baby-sitters. Charley had shrugged, she had muttered that her mind was made up. She hadn't said, couldn't see the point in saying, that she thought them all pathetic and limited, small minded and trapped.

From the bench above the cliff she saw the peregrine preen the pure white of its chest feathers, worrying at them.

Axel had said, "You don't only have rights in this world as some gift of God. If you are given rights, you have to take the downside on board. You have to acknowledge obligation and duty. If the citizen has rights, then the citizen also has obligation and duty. You are the citizen, Charley. Bad luck. You cannot always hand over your obligations and duties to other people. Cannot walk away, cannot cross over the road. I don't have to give you syrup thanks for what you're doing, I don't tell you that we're all grateful to you. I'm not thanking you when all that's asked of you is to perform your duties and obligations as a citizen. I hope you didn't want a pretty speech."

They had sat in his hire car up the lane from the lights of the community, and Danny Bent had come by and stopped to peer in through the misted window and had spat onto the ground when he had turned away. Too right, she had wanted a pretty speech. She had wanted to feel proud, flushed and pleasured, and his quiet and cold voice gave her nothing. She had sent the fax. Three days later, the last evening when she had returned from a day at school, the envelope from the travel agent in London had been on the table in the hallway of Gull View Cottage, beside the telephone, under her photograph, and enclosed had been the ticket to Palermo, via Rome. He had said, cool and devoid of emotion, what she should write in a fax to be sent in the morning, why she was stopping two days in Rome, when she would reach Palermo. He had told her, brusque, where accommodation would be reserved for her in Rome, at what time he would meet her. When she had pushed herself out of the hire car and kick-started the scooter, Fanny Carthew had been watching her. When she had reached home, pushed the scooter up the drive, Zack Jones had spied on her with his binocular lenses. She was turning her back on them, and she knew so little of the man for whom she danced.

Where the sea crashed upon the rocks at the base of the cliffs, a shag bird strutted and held out its wings, drying them in the formation of a blackened cross. It was her place.

Her father had said, "When that Italian telephoned, maybe I should have been a bit firmer with him. Perhaps I should have told him direct, 'She's not coming, there's no question of her traveling to Palermo.' Those sort of people, because they've money, they believe they can buy anything. There's a job down the drain, God knows where you're going to find another one. And what are we supposed to think, your mother and I? But I don't suppose we matter to you. You are treating us like filth, and after all the love we've given you. What are your mother and I supposed to think? You let that American into our house, you skulk out in the garden. You come back from drinking with him, but, of course, your mother and I are not told, and you stink of alcohol. Mr. Bent and Miss Carthew, they both saw you last night, with that American, but we're not told. All we're told is that 'if we talk about it we might be responsible for hurting people.' What sort of an answer is that to two loving, caring parents?"

She had felt then a depth of sadness, and the mood must have been mirrored on her face, because her father had broken his whining attack and her mother had come from the kitchen and put her arm around her daughter. It had been the only time since the American had first come that she could have wept, cried out her heart. Charley had said, head against her mother's chest, looking into the bewilderment of her father's eyes, that she was sorry. She had said that she was sorry, but that she could not tell them more. She had gone away to her room to lay out on her bed the clothes she would pack to take to Palermo. She had not told them that the hostility of the common room had given her raw satisfaction, nor had she told them of the sparse moments of delight when she gained the fast, cracked smile from Axel Moen, nor had she told them of the brutal excitement she felt at the chance to walk away from a life that was trapped on tracks of certainty. She had not told them, "I want out, I want to bloody live." She had gone into her room and laid out on the bed, beside the sausage bag, her best jeans, two denim skirts, her favorite T-shirts, her underwear from Marks and Spencer's, two pairs of trainers and her best evening shoes and a pair of sandals, the severe cotton nightdress that she had been given the last Christmas by her mother, her make-up bag and her washing-bag, two dresses for the evenings, her bear that had been in her bed for twenty years and which still carried the yellow ribbon for the safe return of the Beirut hostages, and the leather framed photograph of her mother and father from their twenty-fifth anniversary, and the airline ticket. She had checked what she had laid out. She had packed the bag.

When she could no longer see the peregrine on its perch, and no longer see the shag bird on the rock washed with the sea, when the darkness had closed over her place, she rode home and back to her small room and her packed bag, and the bungalow was like a place for the dead.

It was raining. The wind drove the rain to run in rivers on the windows. Charley settled in her seat. She didn't screw her face against the glass, she didn't look back, she didn't try to see whether her mother and her father still stood on the Totnes platform and waved. Maybe she was a proper little bitch, and maybe that was why Axel Moen thought he could work with her. A mile out of Totnes station, as the big train gathered speed, the world she had known and felt she was condemned to, was slipping, blurred, away. Behind her was the suffocation of home, the smallness of her place on the cliff, the drear routine of the school. She had thought she lived. The train powered toward Reading. She felt the adrenaline thrill. At Reading she would take the shuttle bus to Heathrow airport. She believed, at last, that she was challenged.

From where he sat at his desk, Dwight Smythe could see the man through the glass of the partition wall and through the open door. Axel Moen was clearing the desk that had been given him since he had come to London. He could see him take each sheet of paper from the drawers, fast read it, then take the sheet to the office shredder and mince it. Each last sheet read and shredded, so that when he boarded the plane he would carry nothing. There were handwritten sheets and typed sheets and, note jottings, and each one was destroyed. Dwight's telephone rang. Ray wanting him. Ray had finally gotten round, taken him four days, to going through the budget figures.

He walked out of his office and across the open area. Axel Moen was sat on his desk and turning a file's pages and seemed not to notice him and he had to maneuver round him, awkward, and Axel Moen never shifted to make his way easier. There was a small bag on the floor beside the desk, and there was an Alitalia airline ticket laid down beside the file that Axel Moen was reading, hard concentration.

Ray hated figures. He was like a bad housewife when it came to accounting. He went through the budget figures as if they might bite him, and scrawled signatures on each sheet, and didn't seem to know what he was signing. Ray pushed the budget sheets back.

"That's a good job, thanks. Thanks for taking the weight. Is he about cleared up?"

"Given him his ticket, given him petty cash."

"What time they going?"

Dwight Smythe peered out of the Country Chief's office and across the open area toward Axel Moen, still bent over the last file.

"Oh, they don't travel together, hell, no. He doesn't hold the hand of that poor kid. She goes British Airways, I was instructed to book him with Alitalia. She doesn't get any comfort treatment. You'd have thought . . ."

"You hooked into his file?"

"I did what I was told."

"There was an area blocked off to you."

A bitter, droll response. "There was an area of the file to which I was not admitted. Not suitable for an administrative jerk."

"I hooked in, but my key code doesn't get blocked."

"That is privilege to aim at, that gives my life a goal."

"You have, Dwight, don't mind me saying it, a rare ability to get stuck in my throat so's I want to spit. He was in La Paz, Bolivia."

"I got that far—have you anything else for me, Ray?"

The Country Chief's finger, a moment, jabbed at Dwight Smythe's chest. A lowered voice. "He was in La Paz, Bolivia, that was '89 to '92. Only the best get to go down to Colombia and Peru and Bolivia. Three year postings for wild guys."

The lip curled. "You talking about cowboys?"

"Don't push. They move into coca leaf production country, where the *campesinos* grow the goddam stuff. There's remote *estancias* up there, with the small airstrips that the cartels use to ship the coca out for refinement in Cali or Medellín. Back in La Paz life is behind razor wire and walls and with a handgun beside the pillow and checking under the car each morning. Up country it's serious shit. Our people have CIs out there, our people try to hit the airstrips when the CIs report there's going to be a shipment. We have to fly with the Bolivian military. A Bolivian helicopter pilot might get to earn $800 a month, he's wide open to corruption, but you have to tell him where you're flying, you have to trust him. You can't reckon to fly with your own people every day. You have to trust. You wouldn't know about that, Dwight, living that sort of stress, waiting for betrayal, and pray to your God you never learn. They were up near the Brazil border, hot news from a Confidential Informant, two Huey loads of Bolivian special forces, Axel Moen and another agent. They came in over the strip and there were three light aircraft being loaded—it's what his report in the file says. Understand, when you come in on a Huey you don't go round a couple of sweet circles for recce, you go in and you hit. It was bad, compromised, it was a fuck-up, ambush time. He, your friend Axel Moen, took a high velocity in the stomach, one of the birds was busted, three Bolivians KIA and six more WIA and that was out of twenty-two of the poor bastards."

"I never found war stories that interesting."

"Hang around. The high velocity in the stomach was flesh at the side. They hadn't much choice but to get themselves off the open strip and to the cover of the buildings. It was quite a fire fight. When they got to the buildings they met up with the Confidential Informant. Couldn't do much talking with her. She was dead. She'd been gang banged. She'd had her throat cut. She'd been nailed up, through the hands, to the inside of the door of the building. Are you hearing me? It's a hard world out there, it's better out there when you don't make emotional relationships with a Confidential Informant, it's better when you're a cold bastard."

"Thanks for checking the budget figures, Ray."

Across the open area Axel Moen fed the last sheet of paper into the shredder, and then a photograph. Dwight Smythe had only the most fleeting glimpse of it.

The photograph seemed to show a slight and inoffensive man of middle age, perhaps at a function or a wedding or a reception because there were others in suits around the small man, whose head was ringed in red chinagraph. The target? Shit, and the guy looked nothing and wouldn't have stood out in the photograph if it hadn't been for the red ring around his head. As Dwight Smythe came across the work area, Axel Moen checked that the band holding his hair was secure then picked up and pocketed his airline ticket, and heaved up his small bag.

Axel Moen waved, desultory, at Ray, and was heading for the door.

Dwight Smythe thought that once the intruder had left then he'd spray an air freshener round the office area. He didn't know the world of Confidential Informants and fire fights and high velocity flesh wounds, and hoped to God he never would. And he thought the girl from the small bungalow was an innocent.

He growled, "I'll see you some time. Have a good flight. I'll see you, maybe—"

"Yes, if I want some expenses signed."

Gone through the door, gone and not closed it behind him.

When the aircraft had lifted, yawed and climbed, as she sat small in her seat and buckled tight, Charley had felt that she crumpled. She had thought then that she was the most miniscule of the marionette puppets locked in the cupboard behind the teacher's desk, not her desk, in class 2B.

As the aircraft cruised, on automatic flat flight, and she sat numbed in her seat beside the honeymoon couple in their best new British Home Stores outfits, Charley felt numbed. The couple did not seem to notice her, and after she had seen the rampant love bite on the girl's lower throat and the girl was younger than Charley, she did not even consider trying to talk to them. What would they have understood of her acceptance of an invitation that would provide access? Damn-all of nothing . . . She sat far down in her seat, refused the tray of food, turned the pages of the inflight magazine and retained not a word of the printed text, not a frame of the glossy photographs.

The aircraft lurched in flight, bounced on landing, swayed in flight and bounced again, and Charley thought briefly of the seabirds on the rocks below the cliff at her place, coming to land without faltering on the water washed rocks. It was behind her. The honeymoon couple, had they bothered to look, but they didn't because they were huddled together in a fear of flying, would have seen at that moment that a stubborn and bloody-minded grimace had caught at her mouth. It was what she had wanted, the chance, what she had chosen, the opportunity. When the aircraft was still, when the music came on, when she had unfastened the waist strap, she strode down the aisle, a small bounce in her step. She was needed, and it had been a long time in her life since she had known the glow of importance, too damn long . . .

Charley walked briskly through the aircraft's door.

"You on secure, 'Vanni?"

"Wait out . . . You there, Bill? OK, I'm on secure."

Bill Hammond, Country Chief of the Drug Enforcement Administration, working out of an office in the Via Sardegna, to the right off the big drag of the Via Veneto, held the telephone tight in a sweaty grip. He was an old hand, heavy experience in the back-pack of his career. The walls behind him and beside him had no further space to carry the commendations and the handshake photographs and the team pictures, of which the operations for Polar Cap and Green Ice were the most recent of the blitzkrieg swoops. His desk, on which his shirtsleeved elbows rested, was thick with paperwork, requests from Washington, cross-references with colleagues in London and Frankfurt and Zurich, reports from the Italian end . . . and there was the closed file bearing his hand-written legend, CODENAME HELEN. His fists sweated, always did and always would, when an operation went live.

"How's it going down there?"

"Don't give me Yankee bullshit." A sharp metallic-toned response.

"You got sun down there? May rain up here, always liable to rain when Easter's coming on."

"Don't pee on me."

"Tried to call you last night. Were you out screwing? Your age and you should watch your heart—"

"What's happening, shit on you, Bill."

He took a deep breath, he had the wide smile on his face. "She's coming. She'd have touched down about now."

"Jesu . . ." A hiss distorted by the scrambler system on the telephone. "How did he get her, How did he persuade . . . ?"

"That's my boy, you know my boy. How? I didn't get to ask him."

"Is she stupid, what is she?"

He was laughing. "Go back to your pit, 'Vanni, dream of big hips and big boobs, whatever you spend your time doing, you *carabinieri* bastards. My boy'll call you. Look after yourself, 'Vanni, stay safe. I don't know whether she's stupid, or what . . ." He replaced the telephone. He flicked the switch to disconnect the scrambler.

The Country Chief had worked with Axel Moen for two years and he reckoned, better than any man in the Administration, that he knew him. He did not know the detail of how Axel Moen had manipulated the young woman, Charlotte Parsons, but he had never doubted that face to face, body to body, eyeball to eyeball, Axel Moen would bring back to Italy the young woman and her baggage of access.

He would have qualified on his knowledge of the career of Axel Moen.

He would have said that he knew the backgrounder—upbringing, home base, education, work before joining the Administration, the postings of the agent before Rome—but that he was short on the motivation that drove the man.

The Country Chief had the backgrounder on Axel Moen from the headquarters confidential file . . . from his meeting two years back with the Country Chief who had run him in Bolivia . . . from sessions when he was in Washington for the strategy seminars, late at night over whiskey, with the people who had run him in New York and Miami. He could tell the backgrounder.

His man, Axel Moen, was thirty-eight years old. From immigrant Norwegian stock, farm people. Reared by his grandfather and his step-grandmother on the Door Peninsula of Wisconsin. Complications in the rearing because his father was away with the oil industry and pneumonia had taken his mother. Lonely childhood because his grandfather was divorced before the Second World War and had brought back from Europe a second wife, Sicilian, but the community on the Door Peninsula hadn't held with divorce and hadn't taken in a stranger. Isolated. Went through the University of Wisconsin, finished in Madison with grades not quite decent. Joined the city police, reached detective, applied to join the Administration. Thought to have an "attitude problem" on the induction course at Quantico, given the benefit of the doubt because the DEA was pushing up its numbers and not looking for course failures. Sent to New York, with fluent knowledge of Sicilian dialect, to sit in the darkened rooms with the earphones on and listen to the Pizza Connection wire taps. Sent to Bolivia, good under stress circumstances, good with the locals, poor on a team operation, superficially wounded. Sent back to New York, reported as a "pain" in an office environment. Sent down to Miami, worked well in deep cover, identified by the cartels, shipped out and sharp. Sent to Rome . . . Bill Hammond had been with Axel Moen for two years, run him, knew the backgrounder. Bill Hammond, who did not lie often, would have confessed that he knew sweet fuck-all of the motivation of Axel Moen.

He himself had been a DEA man since the start. Bill Hammond was coming now, and the dates on the year's work planner behind him were the ever-present reminders, toward the day he dreaded most. He was headed for retirement, for the presentation of the carriage clock or the crystal sherry decanter, for the speeches, for the last photo opportunity of the handshake with the Director. Everybody loved a cop, nobody noticed a retired cop. He was headed for minding the grandkids. Over fourteen years of service he had gathered in the detail of the file biographies of, maybe, a couple of hundred agents—men and women he could evaluate and pass a judgment on. But he did not know the source of the drive force governing Axel Moen. OK, right, sure as hell, as his career wound toward that date on the year planner, he wanted to preside over a spectacular arrest operation and he wanted to have the Director on the telephone, personal, and he had given his authorization to the plan that was CODENAME HELEN and he had basked in an anticipation of glory, but . . .

But . . .

But the kid was now off the plane at Fiumicino. But the young woman was now through Immigration. But the kid was in a taxi and headed for central Rome.

But . . .

The kid, the young woman, was now the property of Axel Moen. And it was Bill Hammond who had authorized it, and Bill Hammond had put his goddam name on the recommendation document that had gone to Washington and onto Herb Rowell's desk. And it was Bill Hammond who had given the big talk and enthused enough for Herb to kick it through the committee that rubber stamped hard point operations. And it was Bill Hammond who had pushed Herb to make the requisition order to the Engineering Research Facility. It was the responsibility of Bill Hammond that the kid, a young woman, was traveling in a taxi toward central Rome. Maybe it would be the glory, maybe it would lie on his conscience . . .

He was old, too old. He was tired, too tired . . . As the bag was dropped down on the floor, his eyes snapped open.

"Good flight, Axel?"

The shrug. "Same as any other."

"She's arrived, Miss Parsons?"

The glint of the eyes, tightening, narrowing. "That, Bill, is a sloppy mistake."

He was in the wrong. He blustered, "For God's sake, Axel, where are we? We are swept, cleaned, hoovered. We can talk—"

"You make a beginner's mistake. You talk a name here, perhaps you get to talk it elsewhere. A beginner's mistake can get to be a habit."

"I'm sorry."

"I don't want to hear it again, that name."

"I apologized . . . 'Vanni, he called her the *uccello da richiamo,* the decoy. We talked about the Trojan Horse. The horse had access. For 'Vanni, she's Codename Helen. Can you live with that?"

Axel, standing loosely, lit a cigarette. "It'll do."

"Where is she?"

"About checking in, I should think. You got my package?"

From the ring of keys on the chain at his belt, he unlocked the bottom drawer of the desk. He took out the padded bag. The bag had come with the cargo on a military flight to 6th Fleet from Engineering Research Facility at Quantico, then had been brought to Rome by a Navy courier from Naples.

"Thanks. I'll be getting on."

Axel Moen held the package and seemed to stare at it for a moment, then dropped it into his small bag. He was turning away.

"Hey, Heather rang for you. Seems Defense Attaché's a party on tonight. I said you wouldn't be able to go, I told Heather that."

"Why'd you do that?"

The emphasis steeled his voice. "Because, Axel, I assumed that Miss Codename Helen, described by you as 'ordinary' and 'predictable,' might be stressed up, might need some care before she goes down there. Aren't you taking her to dinner?"

The shaken head. "No."

"Shouldn't you be taking her to dinner?"

Axel said, "It's good for her to be alone. I can't hold her hand, in Palermo I can't nanny her. She's got to learn to be alone."

It was as the memory had been, the memory she had guarded as a treasure, in privacy, for the last four years.

In the Piazza Augusto Imperatore, in front of the imperial tomb encased in glass, Charley could have shouted her delight. In the Piazza Popolo, surrounded by the rushing river of cars and vans and motorcycles, Charley could have screamed the news that she had returned.

A heady and excited delight caught at her, as a narcotic would have. It was to her, the solitary young woman walking the old streets and scuffing her toes on the uneven cobbles and skipping over the dog dirt and the refuse, an evening of triumph. Around her were the evening crowds of the beautiful people, beside her were the open shops of clothes and designed furniture, above her were the peeling ochre buildings. Like the renewal of a love affair. Like seeing, after long absence, a man standing and waiting for her, and running headlong to him, sprinting to jump toward him and his arms. It was one evening, it was so precious. She found again, as she had found them in the summer of 1992, the little courtyards off the Via della Dataria and the churches with the high doors off the Corso, the steps above Piazza Espagna where the Arab boys sold rubbish jewelry, the fountain of Bernini in Piazza Navona. She stood by the edifice to Vittorio Emanuele and looked the length of the wide street to the faraway, floodlit Colosseum. It was Charley's heaven ... For three hours she ran and walked and ambled through the streets of the *centro storico,* and knew happiness again. When she was tired, bruised feet aching, Charley had to kick herself because the impulse was to find the bus stop on the Corso, or the rank of yellow taxis, and head north for the apartment on Collina Fleming. She had thought, many times, that she saw a younger woman walking with Angela Ruggerio and carrying the shopping bags, a younger woman walking with Giuseppe Ruggerio and smiling up at him as he joked, a younger woman walking with small Mario Ruggerio and holding his hand and laughing with his love ...

She took her dinner in a *ristorante,* a table to herself and was served by grave faced waiters a meal of pasta and lamb with spinach, and she drank all of the gassy water and most of a liter of wine, and she left a tip that was near to reckless and felt her self-esteem.

She strolled from the *ristorante* the few yards back to the hotel in which she had been booked, near to the river, off the Via della Scrofa, near to the Parliament. Outside the narrow door of the hotel, across the alleyway, a radio blared from an open workshop and a man in greasy vest and torn jeans repaired motorcycles. She looked at him, she caught his eye, she winked at him, as if it were her city. In Italian, her best, she asked the *portiere* at the reception for coffee in the morning and a copy of *La Stampa,* and with an impassive expression he had answered her in English that she would indeed have coffee and a newspaper, and she'd giggled like a child.

Her room was tiny and stifling hot. She switched on the TV, habit, scattered her clothes on the bed and the carpet, habit, went for a shower, habit. She let the lukewarm water sprinkle on her upturned face and wash away the dirt of the streets. She toweled herself hard. She would sleep naked in the sheets. She was alone, she was free, she controlled her destiny, and she bloody well was going to sleep naked and she looked, her opinion, bloody good naked. She was standing before the mirror, bloody good and . . .

In the mirror, behind what she thought was her bloody good nakedness, was the inverted television picture. A body in a street, a bustle of photographers pressing on the body and held back by the languid arm of a policeman. The trousers of the body were down at the ankles, the underpants were down at the knees, the groin was as naked as her body and bloodstained, the bare chest of the body was slashed by torture cuts, the mouth of the body bulged with the penis and the testicles cut from the groin. She held the towel now tight against her skin, as if to hide her nakedness from the eye of the mirror and the eye of the television. The commentary on the television said that the body was of a Tunisian man, a pusher of hard drugs, who had tried to trade in the streets behind the *stazione centrale* of Palermo.

Charley lay in bed. The alcohol had drained from her. She heard each shout, each siren, each roar of a motorcycle without an exhaust. Away in the south was the crevice of what Axel called *la piovra,* the source of the spreading and writhing tentacles of the octopus. Palermo.

Could an individual change anything? Answer yes or answer no . . .

Could a single person alter a situation? Answer yes or answer no . . .

Don't know, don't bloody know.

She put the light out. She lay huddled in her bed and she held herself as if to protect her nakedness.

The night lay on the city of Palermo. The journalist from Berlin yawned. Below the apartment windows, muffled because the glass was reinforced and the shutters were closed and the drape curtains drawn, only occasional cars passed. The journalist yawned because he could not see that the interview granted him, so late, would fit easily into the article commissioned by his editor.

The senator said, "You foreigners, you see La Cosa Nostra in Sicily as a 'Specter,' you see it as a character in the fiction of Ian Fleming. It makes me laugh, your ignorance. The reality is a centaur, half a knight in bright armor and half a beast. La Cosa Nostra exists because the people want it to exist. It is in the people's life and souls and bloodstream. Consider. A boy of nineteen years has left school and if he is admitted to the local family, he gets three million a month, security, structure, culture, and he gets a pistol. But the state cannot give him the security of work, can give him only the culture of TV game shows. The state offers legality, which he cannot eat. From La Cosa Nostra he gains, most important, his self-respect. If you are a foreigner, if you follow the image of 'Specter' you will believe that if the principals of La Cosa Nostra are arrested, then the organization is destroyed. You delude yourself, and you do not comprehend the uniqueness of the Sicilian people. As strangers here you will imagine that La Cosa Nostra rules by fear, but intimidation is a minor part of the organization's strength. Don't think of us as an oppressed society, in chains, pleading for liberation. The author, Pitre, wrote, 'Mafia unites the idea of beauty with superiority and valor in the best sense of the word, and something more—audacity but never arrogance,' and there are more who believe him than deny him. To most people, most Sicilians, the Government of Rome is the true enemy. You asked me, does the arrest of Riina or Santapaola or Bagarella wound the power of La Cosa Nostra? My answer, there are many who are younger, as charismatic, to take their place. Do I disappoint you? This is not the war with a military solution that you want."

The journalist blinked his eyes, tried to concentrate on what he was told and to write his long hand note.

The Capo district, the old quarter of the narrow streets and decaying buildings that had long ago been the glory of the Moorish city, was quiet. The bars were closed, the motorcycles were parked and chained, the windows were opened to admit the slight breath of the warm air. In his room Mario Ruggerio slept dreamless and a few inches from his limp and outstretched hand, on the floor beside his bed, was a loaded 9mm pistol. He slept in exhaustion after a day of figures and calculations and deals. A dead sleep that was not troubled by any threat, that he knew of, from any quarter, of imminent arrest. Lonely, without his wife, without the few that he loved, with his pistol on the floor and his calculator on the table, Mario Ruggerio snored through the dark hours.

The time of the change of the guards' shift . . . Pasquale hurried, flashing his ID at the soldiers on the street and the sergeant who watched the main entrance of the block.

Pasquale hurried because he was three minutes late for the start of his shift, and it was laid down that he should have been at the apartment a minimum of ten minutes before the shift of eight hours began. He was late for his shift because it had been the first night that his wife and the baby had been home, and he had lain beside her for three hours, awake and unable to sleep, ready to switch off the bleeped alarm the moment it sounded. The baby had been quiet in the cot at the end of the bed. His wife had lain still in the bed, buried in tiredness. He had not woken either his wife or his baby when he had slipped from under the single cotton sheet, dressed, gone on his toes from the bedroom.

The door was opened. He saw the disciplined annoyance on the face of the *maresciallo*. Pasquale muttered about his baby, coming home, asleep now, and when he shrugged his apology he expected a softening of the *maresciallo's* anger, because the older man had children, adored children, would understand. There was a cold, whispered criticism, and he squirmed the whispered response that it would not happen again.

They knew where the polished floorboards of the hallway creaked. They avoided the loose boards. They went silently past the door behind which the magistrate slept. Sometimes they heard him cry out, and sometimes they heard him tossing, restlessly.

In the seven weeks he had known the magistrate, Pasquale thought the saddest thing he had learned of the life of the man he protected was the going of Rocco Tardelli's wife and the taking of Rocco Tardelli's children. The *maresciallo* had told him. The day after the killing of Borsellino, the month after the murder of Falcone, Patrizia Tardelli shouting, "Sicily is not worth a single drop of an honorable man's blood. Sicily is a place of vipers . . ." She had gone with her three children, as the *maresciallo* had told Pasquale, and the magistrate had not argued with her but had helped to carry their bags from the outer door to the car, and the *ragazzi* had hurried him away from the danger of the exposed pavement and not allowed him even to see the car disappear around the corner of the block. The *maresciallo* had said that afterwards after they had gone, the magistrate had not wept but had gone to work. Pasquale thought it the saddest story he knew.

In the kitchen, among the mess of the heavy vests and the machine pistols, Pasquale filled the kettle in the sink where the magistrate's supper dishes had not yet been cleaned, and made the first coffee of the day. He poured the coffee for the *maresciallo* and himself. Later he would wash the dishes in the sink. They, the *ragazzi,* were not supposed to be the servants of the magistrate, nor his messengers, nor his cooks, nor would they ever be his true friends, but it would have seemed to each of them on the detail to be merciless to sit and watch as the magistrate washed his own dishes, prepared his food alone.

Pasquale asked what was the schedule of the day.

The *maresciallo* shrugged as if it were of no relevance.

"To Ucciardone . . . ?"

Again the shrug, as if it were of no importance whether they went again to the prison.

The forehead of Pasquale wrinkled in puzzlement. It was what had confused him the night before, when he had sat in front of the late-evening television after his wife had gone to their bed and the baby to the new cot. He did not understand.

"The man who tries to be a *pentito,* he was very hard with him. All right, so we are not supposed to hear, to listen, but it is impossible not to hear what is said. 'I can tell you where is Mario Ruggerio.' Nothing happens. It is left. Why? Ruggerio is the biggest catch, Ruggerio is the target of Tardelli, Ruggerio is of international status. Am I very simple?"

"Simple and naïve and with much to learn." There was a weariness in the expression of the *maresciallo.* He held the coffee cup in two hands, as if one hand on the cup might have shaken and spilled the coffee. "There is a saying on the island, 'A man warned is a man saved.' Dr. Tardelli was warned long ago, and he has ignored the warning. But, important, he has not only been warned by La Cosa Nostra, he has been warned also by those who should be his colleagues. He has the quality of honesty, and it is that honesty that humiliates his colleagues. There is no serious effort to attack the enemy, the colleagues stand and watch from safety, and they wait to see Tardelli fall on his arse. How many in the Palace of Justice make certain, Jesu, so certain, that an investigation into La Cosa Nostra never hits their desks? Too many. He is accused of the personality cult, of judicial communism, of denigrating the reputation of Sicily. He is accused by those who have ambition and vanity and envy, but who do not have honesty. Which judge can he trust, which prosecutor, which magistrate, which *carabiniere,* which police officer? Pasquale, can he trust you?"

"That is insane."

"Insane? Really? A judge in Calabria is arrested, mafia collusion. The head of the *squadra mobile* is arrested, mafia association. What is your price, Pasquale, if your wife is threatened or your baby? If a prime minister can be bought, what is the price of a young policeman with a wife and baby? Everywhere is the contamination of the bastards. The former head of International Affairs of the American Justice Department is charged with working for the Colombians. In Germany it is reported that new levels of corruption in public life have been reached. Maybe he trusts us because we ride with him, because we would die with him. He does not trust his colleagues."

"Tell me."

"Each time he offers protection to a *pentito* he has to be certain of the genuineness of the man. He may be dealing with a 'placed' man, he may be sitting opposite a liar. If he diverts resources, the weight of an investigation, in the direction of a 'placed' man or a liar, then he will be weakened. If he is weakened, then he is isolated. If he is isolated, then he is dead. It is necessary for him to go one short step at a time because he walks through a mine field. Heh, what would you prefer, boy? Would you prefer to be directing traffic in Milan?"

The coffee Pasquale drank was cold. He stood. He took off his jacket, and rolled up his sleeves, and ran hot water into the sink and started to wash the magistrate's dishes.

Past two in the morning . . . The night duty manager reflected his annoyance at being called by the porter from his office and his catnap. He studied the computer screen.

"Difficult to help you, Sergeant. That's nearly a week ago. We've had 827 guests through since that night. All right, the date you want . . . 391 guests in residence. Bear with me. Are you sure this cannot wait till the morning?"

But Harry Compton, after another evening beavering at the solicitor's files and archives, had chosen to visit the hotel in Portman Square on his way home. It was what was called, a bullshit expression, a "window of opportunity." In the morning he would be back at the solicitor's papers, so, definitely, it could not wait.

"Well, of the 391 residents, twenty-one declared Italian passports. Wait again, I'll check the details . . ."

The fingers flitted over the computer's keys.

"You said, 'resident in Palermo.' No, can't help. Of the Italian passport holders that night, none declared residency in Palermo. You're being economical. Could you tell me why Fraud Squad is here at this wretched hour?"

He felt the blow, like a punch. He swore under his breath.

"Are you sure?"

"That's what I said, friend—none lists residence in Palermo, Sicily."

"What about the dinner bill? Table 12 in the restaurant, did one of them sign?"

"No can help. That's a restaurant matter. The restaurant's closed, has been cleared for ninety minutes. Have to come back in the morning."

"Get it open."

"I beg your pardon."

Harry Compton, detective sergeant in SO6, reckoned he loathed the languid little creep across the reception counter. "I said, get it open."

They went into the dim-lit restaurant. A *sous* waiter was found, smoking in the kitchen. The keys were produced. A drawer was opened. The receipts and order bills were taken from the drawer. There had been eighty-three diners on the evening that concerned him. He took the bundle of receipts and order bills to a table and asked to be brought a beer . . .

It was near the bottom of the pile, sod's law, the sheet of paper for table twelve, the printout sheet with the illegible signature and the digits of the room number of the resident. He gulped the beer. He strode with the sheet of paper back to the reception desk and trilled the bell hard for the night duty manager.

"Room 338, I want that gentleman's card."

"Are you entitled to that information?"

"I am—and I am also entitled to report to Public Health that a dirty little creature was smoking in your kitchen."

The bill was printed out for him, with the check-in card carrying the personal details of the guest who had occupied room 338. It was an afterthought. Should have been routine, but he was so goddam tired. The night duty manager was disappearing back to his office.

"Oh, and I require a list of the telephone numbers called from that room. Yes, now, please."

"Did you go back, where you were before?"

"I did."

"Never worth it, going back. It seems unimportant, what was once special."

"I walked from the block along past the tennis club and into Piazza Fleming. It was the way that I used to take small Mario to the school bus."

"Going back is time wasted, sentimental."

"If you have any other criticisms to make could we do them in a job lot and get them over with, Mr. Moen? It gets to be tedious, your criticism."

If Charley annoyed him then, he did not show it. If she amused him, he did not show it. They were by the footbridge, high on the promenade above the water, across from the fortress of Sant' Angelo. She had been at the rendezvous on time and then she had waited. It had been ten minutes after she had come to the bridge that she had seen him, coming easily through a traffic flow, stopping then skipping forward, confident. He'd told her that he had watched her through those ten minutes and he'd satisfied himself that she was not followed. He hadn't made a big deal of the fact that, his opinion, she might have been followed, just said it and unsettled her. She gazed down into the slow movement of the green brown water below.

"Are you going to ask me what I did last night?"

"No."

So, Charley did not tell Axel Moen about walking the streets of the *centro storico* and dousing herself in nostalgia. Nor did she tell him of sitting, anarchic and alone, in a *ristorante* and eating till her stomach bulged and drinking the best portion of a liter of house wine. She did not tell him that she had showered, walked naked from the bathroom and seen on the television the picture of a man's body in Palermo whose balls were in his mouth, and didn't tell that the night had been a long nightmare.

"What did *you* do last night?"

The dry voice, as if reciting from a catalog. "Went to a party."

"Could you have taken me?"

"I had someone to go with."

He stood beside her. He held a padded paper bag in his hand. The labels had been pulled from it. She saw the great tree logs and the big branches, debris of the winter floods, now marooned against the piers of the bridge. She looked up at the fortress of Sant' Angelo. She had been round it, alone, in the summer of 1992, tramped the narrow corridors and climbed the worn steps and marveled at the symmetry of its architects, so many centuries ago, in creating the perfect circular shape. It had been then a place of friendship.

"I'm here, you're here, so what happens now?"

"You're on board?"

"Of course I'm bloody on board."

"You don't want to step off?"

She stood her full height. He wasn't looking at her. He was gazing away, distant, toward the dome, misted and gray, of St. Peter's. She took his arm, a fistful of the arm of his windcheater, and she jerked him round to face her.

"For Christ's sake—I came, didn't I?"

He seemed to hesitate, as if he were troubled. Then, he launched. "Terrorism, Charley, is spectacular. Terrorism makes headlines. You know about the bombs in the City of London, you know about Oklahoma City and the World Trade Center, and about hijackings. You know about the charisma of a Che Guevera or a Carlos or an Adams or a Meinhof because the ideology and profile of those people are plastered all over your television. They don't count. For all the resources we throw against them they are minor league. But you, Charley, you don't know the name of an internationally relevant criminal. It's like HIV and cancer. HIV, the terrorist, gets the attention and the resources, while cancer, the crime boss, busies itself with the serious damage, but quietly. With an ideology only of greed, organized crime is the cancer that chews at our society, and it should be taken out at source with a knife. In the ideology of greed there is no mercy if an obstacle—you, Charley—gets in the way . . ."

A small and weak grin. "Is this your effort to scare me?"

"When you're alone, when you're frightened, then you should know what you've gotten into. Down in Sicily, fair to assume, there's a hundred different programs, slants, angles of an operation running. You are one in a hundred. That's your importance. You offer a one-in-a-hundred chance of, maybe, getting up alongside the target. You are Codename Helen, that is the name—"

She snorted and the color ran back into her face. She laughed at him. "Helen? Helen of Troy? Trojan Horse and all that? That is really original—did a genius think up that one?"

"It's what you are, Codename Helen." He flushed.

"What's inside the walls? Who's hiding in Troy?"

"Don't play jokes, Charley, don't. There is a family in the town of Prizzi, that's inland from Palermo. It's a mean little place stuck on the rock. OK, Prizzi is the home of a *contadino's* family. The *contadino* is Rosario and he is now aged eighty-four. His wife is Agata, now aged eighty-three. Rosario and Agata have produced six children. The children are Mario, the eldest, sixty-two . . . Salvatore, sixty, in prison . . . Carmelo, fifty-nine, simple, lives with his parents . . . Cristoforo, would be fifty-seven, dead . . . Maria, fifty-one, married and an alcoholic . . . the youngest, Giuseppe, forty-two, the big gap because old Rosario was called away between 1945 and 1954 to spend time in Ucciardone prison. The name of that family from Prizzi is Ruggerio . . ."

He flicked a cigarette from the Lucky Strike packet. She locked her eyes on the cupola of St. Peter's, as if she thought the mist-shrouded image might strengthen her.

"The family is *mafiosi,* down to the base of its spine, right to the bottom of the root of the weed. But nothing is as it seems. The family has played a long game, which is the style of La Cosa Nostra, to play long and patient. Giuseppe, bright child, was sent by his eldest brother away from Prizzi, out of Sicily, to university in Rome. On to a school of business management in Geneva. To an Italian bank in Buenos Aires. There were connections, favors were called in, work in Rome for one of those discreet little banks handling Vatican funds. Did he seem to you, Giuseppe, to be the son of a *contadino*? Did he tell you about a peasant family? Did he?"

Charley had no answer. Her teeth ground at her bottom lip.

"I said that the family could play a long game. Only a very few in Palermo, and none in Rome, would know that Giuseppe is the brother of Mario Ruggerio. I don't know how many hundreds of millions of dollars Mario Ruggerio is worth. I know what he needs. Mario Ruggerio needs a banker, a broker, an investment manager, in whom he can place absolute trust. It's all a matter of trust down there. Trust is held in the family. The family has the man to wash, rinse, spin and dry their money. The family is everything. The family meets, the family gathers, and the family does not feel the danger of betrayal. Then, and it's rare, the family makes a mistake. The mistake is a letter written by Angela to a former nanny/child-minder—I have a friend down there and you don't need his name and you don't need his agency, and because it's the way in Sicily he does not share with colleagues what he learns, and he learned of the link between Giuseppe and Mario Ruggerio, and he started to run a sporadic surveillance on pretty little Giuseppe, and the jackpot bonus came up when he intercepted the letter, a mistake. I don't know how often that family meets, no idea. I know that the family will come together, that Mario Ruggerio will need, a deep need because he is Sicilian, to be in the bosom of his family. They all have it, the evil, heartless bastards, a syrup streak of sentimentality for the family. You're there, Charley, you're a part of the family, you're the little mouse that nobody notices, you're at the far end of the room, and watching the kids and keeping them quiet, you're access . . ."

She stared at the cupola of St. Peter's. She thought it a place of sanctity and safety, and she could remember standing in the great square on a Sunday morning and feeling humbled by the love of the pilgrims for the Holy Father, minuscule on the balcony.

"A man from Agrigento has disappeared. He led one of the three principal families of La Cosa Nostra. It is assumed he is dead. There is a man from Catania, the power in the east of the island. There is Mario Ruggerio. They do not share power in Sicily, they fight for power with the delicacy of rats in a bucket. Mario Ruggerio is one stage away from the overall command of La Cosa Nostra. One step away from taking the title of *capo di tutti capi*. One killing away from becoming the most influential figure in international organized crime. The target of Codename Helen is Mario Ruggerio."

She felt weak, pitiful. "Is it possible, listen to me, Christ, hear me, is it possible for one person, me, to change anything?"

He said, "If I didn't think so, I would not have come for you."

He took her hand. Without asking, and without explanation, he unhooked the fastening of her wristwatch. The watch was gold. It was the most expensive thing that she owned. It had been given to her by her father, three weeks before he had known of his redundancy, for her twenty-first birthday. He dropped the gold watch, as if it were a bauble and worthless, into his trouser pocket. He still held her hand, a strong grip that was without affection. The envelope was laid on top of the stonework above the flowing river. He took from it a bigger watch, a man's watch, the sort of watch that young men wore, a scuba diver's watch. He told her to think of a story as to why she wore such a watch. He slipped it over the narrowness of her fist, onto the narrowness of her wrist. The strap was of cold expanding metal. He showed her, exactly and methodically, which buttons activated the watch's mechanism, and which button activated the panic tone . . . Christ . . . He told her the life of the cadmium battery in the watch. He told her the signals she should send. He told her the range of the signal of the panic tone. He told her that the UHF frequency would be monitored twenty-four hours a day in Palermo. He told her when she should make a test transmission. He let her hand drop.

"When he comes, if he comes, to meet with his family, Mario Ruggerio, you activate the tone. The only other time that you use it is if you believe that your physical safety is endangered. Do you understand?"

"Where will you be?"

"Close enough to respond." She saw the strength in his face, the bold build of his chin, the assurance of his mouth. She reflected that she was placing her life in that strength.

"You promise?"

"I promise. You have a good journey."

She flared, enough of playing the small and pathetic girl. "Wait a minute, Mr. Axel bloody Moen, how often do we meet?"

Casual. "Every so often."

"That's not good enough. Where do we meet?"

"I'll find you."

He walked away. She watched him go over the bridge, toward the fortress of Sant' Angelo. She felt the tight cold metal of the strap on her wrist.

5

HE HAD SAID, BACK IN DEVON, that she should travel from Rome to Palermo by train. He had explained, chill and staccato, that the most vulnerable time for an agent was in the sea-change hours of going from overt to covert. If she boarded a plane, he had said, a journey like Rome to Palermo, she would step over the gulf in an hour. Better, he'd said, to spread the transition time. Better to use a dozen hours and have the chance to reflect on the sea change and the gulf that was to be crossed.

Charley had taken the train from the *terminii* in the early evening, pushed her way with a rare aggression through the crowds on the concourse. She had booked the sleeper, a single berth, and not cared what it cost because the Ruggerios would pay for it. She had heaved her bag along the corridor and dumped it inside the little compartment of the snake-length train that was alongside those that would leave later for Vienna and Paris. She had chewed on a ham-and-tomato roll, revolting, and sipped from a bottle of mineral water, warm, and watched from the train as the dusk gathered on isolated farmhouses and avenues of high pines and a long, ruined viaduct from the dawn of history.

She had reflected, as Axel Moen had said she should.

She had considered the distance at which he kept himself. She knew nothing of what lay beneath the exterior of his face, beneath his clothes, nothing of his mind. She had not met before, ever, a person of such sealed privacy. She thought, and it perked her up, that he kept a distance as if he were a little afraid of her. So she wanted to believe that she was important to him, that she was the final piece that made the puzzle complete.

It was good to feel that. And, alone in the train, the rumble of the wheels below her, rushing south, the darkness of the night beyond the window, she felt a sense of pride. She had been chosen, she had been challenged, she was wanted. She had lain on the made bed and the glow of excitement had coursed in her. She was needed. She was important ... She had slept, as if an arrogance and an ignorance had caught her.

She had slept through the shunting of the train onto the ferry at Villa S. Giovanni on the Calabrian coast and the docking of the ferry at Messina, slept a dead and dreamless sleep.

The knocking on the door woke Charley. She had slept in her T-shirt and her knickers. She was decent, but she wrapped the blanket around her as she unlocked the door and took the tray of coffee from the attendant. She closed the door and locked it again. She set the tray down and went to the window and released the blind. Charley saw Sicily.

The journalist from Berlin was awake early. He boasted a tidy mind. He believed it important, at the first sober opportunity, to transfer the essentials of the interview from notebook to laptop memory. He had ordered an early call, before the pace of the city moved, because he had first to dissect the notes he had taken over dinner and two bottles of Marsala wine, and the notes would be a mess and scrawled in confusion. He had dined with the mayor of a small town on the west coast down from Palermo. He had anticipated a ringing cry for action against La Cosa Nostra from a man whose father had been killed because he had denounced an evil. Sitting on his bed in his pajamas, the ache in his head, he had read back his notes.

"Quote Pirandello (paraphrase)—draw the distinction between the seeing and the being, the fiction and the reality—the fiction is police activity, ministers and policemen and magistrates on TV, prisoners paraded in front of cameras, the cry that the mafia is crumbling, FICTION. The mafia is not weakened, stronger than ever, REALITY. No serious commitment by the state against the mafia—think what it is like to be Sicilian, abandoned by central government, not supported, to be alone. No big victory is possible—white sheets on balconies after the killing of Falcone as an expression of public disgust, but the disgust is slipping, collective anger is gone. The thread of the mafia is woven through every institution, every part of life—always the stranger must realize that he does not know who he talks to—being a *mafioso* can mean a man belongs to the upper strata of society, does not mean that he is a crude killer. Nobody, NOBODY, knows the depth of mafia infiltration into public life. For the stranger, NEVER BE UNGUARDED ..."

———

The Country Chief drove Axel Moen to Fiumicino for the first flight of the day going south to Palermo, and parked, and went with his man to check-in.

They walked together toward the center of the concourse; there were a few minutes before the flight would be called. Should have talked in the car, but they hadn't, and it had been time lost, but the traffic had been heavy and the Country Chief had reckoned he needed all of his start-of-the-day concentration to keep himself from shunting with the bastards around him who were weaving and overtaking and braking. The Country Chief shouldn't have left the loose ends to the concourse.

"You OK?"

"I feel fine."

"The archaeology . . . ?"

"It'll do and it'll get better."

"You get a shooter from 'Vanni."

"Yes, 'Vanni says he'll fix me a shooter."

Too old and too tired, and the Country Chief thought he played the part of the fussing mother well. "It's shared with 'Vanni, only him."

"Maybe it has to be shared with a magistrate. That guy, Rocco Tardelli, maybe we share with him. He's a good man."

"He's a friend, useful, but don't . . . You know it hurts me, but you put ten Italian law enforcement people in a room, and you share. If you share, you should trust. Do you know everything about them? Do you know which of them's wife's uncle's cousin is going after a construction contract to build a school and needs a favor from the local boss? So you trust none of them. That bugs me, the lack of trust, it makes for corrosive suspicion, but you cannot take the chance."

"I know that, Bill."

"Because it's her life."

In front of him was the face of Axel Moen, a wall of granite, shielding whatever feelings the damned man had.

"I figured that."

"You know what I want?"

"Keep it quick, Bill."

"I want that bastard, I want Mario Ruggerio nailed, and I want it to be by our efforts. Not a big cooperative, but by our efforts. If it's us that nails him, then I believe, what Headquarters says, we can swing the extradition business. I want him shipped Stateside, I want him put into Supermax. I want him to breathe the sweet air of Colorado. I want him in one of those concrete tombs. I want him to know that for sending over all that filth into our country there's a downside. I want . . ."

"I'll stay close, Bill."

"Look after that kid, damn you, with your life."

Axel shrugged and walked toward Departure.

She was not trained, she was not coached. But she did not think herself stupid.

Charley was dressed. She leaned against the grimed glass of the window and the train lurched slowly along. She was gazing inland. She thought that she did not have to be trained to recognize, in that country, how a corpse could remain hidden and how a fugitive could stay free. On and on, displayed from her window, were the steep and harsh cut rainwater gullies that were overgrown with coarse grass and scrub that ran from the track up to the hills. She had bought from the English-language bookshop on Via Babuino, the previous day, after he had left her, a guidebook to Sicily. The book had a chapter on the island's history. In the gullies there could have been the corpse of a Moorish invader, of a Bourbon soldier, of a Fascist official, of a Roman policeman, and it would never be found, it would be food for foxes and rats. Among the scrub were dark-set, small caves, and there were the roofless ruins of peasant homes and the crumbled shelters where once a farmer had put his goats or his sheep, and the ruins and the shelters could have been hiding places for fugitives from centuries back to the present moment. Above the gullies and the caves and the ruins, beyond the hills, were the climbing mountains that reached to the clouds. A great emptiness that was broken only rarely by the white scars of winding switchback roads. A ruthless and hard place . . . A body, her body, dumped into a gully, and she would never be found. A fugitive, Mario Ruggerio, hiding in the caves and ruins, and he would never be found.

She murmured, private to herself, as she fingered the heavy watch on her wrist, "Learning, Charley, learning bloody fast."

She came away from the window. She brushed her teeth. She tidied her sausage bag. She reflected, as Axel Moen had told her to.

They had circled Catania, then come in to land through the early mist. He could see the foothills to the west, but not the summit of Etna, which the cloud held.

He had told her that going back was time wasted, was sentimental.

Palermo, yes, many times, but it was twenty one years since Axel Moen had been at the Fontanarossa airport of Catania. They were old now and they were living far up the Door Peninsula, up between Ephraim and Sister Bay, and eking out their last days and weeks and months. It was twenty-one years since his grandfather and his step-grandmother had brought him to the airport at Catania. Only the name to remember it by because there were new buildings and a new tower and new acreage of concrete. On Arne Moen's retirement he had brought his wife, Vincenzina, and his grandson to Catania and Sicily. Didn't matter if he cared not to think on it . . . Most of the emotion juices Axel was ready for, could control. Going through the airport at Catania, the juices worked on him and hurt him. Arne Moen had come to Sicily in 1943, a captain in George Patton's invasion army, and he'd been the idiot who'd drunk too much brandy for his system one night and had fallen in the gutter while swaying back to the commandeered villa at Romagnolo and broken his goddam arm. The army had leapfrogged onto the Italian mainland and left Arne Moen behind to nurse his plaster-cased arm. Taken into AMGOT, given a job with the bureaucracy of the Allied Military Government, and found himself in a minor heaven as a minor god controlling gasoline supplies and transportation between Corleone and the road junction at Piana degli Albanesi. It had provided what his grandfather called an "opportunity." The story of the "opportunity" had been told in self-pity and with moist eyes at the Catania airport at the end of the week's tour, as if it were necessary for a seventeen-year-old to know a truth.

The emotions wounded Axel because the "opportunity" was corruption. He did not care to remember because the "opportunity" was in the black-market siphoning of gasoline and the taking of bribes in return for permission to run lorries down to Palermo. The money from the corruption and the black market and the bribes had gone back to the Door Peninsula and it had paid, dirty money, for his grandson's education at the university in Madison, and had paid for the house and the fields and orchards between Ephraim and Sister Bay. One day, maybe not too long, because Arne Moen was now in his eighty-fifth year, and Vincenzina Moen was in her seventy-eighth year, he would have to decide what to do with a legacy of dirty money . . . After the tour of the battlefields, precious little fighting done, and the visit to the house in Corleone from which the minor god had run his racket, after the cloying visit to Vincenzina's peasant family, after the journey had come to its end, the story of the "opportunity" had been told.

For Axel it was a sharp memory. He had sat between his grandfather and his step-grandmother in the departure lounge at Catania. His grandfather had sniveled the story of criminality, and his step-grandmother had stared straight ahead as though she heard nothing and saw nothing and knew nothing. He thought, striding that early morning through the airport, that the telling of the story of corruption had withered his innocence. He had sworn to himself, with the authority of his seventeen years, that he would never again allow innocence to cut him . . . Where he'd sat, between his grandfather and his step-grandmother twenty-one years before, was now a left luggage area. What he had learned when his innocence had ended was to trust no man because even a man he loved had a price. Shit . . .

Axel Moen went to the Avis counter for his hire car.

Charley jumped down onto the low platform.

She reached back to drag out her sausage bag.

She was carried forward in the restless rush of passengers surging from the train. Her gaze raked the barrier, and she saw them. She recognized Angela Ruggerio, a little thicker in the hips and a little heavier at the throat and still beautiful, and holding the new baby and holding the hand of Francesca who had been the baby in the happiness summer of 1992, and bending to speak in small Mario's ear and pushing him forward. The boy ran against the flow and came to her, and Charley dropped her bag and held out her arms and let him jump at her and hug her. She held the son of the man who washed and rinsed and spun and dried the money, the nephew of the man who was an evil, heartless bastard. She had arrived, she had gained access. Small Mario fought out of her arms and took the straps of the sausage bag in his hands and scraped it after her along the platform. Charley gave the Judas kiss to Angela Ruggerio and her hands were squeezed. It was a desperate love that she saw in Angela Ruggerio, as if she were a true friend, as if she represented deliverance from misery. She tugged the cheek of Francesca in play and the little girl laughed and thrust her arms round Charley's neck.

"You are very good for time, Charley. I do not think you are a minute late."

She glanced down at her watch, the heavy watch of a diver, instinct. The minute hand of the watch pointed directly to the button for the panic tone.

"No, it is wonderful, we were exactly on time."

Axel took the *autostrada* route across the heart of the island. He was calm. He cruised in the small Fiat hire car along the dual-carriageway A19 through the central mountains, past the small vineyards that had been hacked from the handkerchiefs of ground available for cultivation among the rocks, past the herds of thin goats and leggy sheep that were watched by men with leathered faces and by restless dogs. He stopped at the old hill city of Enna, long enough to see the crooked lines in yellow and

97

orange and ochre of successive mountain ranges to the north, not long enough for the culture of the buildings, sufficient time for a cup of sharp and hot coffee. On down toward the coast, and he allowed the lorries and cars to race past him, as if he had no ambition to compete with speed. When he reached the coast, could see the blue haze of the sea, he swung west for Terminii Imerese, and he drove toward Palermo. Between the road and the shore were orange groves and lemon orchards, holiday complexes that were shuttered and barred because the season had not yet started . . . A prosecutor had talked of "a power system, an articulation of power, a metaphor of power and a pathology of power . . ." The sun burned the road, the light beat up from the tarmac into his face. Away out on the water were small boats, drifting distant from each other, in which lonely fishermen stood and cast small nets, and he saw old men walking on the gray pebble beaches with long shore fishing rods on their shoulders . . . A judge had talked of "a global, unitary, rigidly regimented and vertical structure governed from the top down by a *cupola* with absolute powers over policy, money, life and death . . ." He felt a calmness because he was not deluded by the peace of the mountains and the peace of the seascape. He drove through Bagheria and Villabate and took the ringroad to the south of the city, as if ignoring the close-set tower blocks of Palermo, and then he climbed the switchback road that was signed to Monreale. He was close to his destination.

At the apartment in the Giardino Inglese the morning was spent packing Angela's clothes and the children's bags.

She was told about Mondello and a villa by the sea, the holiday home for the summer. The description of the holiday villa, given by Angela Ruggerio, was curt, and Charley saw already a wan tiredness and distraction about the face and movements of her employer. It was hard for Charley to gauge her mood, but the woman was a changed person: the confidence and humor of four years before were gone, as if the spirit of her were crushed. It was, Charley, thought, as if a wall had been erected. She spent most of that morning in the rooms used by small Mario and Francesca, taking the necessary clothes from drawers and the favored toys from cupboards, but when she had wandered into the principal bedroom and not knocked she had seen Angela at the drawer of a bedside table, taking two pill bottles out, and she had seen a little moment of almost panic because the bottles were noticed, and then Angela had dropped them into a bag. Charley had smiled in embarrassment and said something inane about the number of shirts that small Mario would need, and the little moment had passed.

Charley and small Mario were given the work of taking the bulging bags and cases down in the elevator to the underground parking area. When she came back up and walked into the grandness of the apartment Angela was standing in the center of the living area and was gazing down at a blemish in the beauty of the embroidered carpet and frowning. Then, aware of Charley in the doorway, she replaced the frown by a fixed and tense smile.

The last bags were carried out. The door was locked. In the car park, the bags and cases were pushed into the big trunk of a Mercedes saloon.

Charley sat in the back and held tight to the baby and Francesca cuddled against her as if, so soon, a friendship had been made. They were out of the city, the tower blocks were behind them, they were under the steep might of the Pellegrino mountain, they were passing the first whores of the day waiting in their mini-skirts and plunging blouses at the entrances to the picnic sites, when it struck Charley. He had not been mentioned. Dr. Giuseppe Ruggerio had not been spoken of. It was not for her to ask questions. She should not probe, she had been told, and she should not push and she should not display curiosity.

They drove along the slack crescent road that skirted the beach at Mondello. They went through the narrow streets of the old town. They stopped at big iron gates with black painted steel plates to deny a voyeur's inspection of what lay behind them. Angela slapped the horn of the Mercedes. The gates were opened by an old man, who ducked his head in respect and she drove up a hidden drive, past flowers and shrubs, and braked hard in front of the villa.

She had arrived. Codename Helen was in place. She had taken the opportunity of access. She was the horse, she was treachery. Angela, remote and unsmiling, carrying the baby, went ahead and fished the keys from her bag as she walked to the patio of the villa. Small Mario and Francesca ran after their mother. Charley opened the trunk of the Mercedes and started to heave out the family's bags and cases. From by the gate, leaning on a broom, standing among the fallen winter's leaves, the old man, the gardener, watched her ... She felt small and alone and so cast off.

"There is no change." The magistrate shrugged as if uninterested. "You tell me what you know, when you have told me then I evaluate, when I have evaluated what you tell me then I decide on a recommendation, when I have decided on a recommendation then the committee will determine if you should be given the privileges of the Special Protection Program ..."

Pasquale leaned against the door. The Beretta 9mm pistol was against his hip, and the machine gun was draped on a strap and cut into the small of his back.

"I need the guarantee."

The prisoner was hunched over the table and his furtive eyes roamed around the bare walls, and his fingers shook as they guided his cigarette to his mouth. Outside the door, muffled from passage along the concrete faced corridor, deadened by the distance from the car park, were the shouts and jeers of the men kicking a football, the men who guarded the magistrate and a judge who worked that day at Ucciardone. From the door Pasquale craned to hear the response. The magistrate made the gesture, opened his hands. "If you do not tell me what you know then you will serve a sentence of life imprisonment for murder. It is not for me to offer guarantees."

The prisoner had requested the second interview. Word had again been passed. The prisoner had again been brought by the secret and circuitous route to the bare walled room. The wretch trembled. Pasquale knew the oath that he would have sworn. In a locked room filled with already sworn Men of Honor, the darkness of night outside to conceal their gathering: "Are you ready to enter La Cosa Nostra? Do you realize there will be no going back? You enter La Cosa Nostra with your own blood and you can leave it only by shedding more of your own blood." Pasquale thought the wretch trembled because he would then have been asked in which hand he would hold a gun, and the trigger finger of that hand would have been pricked with a thorn sufficient to draw blood, and the blood would have been smeared on a paper image of the Virgin Mary at the Annunciation, and the paper would have been lit and it would have been dropped, burning into the palm of the wretch's hand and he would have recited the oath and then condemned himself if he betrayed it— "May my flesh burn like this holy image if I am unfaithful to La Cosa Nostra." The wretch would have sworn it, with blood and with fire, and now he squirmed.

"For Ruggerio, I get the guarantee for Mario Ruggerio . . . ?"

The magistrate's fingers drummed on the table. Pasquale watched him. The shoulders were rounded, the chin was slack, there seemed no evidence of the core strength of the man, but the *maresciallo* had spoken, musing, of his courage and quoted as if it were relevant to this man too, the saying of the dead Falcone, "The brave man dies only once, the coward dies a thousand times each day." Pasquale listened. If they were close to Mario Ruggerio, if they threatened the freedom of Mario Ruggerio, they were all endangered—not only Rocco Tardelli's life was hazarded, but also the lives of the *ragazzi* who stood in front of Tardelli and beside him and behind him.

"If, through your efforts, Mario Ruggerio were to be arrested, then I would recommend that you be given the privileges of the Special Protection Program."

The silence hung between the bare walls, eddied with the cigarette smoke toward the single fluorescent strip. Because Pasquale knew the oath that the wretch had sworn, the depths of the oath made with fire and blood, he shuddered. The *maresciallo,* sitting behind the wretch, leaned forward to hear better. The magistrate scratched at the head of a pimple on the side of his nose as if it were not a matter of importance to him. There were tears in the prisoner's eyes.

"He is in the Capo district of Palermo . . ."

"Now, today?"

"I heard it a little time ago, Mario Ruggerio is in the Capo district."

"How long is a 'little time ago'?"

"A few months ago, in the Capo district."

The hardening of the accent of the magistrate, leaning forward across the table and allowing the smoke to brush his face. "How many months ago?"

"A year ago."

Pasquale sagged. There was a sardonic and bruised smile on the face of the *maresciallo.* Rocco Tardelli did not imitate them, did not sag and did not smile. He held the prisoner's eyes.

"Where, 'a year ago,' in the Capo district was Mario Ruggerio?"

"He used a bar . . ."

"Where was the bar in the Capo district that was used by Mario Ruggerio?"

"He used a bar in the street between the Via Sant'Agostino and the Piazza Beati Paoli. Several times he used the bar, but once he ate almond cake in the bar and his stomach was disturbed. He said, I was told, it was a shit bar that served shit almond cake."

"That is what you were told?"

"Yes . . ."

The prisoner's head was bowed. An oath was broken, an oath made on blood and fire was fractured. The tears ran brisk on the wretch's cheeks.

The magistrate said, serene, "May I recapitulate what you have said? It is important that we understand the information you pass me. In return for eighteen million *lire* a month, and for your freedom, and for the ending of the legal process against you that is a charge of murder, in return for that you offer me the information that a friend told you that Mario Ruggerio had mild food poisoning in a bar in the Capo district."

The blurted response. "He would only have used a bar in the Capo district if he lived there."

"If he lived there a year ago." So patient. "That is everything?"

The prisoner's head rose. He looked directly into the face of the magistrate. He wiped the tear rivers from his cheeks. "It is enough to kill me."

Later, after the prisoner had been taken with his face hidden by a blanket back across the yard to the medical center, after they had called a halt to the football game in the car park and loaded into the Alfa and the chase car, after they had emerged from the safety of the perimeter fence of the Ucciardone prison, after they had hit the traffic and blasted a way clear with the siren, Rocco Tardelli leaned forward and spoke quietly into the ear of the *maresciallo*. Pasquale drove fast, using brakes and gears and accelerator, and listened.

"It was of importance, or not of importance? I have my own opinion, but I wish for yours. Or is it not fair for me to ask you? I believe him. I believe Mario Ruggerio would indeed inhabit a rat hole like the Capo district. He has no use for luxury, for gold taps, for silken sheets and suits from Armani. He is a *contadino*, and the peasant cannot change. He would be happy there, he would feel reassured there, in safety. But it was a year ago. A summer has gone, an autumn, and a winter, and now I have to deliberate as to whether to use my authority to divert pressed resources to the investigation of information that is stale. We have to pick at crumbs and pluck at straws as if we starved and as if we drowned . . . It is not fair for me to ask you, I must walk my own road."

They stood back and they watched.

The swing was good and the pivot was good and the contact was good and the flight was good. The ball flew. Before the ball had landed Giuseppe Ruggerio bent to pick up the plastic tee peg, then he went forward and reached down for the divot, cleanly removed like a dropped hairpiece. Now he glanced up to see the final bouncing of his ball on the sand ground of the fairway, then turned to replace his divot.

They murmured as they watched.

"He's useful, can't take that from him."

"Useful, but, God, he doesn't hide that he knows it . . ."

"Where did you meet up, Giles? Where did your paths cross?"

Giles Blake heaved up his bag. The Italian, his guest, was already striding off down the grassed avenue between the dull winter heather and the broken down bracken. "I've known Peppino forever . . . You know there's too many generalizations about the old Italian. Get a good one and you've the best you could meet anywhere. He's a dream to know. He's decisive, knows what he wants. Better than that, no cash-flow problem, loaded with investment funds. I had an introduction in Basle, sort of took it from there . . ."

They walked. Their voices were lowered and they held a pace up the fairway that kept them beyond the hearing of the Italian ahead.

"What's he looking for?"

"That about sums it up. I mean, Giles, lunch was bloody good, I'm not averse to a golf round and a decent lunch, but what's the bottom line?"

"He's pretty good company, I'll grant you, but why are we here, Giles?"

Giles Blake could give the sincere smile, do it as well as anyone, and he could laugh quietly. "You're a hell of a suspicious bunch. OK, he has funds. He needs to place monies. He's like any other banker I've ever known. He moves money and he looks for opportunities that will benefit his clients and stockholders. I think some rather seriously wealthy people use him, people who are looking for discretion . . . Hold on, wait a minute, I'm not talking about 'funny' money, I'm talking about 'quiet' money. For Heaven's sake, it's not 'hot' money. Be quite honest, I've always found him good as gold."

"Where do we fit in?" the banker asked.

"What can he offer that interests me?" the investment manager asked.

"What should I pitch for?" the property developer asked.

"How long have I known you chaps? Barrie, fourteen years. Kevin, since '85. Don, we've done business for nine years. I wouldn't think any of you have had much to complain about. Am I going to see you, you know my track record, short changed? Am I hell. Cards on the table. Meeting with Giuseppe Ruggerio was the best thing that happened to me. Believe me, I'm really happy to have made this introduction."

In front of them, the Italian had stopped by his ball. The ball would have been at least fifty yards ahead of any of theirs. The banker was no golfer, had no clubs, had come for the walk . . .

Barrie, the banker, asked, "What does he want?"

Kevin, the investment manager, asked, "There's no dirty, nasty bit?"

Don, the property developer, asked, "Where do we go?"

They were, all three of them, trusted and tried friends of Giles Blake. They were friends over the business desk and across the social scene. They met for the rugby at Twickenham, for the cricket at Lords, for the opera at Glyndebourne and they shot together. They put business each other's way, they made money. They were the new élite, tolerant of success, intolerant of obstructions.

"Barrie, what I'm saying is this—what he's looking for is an opportunity to move funds into a good UK house where his cash is going to be rather better managed than where it is now. Kevin, we're talking quite substantial funds—do you really think I'd be involved if it were 'dirty and nasty'? Not damn likely. Don, what I know, you've got a hell of a large white elephant sitting in Manchester, short of the top seven stories, and the backers have pulled the rug on you. We're talking about him having twenty-five available for starters. I would have hoped twenty-five million sterling on a three way split with commission . . . I'm sure there would be a little mark of gratitude, would go down as well as that Chardonnay at lunch . . . Of course, I vouch for him. Look, you know what Italians are like, Italians are paranoid about the old tax man back in their own yard. They like their money overseas and they like it held quietly. It's the 'no names, no pack-drill' bit. Can't you live with that?"

"There would be commission?"

"Kevin, certainly there would be commission—it's the way they do business. It's no skin off my nose if you're not interested, chaps . . ."

Giles Blake walked away to his own ball. He would push the matter no further. He had done what he was paid to do. He provided discreet introductions for Giuseppe Ruggerio, the overseas player, who constantly searched for new pipelines through which to feed money. He sought out and befriended contacts who would make double damn certain, in return for commission, that the paperwork on "due diligence" would be ignored. He assumed, and he would not have dared to press the point, that he was one of many used as fronts for the washing of money and its ultimate layering into legitimate finance.

He played his stroke. He watched Giuseppe Ruggerio club his own ball toward the distant green. He called quietly to the Italian to come to him.

They stood at the side of the fairway. The banker and the investment manager and the property developer were in deep talk.

Giles Blake said quietly, "They're jumping because they're greedy. Three way split. They need it, why they're nibbling."

"And quiet people?"

"As the grave, when they've banked their commissions."

"Because if they are not quiet . . ."

The voice died. They walked on up the course toward the green, Giles Blake and Giuseppe Ruggerio ahead of their guests. It was a fine course, used on several occasions a year for championships. Until Blake met the Italian there had been no way, not till hell froze over, that he could have afforded the membership fees. Nor could he have afforded the house a dozen miles away, nor the horses, nor the children's schools. He was owned by the Italian . . .

The threat had been made before the voice died. He thought that Giuseppe Ruggerio understood only too well that the threat did not have to be articulated. He knew of the banker who had unsuccessfully handled the funds of La Cosa Nostra and who had been strangled and then hanged from a rope under a London bridge. He knew of an investment broker in New York who had failed to predict the last great fall in the international markets and who had been found dead on the paving below his balcony. He knew of the import/export man in Toronto who had been found knifed to death off Yongue Street, the hookers' area, with dollar bills stuffed in his mouth. He knew of those who had died after failing La Cosa Nostra because Giuseppe Ruggerio had told him of them.

"A very pleasant day, Giles. I am having a very pleasant day. Before we were joined by your guests we were talking of the opportunity of the antique furniture markets . . ."

Each day the file on Giles Blake had worked lower in the detective sergeant's pending tray. There was a method. Each day the bottom file in the pending tray was retrieved from oblivion, shown the light and placed on the top. Harry Compton, when the Giles Blake file reached the top again, should have given it attention, but the bloody solicitor's paperwork was defeating them. If the paperwork of the bloody solicitor, the bastard, did not give up its secrets then the shit was going to be spinning across the ceiling and they'd be looking, bloody certain, at "harassment," at "wrongful arrest," at "punitive compensation." Over a quick sandwich and tea from a polystyrene cup, he leafed fast through the top file, swore because he had done nothing in the best part of a week, then scribbled a note.

TO: Alfred Rogers, Drugs Liaison Officer, British Embassy,
Via XX Settembre, Rome, Italy.
FROM: SO6, D/S H. Compton.

Alf, Sorry to interrupt the rest module in which you have, no doubt, settled easily, and hope this does not disturb your necessary siesta. Meanwhile, some of us are paid to work, not scratch their blackheads, you jammy bugger!!
If your Italian colleagues have learned how to operate the computer *(if!!)*, get them to P check Bruno Fiori, Apartment 5, Via della Liberazione 197, Milan. Confession, don't know what I am looking for—was it ever different? He stayed last week at the Excelsior Hotel, Portman Square, London W1. See attached copy of hotel reg. form for passport details etc. In haste. All in chains here and hacking at the coal face. I imagine it's tough, too, in Rome.

In envy, Harry.

He brushed crumbs from his shirt, wiped the tea from his chin, handed the scrawl and the photocopy to Miss Frobisher, requested transmission to Rome, then stumbled back to the rooms in which the solicitor's documents and archives were piled.

The last time they had met had been a year before, and they had argued.

There was no love between Mario Ruggerio and the man from Catania.

It had taken a week of bickering by emissaries from the two for the meeting to be arranged. It had been decided after a week of sour discussion that the meeting should take place in a no-man's land in the Madonie mountains. Off a dry, rutted farm track between Petralia and Gangi, in a remote farm building, they met to talk of the future. They were two scorpions, as if in a ring, watching each other.

No love, no trust existed between these two. Each had sent men the day before to sit on the high ground above the farm building, and to look down over the ripening fields and over the flocks of grazing sheep and the herds of browsing goats, to check the security arrangements. Neither Mario Ruggerio nor the man from Catania feared intervention by the *carabinieri* nor by the *squadra mobile,* but they feared the trap and the trick that might be sprung by the other. The man from Catania had come first, driven in a Mercedes and with a following car of minders. Mario Ruggerio had deemed it right that the other should come first and then wait . . . He had made his statement, he had come with two BMW cars filled with his own men but had driven himself in an old Autobianchi, a poor man's car, a peasant's wheels.

Outside the building the two groups of armed men stood apart. All would have known that if it came to war between the two families then they must make, and fast, the decision as to whether to stand and fight in loyalty or to attempt to switch sides. If it were war it would be to the death. It was said—and the minders who stood apart from each other would have heard it—that a thousand men in the defeated factions had died when Riina had killed his way to supreme power. There was no tolerance for a loser . . . Some carried machine pistols, some were armed with automatic assault rifles, some slipped their hands nervously inside bulging jackets as if for reassurance. There was no room inside the organization for shared control.

They talked, the two scorpions maneuvering in the ring for advantage, across a bare board table. Ruggerio spoke of his view of the future, and the view was of increased international dealing in the world of legitimate finance. The man from Catania gave his opinion, and his opinion was that the organization draw in the reach of its tentacles and make a concentration of effort on the island. They talked in fast bursts of dialect-accented words, and they smoked through the long silences.

In the silences were soft smiles. In the silences they smiled compliments and felicitations to each other, and both sought to decide whether it would be necessary, in order to achieve supremacy, to fight. In the matter of body language, of assessing strength, Mario Ruggerio was an artist. It was his quality, through his cold and clear blue and darting eyes, to recognize weakness. In the ring, it was not the time for the scorpion to strike. He thought that the chin of the man from Catania displayed weakness.

Outside the farm building, Mario Ruggerio watched the three cars head away for the long drive back to Catania. His own men watched him for a sign. Franco saw it, and Tano and Carmine. They saw Mario Ruggerio watch the dust clouds billow on the track from the wheels of the cars, and they saw him spit into the mud, and they knew that a man had refused to take second place and that a man was condemned.

The tourists came by bus up the hairpin road from the city to the cathedral of Monreale. They brought to the *duomo* voices that bayed excitement in the languages of French and German and Japanese and English. They came with their blinkered eyes and closed minds to the cathedral and monastery for Benedictine monks built nine centuries before by the Norman king William the Good, and they clucked their pleasure as they stood at his sarcophagus and gazed up at the gold of his mosaics and walked through his cloisters, and marveled at the site he had chosen with such care above Palermo. When they returned to their buses to drive on and away from Monreale, the French tourists and the Germans and the Japanese and the English and the Americans knew only of the past, had learned nothing of the present. No guide had told them of the ownership by La Cosa Nostra of the water they had sipped, of the *ristorante* they had eaten in, of the souvenir trade in religious relics they had boosted. No guide had told them of the priests who had offered hiding places to men of La Cosa Nostra on the run, or of the priests who had perjured themselves in court in offering alibi evidence, or of the priests who had permitted the *super-latitanti* to use their mobile telephones, or of the priests who said that La Cosa Nostra killed far fewer of God's children than the modern abortionists. No guide had told them of the new *carabinieri* barracks in the town that were the base of the *Reparto Operativo Speciale*, nor shown them the plaque on the wall of the barracks of the *polizia muncipale* in the memory of d'Aleo killed by *mafiosi* and of the plaque in the principal piazza in memory of Vice-Questore Basile killed by *mafiosi*. The tourists surfeited on history and did not know and did not care to know of present times.

He had the top floor of a widow's house.

She was a tall and elegant woman and wore the traditional black of mourning, but she told Axel Moen that it was six years since her husband, the surveyor, had died. She led him around the apartment—a bedroom, a living room, a kitchen and a bathroom—and in each room her fingers seemed to brush the surfaces for imaginary dust. He used his actual name with her, and he showed her the doctored passport that had come from the Resources section back in Washington along with the wristwatch, and he told her that he was a lecturer at the university in Madison and that his subject matter was archaeology. She was polite, but she had no interest in digging through the past. The widow, his view, was a fine woman with education and dignity, but she had no complaint when he paid her three months' rental in advance with dollar bills. He thought they might, the dollar bills, go to Switzerland or they might go to a tin under her bed, but sure as hell they would not go onto a tax return form. She treated the payment as if it were a necessary moment of vulgarity and continued the tour of the apartment. She showed him how the shower worked, told him when the water pressure would be high, she took him to a small balcony that looked out over the town and the valley beyond and then to the mountains and it would be his responsibility to water the potted plants. She gave him the keys of the outer door to the street and of the inner door to the apartment. Perhaps because he wore jeans and an old check shirt, perhaps because he wore his hair long in a ponytail, she remarked coolly that she expected a "guest" in her home to be quiet in the evenings, that she should not be disturbed, as she was a light sleeper. She was Signora Nasello. She closed the apartment door behind her. She left him.

He had sat alone in the chair by the open doors to the balcony, alone with his thoughts, before 'Vanni Crespo came.

They hugged. Their lips brushed the other's cheeks.

They were as kids, as blood brothers.

"It's good?"

"Looks fine."

"Not easy to find, a place in Monreale . . ."

"You did well."

He was short of friends. Friendship did not come welcome to Axel Moen. Friendship was giving . . .

"You are the spirit of generosity, Mr. Moen."

Not many others, in Italian law enforcement or in the DEA's place on Via Sardegna, cared to goad Axel Moen. Not many others cared to tease or taunt him.

He had learned from his childhood to exist without friends. After the death of his mother, when his father had gone abroad, at the age of eight he had gone to live for five catastrophic months with his mother's parents. They were from the south end of the state, close to Stoughton. They were big in the Lutheran church and ran a hardware store and had forgotten how to win the love of an abandoned child. Five months of screaming confrontation, and beatings, and Axel had been sent on the bus, like preserved cod going to market, like a bale of dried tobacco leaf going to the factory, away up north to his father's father and the "foreign Jezebel." There had been no friends at the small farm between Ephraim and Sister Bay. In the tight-bound Norwegian community, his grandfather and his grandfather's second wife were shunned. He was a child living as an outcast. He had learned to live without a friend on the bus taking him to and from the school in Sturgeon Bay, and without a friend to make the long journey with down to Green Bay to see the Packers play. Vincenzina, from faraway Sicily, dark and Catholic, treated as a medieval witch and a danger and a threat, existed alone, and taught the young Axel how to ignore isolation. He had learned, alone, to sail a boat and fish and walk with the dog as his company. And Vincenzina had never mastered fully the English language and they had talked an Italian of the Sicilian dialect at home in the farmhouse. They had been, forced to be, their own people. Axel had little trust in friendship.

'Vanni took a Beretta pistol from his waist, and two filled magazines of 9mm bullets from his trouser pocket. He passed them to Axel.

"It's good. I'm an archaeologist. I'm digging for antiquities. I teach at the University of Wisconsin, Madison, I'm over for the summer semester. You'd better believe it."

Axel grinned, and 'Vanni was laughing with him.

Axel had known Giovanni Crespo for a full two years. The first trip with Bill Hammond down to Palermo, called "front line acclimatization," they had been assigned the tall and angular faced *carabiniere* captain as a guide. Bill had said, and believed it, that any Italian policeman should be treated as a security risk. Two days of whispering between the two Americans until the last night, when the big trip was winding down, and they had gone to 'Vanni's flat and 'Vanni and Bill had drunk themselves half insensible on Jack Daniel's and Axel had sipped coffee. 'Vanni had been the first Italian Axel had met who said the sociologists and the apologists talked shit about La Cosa Nostra, that the bastards were simple criminals. He had known 'Vanni was worth the trust because it had been 'Vanni who had held the pistol at Riina's head. Salvatore Riina, *capo di tutti capi*, blocked off in a south Palermo street, and shitting himself and wetting himself, and lying in the gutter with 'Vanni's pistol at his temple as the handcuffs went on his wrists and the blanket went over his head. If a man held a pistol at Salvatore Riina's head, at the squat killer's temple, then Axel had a man who did not compromise. 'Vanni drank, 'Vanni screwed a prosecutor from Trapani and usually in the back of a car, 'Vanni talked too much and didn't know how to protect his back. They were different species, and their friendship was total.

"She's here?"

"She's here, and she's Codename Helen."

"That was mine, I thought of that one."

Between the knuckles of his fingers Axel caught a pinch of 'Vanni's cheek. "She said, 'That is really original—did a genius think up that one?' That's what she said."

Axel told 'Vanni the detail of the watch with the UHF panic tone, and he told him about the range of the pulse signal.

'Vanni had the maps, large scale, of Mondello on the coast, and of the high points of Monte Gallo and Monte Castellacio and Monte Cuccio, and of Monreale. They marked, bold ink crosses, the high points on which the microwave boosters would be placed.

"What have you told her?"

"When she should use the signal—only at the time of a contact with Mario Ruggerio or at a time of risk to her personal safety."

"She accepts that?"

"I think so."

"Think? Jesu, Axel, does she understand what she does, where she goes, with whom?"

"I told her."

'Vanni said, soft, "Is she capable of doing what is asked of her?"

"What I told her, 'Don't think I want someone like you down there, but I don't have the option.' And I told her that if she gave cause for serious suspicion then she would be killed, and I told her that after they'd killed her they'd go eat their dinner."

There was astonishment on 'Vanni's face, "And she is just 'ordinary,' your word?"

"She is ordinary and predictable."

"Don't you have a feeling for what you have pushed her toward—do you not have any goddam feeling?"

Axel said quietly, "It's her strength that she is ordinary. And what was lucky for me, she was bored. She saw her life stretched out, the tapestry of her life was insignificance and under achievement and waste. She yearns to be recognized, she wants excitement . . ."

"Don't you go fucking her, she might go to sleep."

They were in each other's arms. Together, crying in laughter. Holding each other and laughing in hysteria.

'Vanni said, and the laughter dribbled at his mouth, "You are a cold bastard, Axel Moen, and you are a cruel bastard. How close did you say you would be?"

"I said that I would be close enough to respond."

"But that's shit, you know you cannot be, not all of the time."

"It's best for her to believe that, all the time, I am close enough to respond."

As if the laughter had served as a bonding, as if now there was no time for more laughter, they talked together into the night. They worked the detail of the exact locations of the microwave boosters, and where the receivers should be, and what were the codes that Codename Helen might use. They talked of the response team that must be made available, and with whom the information could be shared. Later, 'Vanni would slip out of the apartment and then return with boxed fresh-cooked pizzas. They talked in urgency, into the night, as if a life was suspended from their fingers.

She stood back. *Piccolo* Mario was frantically working open the bolts and locks of the door. Angela was in front of the mirror and she touched her hair and then flicked with her nails to remove something unseen from the shoulders of her blouse. Francesca ran from her bedroom. Charley stood at the back of the hall.

He was a little grayer at the temples. He was, perhaps, a few pounds heavier in weight. He was as she remembered him.

He carried bags and flowers and gift-wrapped parcels. The wide smile on his face as he pecked a kiss at Angela's cheek and swung small Mario high in the air and crouched to cuddle Francesca.

He came forward, across the hall, and he beamed pleasure at the sight of her. She held out her hand, shyly, and he took it and then lifted it and kissed it, and she blushed.

"So wonderful that you could come, Charley. You are very welcome in our small home."

She stammered, "It's lovely to be here . . . thank you."

The man who washed money, whose brother was one killing away from becoming the most influential figure in international organized crime, let her hand drop. She was there, she had been told, because the family had made a "mistake." Angela and small Mario and Francesca, as if according to a ritual on his return and she remembered the ritual, were opening their presents, discarding to the floor the ribbons and the bright paper.

"And you have been in Rome, Charley?"

"Yes."

"Why did you go to Rome?"

She blurted, "For nostalgia . . . because I had been so happy there . . . because it was the best time of my life. It was an opportunity." She felt confident because she thought she had lied well.

A brooch of diamonds for Angela, an electronic game for small Mario, a soft toy for Francesca . . .

"I missed the direct flight, had to change in Milan—delay, of course—fog, of course. You should not have stayed up for me, not until so late."

Charley instinctively, glanced down at her watch. The watch was heavy on her wrist. She glanced at the watch and the button on her watch. She slipped away. She should not intrude. She went to her room. In her bed Charley pressed the watch against her breast and felt the hardness of it, and she wondered where he was, where Axel Moen waited.

6

HE HAD BEEN UP EARLY.

He had seen Signora Nasello, through a ground floor door, in her kitchen and wearing a bright dressing gown, as if in the privacy of her home she did not need to clothe herself in widow's black. In a bar he had taken a coffee and a pastry, and he had gone to the meeting place.

He had not shaved. He was dressed in old jeans and an old shirt, and his hair was gathered back into an elastic band.

Axel waited at the meeting place and gripped a plastic bag close against his thigh, and the Beretta pistol was under his shirt and held by the waist of his trousers. He was off the main street that led down to the piazza and the cathedral. He was high in the town and close to the rock face of the dominating mountain. He stood beside the stall of a man who sold vegetables and while he waited the housewives came and bartered for beans and artichokes and lemons and oranges and potatoes and shrugged and made to walk away and turned back to give the man their money and to take the bags in return. The van came from behind him. It was poor procedure on Axel's part that he did not see the approach of the van. He was jolted by 'Vanni Crespo's sharp whistle. It was a builder's van, the sort that would be used by an artisan working alone, small and dirty and rust flaked. The door was opened for him, and he slid inside and his feet had to find space between a plastic bucket and paint pots, and he needed to duck to avoid the stepladder that jutted from the back of the van out between the front seats. He held the bag on his lap.

"You like it?"

"Taxed, I assume?" Axel grinned.

"Taxed, even insured. Did you sleep well?"

"I slept all right."

"Did you dream?"

"No."

"You didn't dream of her, of Codename Helen, not of her?"

Axel shook his shoulders. "You play CIs, you use them, and when you have finished with them then you pack them off back where they came from, end of story."

"And you did not dream of Ruggerio?"

"No." Axel, quite hard, punched his fist into the side of the Italian's chest. "Hey, big boy, ugly boy, this woman from Trapani, does she have to go with you in the back of this heap?"

"She has, I thank the Virgin, her own car."

They lapsed to quiet. They had come to a four-lane road below the town. He felt the keen thrill of pleasure, like he was dosed on ephedrine, like it was when the adrenaline coursed. The adult life of Axel Moen was divided, sharply, between the good times and the bad times. There were no gray shade compromises.

The university at Madison was bad times, no friends and no tolerance of student life and finding what he rated as juvenile kids, and working alone to get the grades that were necessary. The city Police Department was good times, interesting from the start and better when he'd made detective status and gone to the surveillance team. A Drug Enforcement Administration investigation in Madison that used him as liaison and included him on a covert stake-out, that was good times. Taking the jump, quitting Madison and going to the DEA, joining the recruits at Quantico and being told he had an attitude problem and struggling to stay with the flow, that was bad times.

No warning, 'Vanni swung the wheel. They were checked at the gate by the smart uniformed *carabiniere* trooper. They were passed inside, went under the raised barrier. They were a pair of workmen going on a small contract into the main *carabiniere* barracks on the island. He turned to 'Vanni, nodded his approval. Of course, the comings and goings at the main barracks on the island could be watched . . . They parked away from the main fleet of shining squad cars, near the memorial to the guys shot down in the line of duty. And still they could be watched, and 'Vanni gave Axel a bucket to carry and took the stepladder for himself, and they headed for a side door. He liked 'Vanni because he thought the guy trusted no bastard.

The first assignment with the DEA had been bad times. New York City, and the file had said that he was fluent in the Sicilian dialect, and the Pizza Connection case was going to trial, and there were the hours of wire taps to be listened to and noted, and he had sat week after week, month after month, in a small, darkened room with the earphones on his head and the tapes turning and the light blazing at his notepad . . .

When 'Vanni had fingered in the entry code and they were inside a corridor, they dumped the bucket and the stepladder.

La Paz, Bolivia, that had been good times, working with a small team, running his own CIs, riding in the local Huey birds, getting used to wearing the flak vest and to carrying the weight of an M16. The big shootout, the end of the day, hadn't changed La Paz, Bolivia, from rating as good times. Nor being shipped out on a walking wounded ticket.

They went down a corridor and past the open section of an operations area with consoles and radios. Past a rest room where men sat in chairs and wore casual clothes and the firearms and the vests and the balaclavas were heaped on a table with the coffee cups and the used plates, and 'Vanni told Axel they were the Response Squad of the *Reparto Operativo Speciale*. 'Vanni said, if the panic tone went for real, that they'd be the guys who'd go running. He'd called in a favor, been allocated the team, dragged in a big debt, refused to explain.

Back to New York, three more years, and that had been bad times. They'd said in DEA and FBI and the prosecutors' offices that the American mainland end of La Cosa Nostra was finished. Tommaso Buscetta, turncoat, *pentito,* had blown them away to the federal penitentiary at Marion, Illinois. All over. The Bureau said, on the record, assholes that they were, that the "mafia myth of invincibility" was torpedoed. A prosecutor said, for quoting, "The Sicilian mafia's drug connection has been dismantled." The resources were being drained from the Organized Crime Drug Enforcement Task Force. Three years of scrapping with FBI over investigation priorities and pushing reports from desk to desk, three years of hearing that the Sicilians were a back number by comparison with the Colombians, and wondering then why the streets of Chicago and Philadelphia and Atlanta and Los Angeles and New York and Washington, a short walk from Headquarters, were stacked high with goddam heroin. Bad times, until the posting to Rome . . .

Up a flight of stairs, down another corridor, through a door that could be opened only with an entry code, into 'Vanni's office. Axel looked around him.

"If this is home, Christ . . ."

He thought it was a monk's cell. A bare room, with bare walls except for the photograph of a general in best uniform and a smiling portrait of a little girl, with a bare, plastic topped table and a hard chair, with a bare bed and blankets folded neatly on top of the single pillow.

Axel took from the plastic bag the second of the receivers he had brought to Sicily. The box was a little longer and a little thicker but the same depth as a hardback book. He extended the aerial. He showed 'Vanni the on/off switch. He wrote on a sheet of paper the UHF frequency that was programed into the wristwatch worn by Codename Helen.

'Vanni said, "I am only back-up to take the signal. She is your responsibility."

"I understand that."

"You can take the signal in Mondello, if you sit there, which is not sensible. You can take the signal in Monreale, which is better but you are a long way from her. On the road, in Palermo, you are beyond contact."

"I understand that too."

"In the operations area the frequency will be monitored, through the twenty-four hours, but I cannot tell them the detail of the importance of the signal, I can only lecture them on the priority. At the bottom line, it is your responsibility, Axel."

Axel said, "I told her to make a test transmission this afternoon."

"This afternoon. That is idiot. It's not in place."

"So, shift yourself."

"You think I have nothing else?"

The quiet smile played on Axel's face. "You held the pistol to Salvatore Riina's head—what I think, you'd give your right ball to hold that pistol at Mario Ruggerio's head."

'Vanni reached for the telephone. He dialed, he spoke, he swore, he explained, he gave his rank, he ordered, he laid down the telephone and looked straight into Axel's eyes.

Distant and quiet, 'Vanni said, "It will be, for her, like a bell calling from the darkness . . ."

She half woke when Francesca crawled under the sheet of her bed. A moment before she knew where she was. Charley woke fully when *piccolo* Mario dragged her bear from her arms. She looked at her watch, she laughed and she tugged back the bear from the boy. God, the time . . . She heard a radio playing and the squeals of the children, excited, drove the sleep from her. She went, dazed, to the bathroom. Washed, teeth brushed, she wandered to the kitchen.

The note was on the table.

Charley, you were like an angel in peace. Giuseppe has gone to his office. I am shopping for lunch. Mauro is sleeping, feed him when he wakes. We meet later, Angela.

The whole of her life was a lie. She thought the lie worked well because she had been given, with the children, the run of the villa for the morning. She was accepted, she had gained access . . . She walked out onto the terrace. There was a freshness in the morning air and she hugged her arms across her chest and the tiles were cold under her bare feet. She could see, through the gaps between the shrubs and the trees of the garden, over the high wall that ringed the villa. Beyond the wall were rooftops of other villas and beyond them was the bay. Where was he? Did he watch her? Was he close by? She saw only the glass shards set in the wall and the roofs and the distant blue expanse of the sea.

The children followed her into the kitchen. She pulled open the fridge for coffee and juice and a day old croissant.

Charley thought the villa, its construction, was magnificent, but it was for the summer. Large rooms with high ceilings and floors of tile or marble. Big windows that could open out onto the patios. There was not the furniture to go with the magnificence, nor yet the weather. Angela had explained, seemed to apologize for, the functional furniture that was so mean compared to the fittings of the apartment in Palermo. Angela had said, head dropped, "I had the place aired, of course, the week before we came, but it is built for the sunshine, not the rain and damp of the winter. You have to excuse us for the wetness. I can barely live with the furniture. You see, Charley, we pay a man a hundred thousand a month and he is supposed to watch the security of the villa. Twice this last winter we were thieved from, we were broken into. You would not leave anything of value here through the winter, the thieving is so bad . . ." She washed the cup and the glass and the plate and the knife. She wandered.

She was alone. She walked barefoot on a paved path. She bent to take the scent of the first of the spring's roses. So quiet around her. The cotton of her nightdress was pressed against her by a light wind. She crouched and took in her fingers the fragile petals of a crimson geranium. She went by a small fountain that spluttered water and she held out her hand and let the cascade run cold on her palm. The watch weighed on her wrist. She tried to believe, as if it were her anthem, that it were possible for one person, Charlotte Eunice Parsons, to change something . . . had to believe it. If she did not believe that she could change something then she should have stayed at home, ridden her scooter to school each morning and ridden it back to the bungalow each evening. Should have bloody stayed, if she could not change something. She came round a screen where honeysuckle sprawled over a trellis frame.

He watched her.

Christ, the bloody "lechie" eyed her.

The man who opened the gate, who swept the leaves, who watered the pots of flowers, gazed at Charlie. She felt the thin cloth of her night-dress against her nakedness. She had thought she was alone . . . An old face, lined by the sun and weathered by the sea's salt, and he stared at her and leaned his weight on his broom. She heard the cry of the baby. The old man with the old face and the old hands watched her. She ran on the coarse stones of the path back toward the villa and the crying baby, and it was seven hours until she would make her test transmission.

Where was he? Did he watch her? Was he close by?

They worked with a drill that was powered by a portable petrol driven generator to pierce the rock so that the stanchions could be buried se-curely and be proof against the winds on the higher point of Monte Gallo. When the stanchions were secured, the antennae of the microwave radio link were bolted to them, along with the booster that would enable the pulse of a panic tone to be carried across five kilometers to the higher point of Monte Castellacio.

Only when the sun over the city has climbed high, to its zenith, does the fierce light and warmth reach the cobbled alleys and broken pavings of the Capo district. Most of the day the district is a place of shadows and suspicion. It was the old Moorish slave quarter, and it is where the his-tory of the men of the modern La Cosa Nostra is rooted. In the gray and run-down heart of the Capo district is the Piazza Beati Paoli where, it is said, was the beginning . . . There is a church in the piazza, there is a small hemmed in open space, enclosed by high buildings with damp-scarred and crumbling walls and the night's bedding is draped from balconies. It is said by the historians who rejoice in the nobility of the anarchic Sicil-ian character that the piazza was the safe house of the Beati Paoli, the se-cret association formed more than 800 years ago. The men of the secret society claimed the right to protect the poor against the foreign rulers of the island. Their motto was "Voice of the People, Voice of God." Their meeting place was in the caves and tunnels under the present piazza. By day they practiced normality, worshiped in public. By night they roamed the black alleys, cloaked in heavy coats under which they carried rosaries and knives, and punished and murdered by ritual. From the men of the secret society of the Beati Paoli was born a word, the word was "mafia." Some say the word comes from the old Italian *maffia,* which describes a man of madness, audacity, power and arrogance. Some say the word was the old French *maufer,* which denotes the God of Evil. Some say the word was the old Arabic *mihfal,* which is an assembly of many people. The children of each succeeding generation have been taught the mythology of the secret society, and its fight against the persecution of the unfortunate, and its punishment of the oppressor, and its justification for murder. What began eight centuries ago had spread now from the gray piazza, flowed and eddied into the city, across the island, over the sea, but it began in the Capo district of Palermo.

"The Capo district, I see. You wish, Dr. Tardelli, to cordon off the Capo district . . . Wait, Dr. Tardelli, you have already spoken. Throw a surveillance cordon around the Capo district because—forgive me if I recapitulate—because you have been told by a source that must remain anonymous, that may not be shared with us, because you have information that a year ago an almond cake upset the bowels of Mario Ruggerio. An interesting proposition, Dr. Tardelli."

The grim smile played at the face of the oldest of the Palermo prosecutors. He shrugged, his fingers were outstretched in the gesture of ridicule, his throat burrowed down into his shoulders.

"I request the resources of a surveillance team."

"Now, I, of course, Dr. Tardelli, am not able to devote my life to the investigation of one man." The voice of the magistrate quavered in sarcasm. A tall man, ascetic, his fingers clinging to an unlit cigarette, he rolled his eyes around the table, before bringing them to bear on Rocco Tardelli. "My desk is piled with many investigations, all of which require my attention. I, too, need resources. But on the basis of information that is as old as was, no doubt, the almond cake— No, Dr. Tardelli, I do not seek to make a joke of this—you wish for a special surveillance of the Capo district. There are, my recollection, at least fourteen entrances into that area. Should we have surveillance cameras for each of them? To do a job at all correctly you must have eight men at any one time on surveillance duty. Mathematics, I regret, is not my strength, but with the duty shifts that would take away twenty-four men from other duties. Then, I make a further addition, and I ask whether the eight men on surveillance duty must have the support of back-up. A further addition, those who watch however many cameras we install. A year ago, on the word of your informant, an almond cake made a problem for Mario Ruggerio, and we are asked to divert an army . . ."

"I ask for what can be spared."

"Please, Dr. Tardelli, your indulgence . . . I work in a more simple field, I attempt investigations into the extortion of payments from the public utility companies. To you, Dr. Tardelli, I have no doubt that would seem to be valueless work, it is as if I hunt for many cats and not just one tiger.

The tiger, of course, may by now be toothless and maimed and harmless, but that is another matter. I assure you, the cats have claws and teeth and kill." The prosecutor was younger than Rocco Tardelli, was in his first year in Palermo, had traveled from Naples, and would have seen his appointment as a step on a career ladder. He would not be long on the island of Sicily. "You put in place the valuable resource of a trained surveillance unit, a resource that each week, for my investigations, I beg for, but do you even know what he looks like, the elusive Mario Ruggerio? How— am I being stupid—how can a surveillance team operate, how can video cameras be monitored, if the only photograph of Mario Ruggerio is twenty years old? I do not wish to be difficult . . ."

"The photograph found when his brother was arrested, taken at his sister's wedding in 1976, has now been computer enhanced. We have aged Mario Ruggerio."

"You must not misunderstand me, Dr. Tardelli. I, I can assure you, am not amongst them, but there are some, a few, who would be less than generous to you. Some, and I am not amongst them, would see an unfavorable motivation in your request for these valued resources. They would look, some would look, toward a desire on your part for promoted status. Not me, no . . ." Older than Tardelli, less gray in the visage because he did not live behind shuttered windows and drawn curtains, heavier in the stomach because he ate in the restaurants of the city, the magistrate had long ago sent a signal that had been transmitted, mouth to mouth, and received. He carried out his work, with punctilious care, but always those arrested, charged, convicted, imprisoned, were from a losing faction. ". . . Myself, I believe Ruggerio to be irrelevant, but his capture would play well on television, it would make the headlines in newspapers. The man who claimed credit for that capture would be fêted, by the ignorant, as a national hero. Would the finger beckon, would Rome summon him? Would he sit at the right hand of the Minister? Would he go to Washington to lecture the FBI and DEA, and to Cologne to meet the BKA, to Scotland Yard to take wine? Would he leave us all behind him to go about our daily work in danger, here in Palermo? Some might say that—"

"When you arrest a man of the stature of Mario Ruggerio then you dislocate the organization—it is proven."

They were his colleagues and they mocked him. They might as well have laughed in his face, they might as well have spat upon him. It was what he lived with.

He looked around the table. He raked his eyes over them. He was accused, behind his back, in conversations in quiet corridors, of "careerism" and of chasing "handcuffs for headlines." In his mind was that description of the dead Falcone, "a lonely fighter whose army had proved to consist of traitors." Some of them, he thought, were crushed by the coward's desire to return to normality. But . . . but he should have been more tolerant of cowards. Not every man could make such a sacrifice, pig-headed in righteous duty, as he had done. Not every man could see his wife walk out and take the children, and then go from the silence of a lifeless apartment, in the armored car, to the bunker office. There had been no contribution at the weekly meeting from the representatives of the *squadra mobile* and the *Resparto Operativo Speciale* and the *Direzione Investigativa Anti-Mafia,* as if those men stood aside while the prosecutors and magistrates carped and cut at each other.

Tardelli began to gather together the papers in front of him. There was a hangdog sadness in his face and his shoulders were bowed as if under the weight of disappointment. He spoke with the diffidence that was his own. "Thank you for hearing me, gentlemen. Thank you for your courtesy and consideration. Thank you for pointing out to me the folly of my ambition and the idiocy of my request . . ."

He stood. He placed his papers in his briefcase. It had been the same for Falcone and for Borsellino, and for Cesare Terranova and "Ninni" Cassara, and for Giancomo Montalto and for Chinnici and for Scopellitti, all ridiculed, all isolated, all dead. He had been to the funerals of each of them.

"I will call, in one hour, a news conference. I will tell the world that I have a lead, a slight lead, for the hiding place of the *super latitanti,* Mario Ruggerio. I will say that my colleagues in the Palazzo di Giustizia, and I will name them, do not consider this a matter important enough for the allocation of resources. I will say—"

The bluster beat around him.

"That would be disloyal . . ."

"Unfair . . ."

"We merely pointed to the difficulties . . ."

"Of course there are resources . . ."

When he was out in the corridor, when the door behind him was closed on the hatred, when his *ragazzi* gathered around him with their guns as they did even on the upper floor and questioned him with their glances, the magistrate showed no triumph. Falcone had written, "One usually dies because one is alone, because one does not have the right alliances, because one is not given support," and Falcone with his wife and his *ragazzi,* was dead.

Walking briskly, he said to the *maresciallo,* "I have been given nine men of the *squadra mobile* for the surveillance of the Capo district, three shifts of three, and no additional cameras. I have to hope. I have nine men for ten days. If they find nothing, then I am isolated. We should, my friend, be very careful."

They sweated in the cold wind that hit them. They were at 890 meters above sea level. The wind buffeted them and rocked the stanchion arms. They struggled to hold the antennae as the bolts were tightened. The clear line of sight was established from Monte Castellacio, across the Palermo-to-Torretta road, to the greater height of Monte Cuccio.

In a new block, overlooking the moles against which the big ferries from Livorno and Naples and Genoa docked, Peppino had his office. It was lavishly furnished, modern and expensive-Italian. He sat in the wide room with the picture window that faced out over the harbor. The office was a home from home for him, necessary that it should be of the greatest comfort because Peppino spent fifteen hours out of the twenty-four hours of the day there, six days a week, hugging the telephone between his ear and his shoulder, feeding the fax machine, flicking between the channels on the screen that gave him the market indices in New York and Frankfurt and London and Tokyo. He did not take a siesta in the afternoon as did every other businessman in the city's Rotary or in the Lodge he attended, the third Thursday in the month. He avoided the luxury of a siesta because, single-handed, he managed and moved and placed, each year, in excess of four billion American dollars on behalf of his elder brother.

It was the way of the organization and, in particular, the way of his elder brother that matters of finance should be kept inside the family. It was why he had been brought back to Palermo from Rome. He lived a life consumed by the need to "clean" money. He was the trusted laundryman for Mario Ruggerio. He was a master at his work, the consolidation and placement, the immersion, the layering, the heavy soaping, the repatriation and integration, the spin dry. What Angela did in the utility room off the kitchen, Peppino did in his office in the new block on Via Francesco Crispi. Angela washed and cleaned a dozen shirts a week, a dozen sets of socks, half a dozen sets of underwear. Peppino washed and cleaned in excess of four billion American dollars a year. The office was his home. He could cook and eat in his office. He could shower and change in his office. He could take his secretary, when the businessmen of the Rotary and the Lodge were at siesta, to the stark black couch by the picture window.

If the office were his home, if the scale of his work increasingly kept him from the apartment in the Giardino Inglese and the villa at Mondello, Jesu, it was necessary for him to take his secretary to the couch. What his brother said, Mario said, a wife should never be embarrassed . . . Would Angela have cared? If the condoms had spilled out of his pocket, fallen at her feet, would Angela have noticed? Not since she had come to Palermo. Angela would not be embarrassed by any indiscretion of his secretary because the young woman's father was sick with a carcinoma and the treatment was expensive, and Peppino paid for the principal consultant in the field of that necessary treatment. The rows with Angela came more often now. They lived in physical promixity and in psychological separation. She could have everything that she wanted except divorce, divorce was unthinkable . . . So good in Rome, so different. They maintained an appearance. His brother had said that appearance was important.

His feet, shoes discarded, rested on the glass top of his desk, his leather chair was tilted far back. He talked through the final details of a leisure complex in Orlando with the bank in New York and the construction company's operations manager in Miami. Two phones going, and the talk "in clear" because the money coming down from New York was cleaned . . .

And just as he washed money for his brother, so Mario Ruggerio had immersed and soaped and spun dry the younger Peppino. Sent by his brother away from Prizzi, dismissed from his mother, sent abroad, dismissed from his past, sent into the world of legitimate finance, dismissed from his family. The businessmen that he knew in Rotary and the Lodge, the trustees of the Politeama who sought his advice on financial planning, the charitable orphanage in Bagheria and the priests at the *duomo* in Palermo who sought his help did not know of the connection of his birth, were unaware of the identity of his elder brother. Perhaps, maybe, a few policemen knew. There was a magistrate who knew. One interrogation, one summons to come to the offices of the *Servizio Centrale Operativo* in the EUR suburb, one journey out of Rome. The magistrate who knew had been a pitiful little man, obsequious in his questions, up from Palermo. He had attacked. Was he to be blamed for the accident of his birth? Should he carry his blood as a cross? Because of his brother, he had left home, left the island—what more could he do to break the association? Was he obliged, because of blood and birth, to wear the hair-shirt of a penitent? Was he to be persecuted? He had thought the magistrate, Rocco Tardelli, an insignificant man who had cringed at the attack. He had not been interrogated again in Rome, and not since he had come back with Angela and the children to Palermo. It had been important, in that one session with the magistrates at the offices of SCO, to dominate and kill the investigation of his affairs. He knew the way they worked, submerged with paper, starved of resources, scratching for information that would take them forward. He imagined that the transcripts of the interview, no information gained and nothing moved forward, was now consigned to a file shut away in a basement, was buried beneath a mountain of other sterile interrogations, was forgotten. If it were not forgotten, then he would have been investigated again following his return to Palermo. He felt safe, but that was no reason to drop, ever, his guard. He kept his guard high, as his brother demanded.

The deal was concluded. The papers would go to the lawyers for fine analysis, then the bank in New York would move the money, then the operations manager would move on site. Peppino said when he would next be in New York . . . dinner . . . yes, dinner, and he thanked them.

Peppino looked up at the clock on the wall, cursed. Angela was never punctual, and they were to be at the opera. As a trustee it was necessary for him to be at a first night of the Politeama's spring program.

He called to the outer room, to his secretary. She should telephone Angela. She should remind Angela at what time she should drive into the city, what time she should be in the Piazza Castelnuovo. A wry smile, cool, on his face. No excuse for Angela not to come, because he gave her everything, the brooch of diamonds that she would wear that evening, and he had given her the little English mouse to watch the children.

Charley carried the baby, easily, as if it were her own. She came off the patio as Angela was putting down the telephone.

Charley said, "Please, Angela, I would like to go for a walk later."

"Where?"

Down to the Saracen tower beside the harbor. "Just into the town."

"Why?"

To press the panic pulse button for a test transmission. "Because I haven't been in the town. It would be nice to walk by the sea."

"When?"

Told to send the transmission in an hour and ten minutes. "I thought it would be nice in a hour or so."

"Can't you go now?"

The time was fixed by Axel Moen. "It's too hot now. I think it would be nicer in an hour."

"Some other time. I have to go with Peppino to the opera. I have to leave in less than two hours. Another time."

They would be waiting for the signal to be sent in an hour and ten minutes, waiting with their earphones, twisting the receiver's dials to the UHF frequency. "I'll be here when you go out."

"Charley, the children, and Mauro, they have to be fed, they have to be bathed, they have to be put to bed."

"I can do all that, don't you worry. I'll take *piccolo* Mario and Francesca and baby Mauro with me. They'll like to walk when it's not so hot. You don't have to worry about them, it's what I've come for, to help you."

Charley tried to smile away the unhappiness of Angela Ruggerio. She did not know the cause of the sadness. She was not the woman Charley had known in Rome, the woman who laughed and talked and lay on the beach without the top to her bikini. She did not recognize the new woman.

"Perhaps . . ."

"You should have a rest. Lie down. Don't think about the children, that's for me, that's why I'm here." Here to send panic-pulse transmissions, here to spy, here to break open a family's life and to smash the parts . . .

They were beyond the height to which the shepherds brought the flocks and herds. From Monte Cuccio they could see, direct line of sight, to Monte Castellacio and on to Monte Gallo, and when they turned away from the swaying antennae and looked down the scree slope, and on past the track's limit where the Jeep had been left, there was the ridge line of yellow gray rock that lay above Monreale. One more set of antennae, on that ridge, and they would have made the boosted microwave link from Mondello to the aerial on the roof of the *carabinieri* barracks.

'Vanni Crespo asked gulping air, panting, "It's good?"

The technician pouted. "If a signal is transmitted, on the frequency you have given me, from Mondello, then it will be received in Monreale."

He scrambled down the scree slope, slipping and falling, and when he was on his feet, 'Vanni ran for the Jeep.

Anxiety furrowed the wide forehead of Mario Ruggerio. His fingers tapped restlessly at the keys of the Casio calculator.

The figures, the *lire* totals, were worse than they had been a year ago.

Losses, that column, stood at forty billion a month, the calculation for income was down 17 percent on the previous year and these were the balance sheet figures that were held in his mind. His estimate of outgoings was up by 21 percent. Each time he played the figures onto the calculator's screen the answer came the same, and unwelcome.

He sat at his table in the drab room on the first floor of the house in the Capo district. The figures were estimates, given him by an accountant from Palermo.

He wrote occasional words with figures beside the words that he ringed. He had written "decline in public works expenditure": the new

Government in Rome no longer poured money into the Sicilian infrastructure for roads and dams and the administration offices for the island. He had written "legal fees," and the estimate was that four thousand Men of Honor, from the members of the *cupola* to the *sotto capi* and the *consiglieri* and the *capodecini* and right down to the level of the *picciotti,* were in custody and must receive the best legal representation—if they did not receive the best, and if their families were not supported then there was the chance of men taking the foul option of joining the bastard *pentiti.* He had written "asset seizure," and the figure for the previous twelve months stood, in his careful hand, at 3,600 billion for the state's sequestration of property and bonds and accounts, and the calculator, purring through fast additions and multiplications and divisions and subtractions, told him that "asset seizure" was already up in the first months of the year by 28 percent. He had written "narcotics," and there the figure was down because the habits of addicts had changed to the more recent creation of chemically based tablets, and the organization did not have control of the supply of such products as the LSD and amphetamine range. He had written "cooperation," the payment each year to politicians and policemen and magistrates and the revenue investigators, and the figure alongside the word was five hundred billion. He thought the words and the figures were the result of three years of drift. The drift had begun with the capture of Salvatore Riina, and had continued while others had scratched eyes and killed in their attempts to succeed him as *capo di tutti capi.* When he had control, full control of the organization, then the drift would be halted.

He lit his cigar, and coughed, and he held the flame of his lighter against the sheet of paper on which he had written the words and the figures. He coughed again, deeper in his throat, and tried to lift the phlegm.

Axel saw her.

He sat on the warm concrete of the pier and he looked across the curve of the bay toward the dun tower that was, he guessed, four hundred meters from him.

He saw her, and in his mind she was Codename Helen. She had no other identification. He stripped her, as he gazed across the bay at her, of personality and of humanity. She was the Confidential Informant that he used.

Axel sat with his legs casually dangling over the edge of the pier and the water lapped below his feet. Around him were small fishing boats and men working at the repair of their nets and at the tuning of boats' engines. He ignored their solemn faces, walnut colored from salt spray and the sun's strength. He watched her.

The small boy ran ahead of her the moment they were across the road and she released his hand. A small girl clutched the side of the pram that Codename Helen pushed. There was a bright awning on the pram to shelter a baby from the brilliance of the late-afternoon light. It was so normal. It was what Axel might have seen beside any bay on the island, on any esplanade above the gold of any beach. A hired help, a nanny and a childminder, pushed a pram and escorted two small children. He had good eyesight, no need of spectacles, and he could see her face as a whitened blur. He had reckoned that binoculars could draw attention to himself; without binoculars he could not see the detail of her face, did not know whether she was calm or whether she was stressed.

On Axel's lap, shielded by his body from the fishermen who moved behind him on the pier from boat to boat, covered by his windcheater, was the equipment designated as CSS 900. The crystal-controlled two-channel receiver, the best and most sensitive that Headquarters could supply, had been stripped of its microphone capability and would receive only a tone pulse. In the canal of his right ear, buried from sight, was an induction ear piece, no cable necessary. The equipment, and the earpiece, were activated only when a tone pulse was transmitted. Protruding from under the windcheater, protected from view by his body, was the fully entended aerial of the receiver. He waited.

He thought that he saw her head drop and for a moment the whiteness of her face was gone, and he thought that she checked her watch and he wondered whether she had synchronized with the radio during the day, as he had done, as she should have. His eyes roved over the shoreline, sweeping inland from the tower that had been built by the Moors centuries before as a defensive position and across the piazza where the kids were gathered with their motorbikes and their coke tins and up over the roofs toward the final line of villas set against the raw gray stone of the cliff. Later he would go, on another day, to see the villa. She was at an ice cream counter, and he saw her hand a cone to the small boy and another to the little girl. She did not take an ice-cream for herself.

It was Axel Moen's life. His life was made of waiting for covert transmissions from Confidential Informants. There was, to him, sitting with his feet above the vivid colors of the water that was polluted by oil and above the floating plastic bags and fish carcases, nothing that was particular or special about the CI given the title of Codename Helen. His life and his work . . . Shit. He had no feelings for her that he could summon, was not concerned as to whether she was calm or whether she was stressed. Couldn't help himself, but his head jerked.

The pulse tone rang in his ear. So clear, three short blasts, so sharp. It cavorted through his head. There was little static, and the pulse tone was repeated. It beat within the confines of his skull bone. It came again, a final time, three short blasts.

The static was gone, the silence returned.

He thought she looked around her. He thought she looked for a sign. He saw her turning slowly and looking at the road and at the pavement and up into the town and out across the sea. It was good that she should be alone and good that she should know she was alone. He pushed down the aerial, lost it under the cover of his windcheater.

Axel stood. When he was standing he could see her better. She was going away, alone, with the children and with the pram. She stopped to cross the road, and when there was a gap in the traffic she hurried. He did not see her on the far side of the road because a lorry blocked his view of her.

He walked away.

'Vanni handed the second headset back to the technician. He leaned against the technician's chair as if a weakness sagged through his body. The grit and dust of the scree slope on Monte Cuccio was on his hands and on his face, and on the knees and seat of his jeans and on the chest and back of his shirt. He breathed deeply . . .

The signal had come so clearly, and he had said that it would be for her like a bell ringing from the darkness, like the light of a candle in the black of night. It might just, offer success . . . He wondered where she was, their Codename Helen, whether she shivered in fear, whether she felt the chill of isolation . . . He wrote on a piece of paper the number of his mobile telephone and he told the technician, smacking his fist into the palm of his hand for emphasis, that he must be called every time that the frequency was used, night or day. The number was clipped to the banked equipment in front of the technician.

"You have that? Any hour—whether it is the triple pulse, short and repeated three times, whether it is the long pulse, repeated four times— at any hour, if that signal comes . . ."

The technician, laconic, shrugged. "Why not?"

His fists gripped the technician's shoulders, his fingers gouged at the technician's flesh. "Don't piss on me. The early duty and the late duty and the night duty, whatever *cornuto* sits here, he calls me. If I am not obeyed, I will crack the bones in your spine."

"You will be called."

He loosed his hands. He shook. He had heard a bell ringing in the darkness. He felt the weakness because he believed, for the first time, that the plan might work. Not since they had turned Baldassare di Maggio, not since di Maggio had told them where to look for Salvatore Riina, not for three years had a source been in place so close to the heart of the organization. They would kill her. If they found her they would kill her.

One piece of paper . . . One telephone number scribbled on one piece of paper . . .

The party spilled noisily through the offices. Of all the boxes taken out of the solicitor's premises, and all the plastic bags, one piece of paper had done the business, one telephone number on the back of a commercial property conveyancing draft had launched the party. The solicitor would have been checking a subordinate's work on the draft, and a telephone call would have come through, and he would have been given a number, and he would have jotted it on the back of the nearest sheet of paper. Trouble was, for the solicitor, the number was that of a small and discreet Zurich bank. Further trouble was, for the solicitor, that Swiss banks weren't what they had been. Cold feet in Cuckoo-clock-land, and the small and discreet Zurich bank had not been prepared to fight the recent Swiss legislation contained in Article 305 ll of the penal code which made its directors liable to prosecution if they shielded illegal funds. With the solicitor's name and account number on the top page of the evidence file, and the reckoning of what was stashed there of his clients' cash, the party had started.

Six packs of beer from the off license, and three bottles of wine, and a bottle of Scotch which was the detective superintendent's fast track to getting pissed up, and music from a transistor. They didn't come often, the good ones.

Harry was called.

Harry Compton was called out of the party area and into the administration office. Miss Frobisher, and the place fell apart when she took her five weeks of leave, didn't drink and didn't approve, but she'd stayed put to answer the telephones. She would have read the secure transmission, and she scowled as she handed it to Harry.

TO: Det. Sgt. H. Compton, SO6, London.
FROM: Alf Rogers, DLO, Rome.

Harry, Regards. Assuming they could find it, some nasty soul has been pulling your insignificant pecker. No trace in Milan on available records of BRUNO FIORI. The address provided in Via della Liberazione does not exist. That section of the street was pulled down six years ago for the construction of a mu-

nicipal swimming pool. Details on hotel reg. were totally fic-
titious. Back to your tin/gonics. We, here, are involved in important work and don't need to be diverted from the necessary
with duff info.

Luv, Alf.

Harry took the single sheet of paper to his desk, locked it away, went
back to the party. The detective superintendent was into his joke repertoire
and had an audience, and Harry didn't think he'd take it kindly if his
punchline was interrupted. It would wait till the morning, till they crawled
in with their headaches. He had a nose, that was his bloody trouble, and
the nose was smelling something rotten, but it would be better talked
about in the morning.

7

"How long?"

"I don't know."

"If you don't know how long it would take then, Harry, leave it to the locals."

Maybe it would have been better the night before, perhaps it would have been better to have crashed the boss when he was in his joke session. Water under the bridge, because Harry Compton had let that moment go.

"I don't want to do that."

"Did I hear right? 'Want'? Don't 'want' me, young man."

The morning after, and the SO6 office was a dead ground. Miss Frobisher, of course, had been in early, before seven, and she'd removed all the plastic cups and emptied the ashtrays and wiped the bottle stains off the desks, but the place still stank, and their heads ached. He thought the detective superintendent's head hurt worse than most because the bossman's mood was foul.

"What I'm trying to say—"

"Rein in, young man. What you are 'trying to say' is that you want two days down in the country. Well, we'd all like that, wouldn't we?"

"It should be followed up."

"The locals can follow it up."

Harry stood in the detective superintendent's office. The boss was hunched over his desk and he had a second coffee mug in front of him and the heartburn pills that squeezed off a little tinfoil platter. He held in his hand the message received the last evening from Alf Rogers, and the hotel registration sheet, and the printout from the night manager of telephone calls made from the room occupied by Bruno Fiori, alias for Christ only knew. He was on a short fuse that was getting shorter. His wife, Fliss, had bitched at the time he'd come in. Hadn't he remembered that they were supposed to be going out shopping for the new living room suite? Wasn't there a telephone he could have used? He'd an accountancy exam, first part, coming up, and wouldn't he have been better at his books, after late-night shopping then lurching in smelling foul from drink? Why'd he forgotten to put the cat out? the cat had been shut in the kitchen and crapped on the floor. God.

"The locals down there are useless, they're parking-ticket merchants."

"You've got nothing, nothing, that warrants me kissing you good-bye for two days."

"It's worth doing."

"How many files on your desk?"

"That's the bloody point, isn't it?"

"What's tickling up your arse, Harry?"

"It's trivia, that's what's on my desk. It's nothing stuff. It's corrupt little men, high street dwarfs, fiddling pensions, fiddling savings."

"Those pensioners, those savers, they just happen, young man, to pay fucking taxes. Those taxes are your wages. Don't you get on a high-and-mighty horse and forget where your bread comes from."

For a moment Harry closed his eyes. He squeezed the lids tight shut. He took a big breath.

"Can I walk in again? Can we start again?"

The coffee dribbled from the sides of the detective superintendent's mouth. "Please yourself, and keep it short."

"What I'm saying is this. We have a trace that is just routine on this tosser, Giles Blake, bank disclosure on a cash deposit. We run the check on his accounts. Nothing special, no alarms, except that it's not clear where the wealth comes from. Ninety-nine times out of a hundred, we'd say that's as far as it runs, file it and drop it. But, you authorize an evening's surveillance, and Mr. bloody Blake takes an Italian to dinner, and they talk about nothing that is illegal. File it and drop it. But the Italian says he's come from Palermo. But the Italian has given the hotel a false name, a false address. We don't know who he is. But his telephone records indicate that from his room he called a travel agent for his flight back to Milan and the non-existent address, to a limousine company for a ride to the airport using the fictional name. But there was one more call from his room. He rang a Devon number. He rang a number listed as belonging to David Parsons. That's where I want to go, to see Mr. David Parsons."

"Why can't the locals—?"

"Christ, don't you understand?"

"Steady, young man."

"Don't you understand. I repeat myself, what we do is trivia. Trivia are good for the statistics. We lift enough second-rate people on second-rate scams and you get to make commander, and I get to make inspector, and we get pissed together, and we are achieving damn-all. But, don't worry, it's easy and it gets fast results, and aren't we bloody clever?"

He was on the edge. Over the edge was insubordination, was a bollocking, was a mark on his file. Maybe it was last night's drink, perhaps it was the tiredness, could have been the row with Fliss. It didn't seem to matter to Harry Compton that he was on the edge.

"Then, onto your plate falls something that might just be interesting. Can't quantify it, can't put bloody time and motion to it, can't put a balance sheet on it. Might spend a week or two weeks or a month, and might get nothing. No, it's not for the locals, it's our shout and I want to go to Devon."

The boss man hesitated. It was always that way with the boss, because the man was a bully. If the boss's shin were kicked, if he had pain, then he usually crumpled, what Harry had learned. "I don't know . . ."

"If you're trying to send a message then the message is being heard. Looks to me that you're saying that Fraud Squad can chase greedy little bastards with their fingers in the pensions accounts and the savings accounts, but we're not smart enough for the international scene. I hear you. The big time is too complex for SO6, like we're not fit enough to run on dry sand where it gets to hurt. I hear you."

"For two days, when you've got your in-tray down to half empty, not before," the Detective Superintendent said, sour. "And get the fuck out of here."

Four days gone, and the excitement had drained. Four days gone in a numbed routine of getting up, getting the kids dressed, getting the kids their breakfast, getting small Mario to school, getting Francesca to kindergarten, getting baby Mauro changed. Charley was four days into the routine and was bored. She sat at the iron legged table on the patio and she wrote her first postcards.

It was four days since she had gone down to the town and stood by the Saracen tower and pressed the button on her wristwatch, and looked around and tried so desperately to see him and failed. That had been the last moment of excitement. For God's sake, she hadn't come to Sicily to walk the kids to school and kindergarten, to deal with a baby's stinking backside, to skivvy for Angela Ruggerio. She'd come, spit it out, sunshine, she'd come to gain the access that would lead to the capture of Mario Ruggerio. Who? What for? Why? A postcard for her mother and father, and another for her uncle, and another for the 2B class. All the week Peppino had been in Palermo, not come to Mondello, and Angela said that her husband had too much work in the city to be able to come back to them in the evenings. Now that was just plain ridiculous because it was twenty minutes' drive in that big bloody fast car from central Palermo to Mondello.

On the postcards Charley didn't say that she was bored out of her mind. Having a wonderful time—weather brilliant—soon be warm enough to swim, Love, Charley. The same for her parents and for her uncle and for the 2B class.

She had come because she had decided she was trapped at home, netted at work. But nothing bloody well happened here either, except that she fussed round the kids and changed the baby and swept the bloody floors. God. Come on, speak the bloody truth: Charley Parsons had come to Sicily because Axel Moen had told her to. She wrote the addresses on the cards, a fast and clumsy hand. Damn Axel Moen. What did he mean to her? Meant nothing, and she threw the pen down onto the tabletop. God, and just once he could have said something decent, could have given her something that was praise, something that was bloody compassion.

She had come with the excitement holding her. Like when she had gone to the home of the lecturer at college, the first time, and known his wife was away, and worn the sheer blouse and no bra, and drunk his wine, and stripped for him in front of the open fire, and climbed on him as they did in the films. That had been excitement, till the dull fart had cried. Like when she had walked to the caravan at the edge of the camp site at Brightlingsea, where the long term activists lived who each day tried to break the police cordons and halt the trucks carrying the animals to the continental abbatoirs, gone to the caravan where Packy slept, with the cap in her hip pocket, walked to his caravan because the other girls said he'd a prick bigger than a horse's. That had been excitement, till the stupid bugger had spurted before he'd even got over her. Hey, sunshine, excitement's for books. The villa was a mortuary, it was the death of excitement.

It was the third day that *piccolo* Mario and Francesca had been to school and kindergarten, and Charley thought they were like a pit-prop to their mother. She seemed to weaken when they were gone from her sight. Charley, too damn right, she'd tried. Tried to make conversation, tried to earn some laughter back—a lost bloody cause. Some mornings

Angela went into Palermo, some mornings she stayed in her room. Some afternoons Angela walked with the children, some afternoons she went, remote, to a sunbed at the bottom of the garden. Charley tried, Charley failed, to get through to her. Charley giggled, Charley remembered the face of the mistress at school who taught sixth-form history and who'd come to hammer the Civil War into them the morning after the miserable cow's husband had moved out to set up home with a nineteen-year-old boy, same school. God, that was bloody cruel, but it was the face of Angela Ruggerio, struggling to keep the appearance, and tortured . . . Charley would try, and fail, and try again. As though she were haunted, as though . . .

The gardener watched her. Whenever Charley was outside the gardener was always close, with the hose for the plants, with the broom for the paths, with the fork for the weeds, always near to her, where he could see her. One day, bloody certain, one day she'd put a towel on the grass and lie on it, and give the "lechie" something to look at. One day . . .

"Charley. Do you know what is the time, Charley?"

She turned. She looked toward the open patio doors.

"It's all right, Angela, I've not forgotten the time, about ten minutes, then I'm off for them."

Angela Ruggerio stood in the doorway. It made Charley miserable to see her, to see her drawn face, to see her attempt to smile, to see the woman pretend. There was no love, Charley reckoned, and there had been love in Rome. But not her problem.

"I was just doing some postcards, friends and family . . ."

Angela repeated the word, rolled it. "Family? You have a family, Charley?"

"Not really, but there's my parents and there's my mother's brother, lives up in the north of England. We hardly see him . . . I'm afraid we're not like Italians in England, family doesn't matter that much. But—"

The bitterness snapped in Angela's voice, as when a mask slips. "Find a Sicilian, and you find a family."

She must never pry, Axel had said, never push. "I suppose so."

"When you were with us in Rome, you did not know that Peppino was Sicilian?"

"No."

"With a Sicilian there is always a family, the family is everything . . ."

She was gone. Angela went as quietly as she had come.

Charley finished the addresses on the postcards. She had come into the villa to find Angela, to ask at when the post office closed and whether she would have time to buy stamps. She moved, barefoot across the marble of the living area and the tiles of the hallway at the back. She moved without sound. Angela lay full-length on the bed. Charley saw her through the open door. Angela lay on her stomach on the bed and her body convulsed in weeping. She knew of the family. The family was Rosario and Agata in Prizzi, and Mario who was hunted and Salvatore who was in prison, and Carmelo who was simple, and Cristoforo who was dead and Maria who drank, and Giuseppe who washed the money. She knew of the family because Axel had told her. Charley watched the woman weep and sob. She felt humbled.

She left the villa, the prison, and walked with the baby in the pram into the town to collect small Mario and Francesca.

"You'd like a coffee?"

"Yes, I'd like that, *espresso,* thanks."

"Three coffees, *espresso,* please."

The policeman bobbed his head in acknowledgement. He was an old tired man, in a uniform that bulged over his stomach. He looked to be the sort of fixture in the upper corridor of the Palazzo di Giustizia that they had in the same upper corridors at Headquarters. He wore a pistol in a holster that slapped his thigh, but his job was of little more importance than bringing coffee for guests.

The magistrate gestured that 'Vanni should go first through the outer door. Axel followed. There were minders on the outer door and minders on the inner door. Both the doors were steel-plated. There had been razor-wire coils on the walls around the compound in La Paz. They had lived in Bolivia, and worked, with a pistol at the waist, with constant apprehension. They had been careful in their movements, avoided nighttime car journeys. The screen around the magistrate, Dr. Rocco Tardelli, even on the top floor of the Palazzo di Giustizia, jolted Axel and he tried to imagine what it would be like to live a half life under guard. It was over the top, above anything he had seen on the previous trips down to Palermo. The inner door, steel-plated, was closed behind them, his view of the harsh and suspicious faced guards was lost. He blinked in the low light of the room. Behind the drawn blinds there would have been shatterproof and bulletproof glass . . . A shit of a way to live.

The man was small and so bowed and while he tried to play at the necessary courtesies his eyes flickered in a constant and moving wariness. Axel knew the phrase the "walking dead." He could laugh about the "walking dead" in Rome, make gas chamber humor of it, but not here, not where the reality confronted him. His Country Chief rated Dr. Rocco Tardelli, took him to lunch when he was in Rome. Headquarters rated Dr. Rocco Tardelli, flew him to the Andrews USAF Base once a year on a military transport and had him talk to the Strategy teams, poor bastard. The Country Chief said, and Headquarters said, that Dr. Rocco Tardelli was a jewel—but not precious enough to share with . . .The poor bastard seemed, to Axel, a caged creature.

A knock at the door. The coffee tray was set down on the desk, and the machine pistol of the young guard swung on its strap and clattered against the desktop. Shit, the goddam thing was armed, and the magistrate seemed to wince.

"Careful, Pasquale, please."

They were alone.

The soft voice. "So the DEA has come to Palermo. May I be so impertinent as to ask what mission brings you here?"

Axel said, "We have an operation going, the target is Ruggerio."

"Then you are one of so many. What is the scope of the operation?"

Axel said, "We hope to mark him. If we mark him, then we send for the cavalry."

Said dry, with a gentle smile, "Of course you would expect that we have plans for the arrest of Ruggerio. What is the range of the operation from which the DEA believes it will taste success when we eat failure?"

"This is what you'd call a courtesy call. We have a small range of facilities organized by our friend. 'Vanni is looking after our interest." Axel shifted awkwardly in his chair. "I'd rather not be specific."

The smile widened, warmth flowed and there was a brightness in the magistrate's eyes. "Do not be embarrassed—I am the same as you. I trust very few people. You would not expect me to tell you of the locations of the physical surveillance and the bugs and the cameras, where we watch for Ruggerio . . .You would not expect me to tell you what information I have from the *pentiti*. But it is a sad game to play when there is no trust."

"It's not personal."

"Why should it be. So, we are engaged in competition. You wish to achieve what we cannot. You wish to show the Italian people that the power of the United States of America is so great that they can succeed where we fail." The smile was long gone, his eyes fixed on Axel. "If you succeed where we fail, then I assume you would seek the extradition of Ruggerio, and fly him back in chains to your courts as you did with Badalamenti."

"We have charges to lay against Ruggerio. It would be a message because we'd lock him up till he was dead."

"There are many here who would appreciate such a situation, and the poison whispers would pass in these corridors that Tardelli, the seeker after glory, was humiliated. You have put an agent into Palermo?"

What he'd heard, more prosecutions were blocked by the jealousies, the ambitions, the envy, of colleagues than by the efforts of La Cosa Nostra. The man yearned for a rope to be thrown him. Axel looked away. "I'd rather not."

"My assumption, Signor Moen, you have put an agent of small importance into Palermo. I do not wish to insult you, but if it were an agent of big importance then Bill himself would have come, but only you have traveled . . . Do you know of Tom Tripodi?"

Axel scratched in his memory. "Yes, didn't meet him, gone before I joined, I heard of him. Why?"

"He was here in the summer of 1979, not too long ago for lessons to be remembered. He was the star agent from Washington, and he worked with *vice questore* Boris Giuliano. He posed as a buyer of narcotics, he found himself an introduction to Badalamenti, who was then *capo di tutti capi*. For those who made the plans in Washington it would have seemed so simple. An agent in place to achieve what the Italians could not. So sad that there was disappointment, that Badalamenti did not bite. It ended with Tripodi running for his life, taken to the docks by Boris Giuliano, with escort cars, with a helicopter overhead. We paid a heavy price, maybe because of Tripodi and maybe not, on the twenty-first of July of that year. Some days, a few days, after Tripodi ran from Palermo, *Vice questore* Giuliano went to his usual bar for his usual coffee early in the morning, and he did not have the chance to reach for his gun. But, of course, Signor Moen, the danger to your agent and to those who work with you, and to yourself, will have been carefully evaluated in Washington . . ."

There was steel in the magistrate's eyes, there had been the rasp of sarcasm in his voice.

Axel said brusquely, "We have made an evaluation."

"I am very frank with you, Signor Moen, I do not have an agent in place. I do not have an agent close to Mario Ruggerio, nor do I try to put an agent in proximity to that man. I would not wish it to lie on my conscience, the danger to an agent. Unless your agent is scum, a creature of the gutter, whose life is held to be of small importance . . ."

Axel stood. "Thank you for your time. Bill wanted to be remembered to you. It was only a courtesy."

The magistrate was already at the papers on his desk as they closed the door on the inner office. God, and he wanted to be out of the goddam place, like it was a place where he could suffocate on foul air.

The guards watched them go, and drew casually on their cigarettes and stopped the card game. Axel led, pounding down the corridor, past the policeman who had been instructed to bring them coffee. Didn't wait for the elevator, but skipped down the wide stairs.

Out into the fresh air, the goddam building behind him. He turned his back on the great gray white building, Fascist architecture and a crap symbol of the state's power. He strode between the high pillars that were built to impress, through the parked and armor reinforced cars that offered status.

"What I cannot comprehend—"

"What you cannot comprehend, Axel, is how small brother Giuseppe is not a priority to Tardelli's investigations. I tell you, he works alone. He does not trust a staff. He works from early in the morning till too late in the night. He pushes paper until he is exhausted, because he does not trust . . . A long time ago he talked with little brother Giuseppe, in Rome, and was satisfied with what he was told. Think, how many meters of paper have crossed his desk since then? His mind is governed by priorities, and what he dismissed four, five years ago is low with priority. Of course he should target the family, every root of the family, but his mind is cluttered, his mind is tired, he has lost track of the distant root of the family. Do you complain that I don't help him? We are not the wonderful DEA, Axel, where colleagues are trusted, where work is shared. We are just pathetic Italians, yes? We are just food for your prejudices, yes?"

He did not look back to see the troops on the flat roof with their machine guns, he did not glance sideways to see the troops patroling the outer fence, he went by the troops at the gate ignoring them as they pushed the anti-bomb mirror on the pole under a car. 'Vanni had to run to keep up with him, and Axel pitched himself into the traffic flow, and the protest blasts of the horns beat in his ears. On the far side of the street, Axel swung round and he gripped 'Vanni's shirt front.

"Why did he do that, why did he piss on me?"

'Vanni was laughing. "He goes to all the funerals. Maybe he is too busy to go to your funeral or the Codename Helen's funeral. Maybe he was telling you to be careful because he does not have a hole in his diary."

He thought of her, standing beside the Saracen tower, looking for him, alone, not finding him.

Carrying the small bag, with a raincoat sagging from between the straps, Mario Ruggerio walked out of the Capo district.

He came from behind the Palazzo di Giustizia. There was no expression on his face as he went past the building site backing onto the building where new offices were under construction for the sprouting kingdom of the magistrates and prosecutors. An old man with a small bag and a check cap on his head and a gray tweed jacket on his peasant's shoulders drew no interest from the soldiers of the *bersagliere* regiment on the roof, on the gates, beside the fence, on the pavement corners. In front of the Palazzo a policeman strutted importantly into the traffic flow and blew an imperious whistle blast, stopped the cars and vans and allowed the old man and others to cross safely over the Via Goethe.

He walked a full 750 meters along the Via Constantino Lascaris and the Via Giudita, and he did not turn his head to see the approach of sirens behind him. He walked until the breath was short in his lungs, until the tiredness was in his legs. The figures from the Casio calculator played in his mind, absorbed him. His concentration on the figures was broken only when he rested and faced a shop window, when he turned to watch the pavement behind him and the pavement across the street, when he checked to see if a car dawdled slowly after him. Near to the junction of the Via Giudita and the Via Giuglielmo il Buono, tucked away behind an apartment block, was the garage.

At the entrance to the garage, by the high gates that were topped with wire, he turned again and checked again.

The cousin of the owner of the garage had shared a cell in Ucciardone, four years before, with Salvatore Ruggerio. The cousin had received the protection of Salvatore Ruggerio. Four years later, in return for that protection, a debt was called in.

The garage was a good place to meet. He went between the cars parked out in the forecourt and into the building that was alive with the music from a radio and the hiss of the welding burner and the clatter of spanners and the clamor of the panel-beating mallets. He carried his bag into a back office and the owner of the garage looked up, saw him and immediately cleared the papers from his desk and dusted the chair, as if an emperor had come. He was asked if he wished for coffee or for juice, and he shook his head. He sat on the cleaned chair, and waited.

It was a good place for a meeting with Peppino. It was where Peppino had, for the last year, brought his car for servicing. He lit a cigar. He assumed that Peppino, though he denied it, was under sporadic surveillance.

When Peppino came, they embraced.

"You are well?"

"Fine."

"A good journey?"

"London was for me, for us, very good."

They talked the business. Peppino told his brother, close detail, down to each contractor's percentage, of the deal for the leisure complex at Orlando in Florida. Peppino spoke of the money that would be moved from Vienna to the account of Giles Blake in London and then invested with a merchant banker and a broker and a building contractor who needed the funds to complete seven stories of a Manchester office block. He said what arrangements were made for the visit of the Colombian from Medellín who managed onward shipments into Europe. And there were the Russians he would meet the week after in Zagreb.

And Mario thought his brother spoke well. Only rarely did he interrupt. What was the commission for the clients of Giles Blake? Where would the meeting be with the Colombian? What percentage, down to a quarter of a point, would the Russians pay? He loved the younger man, so different from himself, and every phase of the differential had been planned by him, as though he had made and fashioned each stage of Peppino's life. He could smell the talc on Peppino's body, and the lotion on his face. The suit was the best, the shirt was the best, the tie was the best and the shoes of his brother. The irony was not lost on Mario Ruggerio. Wealth and success clung to Peppino. Their parents lived in the old terraced house in Prizzi with Carmelo. Salvatore rotted in a cell in the prison at Asinara. Cristoforo was dead. Maria was cut off from them because the alcohol made her dangerous. His own wife, Michela, and his own children, Salvo and Domenica, were in Prizzi, where she looked after her mother. Only Peppino lived the good life.

Nothing was written, everything was in their heads. He told Peppino of what the accountant had said, recited the figures of declining income and increasing outgoings.

"You should not listen to him. If you were a small man, if you were concerned only with investments and product on the island, then this would be perhaps important. Your portfolio is international. You are better without him."

"There are some who say that I do not interest myself enough in the opportunities given by Sicily."

"I think in Catania they say that, where there is a small man—as the man in Agrigento was a small man . . ."

It was, for Giuseppe Ruggerio, the confirmation of a death sentence. "It is possible for a small man, as from Catania, to obstruct progress. If a tree falls in the wind and blocks a road, it is necessary to bring the saw, and to cut the tree, and to burn it."

"Burn it with fire."

They laughed, the chuckle of Peppino merging with the growled snigger of Mario Ruggerio. They laughed as the sentence of death was confirmed.

And the smile stayed on the old and lined face. "And how is my little angel?"

"*Piccolo* Mario, the same as his uncle, a rascal."

"Francesca and the baby?"

"Wonderful."

"I hope very much soon to see them. I have their photograph. I carry their photograph. I do not carry a photograph of your aunt, nor of Salvo and Domenica, but I have with me the picture of Francesca and the *birichino*. The day you went to London, I was near to the Giardino In-glese, I saw the rascal. I have few enough pleasures. And Angela, how is your wife, how is the Roman lady?"

"She survives."

He noted the coolness of the response. He shook his head. "Not good, Peppino. Sometimes there is a problem if the wife of someone like your-self is not happy, sometimes there is an unnecessary problem."

Peppino said, "In Rome we had a girl to help Angela with the chil-dren, an English girl. Angela became fond of her. I have brought her back, to the villa in Mondello, to make Angela happier."

The eyebrows of the old man lifted sharply, questioning. "That is sensible?"

"She is just a girl from the country. A simple girl, but she is company for Angela."

"You are sure of her?"

"I think so."

"You should be certain. If she has the freedom of your home, there should not be doubt."

When Mario Ruggerio left, he walked from the garage to the corner of Via Giuglielmo il Buono and Via Normanini. He had the time to go into the *tabaccaio* and buy three packets of his cigars, and then the time, while he waited on the corner, to think of the small man from Catania, a tree that blocked the road and should be cut and burned, and more time to think of the family that he loved and the rascal boy who was named in respect of him. The Citroën BX came to the corner. The driver leaned across to push open the passenger door. He was driven away. A dentist had moved from Palermo to Turin and the apartment on Via Crociferi that was now vacated would be the safe house, for a week, used by Mario Ruggerio. At least he would sleep there, be free of the shit noise of the Capo district.

He could not sleep. He stood at the window. Behind him was the bed and the sound of his wife's rhythmic snoring—he had not told her. In front of him were the lights of Catania, and out at sea were the lights of the approaching car ferry from Reggio. He could not talk about such mat-ters with his wife. Never in thirty-two years of marriage had he talked of such matters, so she did not know of his fear and she slept, and snored. Alone, unshared, was the fear. Because of the fear, the loaded pistol was on the table beside his bed and the assault rifle was on the rug under the bed. Because of the fear, his son had come from his own home and now slept in the adjoining room. The fear had held him since he had come away from the meeting in the Madonie mountains with Mario Ruggerio. Other than his son, he did not know now in whom he could place his faith. It would come to war, war to the death, between his family and the family of Mario Ruggerio, and each man of his family, in his home and his bed, would now be making the decision as to which side he would fight on. He knew the way of Mario Ruggerio. It was the way that Mario Ruggerio had climbed. From among his own family of men there would be one who was targeted by the bastards of Mario Ruggerio, targeted and twisted and turned and bent to compliance.

One of his own family of men would lead him to death, and he did not know which one. The fear, in the night, ate at him.

"I don't want Pietro Aglieri, I don't want Provenzano nor Salvatore Minore, I don't want Mariano Troia. You see them, you light a cigarette for them, and you offer them gum, but you don't show out."

A weak and nervous ripple of laughter played in his office. Rocco Tardelli believed that each man on a surveillance team should be in at the briefing. He reeled off the names of the *super-latitanti* and grinned humbly. They would have thought him an idiot. They stood in front of his desk, seven and not nine of them because one was on holiday and one claimed illness. He turned over the photograph on his desk, showed it to them.

"I want him. I want Mario Ruggerio. Aglieri, Provenzano, Minore, Troia are men of yesterday, gone, spent. Ruggerio is the man of tomorrow. There are insufficient of you. We have no more cameras than before. We do not know where to put audio devices. The photograph is twenty years old, but it has been through the computer. I do not know now if Ruggerio has a moustache, I do not know whether he routinely wears spectacles, I do not know whether he has dyed his hair. You are going into the Capo district, which is the most criminally aware sector of Palermo, I believe, more so than Brancaccio or Ciaculli. The prospect of your maintaining a cover for ten days is minimal, and you know that better than I. The information I have is that Ruggerio took an almond cake in the bar in the street between the Via Sant'Agostino and the Piazza Beati Paoli which caused him to shit, but that was a year ago."

The men of the *squadra mobile* surveillance team laughed at the magistrate, which was the intention of Rocco Tardelli. The surveillance teams, whether from the ROS or the DIA or the *Guardia di Finanze* or the *squadra mobile,* were in his opinion the cream. They looked so awful, quite beyond salvation—they were like street thieves and like beggars and like pimps for whores and like narcotics pushers. They looked like the filth of the city. But, his *maresciallo* knew them all, and had sworn on the loyalty of each of them. He wanted them to laugh at him. He needed them to reckon that what was asked of them was idiot's work. Others would have lectured them, others would have minimized the problems. Rocco Tardelli challenged them.

"And, of course, you should know that you are not alone in hunting Ruggerio. Every agency has a plan for his capture. You know, even a foreigner has come to me, as a matter of courtesy, to inform me that he is on the ground and hunting *il bruto.* You are considered to have the least chance, you are at the bottom of the priority heap, you are assigned to an obsessional and neurotic and vain investigator. You are given to me."

They gazed at him. The time of laughter was over.

He said quietly, "If he is there,—if,—I know you will find him. Thank you."

Peppino had come home the night before, late.

When she made breakfast for Francesca and small Mario, while she heated the milk for baby Mauro's bottle, Charley had heard the sounds of the lovemaking from the main bedroom of the villa. Tried to concentrate on what measure of cereal for the children, and what temperature the milk should be heated to, and she had heard the groaned whisper of the bed. It was eight months since she had had sex, been screwed by the creep in the caravan who'd come over her stomach before he was even inside her . . . She turned the radio up loud. On the radio was the news of a train strike and a rail strike and an airline strike, and a man had been shot in Misilmeri, and there was a demonstration of pensioners in Rome, and an excavator digging a drain's trench in Sciacca had uncovered the buried bones of four men, and the treasurer of the Milan city administration had been arrested for taking the *bustarella,* and . . . Christ, it was better listening to the sex. All through the breakfast of the children, all the time that she chewed on an apple and peeled an orange for herself, all through feeding the baby, Charley heard the whisper of the bed.

When she was ready to take the children to school and kindergarten, when she had laid the baby Mauro in the pram, and taken the housekeeping purse from the drawer and Angela's shopping list from the table, there was the sound of the shower running. She didn't call out. It had sounded like good sex, like the sex the bloody girls at college had bragged of, like the sex Charley hadn't known with the bloody lecturer and the bloody man in his caravan, like the sex she never heard from her mother's bedroom. She went down into Mondello and she saw Francesca into the kindergarten class and she kissed small Mario at the school gate and saw him run inside.

She walked in the street behind the piazza, where the bars were open behind scrubbed and sluiced pavements, where the *trattorias* and *pizzerias* were being prepared for the day with swept floors and laundered table-cloths. She bought salad things from a stall, and cheese and milk and olive oil from the *alimentari,* and some fresh sliced ham. She ticked each item on Angela's list.

Every morning, when she took the children to school and kinder-garten, and shopped, she looked for him, and never saw him.

That morning she did not linger in the town. Her shopping was com-pleted. She pushed the pram with the sleeping baby back up the hill, past where the workmen were repairing the sewerage pipes, past the leaping and barking guard dogs, back to the villa. She whistled sharply at the gate, like she was in charge, and she had learned that the bloody "lechie," the miserable toad, the gardener, came running when she whistled and opened the locked gate for her. She didn't thank him, ignored him and walked past him. She left the baby, sleeping in the pram, on the patio that was shaded from the rising sun. In the kitchen she put the salad things and the cheese and milk and ham into the refrigerator and the olive oil into the cupboard. She wanted her book.

She almost crashed into him.

The door to her bedroom was open. Peppino stood in the corridor beside the open door.

He said that he had come to look for her. He wore a loose towelled dressing gown. The hair was thick on his legs and on his chest, and he had not shaved. He said that he had not realized she had already gone with the children and with the shopping list. Well, she hadn't wanted to disturb him, had she? Wouldn't want to muscle in on a good fuck, would she? He said that he wanted her to buy flowers, fresh cut flowers. Very good, sex and flowers to buy off Angela's misery, no problem in tramp-ing down to the town again and buying flowers. He was sleek headed from the shower, and the talc dust was a frost on his chest hair. She thought it amused him, using her as a messenger, a fetcher and carrier. She won-dered if Angela, back in the bedroom, smiled or cried, whether a fuck changed her life, whether flowers would lift her spirits.

She took the purse from the kitchen drawer. Back down the path be-tween the flower beds, back past the gardener, back through the gates, and she slammed them behind her and the lock clicked into place. Back past the fury of the guard dogs, and past the workmen who leered at her and stripped her from the sewerage trench. Back to the piazza . . .

Right, Giuseppe Ruggerio, right. Expensive flowers. At the stall she took from the housekeeping purse a note for 50,000 *lire*. Not enough. She took a note for 100,000. She gave the 100,000 *lire* note to the man. What would the *signorina* like? She shrugged, she would like what she could have for £40 sterling, and he should choose. She took the wrapped bunch, chrysanthemums and carnations, and crooked them on her elbow. She was walking away.

"Go down to the sea front."

The voice was behind her.

"Don't look round, don't acknowledge."

The voice, quiet, belted her.

Charley obeyed. She didn't turn to see Axel. She fixed her eyes ahead of her, took a line between the Saracen tower and the fishermen's pier. She assumed he followed her. The American accent had been sharp, curt. She walked through the piazza. She waited for the traffic and crossed the road. She stood beside an old man who sat on a stool on the pavement, and in front of him was a box of fresh fish with ice around them and he held up an ancient black umbrella to shadow his fish.

"Keep walking, slowly, and never turn."

Charley walked. The sea was blue green, the boats in the sea rolled at their moorings.

She thought he was very close, near enough to touch her. The voice behind her was a murmur.

"How does it go?"

"Nothing goes."

"What does that mean?"

"Nothing happens."

Said cold, "If it happens, anything happens, it'll be quick, sudden. Is there any sign of suspicion?"

"No." She looked ahead, out over the sea and the boats, and she tried to show him her defiance. "I'm a part of the family, it's just a damned miserable family, it's—"

"Don't whine . . . and don't ever relax. Don't go complacent."

"Aren't you going to tell me?"

"Tell you what?"

"The test? Did your gadget work?"

"It was OK."

She flared, she spat from the side of her mouth, but the discipline held and she did not turn to face him. "Just OK? Brilliant. I've been wetting myself. If you didn't know, it's my link. My road to the outside. It's like a morgue in there. I feel so much better to know that your gadget works OK. Not magnificent, not incredible, not wonderful."

"It was OK. Remember, because it's important, don't be casual. Keep walking."

"When'll I see you again?"

"Don't know."

"You bastard, do you know what it's like, living the lie?"

"Keep walking."

She was able to smell him, and she heard the light tread of his footfall behind her. She walked on with the flowers. The tears welled in her eyes. Why, when she cried out for praise, did he have to be so damned cruel to her?

She could no longer smell him, no longer hear him. She wondered whether he cared enough to stand and watch her go. She smeared the tears out of her eyes. She carried the flowers back to the villa. Bloody hell. In less than an hour and a half she would be going again into the town to collect the children. Peppino was dressed. Peppino thanked her and smiled gratitude. He told her that she was very welcome in their home, and that they so much appreciated her kindness to the children, and she had not had a day off, and she should go tomorrow on the bus to Palermo, and he winked and took a wad of notes from his pocket and peeled off some for her and told her of a shop on the Via della Liberta where the girls went for their clothes, young girls' clothes. He was sweetness to her, and he took the flowers into the bedroom to Angela. Charley went for her book.

Her book, on the table beside the bed, alongside the photograph of her parents, had been moved.

She felt the cold running over her.

Only slightly moved, but she could picture where it had been, a little over the edge of the table.

She could tell nothing from the clothes hanging in her wardrobe. She could not recall exactly where her sausage bag had been on top of the wardrobe.

She thought that her bras had been on top of her pants in the middle drawer of the chest, and now they were underneath.

Charley stood in her room and she breathed hard.

"Is that all you said?"

"I said the test transmission had been OK, I told her that she was not to relax. Because nothing has happened she should not be complacent."

"That's all?"

"There wasn't anything else to say."

The archaeologist was hunched down on the stone slab and his back was against the square fashioned rock that was the base of the cloister column. He sketched rapidly, and to reinforce the detail of his work he used a tape to measure height and width and diameter. It was natural, when an expert came to the *duomo* and studied the history of the construction of the cathedral, that a busy-minded and prying bystander should come to talk with him, question him, disturb him. So natural that none of the tourists or the priests or the guides took note of the archaeologist and the bystander. There was a bag by the feet of the archaeologist, and from the bag a chrome aerial was extended to its full length, but the aerial was wedged between the spine of the archaeologist and the base rock of the column and was hidden from the echoing flow in the cloisters of the tourists and the priests and the guides.

'Vanni said, "You make it hard for her, very hard."

Axel did not look up from his sketch pad. "She has to find her own strength."

"You gave her no comfort."

"That's crap."

"Did I tell you the story about dalla Chiesa?"

"General dalla Chiesa is dead."

'Vanni grinned. "I don't wish to be impertinent to my friend, to the eminent *archeologo,* and I think you are most sensible to pursue the cover, give it authenticity. I think it is right you are not 'complacent'—but an *archeologo* takes lessons from the past, and General dalla Chiesa is of the past and offers lessons."

"It is difficult to study detail when one is subject to the boring interruption of a stranger, don't you think?"

'Vanni said, conversational, "There was a story that the general told of when he was a young *carabiniere* officer in Sicily, some years before he achieved the fame of destroying the *Brigate Rosse.* He had a telephone call from a captain under his command who was responsible for the town of Palma di Montechiaro which is near to Agrigento. The captain told dalla Chiesa that he was under threat in the town from the local *capo.* He went to the town, he met the captain. He took the captain's arm, held his arm, and walked with him up the street of Palma di Montechiaro, and back again. They walked slowly so that everyone in the town could see that he held the captain's arm. They stopped outside the home of the *capo.* They stood in silence outside that house until it was quite clear, no misunderstanding, that the captain was not alone. Do you still listen to me, my friend the *archeologo?*"

Axel did not look up from his sketch pad and his calculations. "I listen to you."

"Years later, General dalla Chiesa came to Palermo to take the post at the Prefettura. He found himself mocked, sneered at, obstructed and alone. Each initiative he tried to make against La Cosa Nostra was blocked by the corruption of the Government. In desperation he telephoned for a meeting with the American consul in the city. I drove him there, to see Ralph Jones. I sat in on the meeting. The general begged of Jones that the Government of the United States should intervene with Rome, 'do something at the highest level.' At the finish of the meeting, the general told Jones the story of Palma di Montechiaro, and he said, 'All I ask is for somebody to take my arm and to walk with me.' I drove him back to the Prefettura. At the end of the day he dismissed me. His wife came to take him home. He was killed, with his wife, that night in Via Carini. He was killed because he was alone, because nobody had taken his arm and walked with him."

"What do you want of me?"

'Vanni's voice was close and hoarse. "Should you not take her arm, Codename Helen's arm, and walk with her when she is alone, and give her comfort?"

"I can't give her the strength. She must find it for herself."

The bystander walked away from the archaeologist, left him to his research.

"No."

"I'm sorry, Mr. Parsons, but I have to be quite clear about this. My question was, did you have a telephone call a week ago from Bruno Fiori?"

"Same answer, no."

They sat across the fireplace from Harry Compton. He thought they were scared half out of their minds.

"And you don't know an Italian who uses the name of Bruno Fiori?"

"No."

"Would you care to look at this, Mr. Parsons?"

He was deep in his chair in the small front living room, and reaching into his briefcase, and he passed to the man the printout list of the telephone calls. The woman sat close to her husband and her eyes were down and staring at the card he had given them. His card had that effect on people, "Metropolitan Police Fraud Department, Harry Compton, Detective Sergeant, Financial Investigator" frightened the shit out of them. The man glanced at the list of calls made from the hotel room, two London numbers and his own number.

The man glowered back defiantly, like he was trying to show that he wasn't scared half out of his mind. "Yes, that's my number."

The woman said, eyes never leaving the card, "It was Dr. Ruggerio who called."

The man's glance flashed at his wife, then, "We were telephoned by Dr. Giuseppe Ruggerio. And may I ask what business that is of yours?"

"Better that I ask the questions. Why did this Giuseppe Ruggerio telephone you?"

"I'm not going to be interrogated, without explanation, in my own home."

"Please, Mr. Parsons, just get on with it."

He wrote a fast shorthand note. He heard the name of Charlotte, an only daughter.

He could see from his chair out through the open door of the living room and into the hall. He could see the photograph of the young woman in her graduation gown and her mortarboard at a cheeky angle. He heard the story of a summer job in 1992. And a letter had come, and the invitation for a return to minding children. The information came in a slow and prompted drip. Charlotte had given up her job and was now in Sicily. The wife had gone to the kitchen and come back with an address, and Harry wrote it on his pad and underlined the words "Giardino Inglese."

The father said, "Dr. Ruggerio telephoned but Charlotte was . . . she was out. I spoke to him, he just said how much they wanted her. I was against it, her going. She's thrown up a good job. God knows what she's going to do when she gets back. Jobs aren't on trees."

The mother said, "They're a lovely family. He's such a gentleman, Dr. Ruggerio, very successful, banking or something. David thinks that life is all work, and what's work done for him? Chucked out without thanks, redundant. I said that she would only be young once. They treat her like one of the family. If she hadn't gone she'd have been old before her time, like us."

He closed his notebook, slipped it into his pocket. He stood. He was asked again why he had an interest in Dr. Giuseppe Ruggerio, and he smiled coolly and thanked them for their hospitality, not even a bloody cup of tea. He went out into the hall. He looked at the photograph of the young woman and made a remark that she was a grand-looking girl. He took his coat from the hook. The man opened the door for him. He could hear the sea beating on a shingle away in the evening darkness. A woman was across the lane, clinging to a dog's leash and staring at him as he stood under the porch light. He saw a man hunched in a lit window across the lane and peering at him through small binoculars. Behind a board advertising bed-and-breakfast (Vacancies), a curtain fell back to its place. God, what a dreary and supicious little backwater. He started down the path to the gate.

The hiss of the woman. "Aren't you going to tell him?"

The man's whisper. "It's not his business."

"You should tell him."

"No."

"You should tell him about the American ..."

Harry Compton stopped, turned. "What should I know? What American?"

To: Alfred Rogers, DLO, British Embassy, Via XX Settembre, Rome.

From: D/S Harry Compton, SO6.

Please get your leg off the beautiful women and ditch the bottle you will inevitably be busting open. Do me SOONEST a P check on Dr. GIUSEPPE RUGGERIO, Apt 9, Giardino Inglese 43, Palermo, Sicily. Ruggerio believed to be in finance, banking? Interests me because he uses alias of BRUNO FIORI. Don't break a blood vessel at the chance of actually doing something useful. Come up with the goods and I'll stand you a half-pint at the Ferret and Ferkin on your next extended (!) leave.

Bestest, Harry.

He had the scent, the smell was in his nostrils. He gave the sheet of paper to Miss Frobisher for transmission to the DLO, jammy sod, in Rome. Bloody good job, that one, soft old number. His detective superintendent was out of the building. It would have to keep, what he had to share, but there was a good bounce in his step. The day that the invitation to travel down to Palermo had reached Charlotte Parsons there had pitched up on her doorstep an American from the embassy, from the Drug Enforcement Administration. "He said that if I talked about him, what he said to me, then I might be responsible for hurting people." He'd bloody well find out, too right, what Americans were doing running round foreign territory to scoop up compliant and untrained agents. Charlotte Parsons's father had said that his daughter was "pressured" to travel. The boss would like it. Harry's boss had been skewered and minced and chewed by the FBI the last summer at the Europol fraud conference in Lyon. He'd come back bruised from France, worked over for suggesting that international crime was a figment of American imagination. He'd said, loud, at a seminar that international crime was a fantasy-land, and been told for all to listen that he was talking rubbish and that the Brits were just part-time players. Harry had heard it from the inspector who'd traveled as the detective superintendent's bag carrier. If the Americans had taken an English girl, "pressured" her, dragged her in, then his boss would not mind hearing of it, too right.

and heard, nothing written down, and then he walked from the park and along the Via Papireto and he would stop at the post office and buy the stamps for Germany. He would send the money. At the Palazzo di Gius-tizia he would show his identity card, walk past the soldiers, climb the wide steps, go to the rest room and open his locker and change into his uniform, and then he would go to the armory and draw his firearm and the holster, and then he would take the elevator to the upper corridor where he saw and he heard, and he would bring the small cups of *espresso* coffee to the magistrates and prosecutors. One morning each month his dream of buying the *pizzeria* in Hanover came closer.

A man stood beside him, and asked with courtesy whether he had a match for a cigarette, and they talked, as men talked who stood in a park and watched the mothers with their children and their babies.

The policeman said, ". . . He spoke in Italian, but the accent was Amer-ican. 'Yes, I'd like that, *espresso,* thanks.' He was not Italo-American be-cause he had a fair skin and gold hair. I recognized the one who brought him, that was Giovanni Crespo who is of the ROS in the Monreale bar-racks. He was not an American journalist because Tardelli never sees journalists, and when I brought the coffee I was not permitted by Tardelli's guards to take the tray inside myself. The tray was carried inside by Tardelli's man. I remember last year, in the winter, when an American came and I was not permitted to take the coffee inside, and then I heard the guards say that the American was the Country Chief of the DEA from Rome. The American was with Tardelli for fifteen or twenty minutes. What I can tell you of Giovanni Crespo, he is with the squad of the ROS that searches for the *super-latitanti.* The American wore casual clothes, not the clothes that are worn for a meeting with a person of the position of Tardelli, jeans and an open shirt, it surprised me, and he did not carry a briefcase but a small bag. I cannot be certain, I think there was a firearm in his waist but under his shirt. I estimate that he weighed near to 80 kilos, a height of perhaps 1.80 or 1.85 meters. He wore his hair long, like a hippy, and his hair was taken at the back with an elastic band, fair hair. I won-dered how it was possible that such a man could be brought to meet Tardelli . . . I know also that Tardelli has met with a team from the *squadra mobile,* they were dressed very roughly, so it is a surveillance team. Again, I was not permitted to take in the coffee. The story on the corridor, but it is only gossip, is that Tardelli had the big argument with the prosecu-tors and magistrates, I don't know . . ."

An envelope was passed. The policeman talked of the information scraps he had gained in a month of the work of other magistrates and other prosecutors.

IN TWO YEARS, NOT MORE THAN three years, he would have sufficient money to buy the *pizzeria*.

Each time that he was paid, in American bills, he sent them by post to his son. He had enough money already to buy a *pizzeria* in Palermo, nearly enough money to buy a *pizzeria* in Milan or Turin. But to buy a *pizzeria* in Hanover, near to the railway station, was more costly. His son and his daughter-in-law and his grandchildren lived in Hanover. They were, and he thought it was quite shameful to his own dignity, a part of the immigrant underclass in Germany. His son worked at night in the kitchen of a *trattoria* in Hanover, his daughter-in-law went to the *trattoria* in the mornings to clean it and to lay the tables. When there was sufficient money his son would use it to buy a *pizzeria,* and he would go to Hanover with his wife and with his daughter and he would live the last of his days there. The *pizzeria* in Hanover was the limit of his dream, and he and his wife and his daughter and his daughter-in-law would take it in turn to sit behind the cash desk. In return for the money, a thousand American dollars a month, he supplied information. The money came to him each month whether the information he supplied was important or whether it was insignificant. The money was a certainty, just as it was a certainty that he could not cease to provide the information. Trapped, corrupted, he stood one morning each month in the park in front of the Palazzo Reale and he watched the mothers with their children and their babies and waited for the contact to be made. He did not know the name of the man who came to him, nor did he know to whom the information was delivered. One morning every month he reported on what he had seen

He went on his way to the post, and dreamed of the *pizzeria* near to the railway station in Hanover, then to the Palazzo di Giustizia.

Her mother would have said that she should not have taken the money, and her father would have said that it would have seemed ungrateful to refuse the money. The purse in her handbag bulged with the roll of notes. Her mother would have said that it was simple human nature, like it or not, for people to look in the drawers of a guest, and her father would have said that she had probably forgotten where she had laid down her book and whether her pants had been on top or below her bras.

Charley had the money, and she wore the handbag draped from her shoulder across her chest. She didn't know.

She could not know, and all through the night she had tossed and twisted it in her mind, whether the movement of her book and her clothes was the mark of suspicion against her, or was in innocence, or was her bloody imagination. The taxi driver in Mondello had quoted her 20,000, sod that. She had come on the bus along the road that was shadowed by the height of Monte Pellegrino, on the road that skirted the La Favorita park where the whores were already gathered, on the road that cut through the high rise blocks. Where the Via della Libertà merged into the Piazza Crispi, Charley had pushed her way to the bus door.

Better to think it was her bloody imagination. But, he had said, the damned faceless man creeping behind her, "Don't ever relax, Don't go complacent." She felt a freedom, as if the garden gate of the villa when it had slammed shut behind her, had been a jail's gate. She walked along the Via della Libertà. They were beautiful shops, they were better than any of the shops in Plymouth or Exeter. The temperature was near to the seventies, and the women around her had fur coats hoisted loose on their shoulders, and the men wore their best *loden* coats. It was so bloody hot, and she was in a blouse and jeans with a light cardigan tied to the strap of her handbag, bloody peacocks around her. The women had their jewelery on, rings and bracelets and necklaces, as if they were out for an anniversary dinner and not merely promenading, and Charley only wore the thin little chain of poor gold that her uncle had sent down to her for her eighteenth birthday . . . And bugger Axel Moen who was a cold bastard . . . She had bounce in her stride, she had control. There was no street like the Via della Libertà in Plymouth or Exeter. Three lanes of traffic running in each direction and a wide center area with benches under the shade of trees. To Charley Parsons it was a little piece of joy. She heard the shouting. She looked across the traffic lanes and the center area, and she saw a street leading away in which there were no vehicles parked, and a soldier was gesturing with his rifle, and playing dumb innocent was a squat little man with a pickup truck loaded with builder's gear. She watched the yelling soldier and the obstinate little man trade insults. She murmured, "Go on, old boy, give the pompous bastard stick," just as they had given stick to the bloody policemen in their battle gear at the harbor in Brightlingsea. She had been free then, on the picket line and trying to block the lorries carrying the animals to Europe. She could have clapped because the squat little man had won the day, and the soldier stood, threatening, over him with the rifle, had gained the right to park his pickup and to unload his sacks of concrete mix. She grinned, she moved on. Her mother would have said that she had insufficient respect for authority, her father would have said she was a damned little anarchist . . . She held tight to her bag because Angela had told her she should.

Not the Via Siracusa, the next street off the Via della Libertà from the Via Siracusa. She couldn't think when, if ever, she had had as much cash, as thick a roll of notes, in her purse. She saw the sign of the boutique, where Peppino had said it would be. She was flushed, a little thrilled. God, that amount of money to spend on herself. What would the cold bastard have said? She stopped outside the boutique, in front of the window of clothed model figures. She looked around her. As with a child's guilt, she looked for Axel Moen. Did not see him. Nor did Charley see the young man who sat astride a motorcycle, up the street from her.

The prices on the model figures were just incredible, out of this bloody world, but she had the money in her purse. Best foot forward, ma'am. She pushed open the door of the shop. Go hack it, Charley. She did not see the young man astride the motorcycle, the engine idling, slide down the smoked black visor of his crash helmet.

Soft music played. The lighting was clever. She was of importance. God, eat your heart out, British Home Stores in Exeter, Marks and bloody Spencer in Plymouth. She tried four blouses, her mind played the calculations of translating from *lire* to sterling. Christ, Charley . . . Big breath, deep breath. She chose a blouse of royal blue, and the touch of it on her fingers was so soft. She tried three skirts, short minis, and they'd be better when she'd done time on the beach and burned the whiteness off her knees and thighs. She chose a skirt in bottle green. She paid, stripped the notes off the roll. She took the bag they gave her. Bugger where the money had come from. Bugger that Giuseppe Ruggerio washed money. She had enough in her purse to go on to find a throat scarf and maybe a good pair of dark glasses. She came out of the shop, and she did not see the haughty smiles of the sales staff, as if they thought her an *ingenua*. She stood on the pavement, savoring the moment. Her mother would have said that it was criminal to spend that much on clothes, her father would have said they were the clothes of a spoiled child. She did not see the young man, head hidden in the crash helmet, nudge his motorcycle forward.

It was a few yards from the open space of the pavement of the Via della Libertà . . .

Meandering past a shoe shop . . .

Heard nothing and seen nothing, and the blow belted her.

As if her chest was torn apart, as if the strap of her handbag cut into her back and her breast.

She clung to the strap. Trying to scream, and spinning, and there was the roar of the motorcycle against her, and the black shape of the crash helmet was above her.

Falling, and the boot came into her face. The boot came from below a scarlet painted fuel tank, and on the tank was an eagle's head. The boot savaged her. She held the handbag strap and she was dragged on the pavement. Kicked again, and letting loose of the strap and covering her face.

On the pavement and the foul filth of the motorcycle exhaust blasting at her, choking. The gloved hand came down, crude, bulged fingers, and caught at the necklace that was the present of her uncle, and ripped at it, and it broke and it was coiled in the gutter beside her.

Charley lay on the pavement and under her body was the shopping bag. She sobbed into the dirt of the pavement.

The motorcycle was gone.

A man walked past her, and looked away. She sobbed and she swore. Two women, queens in their finery, quickened their step and hurried by her. She wept and she cursed. Kids were going by her, fast little trainer shoes scurrying. After them were high heels and shoes of worked leather. In pain, she wept. In anger, she cursed. The pain was in her chest and her face and her elbows and her knees. The anger was for all of them, the fucking bastards, who hurried by. She pushed herself to her knees, Christ and it hurt because her knees were red-raw from being dragged, and she could see right down to the Via della Libertà and across she could see a soldier on the far corner with his rifle held in alertness and he didn't come to help her. As if she carried a yellow flag, bloody leprosy, bloody HIV, was quarantined, they went by her, the fucking bastards. She was on her feet, she staggered, she lurched toward a man and she saw the horror on his face, and he pushed her away. She fell. She was on the pavement.

"Are you all right?"

" 'Course I'm not bloody—"

She looked up at him.

He was bent down and close to her. "You are a tourist, yes? English, German?"

"English."

He was young, maybe a couple of years older than herself. Concern was on his face, and sincerity, sympathy.

"Nobody helped me, nobody tried to stop him."

"People are afraid here, afraid to be involved."

"Bloody bastard cowards."

"Afraid to interfere. It is different to England, I apologize."

Such kindness. He was tall. He had a fine angled face, strong bones in the cheeks. He pushed the falling hair back from his forehead.

"I haven't broken anything. I just feel so angry. I want to get him, kick him. There was a soldier across the road, a bloody great gun, didn't move."

So soothing. "He could not help you. It might have been a diversion. In Palermo anything is possible. You are a foreigner, you would not understand. Can I help you? Take my hand. The soldier would have been disciplined. If he had left his place and come to you, it could have been a diversion, it could have been an attack on the home that he guards. It is Palermo."

He took her hand. He had long and delicate fingers. She felt them close on her hand. He lifted her up. The anger had gone. She wanted to be held and she wanted to cry. He picked up her bag from the shop.

"It happens every day in Palermo. They target tourists."

"I'm not a tourist, I've come here for a job. It was my first day in Palermo. The job's in Mondello. I'm sorry that I swore. I am Charley Parsons."

He grinned, embarrassed. "But that is a man's name."

A smile cracked her face. "Charlotte, but I am Charley to everyone."

"I am Benedetto Rizzo, but I am called Benny. You are sure there is no bad injury?"

"I am not going to hospital. Damn, shit, fuck. Sorry, and thank you."

"I was in London for a year, people were very kind to me. I worked in the McDonald's near Paddington railway station. I apologize that this is your first experience of Palermo."

Charley said, "Trouble is, I feel like a fool. I was warned to be careful, I was bloody miles away. I just feel, humiliated. I was warned, and I forgot. Excuse me, you said that in Palermo people are afraid to be involved, afraid to interfere, but you were not afraid."

"It is our city, our problem. You should not dissociate yourself from responsibility from a problem. If nobody does anything, then the problem will never be solved, it's what I believe."

She looked into his face. "Small people can change something, is that what you think?"

"Of course."

He crouched. His hand, the long fingers, were in the gutter and the filth, and he lifted up the broken chain of poor gold. He seemed to Charley to recognize its value to her. He lifted it with care and he placed it in her hand.

"I'm sorry, I am a teacher, I . . ."

"I was a teacher in England."

"Then you will know—I have to be back. I have my class, at the elementary school behind the Piazza Castelnuovo." He grinned. "Maybe if I am not back, there will be a riot of the children, maybe the police will have to come with gas."

Her face was puffing from the bruises, her elbows were scraped, the knees under the tears in her jeans were oozing blood.

Charley grimaced. "I can't go to a bar, not looking like this. I am really grateful for what you did for me, for your kindness. When I am repaired, can I buy you a drink? Please let me."

He wrote for her his address and a telephone number, gave it to her.

"But, you are all right, Charley?"

"I'm fine, Benny. It's just my bloody dignity that's damaged."

Aching throughout her body, Charley limped with her shopping bag toward the bus stop. Only when she stood at the bus stop did she realize that the bloody bastard hadn't gone for her watch, that the watch was on her wrist.

Axel watched the bus come.

He saw her, in pain, drag herself up onto the bus.

As the bus drove away, the bus for Mondello, her face was in the window for a moment in his vision. She was white-faced except for the vivid bruising where the boot had caught her, and she seemed to him to be in shock.

He was on the pavement, a few feet from the bus, close enough to see the markings on her face.

Axel had seen it all. He had seen her, Codename Helen, come out of the boutique, carrying her bag, alive with pleasure, and he had seen the motorcycle accelerate down the side street toward her, and then weave through a gap in the parked cars and come onto the pavement. He had seen each detail of the attack, the snatch of the bag, her being dragged behind the motorcycle, the motorcycle stopping on the pavement and the boot going into her face, and the gloved fist going for her throat, and the motorcycle accelerating away down the pavement before it cut between the cars and out onto the side street.

He had not tried to intervene.

He would have intervened if it had been life threatening. If he had intervened, if it had been life threatening, if he had used his firearm, if the police had been called, then his cover was broken.

He had recognized the situation from the moment the motorcycle had moved on her. It was a bag snatch, it was the life of Palermo. It was not worth the breaking of his cover. From his viewpoint across the side street he had satisfied himself that the situation was, by the terms on which he operated, harmless. The young Palermitan had come to her and helped her, and he had seen her weep and then curse and then soften as she was dosed in his sympathy, and at the end he had seen the small and rueful grimace on her face. She had not needed him.

And Axel did not need the smart talk of Dwight Smythe who pushed paper in the London embassy, nor of Bill Hammond in a safe billet on the Via Sardegna up the road from the Rome embassy, nor of 'Vanni, nor of a magistrate who had probed and warned of responsibilities. Didn't need them whining their consciences at him . . .

He had been to Mondello each morning. Each morning he had seen her come from the villa with the children. He had tracked her, unseen, each morning. Surveillance tactics were the skill area of Axel Moen, always behind, always on the far side of the street or the piazza or the alleyway. Each morning he followed her, Codename Helen, stayed back from her. He did not need any hand-wringing bastards to tell him of his responsibility. There had been a girl crucified on the back of a door, and he had used the pliers and a claw hammer from the tool kit of the Huey's pilot to get the nails from the palms of her hands. He did not need to be told about his responsibilities.

He walked away. He wore a cap so that the long fall of his hair was tucked up inside it. He had sunglasses on. The windcheater was not one she had seen him use.

She could have panicked, could have pressed the pulse tone button that was the alarm on her wristwatch. She'd done well. She had shown good sense. He thought the best of her and it did not cross his mind that she had simply forgotten that she wore the wristwatch with the panic alarm. He went to a shop and brought some sketch pencils with soft lead and buried them in the bag with his sketch pads and his tape measure and the CSS 900 receiver. He was heading for his car. By the late morning he would be back and protecting his cover at the cloister aisle of the *duomo* in Monreale. He used people, and he goddam well knew it, used them and squeezed them and dropped them.

There was a parking ticket on his car, pinned under the wiper on the windscreen. He glanced at it. He tore the ticket into small pieces and dropped them into a street drain. It would be several weeks before the

office where the duplicate tickets were lodged stirred themselves to trace
the registration back to the hire company at Catania's airport, and by then
Axel Moen would be back in the Via Sardegna office. It could not last
more than a month, his reckoning, she could not survive the lie for more
than a month. The Confidential Informant designated Codename Helen
would, in several weeks, have been used and squeezed and dropped.

It had been a shit shift, but the next shift would be worse. The shift from
six in the morning until two in the afternoon was difficult, but at least
the street stalls were up in the Capo district, and it was possible for Giancarlo to walk between the stalls and to finger a lemon or a pear or turn
over an apple and to look at faces, and to drift on. The shift from two in
the afternoon until ten in the evening was worse shit because the stalls
had done their trade for the day and were packing and emptying the alleyways, and it was harder in the afternoons and the evenings to hold
cover. He had not yet been assigned to the shift from ten in the evening
until six in the morning, and that would be the worst shit duty, and Jesu
alone would know how to hold cover in the bastard place when the alleyways were darkened, when people hurried, when the *bambini* roamed
over the cobbles on their scooters. Maybe, Jesu would tell him, when he
had the shift through the night . . .

A man brushed against his shoulder.

"Anything?"

A sardonic smile. Giancarlo coughed on his cigarette. He spoke from
the side of his mouth. "That has to be a joke. Perhaps, a better joke. Yesterday I took home three lemons, a pear, a quarter kilo of cheese and an
artichoke. Today I take home one lemon, three apples, and a cauliflower."
He held up the plastic bag. "My wife said last night that I intruded on
her lifestyle. You would think you would be thanked for doing the
shopping."

"But you don't bring home *il bruto?*"

"The photograph is twenty years old. He could walk past me."

"We need the *buona fortuna.*"

"I think, more than luck, I need to have a taste for lemons."

A sharp smile between them. They were chosen, this team from the
squadra mobile, for the quality of their patience. The patience bred an attitude to their work. They could go each day to a street, to an apartment
that was used for observation, they could sit in a car and in a closed van,
do the shift for a week or for a month and watch the same view and look
for the same face. They did not fret and they were not bored, and that
was the training bred into them.

Giancarlo left the Capo district. The sun was now on his face, and the smells of the dog shit and the rotting food bags and the old drains were out of his nose. There had to be patience. The guys of the DIA had watched a shop for eight weeks before Bagarella was spotted, and the ROS team of the *carabinieri* had watched a street for eleven weeks before Riina was seen. He went for his bus.

He was an anonymous figure riding the bus home. He bought the clothes for work in such a place as the Capo district from a charity shop. He was forty-seven years old, had served eighteen years in the *squadra mobile*, had volunteered four years back for work with the team specializing in the *sorveglianza*. They had moved home then. In the apartment block where they had lived before it had been known on the landings that he was a police officer. They had moved on when he had taken the surveillance work. It was the cross that his wife carried, in the new apartment, that he seemed to their neighbors to be another of the city's *disoccupati*. Better that he should appear as one of the city's unemployed or as a casual tradesman . . . He promised his wife that there would be one more year and then they would move again. It was hard for his wife, difficult for her. She had to tolerate his shabby old handed-down clothes. She had to exist alongside the pistol in the holster and the radio carried in a harness against his skin that were permanent to him when he was on assignment. She had to tolerate the fruit, the vegetables and always the lemons that he bought to hold his cover and dumped on her.

Even on the bus, he watched faces. But the photograph that Giancarlo tried to match to the faces was twenty years old. Faces riding with him, faces on the pavement, faces in cars.

Another day's work finished. There were some operations when Giancarlo, and the guys in the team with him, would feel the chance of a success strike was good, and there were others . . .

Small Mario ran back into the house and shouted for his mother to come.

Francesca stood rooted to the patio, clutching her toy.

The gardener eyed her as he methodically closed the gates behind her.

She struggled up the the drive and then up the path between the flower beds, and then onto the patio. Charley grimaced when Angela came through the open doors. She saw the collapse of Angela's mouth and chin, as if in shock. Angela had come to her, hurrying, and took Charley in her arms. Charley wept. The tears streamed. Charley hung in Angela's arms, as if she were held by a friend. The tears were wet on the shoulder of Angela's silk blouse, staining it, and she tried to make an apology, and Angela would not have it, and held her. It was a moment of bonding. The tears flowed down Charley's cheeks. Small Mario had taken the cue from his mother and clutched at her waist, as if that were his own gesture of comfort love, and Francesca held herself tight against Charley's legs and cried with her. They went together inside the villa. Charley felt as though, now, she was protected by Angela and small Mario and Francesca. She was taken through the hall and as they passed the full length mirror they saw the pavement dirt in the confusion of her hair and the bruising on her face and the grazing on her elbows and the ripped material at the knees of her jeans. She was sat on a chair in the kitchen. When Angela loosed her, to put on the kettle to get hot water, to find the medical box and the cotton wool, the children still held her. Charley tried to blink away the tears. She wore the wristwatch. She spied against their love.

"You were robbed?"

Trying to be brave. "Afraid so."

"You are hurt, badly hurt?"

"Don't think so. I didn't go to the hospital, didn't seem necessary."

"The physician will come—robbed of your bag?"

Angela gathered the medical box, the plasters, the ointments, the cotton wool pad on the table and she waited for the kettle to boil.

"When I came out of the shop, which Peppino had recommended—I still have what I bought, they're lovely—I just didn't see him come. He must have been watching me. As I started to walk, he came from behind me."

"It's a foul place."

"I had the strap of the bag across me, when he pulled the bag I was dragged . . ."

"It's a place of the jungle, home for animals. What have you lost?"

"Nothing that's life-threatening. A diary, that's a nuisance. A credit card, boring. Make-up, thank God, I'd spent most of what Peppino gave me. He got nothing."

The water from the kettle was poured into a bowl. Angela, so gentle, began to clean the wounds.

"He stopped the bike. He kicked my face. That was when I let the bag go. He didn't have to, he had my bag. He leaned down and he snatched at the necklace. It broke."

She took the necklace, broken, from her pocket. She put it on the table. It seemed to her so cheap, so trivial, and the necklace of Angela was heavy gold and dancing in front of her eyes as Angela bent across her to dab the soaked hot cotton wool on her face.

"For what happened, I feel ashamed. Did anyone help you?"

"Most didn't, one did. He was very kind, a teacher."

"I am so sorry, Charley. I will call Peppino. It is a foul place, Charley, because the society is bred on violence, a city that makes fear. I feel so great a responsibility."

"Please, please don't," Charley said.

The whisper of desperation. "You won't go back to England, because of this, you won't—?"

"No."

Angela kissed Charley. The children held her. She would not go home because she was a spy. She thought the watch on her wrist was a talisman of treachery. She was under the control of the cold bastard Axel Moen, who had not been close by, who had not protected her. It was not the filth of the gutter in her hair that dirtied her but the watch on her wrist. The kiss was love, and the children held her in love.

The baby was crying when Pasquale came home, and Pasquale was dead on his feet. A bad night broken by the alarm at four, little sleep before the alarm because the baby then had been crying. And he couldn't tell whether the tiredness on his wife's face was because of the baby's crying or because of her anxiety for his work. Her mother was in the kitchen and trying to quieten the baby, and failing. He didn't want to talk in front of her mother, so he went to the bedroom, and he lay on the bed staring at the ceiling light. He didn't want to tell his wife, in front of her mother that he had received snapped criticism from the *maresciallo*. "If you are tired, you are useless, if you are a zombie, you endanger us all. Don't think you are the only one that has fathered a baby that cries in the night." He should pull himself together, remember that he was a part of a team. The *maresciallo* had said that he had the promise from Tardelli, the magistrate was working at home that afternoon. They could manage, once, without Pasquale. If Pasquale were again found yawning, blinking tiredness, then he would be off the team, the *maresciallo* had said. He had gone home, feeling shame, and he lay on the bed and could not sleep.

His wife came into the bedroom and she carried a glass of juice for him.

"Is there no overtime? You are early."

"I was sent home."

"What had you done?"

"I was told I was too tired. I was told I was not effective. I was told I endangered the team."

He could not tell whether it was the exhaustion or anxiety that made the lines at her mouth and the bulging bags under her eyes. He did not know whether the end of her prettiness was marked by the birth of the baby or by his joining the team that protected a "walking corpse."

"They will get rid of you?"

"I don't know."

"If they got rid of you . . . ?"

"Then I could patrol outside the Questura, I could stop the traffic for schoolchildren, I could be on the pavement and watch the sirens go by."

"What do you want?"

"I want to be with him and stand beside him."

The magistrate had been in the living room of the apartment, when the *maresciallo* had spat the criticism at Pasquale. The living room was his office. The desk where he worked at his computer screen was on the far side of the room from the reinforced plate glass of the windows. The room was always in gloom because the shutters were across the window and the curtains were drawn. When he had left, been sent home, he had passed the door to the living room and seen the magistrate hunched over his computer with the mess of files on the desk and opened on a chair and on the carpet around the desk. He had felt humility toward the magistrate because all the team knew that the phone call had been made at dawn to the magistrate's wife in Udine and the telephone had not been picked up by Patrizia Tardelli, nor by the children, but by a man. All the team had heard the poor bastard stammer to a man whose name he did not know, in his wife's house at dawn. A bad time of the day to learn, for sure, that a marriage had foundered, that his wife was fucked by a stranger.

"And me? Do you want to stand beside me? And do you want to stand beside our baby?"

"That is stupid talk."

"So I am stupid. Each day that you go out, when I am left, I have to consider whether, again, I will see you."

"He asks of you each day, and he asks of the baby. Each day he remembers you."

"Each day, Pasquale, I am so frightened."

"He asks after you, as if he blamed himself for your situation." Pasquale pushed himself up on the bed. He spoke in bitterness. "What would you have us do? Would you have us walk away from him, abandon him?"

"Is he so stubborn?"

"He has the fear, we all have the fear. He jokes of the fear, he has learned to live with it. As I try to, as you have to. Stubborn? Will he surrender to the fear? He is stubborn and he will not give in to the fear."

"Is the danger very great?"

He looked away from her. His shoulders dropped back to the bed. He gazed up at the ceiling light. She sat beside him and she held his hand. He thought that she struggled to reconcile their fear with her own fear.

"You have the right to know. We are not supposed to talk of it, not even in the home, but you have the right. He could compromise, he could exist, he could move paper across his desk, he could ride through the city in safety, and we could go in safety with him. The *maresciallo* says that a man such as Tardelli faces real danger only when he has become a threat to those people."

"Please."

"I should not tell you. There is a prisoner in the Ucciardone who seeks the privilege of the *pentito* program, and he has given information about Ruggerio, the target of Tardelli. The information is not good but if it is acted upon, it could threaten Ruggerio."

"I listen."

"An American came from Rome, an agent of the DEA, to see Tardelli. If he sees Tardelli, then it is connected with Ruggerio, so the threat increases."

"Tell me."

"There is a third factor, the *maresciallo* says. It is a time of great danger to Tardelli. Ruggerio seeks to be the *capo di tutti capi,* he looks for absolute control. There is a rival in Agrigento, disappeared. There is a family in Catania, but they will be destroyed. When, the *maresciallo* says, the control of Ruggerio is absolute, then he will demonstrate his new power with a strike against the heart of the state. It could be the life of Tardelli because that is the man who most threatens him . . . You wanted to know."

"I asked . . ."

"Are you better for knowing?"

She loosed Pasquale's hand. She left him in the dim lit room. He slept with his mind dulled to dreams. Later he would wake. Later he would find her sleeping beside him, and the baby asleep in the cot at the foot of the bed. Later he would shower and dress and strap onto his chest the pistol holster. Later, he would go into the kitchen to make himself coffee to clear away the sleep taste from his mouth and he would find the small bunch of flowers on the table and he would read the note his wife had written. "Please give them to him, and thank him for asking after me each day and after our baby. God keep you." Later, Pasquale would go to work.

The boy was sat in a chair.

His arms were tied tight behind his back and the rope chafed against skin. The boy's ankles were strapped to the legs of the chair. The gag his mouth. He did not understand . . . He was of the Brancaccio t. He came from the high blocks of crumbling apartments. He had never been employed, nor had his father ever been in work. He thieved to keep his family, stole the bags of the tourists.

He did not understand . . . He paid the *pizzo* each month to the Men of Honor in Brancaccio. He never failed to give them the percentage from what he took out of tourists' handbags.

He did not understand . . . He had been told that one day, perhaps, he would be invited to join the ranks of the *picciotti,* that a final decision would be made when he had completed tasks set for him by the Men of Honor in Brancaccio.

He did not understand . . . A task had been set for him. He had taken the handbag. He had brought the handbag to the address given him. A pistol had been pressed against his neck, he had been strapped to the chair. The handbag was now in front of him on a bare wooden table.

He did not understand . . . The money from the handbag was in a neat pile. Two men were looking carefully at the diary from the handbag. Their hands, which held the diary, passed it between them, were protected by transparent plastic gloves. They examined the diary with minute care.

The boy was condemned. They had not hooded him and they had not blindfolded him. He had seen their faces. He could not know whether they would strangle him or knife him or shoot him, whether they would put him in acid or in concrete or whether they would dump him, under cover of darkness, in an alley. They did not seem to notice that the piss ran hot on his thigh and he shivered without control. He did not understand . . .

As a child, he had been told by his father, Rosario, an old saying of Sicily. "The man who plays alone always wins."

Any detail relevant to his personal security was passed to Mario Ruggerio. He alone would decide the importance of information. The message came by word of mouth to the apartment off the Via Crociferi. In conditions of secrecy the magistrate, Tardelli, had met Capitano Giovanni Crespo of the *carabiniere* ROS, and the *capitano* had brought with him an unnamed American. Alone in the apartment, in the kitchen, he heated up his favorite meal of *trippa* that he would take with a sauce of boiled tomato. A woman had come to the apartment the day before he had moved in, and cleaned it and filled the refrigerator with sufficient small and simple-to-prepare meals that would last him for a week. He would be gone after a week, and then the apartment would again be scrubbed clean. He could search in the far recesses of a huge memory. The recesses of his memory were compartmentalized so the name of Giovanni Crespo, of the *carabiniere* ROS, was not obscured by the bank of information held on financial movements and cash investments and future strategy and opponents and affiliates. He could sweep aside his thoughts on the plans of an explosives expert, and on the matter of a handbag thief, and of a meeting with a Colombian who was skilled in the movement of refined cocaine to Europe, and of discussions with the new men from Russia.

He remembered the name of Giovanni Crespo, and there had been a photograph, which was blurred, of a white and tensed face, published in the *Giornale di Sicilia,* beside the blanket-covered head of Riina as the big man was driven away after his arrest from the *carabinieri* barracks. The memory was dismissed. He considered what he had been told of an American, poorly dressed, unnamed, perhaps armed, admitted to the inner office of Tardelli. In his mind he turned over the information, analyzed it, pondered it. If the Americans mounted an operation in Palermo, if an agent came to visit Tardelli, then he believed that only he could be the principal target.

The water in the saucepan boiled around the *trippa.* The sauce made from boiled tomatoes bubbled in a second saucepan. He took a bottle of Perroni beer from the refrigerator. He was ready to eat. There were times that he yearned for the cooking of Michela, and to be surrounded by his family, and to sit the little boy, his nephew, who was a rascal and who was named after him, on his knee . . . So much to think off . . . He took the *trippa* from the saucepan and spooned the sauce of tomato over it. He poured his beer. He seemed to imagine that his wife, Michela, put the plate on the table in front of him. It was a compartment in his life. All his life was in sealed compartments, and that was his strength. He allowed three men, Carmine and Franco and Tano, to be close to him. It was what he had learned in his climb to power. There should always be three, because two men could agree, in secrecy, on conspiracy, never three. The three men competed with each other, in insecurity, for his favor. Carmine would look to the matter of the *carabiniere* officer, Giovanni Crespo, and the association with the American. Franco had already been given responsibility for the security of the meeting with the Colombian. Tano liaised with the expert in explosives. He divided them, and he ruled them. He must be strong.

There was an old saying in Sicily that his father, Rosario, had told him. "A man who makes himself a sheep will be eaten by the wolf."

he physician, elderly and elegant and expensively considerate, had ex-
ned Charley with soft and cool fingers, probed at her grazes and
es, and told her with a distant smile on his lined face that her in-
though painful, were superficial. He had congratulated her on the

good fortune that her experience had not led to serious hurt. Charley thought of what it would have been like in England, waiting in Casualty or at the general practitioner's clinic. Bloody hideous it would have been. But she had been calmed by the physician. She lay on her bed.

He knocked. Peppino was smiling sympathy at her from the door.

"You are better now?"

"I feel a bit of a fraud."

"Angela tells me that you were very brave."

"Just wish I'd been able to scratch his eyes out or kick him in the bloody balls. Sorry, I mean leave him something to remember me by."

Peppino chuckled with her. "It would have been nice. I am so sorry that I could not come at once. Have you reported this matter to the police?"

"I just couldn't face it."

"Of course. It happens all day and every day in Palermo. The beauty of our city, its heritage, is despoiled by such crime, and the police can do little. If you report to the police, then you invade the world of their bureaucracy. Believe me, they are not fast."

"But, for the insurance, shouldn't I have a chit from the police?"

He sat on the end of the bed, friendly, kind but not familiar.

"What exactly did you lose?"

"There was my purse. I'd spent most of what you gave me . . . You'd like to see?"

She swung off the bed. She took the blouse and the miniskirt from the bag. She held them in turn in front of her. She thought it was what she should do, what would be expected of her, what was expected of a spy. He nodded his approval.

"When there is a special occasion, please, you will decorate it. What was in your bag?"

"Not much. My purse and thirty or forty thousand, my lipstick and the powder compact and the eye stuff, some keys. There was my Visa card, but I can get that canceled, and there was my diary with phone numbers and addresses."

"You see, Charley, these scum are only interested in cash, probably for drugs, and they are very impertinent. Many times, after they have taken the money they will dump the bag in a rubbish collector very close to the Questura. It is possible, I cannot say probable, that your bag will be found. And I would not wish you to be concerned about your card. Allow me to take care of it. Angela said there was a necklace."

"He tried to snatch it, broke it. Just of sentimental importance, a present from my uncle."

She pointed to the thin chain that had luster. The chain was on the table beside the book that she thought had been moved.

And across the room was the chest, containing her underwear that she thought had been taken out of the middle drawer and replaced. Maybe it was her imagination. Maybe it was a vicious lie of Axel bloody Moen. Maybe. She was the spy in their home.

A frown, questioning, was on his forehead. "You see, Charley, how greatly Angela depends on you. It is not easy for her here. It is a different culture from her life in Rome. It is impossible for her, in Sicilian society, to recreate the freedom of Rome. To her, your companionship is so important. Why I say that, very frankly, we hope you will not wish immediately to return to England."

"I didn't consider it—and God help the next low-life who tries anything."

He asked her to describe the handbag. He told her that he knew a man in the Questura and he would go directly to see the man and himself report the theft of the bag. For a moment his hand rested on the cleaned wound on her knee.

"All of us, Charley, we admire your courage."

The detective superintendent winked across the table at Harry Compton, like it was going to amuse him. He cradled the telephone between his cheek and his shoulder to free his hands to light a cigarette.

". . . I quite appreciate you're a busy guy, Ray. When you've a moment . . . I know how busy you DEA people keep yourselves. Won't take more than a moment, just something that's come up, needs clarification. I'll fit in with you. Down here at SO6 we're not that stretched, not like you are. Keep for a couple of days? I should think so . . . Oh, yes, the Bramshill conference would be excellent. I'll see you there. Very good of you, Ray, to get me on board your schedule. I appreciate that. See you then, Ray . . ."

9

"... I TURN TO THE ISSUE OF OR-
ganized and international crime. The international scene is developing
with increasing pace and we cannot afford to get left behind. Borders are
coming down, trade is expanding, financial markets and services are becoming integrated. In short, we are no longer an island protected by the
sea from unwelcome influences ..."

So, you got the message, sir, and about time. The Country Chief eased
back in his chair. It was a chore of his work that he should attend the set
piece speeches of the Commissioner of the Metropolitan Police. But he'd
get a good lunch, and over lunch he'd have the opportunity to bend the
ear of people who were useful to him, and he was out of London, and in
spring the gardens at Bramshill College which hosted senior men's courses
were rather fine.

"... We should be in no doubt that organized crime will exploit every
opportunity, technological advance or weakness in order to expand. Organized crime, with its international links and quasicorporate structures,
is responsible for flooding the streets with dangerous drugs, undermin-
ing financial systems, and by the sheer financial muscle it has available, it
is a real threat to the integrity and effectiveness of the rule of law and is
becoming ever more complex and sophisticated ..."

Good to have you on board, sir. The Country Chief looked out of the
window, at the view of the daffodils and crocuses in flowered islands in
the lawns, and around the lecture room. The guy from the National
Criminal Intelligence Service was listening, and impassive. That was the
guy who had told Ray, a year back, that there was no Sicilian La Cosa

Nostra problem in little old UK. About time they grew up and joined the real world.

"...There is the question of the role, where appropriate, of the Security Service, and the future involvement of the Security Service in matters which have historically been the responsibility of the police. There is great strength in exploiting fully the experience, methods, powers and potential of different agencies in tackling common problems. The challenge is how to take advantage of diversity without creating confusion ..."

Heh, come to Washington, sir. Come and see the "confusion" when the FBI and the CIA and the DEA and the ATF and the Revenue and the Customs get their noses onto the same scent. Come and see the cat-fight when the agencies get to hunt the same target. He knew the guy from MI5, a languid dick of a guy, sitting a row behind the NCIS man. Always looking for new territory. Take my advice, sir, keep the bastards at arm's length.

"...Time is not on our side. I do not think our current structures allow us to punch at our full weight and the *status quo* will not serve us well in the next century. Our European and indeed world partners will run out of patience if we do not evolve a one stop shop approach to their involvement with us. I hope we will develop an appropriate mechanism to do justice to this formidable challenge. Thank you, ladies and gentlemen."

Spoken like a man, sir, because patience was certainly wearing thin. Put bluntly, and Ray liked to speak his mind, he thought he found in little old theme-park UK a quite stunning complacency. He could have pointed to specialized police units that were starved of resources, to the Customs and Excise investigators who were driven by the culture of statistics, to the financial institutions in the City who blandly ignored the matter of dirty money. He applauded politely.

Time for coffee.

He was in the queue and talking banalities with a man from Drugs Squad.

"Morning, Ray."

The man from SO6 was beside him.

"You were looking for a word. How you doing?"

"Coffee's usually pretty revolting. Let's walk and talk."

The Country Chief, good ears, caught the snap in the voice of the detective superintendent.

"You go without, please yourself, I'm taking coffee."

So he stayed in the queue, made his point, had his cup filled, balanced it on the saucer and walked to the door. The detective superintendent was ahead of him. They went across the wide hallway and out onto the driveway where the chauffeurs waited with their bullshit cars. He liked to say that DEA had a "blue collar" mentality, and chauffeur-driven black cars didn't fit the work ethic he believed in. They walked on the lawns and skirted the daffodil clumps and the crocus carpets.

"Nice time of year. So what can I do for you?"

The detective superintendent was smiling, but malevolent. "Just something that crossed my desk. You have an agent called Axel Moen on your staff—"

"Wrong."

"I beg your pardon?" The smile had shifted, the face had hardened.

"Put in one-syllables," the Country Chief spoke slowly as if to an idiot child, emphasizing while his mind racheted, "I do not have anyone of that name on my staff. Does that settle your problem?"

"An agent with DEA accreditation named Axel Moen."

"We have around twenty-five hundred special agents, can't know all of them."

He never lied. He could divert, interrupt, head off, but he would not lie. He knew, from his deputy who had been to Lyon, that quite the most memorable twenty minutes of the Europol conference had been when Garcia, FBI out of Moscow, had put down the Brit from SO6. The man's throat was tightening, and the veins were up on his forehead.

"Did you know that a special agent, Axel Moen, traveled down to Devon a bit more than two weeks ago?"

"Maybe I did."

"Where's he out of?"

"Is that your business?"

"Don't fuck me around."

"If it's your business, he's out of Rome."

"Working with your facilities?"

"Maybe."

"With your knowledge?"

"Maybe. I'd kind of like to catch the next lecture." The Country Chief threw the dregs from his cup down onto the grass. The lawns around them, between the islands of daffodils and the carpets of crocuses, had just been given their first cut. The dew damp flecked his shoes. "What's your concern?"

"He went to the home of a young girl, a school teacher."

"Did he?"

"She had received an invitation to go and work for a Sicilian family."

"Had she?"

"Her parents say that your man, Axel Moen, "pressured" her into accepting that invitation."

"Do they?"

"The man who has offered her employment has just traveled to the UK under false documentation."

"Has he?"

"You want it, you'll get it. We reckon you are running some sort of anti-mafia job. We reckon you have trawled round for someone to do the sharp end for you, and you've got your sticky fingers on some poor girl."

"Do you?"

"You have taken it upon yourselves, you arrogant bloody people, to pressurize and then send a small town girl to Palermo for some bloody operation you've dreamed up. Who've you cleared it with?"

"Among your crowd, I don't have to."

"You are running some naïve youngster, filled with crap no doubt, down in Palermo. So help me, I'll see you—"

"Should have listened to what your fat cat said. Your world partners will run out of patience. Maybe they already have."

He remembered what Dwight Smythe had said. The words rang in his mind. "He elbows into a small and unsuspecting life, a young woman's life, and puts together a web to trap her, and did it cold." He remembered what he himself had said: "And maybe we should all clap our hands and sing our hymns and get on our knees and thank our God that He didn't give us the problem." He looked into the flushed anger of the Englishman's face.

"Have you thought through the consequences? Do you take responsibility for the consequences?"

"It's something you shouldn't get your noses into."

"That's shit, that's not an answer."

"It's the answer you're getting, so back off."

The Country Chief walked away. He went back into the hall and gave his cup and saucer to a waitress.

He didn't have the heart for the session from the Italian attaché on preventative measures being taken by the Banco d'Italia concerning disclosure, nor for lunch, nor for the afternoon session when they would be "entertained" by the police colonel from St. Petersburg. He felt bad, and he wanted to get the hell out. He felt bad because he had said himself that it was a good plan, a plan that might just work. He had justified, himself, the use of a pressured innocent. He took his coat from the cloakroom. The poor goddam kid . . .

She had stayed in the villa the day before, fussed over by Angela, lain in the sun while the gardener worked around her, but she had argued that morning with Angela. Yes, she was quite fit enough to take small Mario to school and Francesca to kindergarten. Yes, she was quite able to do the day's shopping. Yes, she would be able to walk the children to school and kindergarten, and do the shopping, before the threatened rain came.

Shouldn't make a bloody drama out of a bloody crisis.

She walked the children, with the baby in the pram, down from the villa and into Mondello. All her childhood, the star who was the center of attention, she had learned to milk a crisis. Perhaps it had been her going to Rome for the summer of 1992, perhaps it had been leaving home and living lonely at college, but the thought of draining sympathy from others now disgusted her. She could reflect, viciously, that her father had whined drama out of the redundancy crisis, made a growth industry from it. Her mother complained drama out of the cash-flow crisis. God, it was why she had gone away. She thought, cruelly, that her parents fed off drama, drank off crisis.

Shut up, Charley, close it down. What was drama to Axel Moen, what was his definition of crisis? And where was he? Wrap it, Charley, forget it . . .

She dropped small Mario at the school gate, bent down so that the child could kiss her. He ran, as he did each morning, through the playground to his friends and was engulfed by them. He was a happy and sweet little boy. If the plan worked, Axel's plan, then the drama would hit the child, the crisis would come with the arrest of the child's father and the child's uncle. She wondered who would play with the child at school the morning after the arrest of his father and his uncle, and the thought hurt deep. So considerate of those children, lying little bitch that she was, Charley acknowledged the growing strength each day of the sun, and she adjusted the parasol over the pram to keep baby Mauro in shade and she had Francesca walk in the shadow of her body. The forecast on Radio Uno had claimed there would be rain later, then promised clear weather for the rest of the week. In a couple of days it would be warm enough to lie on the beach and go into the sea, and get some of the bloody sun onto the white of her legs and onto her arms and shoulders, and onto the bruises and scabs. Put it on the list, Charley, sun lotion. The children would like it, going to the beach. She left Francesca at the kindergarten.

Through the shopping list. Tomatoes, cucumber, salami, non-fat milk, potatoes and oranges, apples . . . She ticked each item on her list. There was a *farmacia* on the road below the piazza, near to the Saracen tower.

She wondered if the habit of coming each morning with the children and the baby to the piazza and the shops and the school and the kindergarten meant she was now recognized. The old man who sat on his chair under the black umbrella that protected the ice blocks around his fish, he nodded gravely to her, and she flashed him her smile. Angela only bought fish on Friday mornings, and then from a shop. Charley promised herself, if Angela were out for lunch one day, if Charley had the responsibility to make a hot meal for the children, then she'd buy fish from the old man with the black umbrella. She was on her way to the *farmacia* for the sun lotion when she saw the photograph.

On the newspaper stall, on the front page of the *Giornale di Sicilia,* in color, was the photograph.

The photograph leapt at Charley, caught at her throat. She stood numbed in front of the newspaper stall.

In color, in the photograph . . .

An old woman with thick legs held in bulging stockings wore the widow's clothes of black. She sat on a small household chair and her arms were held out and her head was raised as if she screamed anguish. Behind her was a priest, behind the priest was a crowd of watching men and women and children, behind the crowd were the tall and wide symmetrical lines of the close set windows and narrow balconies. In front of her was the motorcycle that tilted on its stand. In front of the motorcycle with the red fuel tank and the eagle's head was the body. In the foreground of the photograph, in color, was the head of the body. Blood was spread on the ground from the mouth and throat of the head of the body.

She rocked on her feet. The eyes of the woman behind the counter of the newspaper stall glinted at her.

It was a young head. She had not seen the bloodied head before. The head had been hidden from her by the helmet with the dark visor. A young and thin-faced head that was topped with a wild mat of close curled hair was clear in the photograph. Charley knew the motorcycle. When the boot had lashed her, when she had loosed the strap to her handbag, when the glove had groped for her necklace, her face had looked up at the motorcycle.

Her words, Charley had said to Giuseppe Ruggerio, "Just wish I'd been able to scratch his eyes out or kick him in the bloody balls."

Her words, said to show that she was the big brave kid, "I mean to leave him something to remember me by."

She turned away. She thought that if she stayed to look at the photograph, in color, she would vomit on the street in front of the newspaper stall. It was the motorcycle she remembered, definite. Charley walked past the old man who sold the fish from under his black umbrella. She pushed the pram to the pier where the fishermen worked on their nets and at their boats. She stared out over the water. Such peace. As if it were a place for poets, a place for lovers. Scattered cloud shadows of turquoise on rippled water. Christ, she understood. The power of life and the power of death was around her. Axel had told her of the power. No poets around her, no lovers. Men were around her who would kill a boy, cut his throat, leave him with his motorcycle outside the block where his mother lived, and go to eat their dinner.

She murmured, "Don't worry, Axel Moan, I am learning. I am learning that there is no love, no kindness. Satisfied, you cold bastard? I am learning to be a lying bitch. I am learning to survive. That boy had, Axel Moen, quite a decent young face and probably where he came from there was no bloody chance of work or opportunity, what I've had. So he's dead, and I am learning. I am learning that any bloody sentiment is just a luxury for tossers. My promise, I have forgotten the kindness of Angela Ruggerio and the love of small Mario and Francesca, I will stitch them up, do my best. It's what you wanted, right? You wanted me to learn to be a lying bitch. Satisfied?"

She pushed the pram to the *farmacia* and she bought the sun lotion for the beach. She pushed the pram to a bar where there was a telephone and she rang Benedetto Rizzo and told him when she had next had a free day, and she didn't speak of love and kindness. Charley doubted that, until the day she died, she would forget the photograph in color. While the first drops of rain fell, she pushed the pram back up the hill to the villa.

As snails and slugs come out after rain has fallen and leave tacky and shining tracks on concrete paths that merge and cross and meander, so too moved the surveillance teams.

The man from Catania was first followed by a taxi driver as he went in search of a declaration of loyalty from his brothers. When the man from Catania journeyed on across his territory to gain the same declaration from his wife's brothers, he was watched by three *picciotti* on motorcycles. The driver of a bread delivery van shadowed the man from Catania as he drove the big Mercedes, weighed down by the reinforced windows and by the armor plating inserted in the doors in his cousin's repair yard, reported on a meeting with his *consigliere*. A student from the medical school of the university watched the home of a *capodecino* in the Ognina district of the city to which the man from Catania came. All of them, the taxi driver and the *picciotti* and the driver of the bread delivery van and the student, were paid by the man from Catania. All of them betrayed him and reported his movements to Tano who belonged to Mario Ruggerio.

Slugs and snails, after rain has fallen, move from their cover, leave the

177

slime of their tracks, ignore the hazard of poison pellets, crawl forward to kill the plants that have no defense.

Slugs, on their bellies, on the move . . . A woman who cleaned the living quarters in the *carabinieri* barracks at Monreale had met with Carmine before her slow and labored walk to work. Her husband's first cousin's son, from Gangi in the Madonie mountains, was held awaiting trial in the Ucciardone jail . . . Her security clearance to clean the living quarters of the barracks had not picked up the blood association, but the vetting had not been strict as her work did not give her access to sensitive areas of the building. On her knees she scrubbed a floor. Two pairs of feet were in front of her, waiting for her to move her bucket of soaped water. When she looked up she saw the uniformed *carabiniere* officer and his colleague who was dressed in the clothes of a building artisan. With reluctance, she pulled the bucket to the side of the corridor. They passed her by, as if they did not notice her. She knew the names of all of those officers whose rooms she was not given access to, and the door of the room of Giovanni Crespo was locked to her. When she reached the end of the corridor, where the doors opened out on to the car park behind the barracks, she could see the small builder's van, washed in the driving rain, with the ladder tied to the roof frame and with the stepladder jutting up between the seats. The cleaning woman had a poor memory. In pencil, on a scrap of paper, she wrote the registration number of the van. Without the help of a good lawyer, her husband's cousin's son would spend the next eight years of his young life in the Ucciardone jail.

Snails, crawling in their slime, on the move . . . The leader of the surveillance team of the *squadra mobile* had read the reports of each of the teams working the Capo district, pitifully brief reports. He took those reports to the apartment of the magistrate. Three days gone, seven days remaining, nothing seen that related to Mario Ruggerio. The magistrate smiled his thanks, seemed to expect nothing else, as if he realized that only ten days of surveillance with only three teams of men, only three men to a team, made the task impossible. What surprised the leader of the surveillance team, there was a brightness in the gloom of the room that the magistrate had made his workplace. The brightness was from flowers. He knew, everyone knew, that the magistrate's wife had gone north with the children, but the flowers were a woman's choice. The flowers were on the magistrate's desk, right beside the computer. He told the magistrate that his men were the best, that they were all committed, but that the time and resources given them were inadequate. When he left the magistrate, he went through to the kitchen where the bodyguards smoked and played cards and endlessly read the newspapers' sport pages and drank coffee, he asked after his friend, the *maresciallo*. But his friend was away on a course. There was nothing more to keep him in the apartment. He left the guards and the lonely and isolated man. He hurried through the splattering rain to the Capo district and his own shift. It would be a bastard, wandering through the labyrinth of alleys in the rain.

It was three years since Peppino Ruggerio had needed to drive to Castellammare del Golfo. Then to eat a meal with his brother and to meet with a foreigner, today to take lunch with his brother and to meet with a foreigner. It was the Spanish language that Mario had needed three years before, and again today . . . There was a direct route from Palermo to Castellammare del Golfo, on the *autostrada* to Trapani, and there was the country way. His choice, today, was to use the remote road, narrow and winding, that went south of Monte Cuccio and north of Monte Saraceno.

The clouds had gathered from early morning, darkening and spreading from the west. The rain had hit the car as he approached Montelepre. Not until he had driven his big car out through the villa's high gates had he made the snap decision to go to Montelepre on his way to Castellammare del Golfo. He came as a pilgrim to Montelepre, the town hanging as if on crampons from the rock face. He came today to Montelepre to see the birth place and the living place of Salvatore Giuliano. It was right that he should come to Montelepre as a pilgrim and consider and learn the lessons of the life of the bandit, and of the death. Nothing changed in Sicily. The lessons remained, as apposite now to Peppino and his brother as they had been nearly half a century before to Salvatore Giuliano. He came in humility, as a pilgrim, that he might better learn the lessons.

Peppino parked his car outside the Pizzeria Giuliano at the top of the town, where the roofs were merged with the cold rain cloud. He looked around him. He was huddled under the drop of his raincoat, which he had draped over his head and his shoulders. The rain bounced from the cobbles and spattered his shoes and the legs of his suit trousers.

There was no money in the town, no opportunity, no work. The rain water gushed down the steep alleys around the Chiesa Madre and the terraced homes faced with cracked ochre plaster seemed to crumble before his eyes. A lesson: there had been money in the town when Salvatore

Giuliano, the bandit, had lived here, but with his death it was gone. A lesson: Salvatore Giuliano had been hunted by many thousands of *carabinieri* and troops from the regular army, and it was said he was responsible for the killing of more than four hundred men, and he had been destroyed when his usefulness had expired. He did not know where in the town Giuliano had lived, did not know in which piazza Giuliano had organized the firing squads that executed men for "disrespect of the poor." A lesson: Giuliano had been the master tactician, the expert in the art of guerrilla warfare, and he had been an angel to the poor of the town, and he had been the handsome idol of the young women, and nothing could have saved him. A lesson: far from home, abandoned by those who claimed to be his friends, in Castelvetrano to the south, the cheek of Giuliano had been kissed by the Judas-man Gaspare Pisciotta. A lesson: a man who had been a king was shot to death as a dog in a gutter. Peppino stood in the high streets of Montelepre and the rain ran in his shoes and wet his socks and soaked the trouser legs at his ankles. It was important to him to learn the lessons. Power ended when usefulness expired. A man climbed fast, reached beyond himself, and fell fast. Trust was a kiss and a kiss was followed by a bullet. He felt the better for it, felt as though the lessons learned by a pilgrim made him wise and more cautious.

Old men hurried past him, sheltering under black umbrellas, and they would have clapped when Salvatore Giuliano had stood in the piazza, and they would have spat when the news had come of his death like a dog in a gutter. A girl watched him. She had a young plain face, she was fat at the ankles, she wore a cotton dress and had no coat against the rain. She stood outside an *alimentari* and held a plastic shopping bag. Her father would have told her, and her grandfather, of the fate of the man who climbed too fast, ended his usefulness, and was betrayed. Her mother would have told her, and her grandmother, of the beauty of the face of Salvatore Giuliano. He wondered if the girl dreamed of the bandit. When the rains were finished, when the evenings were hot, did she go to the cool grass under the olive trees, did she look for him? For her, did Salvatore Giuliano live, a fantasy between her thighs? Did she worship him, conjure him to her, an imagination in the hair of her belly, when she was alone in the darkness? He laughed, in grimness, in privacy, as he looked at the young woman's face. Ridiculous. OK for the Americans, OK for the Presley freaks . . . Another lesson: after the Judas kiss and the death like a dog in the gutter, perhaps there was no memory of him other than the fantasy and imagination of a girl with fat ankles. He walked back to his car. There was a last lesson to be found by the pilgrim in Montelepre: Gaspare Pisciotta, the trusted deputy of Giuliano, had betrayed him, had died in the medical room of the Ucciardone jail in shrieking agony, poisoned by strychnine. It was important to learn the lessons of what had gone before.

He drove down the switchback road out of Montelepre, away from the rain-drenched homes and the legend of Salvatore Giuliano.

He went through Partinico, and on through Alcamo, where there had been the first refinery for Turkish poppy paste, and his brother's share of the wealth from the refinery in Alcamo had been the beginning of the cash cascade that had paid for an education at the university in Rome and the school of business management in Switzerland. Alcamo stank of sulfur fumes, said to have been released by the fractures caused by a minor earthquake. Money held in the cash deposit markets in New York and London, good and long-term and steady-earning money, had come from the refinery in Alcamo.

He drove down toward the sea.

He would not have dared to ask his brother whether he ever hesitated to consider the lessons to be learned from the life and death of Salvatore Giuliano. Would not have asked Mario whether he had climbed too fast, whether his usefulness could expire, whether he feared the Judas kiss, whether he believed that death would come in the way that a dog was shot in the gutter. He had the same fear of his brother that infected all men who met Mario Ruggerio.

He took the road that bypassed the old town and the harbor.

Each time he was in his brother's company, Peppino guarded himself. He was held at the same distance as Carmine and Franco and Tano, and the other heads of families, and the affiliates. When his brother smiled or praised, then Peppino was the same as every other man and felt the warm flow of relief. When his brother glanced at him in savagery, then Peppino felt the same terror as every other man. He could not quantify the personality of his brother, could not determine the chemistry that made him, and every other man, flush with relief at a smile and cringe in fear at a criticism. His brother had control over him, over every other man. Peppino knew that he could never walk away from his brother.

He parked in a lay-by above the town. Below the crash barrier and the wilderness of wild yellow flowers was the sharp crescent of the harbor from which once, in the good times, the fishing fleet had sailed for the tuna grounds, but the tuna had been fished to near-extinction. In better times, the same boats had left the same quayside and gone to sea at night without lights and collected the floating bundles of Turkish opium paste dropped by merchant ships, but there were no longer refineries on the island. The small town, shrouded in rain mist from Peppino's vantage point, with its good times, and better times was solid in the heritage of the organization his brother would control. It was said that in a single decade, from 1900 to 1910, one hundred thousand immigrants had sailed from that small harbor to the promised land of America and made the bedrock of the associations that Mario now collaborated with. It was said of Castellammare del Golfo in the 1940s that four out of every five adult males had been in jail. It was said in the 1950s, in the first great war between the families, that one of every three male adults had committed murder. Nothing was said of Castellammare del Golfo today, it was a town from which history had passed on. Peppino waited . . . Often he looked in the mirror in front of him, and he checked the side mirrors, and he saw no indication of surveillance.

Franco drove the car that came alongside.

In the backseat and sitting low down, uncertain and insecure, was the Colombian who had made the long journey.

Tano was in a second car, with more men.

Franco made the gesture for Peppino to follow. He eased his car forward, nudged down the steep road after their brake lights. Franco and Tano would know the same thrill when praised by his brother, and the same hopeless fear when caught in the savage glance of his brother.

Close to the Norman castle, at the heart of the harbor's crescent, facing onto the small blue-painted boats that no longer fished for tuna, was a *ristorante*. On the door of the *ristorante* was the sign CHIUSO.

They went quickly from the cars, the rain beating on them, into the *ristorante,* and Peppino saw the way that the Colombian's eyes flickered around him in nervousness. Carmine met them, and they walked straight through the empty interior, past the empty tables, to a back room. Peppino saw, dumped on the floor, the open box that housed the counter measures receiver. The back room would have been swept the night before, and again that morning. Everywhere that Mario Ruggerio did business was cleaned first to his satisfaction.

His brother rose from the laid table. His brother smiled with kindness and friendship and held out his hand to the Colombian and he gestured for the Colombian to sit and, himself, eased the chair back.

Peppino sat opposite Mario and the Colombian, from where he could lean forward and translate the Sicilian dialect into Spanish and the Spanish into the language Mario understood.

Because the Colombian, Vasquez, merely toyed with his food, Mario Ruggerio ate all that was in front of him. Tano never left the back room, Franco brought the food from the kitchen. Because the Colombian snatched at morsels, Mario ate slowly. Because the Colombian gulped the Marsala wine, Mario drank only water. His demeanor was of respect, offering the warmth of hospitality, but he dominated. Peppino watched and admired. The Colombian, Vasquez, had come to Sicily, made the long journey because the expertise of Mario Ruggerio was needed. Peppino felt a certain pride for his brother who had never traveled outside the island. The questions he translated, spoken by Mario in a tone of unmistakable gentleness, were the snake's questions.

"From your journey, you are not too tired?"

The Colombian had flown from Bogota to Caracas, from Caracas to São Paolo, from São Paolo to Lisbon, from Lisbon to Vienna, from Vienna to Milan. He had driven from Milan to Genoa. He had sailed on the ferry from Genoa to Palermo.

"Is there such a great problem when you travel?"

There were many problems.

"What is the reason for the problems?"

The Americans were the problems.

"In what way are there problems from the Americans?"

Because the DEA were in Colombia.

So mildly, as if he was an old man who was confused, as if the Americans were not a problem that concerned him in Sicily, Mario Ruggerio shook his head in surprise.

"And I hear that there is crop destruction paid for by the Americans, is that so?"

The Americans were paying to have the fields of coca sprayed from the air.

"And I hear, also, that Gilberto Rodriguez Orejuela has been arrested, is that true?"

He had been arrested.

"And his brother, Miguel Rodriguez Orejuela, arrested?"

Both the brothers were under arrest.

"And Henry Loaiza Ceballos?"

He, too, had been arrested.

"And the treasurer of the cartel?"

He had surrendered.

"Were they careless? How is it possible for so many principals to be arrested?"

They had been arrested because they had used telephones, and the DEA had brought in interception technology.

A sad smile of sincere sympathy seemed to spread on Mario Ruggerio's face. He made a gesture with his hands that implied he himself would never have been careless and used a telephone. Peppino translated. He recognized the domination his brother achieved by making the Colombian confess to the weakness of his organization.

"You are disrupted?"

Business continued, with difficulty.

"What weight can you provide?"

They could provide five tons.

"Refined?"

It would be five tons refined.

"Where is delivery?"

The delivery would be on the European mainland.

"The price, what is the price?"

The price was $6,000 a kilo.

He had taken, as he had asked the question, as Peppino had translated the question and the answer, his Casio calculator from his pocket. His finger, for a brief moment, hovered over the "on" switch. He listened to Peppino's translated answer. He was laughing. He put the calculator back in his pocket. His rough hand was on the Colombian's arm, squeezing it as he chuckled.

"I hope you have a good journey home. Before you go home I hope you will find someone else to do business with, and I hope you enjoyed our humble hospitality. There was a dear friend in Agrigento with whom you might have made a deal, but he has disappeared. There is another dear friend in Catania, but I hear he has lost the stomach for such trading. Of course, if you have a vest to deflect the bullets, if you have a tank to travel in, you could go to Moscow. You know that if you do business with me, then it is honest business. There are others in many countries who would like what you have on offer, but you would have to be confident that you would not be cheated. If you do business with me then there is no possibility of deception." What was the price he could offer?

The Casio calculator was back on the table. The screen lit. Mario's thick fingers were off the Colombian's arm and tapping the keys.

"Four thousand per kilo. Do you take it or do you leave it?"

The figure was acceptable.

"Four thousand per kilo, delivery over six months, through Rotterdam and Hamburg docks. You can do that?"

That, too, was acceptable.

"I pay on delivery. You understand that I cannot pay for what is not delivered past Customs at Hamburg and Rotterdam?"

That was understood.

"How do you wish to be paid? I can send you heroin, refined or unrefined, for distribution in the North American market. I can make available aircraft, 707s, a Lear executive, whatever, that you can sell on. I can pay through cash transfers, or in stocks or government bonds, whichever currency. How do you wish it?"

The Colombian, Vasquez, wished it in cash, invested and cleaned in Europe.

"For cash, invested and managed in Europe by ourselves in proxy for you, we charge commission of 10 percent of profits. Do you wish to use our facilities?"

The offer was accepted.

Peppino did not need the calculator. His mind made the calculations. For five tons of cocaine, refined and delivered through the docks at Hamburg and Rotterdam, the Colombians would be paid the sum of $20 million. Five tons of cocaine would be sold on to the dealers and pushers and peddlers for a minimum of $45 million. When the dealers and pushers and peddlers released it on the streets of London and Frankfurt and Barcelona and Paris it would be worth $70 million. Initial profit, for minimum risk, was $25 million and the little bastard, the Colombian, would have known that the old man beside him was perhaps the one individual boss in Europe in whose word he could place trust. Plus $20 million dollars for investment, a profit margin of perhaps 8 percent a year for total safety. A further income of $0.16 million . . . There had been no raised voices, no vulgar bartering. It had been, Peppino thought, a demonstration of mastery and control. The deal was closed with a handshake, the Colombian's small-boned fist wrapped tight in Mario Ruggerio's broad fingers. The number of a post-office box on the island of Grand Cayman was given for further communication.

The Colombian was led away.

Mario lit his cigar and coughed. Peppino made the equation. His brother's deal would make a profit of $25 million, plus the commission on the investment, and his brother had no requirement for the money. There was no luxury that he sought, no means to spend the money. The money was the symbol of power. As if to tease Peppino, because Peppino wore a good suit and a good shirt and a good tie, his brother spat phlegm onto the floor and laughed.

Then, like it was an afterthought, something that could so easily have slipped his mind, Mario bent toward the floor and lifted a supermarket shopping bag from beside his feet, put it on the table, pushed it toward Peppino and tipped a handbag from it. Each stitch of the handbag had been sliced, each panel of the handbag had been cut open. With the handbag were a purse and keys and cosmetics and a credit card and a diary, and tied to the strap was a thin cardigan.

"She is what you called her, a simple girl, but it is necessary always to be careful."

Peppino took the *autostrada* back to Palermo. When he saw the road

185

sign for Montelepre he slowed and he looked up toward the mountains. He could not see the town that was built against a rock fall because the rain cloud was too low. What always astonished him about his elder brother was his capacity to merge the broad frame of strategy with the minutiae of close detail, the strategy of a deal with a profit margin of $25 million along with investment commission, and the detail of a hired help's handbag. He had gone that morning to Montelepre, stood in the rain and walked on the cramped streets, to search for lessons. He accelerated when he was past the turning. His brother had learned all the lessons that could be taught.

The journalist from Berlin had to run to keep alongside her, and her small floral print umbrella covered only her head and shoulders. The rain ran on his head and his neck. To the journalist it was quite ludicrous that he should have to conduct what he regarded as an important interview on the street and in the rain with the woman who claimed to have founded the first of Palermo's groups for anti-mafia education. He had waited a week for the interview. Three times it had been postponed. She was a finely built middle-aged woman, dressed well, and she constantly covered with a slipping scarf the jewelery at her throat. While she talked, while she gave him his interview, she was incessantly yelling into a mobile telephone. The journalist from Berlin was a respected correspondent of his newspaper, he was a veteran of the Russian invasion of Chechenia and of the Gulf War and of Beirut. Palermo defeated him. He could not see the mafia, could not touch it, could not feel it. The woman he had waited to interview did not help him to see, touch, feel. A passing car's tires carved through a rain lake and drenched his trousers.

"... I founded the anti-mafia group in this city at the time of Falcone's *maxi-processo* in 1986. I believed the trial of four hundred mafia men would make a turning point. I was a systems manager with Fiat in the north, but I gave up my job, very well paid, to return to Palermo. I have big support in some of the most hard suburbs of deprivation, I am particularly well known in Brancaccio. My car, my Audi, I can leave it in Brancaccio and it will not be destroyed ... I accept that the mafia offers more to young people than the state offers, but it is possible to go forward through education, through the school environment ... I have to accept also that progress is very slow, and the culture of the mafia is very strong, but a sense of duty drives me to continue ... I can take you to Brancaccio next week, and you may sit with me while I meet mothers of young boys who may be exposed to the contamination of the mafia, that would be most interesting for you ... I beg your pardon? Do the criminals regard us as a threat to their way of life? Of course we are a threat to them, through the policy of education and group meetings . . . If I am a threat why am I not silenced? I think you are impertinent, I think you are not truly interested . . ."

Charley sat on the patio.

The rain of the day had gone, its legacy fresher and keener air. The light came low and settled as a creeping bloodred rug on the water of the bay. It should have been a vision for her to marvel at, it should have been a place where she sat and enjoyed a vista of magnificence, but she was alone and she could not find beauty in the sun's fall across the crescent bay. She had given the children their meal, they were in their rooms. Later she would read to them. Angela had taken the baby to the main bedroom. Most of the day Angela had been in the bedroom. Perhaps company enough for her was the sleeping baby and the pill bottles. The joy of the Roman summer had been in the company of Angela Ruggerio, and the woman was now withdrawn, as if overwhelmed. One reference only, fleeting, to the great bloody god of family, and nothing to follow it. Sitting in the fresher and keener air, turning the reality in her mind and twisting it, Axel Moen's concept of a visit to the villa by Mario Ruggerio seemed to her to be laughable. She murmured, "Sold a bum steer, Charley, sold shop-soiled goods." Her fingers rested on the button of the wristwatch. Would he hear her? Would he be running? Such a small action, to press the fast code onto the button. The sun far out and bloodred on the bay was losing strength. So bloody alone . . .

The car came.

The gates were opened.

The car came forward. The gates were slammed shut, a jail's gates closing.

The car came up the drive and stopped.

Peppino was home. He was half across the patio when he saw her alone and in the shadow. He stopped, he turned, and the smile spread on his face.

"Charley, on your own—you are better?"

On her own so that she could better think of reality and cure herself of the danger of complacency, and better live the lie. "Been a long day, just sitting quietly."

"Where is Angela?"

The villa was in darkness. Angela was in her room and maybe she was weeping, and maybe she was at the pills. "Having a little rest."

"I have some good news for you."

Good news might be that there was a ticket for a flight, that she was being sent home, that she was returning to a room in a bungalow, to a classroom in a school. "What's that?"

As if he played with her, as if he mocked her. He laid his briefcase on the patio table. He went to the doors and switched on the patio light. The light on the patio made the night fall around her. He opened the briefcase. Smiling such sweetness.

"I told you there was a small possibility that your handbag might be dumped. We are very lucky. It was left near the Questura. Damaged, but containing your possessions."

So close to her, his waist and his groin beside her head and her shoulders. He took her handbag and her cardigan from the briefcase, and each panel of the bag had been cut, and he said that the thief must have searched for a hidden compartment and something more valuable, and he put the handbag on the table. He gave her the keys and the lipstick and the powder box, and the credit card, and the diary, and he said that thieves were interested only in cash, and he gave her the purse, empty.

Peppino said, "I am really so sorry, Charley, for your experience."

She blurted, "He's dead. The boy who robbed me, he's dead."

His eyes narrowed. She saw the tension in his body. "How can you know that?"

Axel Moen would have kicked her. Axel Moen would have slapped her. For a moment she had played the clever bitch. She had come out into the shadows of the patio, into the keener and fresher air, to clear her mind, and bloody waded in with two feet. She hesitated. "I'm being silly. There was a photograph in the paper. A boy was dead in the street in Brancaccio."

Soothing. "But you did not see his face, you said he wore a helmet."

Retreating. "I thought I recognized the bike . . ."

"They are scum, Charley. They live on drugs to give them the courage to rob young girls and old women. They steal many bags in a day to feed their revolting habit. Perhaps, before he had stolen from you, or afterwards, he thieved from a young girl or an old woman whose father or sons had influence. They lead a very dangerous life. You know, Charley, once there were some young boys, not aged more than sixteen years, and they stole the bag of a woman who was married to a *mafioso*. This criminal identified the boys and had them strangled and had their bodies left in a well. You are a caring person, but you should not concern yourself with the life or death of such scum."

"Maybe I was wrong about the motorcycle. I am very grateful to you for taking so much trouble."

His stomach and his groin rested against her shoulder. Always the smile on his face. He took another handbag of soft leather from his briefcase and laid it in front of her.

"But you have no handbag. I took the liberty, Charley, to replace your handbag. Please, open it. You see, I remember also that your necklace was broken. I cannot replace its sentimental importance to you, but I do my poor best."

Angela stood in the doorway, and her hair was disheveled from sleep and the blouse hung loose from the waist of her skirt and she was barefoot. Angela watched.

Inside the handbag was a thin jewelery box. Charley opened the box. The necklace of gold shimmered. She took the necklace in her fingers, felt the weight of the gold links. As she lifted it and draped it at her throat. Peppino, so gentle, took it and fastened it, cold against her skin.

Angela turned away.

"Thank you," Charley said. "You are very kind to me."

Peppino asked her to excuse him. He said that he was away early in the morning, that he must pack his bag.

She sat under the patio light, alone, and gazed out over the darkness. God, she wanted so much to be loved and to be held . . .

TO: D/S Harry Compton, SO6.
FROM: Alf Rogers, DLO, Rome.

GIUSEPPE RUGGERIO, Apt 9, Giardino Inglese 43, Palermo, interesting because the heroes of the *carabinieri* do not have files on him, Guardia di Finanze likewise, BUT a lady from SCO no doubt fancies my body. RUGGERIO is a financial fixer, listed by SCO as living at Via Vincenzo Tiberio, Rome. No criminal history. (Unsurprised that locals have lost him—workload, long lunches and inadequate resources to track movement, cannot cope.) BUT, BUT if we talk about same joker, he is younger brother of MARIO RUGGERIO (Grade A mafia fugitive). Because I am overworked, underpaid, reliant only on my considerable charm, difficult for me to learn more. DEA/FBI (Rome), underemployed and overpaid, have big dollar resources hence greater access than me—do I check with them for more GIUSEPPE RUGGERIO information?

Two pints, please, in Ferret and Firkin.

Luv, Alf.

Harry Compton stood over Miss Frobisher as she typed the reply for transmission to Rome. She oozed her disapproval, as if in the days of her youth, the days of carrier pigeons, certain standards prevailed in communications. And he didn't care what she thought and ignored her curled upper lip because the excitement ran with him.

TO: Alfred Rogers, DLO, British Embassy,
Via XX Settembre, Rome.
FROM: D/S Harry Compton, SO6.

Two half pints coming your way. We concerned about use of your body with lady from SCO—could lead to Post-coital Stress Disorder and her requirement for counseling. Do not, repeat NOT, share our interest in GIUSEPPE RUGGERIO with Yankee cousins, nor with locals.

Bestest, Harry.

10

"DO I REALLY NEED TO KNOW this?"

The grievance, the story of the "pressurization" of a young girl from south Devon, was climbing the ladder. From detective sergeant Harry Compton to his detective superintendent. From the detective superintendent to the commander of SO6. From the commander to the Assistant Commissioner (Specialist Operations). At each step of the ladder the grievance was elaborated.

"I rather think, Fred, that you do—and I'd like to hear the views of colleagues."

Around the polished table, bright in spring light thrown through the plate glass windows, in a room on the sixth floor of the New Scotland Yard building, were the commanders who headed what they believed to be the élite specialized teams of the Metropolitan Police. Comfortable in their chairs, at the end of their monthly meeting, were the men who ran Anti-Terrorist Branch, International and Organized Crime, the Flying Squad, Special Branch, Royal and Diplomatic Protection and SO6.

The Assistant Commissioner moved behind them, refilling the coffee cups from a jug. "Right, shoot then."

"Am I peeing in a gale? None of you knew that the DEA, our American friends, were recruiting in this country?"

Gestures and shrugs and shaken heads from Anti-Terrorist Branch and Special Branch and from Royal and Diplomatic Protection, hardly likely to have been blown past their desks. The Flying Squad man said that he rarely dealt with Americans, when he did it was FBI and, snigger, then when he was short of a good meal on expenses. International and Organized Crime denied flatly that he had joint operations with DEA currently in place.

"Get to the point, please."

"Of course, Fred. I am not a happy man, I regard this situation as intolerable. American agencies are based in this country on the very clear understanding that they operate through us, and that means they do not have the right to run independent operations. What we know, no thanks to them, is that a DEA operative flew here from Rome in pursuit of a letter sent from Palermo to a Miss Charlotte Parsons, teacher and first job, aged twenty-three, just a naïve youngster. The letter the DEA tracked was an invitation to Miss Parsons that she should go to work for a Palermo family as a childminder and nanny. The DEA wanted that girl in that household, they worked her over, they put quite intolerable pressure on her. A member of my team has established, at stiletto point, from Devon and Cornwall, that the locals behaved like cowboy bullies at the DEA's request, took the girl on a tour of druggie housing estates, to a morgue to gawp at an overdose victim, to a hospital to visit a narcotic-addicted baby. That is disgusting abuse of influence."

"I've not heard anything that I want to know."

"It is our belief that Miss Parsons is now exposed to real hazard. Whether you want to know it or not, sir, you'll hear it. Sorry, but this gets up my nose. Not any old family, no, but a quality, tasty, mafia family. Miss Parsons has been kicked by the DEA's boot into the Ruggerio family. She has gone to work for the younger brother of Mario Ruggerio."

The commander paused for effect. Not that Royal and Diplomatic Protection, paring his nails, knew who the hell Mario Ruggerio was, nor Anti-Terrorist Branch who was swirling the coffee dregs in his cup, nor Special Branch. Flying Squad was gazing at the ceiling, frowning, trying to gather in a memory of that name. He gestured to International and Organized Crime.

"Yes, I know the name. It's in most of that interminable stuff the Italians chuck at us. Mario Ruggerio is coming through, fast-track, to fill the vacuum created when the Italians finally put a bit of their act together and lifted Riina and Bagarella. Same mold as Liggio or Badalamenti or Riina, a peasant who's made the big time."

"And a killer?"

The commander of the International and Organized Crime unit grimaced. "That's integral to his job description. Riina had a hundred and fifty killings down to him, forty done himself, mostly manual strangulation. Goes without saying."

"Kills without hesitation, kills what threatens?"

"Reasonable assumption."

The Assistant Commissioner rapped his silver pencil on the table, hard. "Where are we going?"

"When challenged their Country Chief gave us a right put-down. I'll tell you where we're going. The DEA, the Americans, have inserted this innocent young woman, untrained and with zero experience of under-cover, into a prime and vicious mafia family. Stands to reason, the Amer-icans see her as an access source. Christ, down there the Italians cannot even protect their own judges and magistrates who're ring fenced with hardware—what sort of protection are they going to be able to give this young woman? Nil."

The lips of the Assistant Commissioner pursed. "Do I not hear a lit-tle of injured pride? Wasn't there a word of a little spat in Lyon last year, the Europol conference, rather a public put-down of one of your peo-ple? I would hope, most sincerely, that we are not edging into vendetta country."

"I resent that."

The Assistant Commissioner smiled, icily. "And we are, I believe, sup-posed to be on the same side, wouldn't you agree?"

"There are potential consequences. Because of the possible conse-quences, I felt it my duty to raise this matter. A naïve and pressurized young woman has been inserted into an area of hazard. Take the bad side. She's blown out. Our little Miss Parsons, of south Devon, schoolteacher, ends in a ditch with her throat cut and her body showing all the marks of sadistic torture. Italian media with their cameras crawling all over her body, our papers and TV picking it up. Going to try and wash our hands of responsibility, are we? Going to say, are we, that she was put in this po-sition of real danger from right under our bloody noses, and we did noth-ing? A lamb to the slaughter, and we did nothing. Would you, gentlemen, sit on your backsides if it were your daughter? 'Course you bloody wouldn't, you'd raise the bloody roof."

"What do you want?"

The commander of SO6 said, "Try me on what I don't want—I don't want bloody Americans running riot in this country on recruitment trawls, short of consideration of consequences."

"I said, what do you want?"

"I want Charlotte Parsons extricated. You postured that we were on the same side. The same side is cooperation. They didn't cooperate. I want the Americans sent a message. I want Charlotte Parsons brought home."

"Shit in the fan," from Special Branch.

"Would kind of knock down bridges," from Royal and Diplomatic Protection.

"Poor friends the Americans if peeved. They'd not enjoy interference," from Flying Squad.

"I rely on their help, be reluctant to see them offended," from Anti-Terrorist Branch.

"I'm taking SO6's position, we'd be hung on lampposts if it went sour, if she came back in a box," from International and Organized Crime.

"I want her brought home, before harm comes to her."

Silence fell. The Assistant Commissioner stared out of the window. Where the buck should stop was in front of him, in front of the neatly piled papers on which his silver pencil beat a slight tattoo. The commander of SO6 watched him. The commander was going no higher, but the Assistant Commissioner was five years the younger and would have his eyes on the top job and the knighthood. Squirming, wasn't he? Working over the tangent lines of consequences. Wriggling, wasn't he? The commander of SO6 felt himself in good shape because the responsibility for consequences was now shared with his superior and with his colleagues . . . But the bastard, true to form, fudged.

"Before we confront the DEA, I want more information on Mario Ruggerio."

"Like what he has for breakfast, what color are his socks?"

"Steady, my friend—detail on Mario Ruggerio. There's a slot in my diary same time next week, just the two of us. I'm sure it'll keep for a week. Don't want to run before we can walk. And, so that I can better evaluate, I want to know more about this girl."

"Hello—wasn't any trouble finding it."

She had lied again, but then the lying was a habit. Good at lying, Charley had told Angela that it was important for her to go again to Palermo. So reasonable a lie, so fluent. "It's the same as if you've been a driver in an accident, Angela, then you have to get back behind the wheel as quickly as possible. It's really kind of you to offer, but I need to be alone, just as I was alone then. I don't want anyone with me. I want to walk the streets, get it out of my system. Tell you what, Angela, I'm not taking that lovely bag that Peppino bought, I'm going to buy one of those stomach things that tourists have. I don't know what time I'll be back . . . I have to do this for myself, I have to put it behind me."

The gardener had let her out of the gates, the bloody "lechie," and she had almost run down the street from the villa in impatience to get clear of the place. Peppino was long gone, driven away while she was still asleep. She had already taken the children to school and kindergarten. The baby was sleeping. When she'd talked to Angela, lied, she'd thought that Angela was close to spitting out the great confidences. Little Charley, she could be a vicious little bitch, she hadn't wanted to hang around and hear the confidences, nor the weeping. Stick to the pills, Angela, keep popping them. She had run to get the bloody miserable place behind her . . .

"You are well, recovered?"

"Do I look awful?"

"The bruise has gone, the scratches are good." He was so damn solemn. "You do not look awful."

"Aren't you going to invite me in?"

She grinned, she felt mischief. He was so damn solemn, and so damn shy. He stepped aside with courtesy.

"It is a big mess, I am sorry."

"No problem."

She was early. Because she had lied well and run fast down to the sea shore in Mondello she had caught the bus before the one she had planned to take into Palermo. She wore her tight jeans that hugged her waist and contoured her stomach and thighs, and the T-shirt with the wide cut at the neck that left her shoulders bare. She stepped through the door. She had taken time, unusual for her, with her lipstick and with her eyes, and she wondered now, as Benny let her into his apartment, if Angela would have registered that she had been careful with her cosmetics, might have known she lied. Perhaps it was a mistake to have been careful with the lipstick and with her eyes, and maybe Axel bloody Moen would have slagged her off for it. The apartment was a single big room of an old building. A small cooker in a dark corner beside a washbasin that was filled with dirty plates and mugs, a wardrobe and a chest, a single bed not made and with the pajamas lying dumped on it, a table covered with papers and a hard chair and an easy chair that was covered with clothes. There were posters on the walls.

"I was going to clean it, but you are early." Said as an apology, without criticism.

"It's lovely. It's what I don't have . . ."

It was what she yearned for, her own place and her own space. A place, space, where she was not a lodger in her mother's home, not a paid guest in Angela Ruggerio's villa.

She was a lying little bitch and a bullying little bitch. She had invited herself into his life. She went to the basin and ran the water till it was hot. She didn't ask him if he wanted his plates and his mugs cleaned, she did it. She ignored him and he hovered behind her. The poster on the wall above the basin was of a pool of blood on a street and the single slogan, "Basta!". When she had finished at the washbasin she went to the bed and stripped back the sheets and saw the indentation where his body had been, and she made the bed neatly and folded hospital corners as her mother had taught her. She put his pajamas under the pillows. It was a narrow bed, a priest's bed, and she wondered if it whispered when his body moved on it, a chaste bed. The poster, fastened with Sellotape to the wall above the bed, was of white doves rising. She didn't look at him, it was her game with him, and at the chair she started to fold the clothes and to take a suit back to the wardrobe. In the bottom of the wardrobe she found dirty shirts and socks and underpants; she assumed he went back to his mother every week with a bag of washing. She turned. Beside the door was a poster on the wall showing, black and white, the long snaking column of a funeral and mourners. Her hands were on her hips, Charley grinned. It was her cheek.

"Another Sicilian boy who needs a woman to look after him. Christ, how did you survive in London?"

She had embarassed him. "Where I lived, there were men and there were women. I used to bring back the left over chips at the time we closed the McDonald's—they would have been thrown away. I fed the women, the women did my washing and they cleaned my room."

"Grieves me to hear there's a male chauvinist piggery alive and well in London."

He did not understand. He stood awkwardly. What she liked about him, he seemed so bloody vulnerable.

"So, that was me saying thanks, saying you were brilliant. Thanks for being brilliant when everyone else looked the other way. Now, I've been really conscientious, I've read the guidebook. I want to see the *duomo,* the Quattro Canti on the Marqueda, the old market in the Vucciria. I want to get to the Palazzo Reale for the Cappella Palatina. I reckon we can do the Palazzo Sclafani as well before lunch. Big lunch, a good bottle, then if we've the stamina—"

"I am sorry . . ."

"What for?"

"You did not give me a telephone number for you. I could not telephone you." He hung his head. "I do not have the time to walk in Palermo."

Charley blinked. Trying to be casual, trying not to show that she had looked forward to the day, the escape, ever since she'd rung him. "So you got your room cleaned up and you don't have to do the guide bit, lucky old you. I suppose that makes us quits."

He fidgeted. "I have the day off from the school. It was my intention to escort you around Palermo. I have the school, and I have another life. For the work of my second life I have to deliver, urgently, some things."

"I'll come."

"I think, Charley, you would find it very boring."

As if he sought to dismiss her. Shit. She could turn round and she could walk out of the door. As if he told her that she intruded.

"Try me. What's the second life? I've nowhere else to go. I mean, the *duomo* has been there best part of a thousand years, expect it'll keep another week. Where have you got to go?"

"I have to go to San Giuseppe Jato, and then to Corleone . . ."

"Heard of Corleone. Interesting, yes? Never heard of the other one. Is that countryside?"

"It is into the country." He seemed to hesitate, as if undecided. She gazed back into his quiet almond colored eyes. Come on, Benny, don't play the bloody tosser. She could not tell him about the claustrophobia she had fled from for a day. "I am a teacher, but I have also other work. I have to see people in San Giuseppe Jato and in Corleone, and I think you would not find it interesting."

"Then I'll sit in the car."

"My other work is for the Anti-Mafia Co-ordination Group of Palermo—how can that be of interest to you? Can we not fix another day?"

Her chin jutted. Axel bloody Moen would have told her to run, not to bother to close the door, run and keep running. The watch was on her wrist. His fingers, twisting, were fine and gentle, a pianist's. She should never relax. His face was of narrow angles, but without threat. She understood the posters on the walls of the room. She challenged him.

"I think that might be of more interest than the *duomo*. I think I might learn more about Sicily than from the Quattro Canti and the Cappella Palatina, yes?"

As a response he went to the door and unhooked his anorak. He looked around him, as if his room had been invaded, as if he had been boxed and bullied, as if he were too polite to complain, from the basin with the cleaned plates and mugs, to the chair from which the clothes had been taken, to the bed that had been made. He led her outside and onto the wide landing above the old staircase. He turned two keys in the heavy mortice locks.

"Safer than Fort Knox."

So polite. "I'm sorry, I don't understand."

"Just something you say, forget it, something silly. Benny, why do you work against the mafia?"

He started to walk to the staircase. He said, matter-of-fact, "Because the mafia killed my father. When he was driving me home from the school, they shot him."

———

Pasquale had run along three blocks from where the bus had stopped, and run into the building, and not waited for the elevator, and run up three flights of stairs, and leaned panting against the wall while he waited for the apartment door to be opened. He was three minutes late. He had not overslept, he was late because his car had not started, battery gone, and the man on the floor below who had the jump leads was not at home, and . . . He was let inside. Jesu, and they were waiting for him, and they wore their vests and they carried their guns. The magistrate, Tardelli, sat in a chair in the hall with his coat on and his briefcase between his feet, and he looked up at Pasquale and there seemed to be sympathy on his face. The one who drove the chase car scowled and looked at his watch pointedly. The one who rode passenger in the chase car stared at the ceiling as if he did not wish to have a dog in this fight. The one who sat in the back of the chase car stared at him hard and without pity.

The *maresciallo* said, "We would have gone without you, but it is against regulations to go when we do not have the full complement. Dr. Tardelli has been obliged to wait for you."

Panting hard. "Car didn't start—battery gone—my apologies, *dottore*—one minute, please, one minute . . ."

He felt sick. He felt like dirt. He stumbled away to the spare bedroom, still decorated and furnished for two of the children taken by their mother back to the north. Beside the wardrobe, empty, was the reinforced-steel gun box, full. Fumbling for the key that opened the gun box, and knowing the angered presence of the *maresciallo* behind him. Jesu, the wrong key. Finding the correct key. Taking out the Heckler & Koch, dropping a magazine that clattered on the wood floor. Blessings to Mary the Virgin that he had refilled the magazine the previous evening because it was routine that magazines must be emptied at the end of each shift or the mechanism might jam, groveling thanks to Mary the Virgin that he had refilled the magazine. Snatching the Beretta 9mm with the shoulder holster from his numbered hook, and more magazines for the Beretta, and a box of bullet shells for the Beretta because he had not filled those magazines. Crouching down and searching in the heap for the bulk of his vest. He stood. He had to peel off his coat, sling the harness of the holster for the Beretta. He had to heave the vest over his head, heavy onto his shoulders. He had to throw on his coat again. The box of bullet shells for the Beretta into the coat pocket, and the emptied magazines. He slapped one magazine into the machine pistol, and the eyes of the *maresciallo* were fixed on him, and, thank Jesu he remembered to check that the safety was on. He breathed hard. For a moment he stood. Blessings to Mary the Virgin. He came back into the hall and they all stared at him, and there was no movement to the front door, still business to be completed inside, and the expression of the magistrate was sympathy and the shrug which said the matter was beyond his intervention.

The *maresciallo* beckoned with his finger, an instruction to follow. Pasquale went after him into the kitchen. The *maresciallo* pointed with his finger. The flowers his wife had bought, the bright flowers he had taken to the magistrate's apartment, were dumped in the trash can under the sink. Alive, still with color, thrown away.

"You are, Pasquale, pretend to be, a close protection guard. You are not the servant of Dr. Tardelli, nor are you his friend. Whether you have sympathy for him or a dislike of him, you do your job, and you take your money, and you go home. What you do not do is snivel sentiment. I will not have on my team any man who, remotely, becomes emotionally involved. I come back from three days away and I find that little presents, little gifts of flowers, have been given. Your job is to protect Dr. Tardelli, not to make a friendship. He is a target, a principal target, and the best way to protect him is to remain aloof from him as a personality. We do not travel each day with a friend, but with a *paccetto*. To you he should be just a parcel that is taken from here and delivered safely to a destination. You should not try to wrap ribbons around a parcel. You are on assessment, on probation, and I remember everything. If you are ready may we, please, leave?"

Pasquale stumbled out into the hall. He had told his wife how much the magistrate, poor lonely man, had appreciated her flowers. There was the clatter of the guns being armed, the static and distorted chatter of the radios. They took the *paccetto* down to the street, to the cars.

"Do you want to wait in the car, or do you want to come in?"

"I think I'd like to walk around the town—I mean, it's sort of famous, isn't it?"

Benny said, somber, "You should not walk alone around the town. Afterwards, if you want, I can show you the town. For now you should come inside with me or you should wait in the car."

Charley said, sullen, "If I should not walk around the town without an escort, then I will come with you."

She snapped her body out of the tiny AutoBianchi car. She stretched and felt the sunlight. Of course she had heard of Corleone—she had seen the first film at college with Marlon Brando starring, and she had seen Godfather III on video with Al Pacino starring. They were parked near the *carabinieri* barracks. Pretty bloody ordinary it looked to her, Corleone. They had come into the town on a wide open road from San Giuseppe Jato where Benny had left her in the car while he collected a photocopier from a small house. He hadn't talked much as he had driven through the countryside between San Giuseppe Jato and Corleone. Axel Moen would have kicked her backside because she had bullied her way into Benedetto's day. It had been spare and empty talk on the road after they had left the confined tight streets of San Giuseppe Jato. They had talked of the horses that grazed the grasslands in the expanses between rock outcrops, and of the wild flowers of yellow and burgundy, and of the handkerchief sized plots of vines growing where a vestige of cultivation could be scratched in soil above the stone, and there had been hawks climbing above the outcrops of rock which she recognized as the kestrels and buzzards of home. Benny didn't know what the horses were used for, didn't know what the flowers were called, didn't know what was the sort of grapes grown here, didn't know about the hawks. She had been talking, nothing talk, about the hawks on the cliffs at home, when he had told her abruptly, almost with rudeness, to be quiet, and he had slowed, and then she had noticed the military road block, and they had been waved through, boring . . . If Sicily was a battleground, if it were the place of Axel bloody Moen's war, then she had only a single military road block to tell her of it. They had driven into Corleone on a broad street and past a street market that seemed to sell everything from clothes and furniture to vegetables and meat. No troops and no police, nothing that was familiar from television of war on the streets of Belfast. The sun was on her back and she walked after Benny as he carried the photocopier.

So she had annoyed him by pressing her presence. So he could bloody well put up with her. Doggedly, she followed.

They went by a school and there was a clamor of kids' voices from inside. There was an emblem on the wall of the school, not large and not ostentatious, of doves flying. She read "AI MARTIRI DELLA VIO-LENZA"—hardly a monument to war, not much of a mark for a battleground. He went through the open door of a house. Quite sharply, he gestured for her to sit on a hard chair in the hallway, and he left her there as he went through to an inner room. She heard the excitement of women's voices, and two women came into her view and were hugging Benny and thanking him and he carried the photocopier into the room where she could not see him. Their voices clattered in her ears. She thought she was excluded—bugger that. She stood, she walked to the door. They were bent over the old photocopier and Benny was on his knees and plugging it to a socket. Their voices died. She was excluded because she was a stranger. There were the same posters on the walls that she had seen in his Palermo room. Benny flushed. He told the women that the Signorina Parsons was English, that he had met her when she was attacked in the street, that he had promised to show her the antiquities of Palermo, but the photocopier had to be delivered.

"So she is a tourist in Corleone?"

"So she comes to see the wickedness of Corleone, and perhaps to send a postcard?"

Charley rode the sneers. She turned away, defiant, and took her seat again. She heard their laughter from the room.

Perhaps they teased Benny, for bringing a tourist. He was distant when he came out of the inner room and each of the women made a show of kissing him on the cheek, and she thought their politeness to her was a charade. Did he screw them? Did he screw anyone on that narrow little priest's bed? Did Axel Moen fuck anyone on any bed? She smiled, lied her simplicity with a smile.

Out in the street, innocent and simple, "What do they do?"

"They have a newsletter to issue, but the photocopier is broken. They produce a newsletter for the Anti-Mafia Co-ordination Group of Corleone."

"Is it a big circulation?"

He matched her innocence and simplicity, but there was no lie. "Very small, very few people, which is why we have such humble resources, a room and two women and a photocopier. In Corleone is the culture of the mafia, but you would not know that. It is the heart beat of the mafia— from Corleone to Palermo, from Palermo across the island, from the island to the mainland, from the mainland to Europe and over the ocean to America. It is why we speak of the octopus, with many tentacles, but the heart beat of the beast is here. The *sindaco* speaks against the mafia, the priest denounces the mafia from the church, but that is politics and religion, and they change nothing."

"When will something change?"

He smiled, innocent and simple. "I will know that something has changed when we need two, three photocopiers."

"Tell me about Corleone. Show it to me."

He looked at her. His eyes that squinted against the sun were grave as if he feared that she mocked him. "Forgive me—so that you can buy postcards and boast to your friends at home that you were in Corleone?"

"Please, walk me through the town?"

"Why?"

Axel bloody Moen would have kicked her arse, would have said that she lurched on the edge of disclosure, would have snarled that she was at the cliff face of complacency. "It's just, what I've seen, a street and a market and a school and blocks of apartments and a barracks. I can't realize what you are fighting against."

"I think you would be bored."

"I want to understand."

They walked to the piazza. Old men watched them from under the bars' awnings and youths sat astride their motorcycles and eyed them from under the shade of palm trees. The sun beat on Charley's arms and on her shoulders.

"It is the town of Navarra and then of Liggio and then of Riina and then of Provenzano. Now it is the town of Ruggerio. To you, the stranger, it will appear like any other town. It is unique in Sicily because here no businessman pays the *pizzo*. Literally that is the small bird's beak that pecks for a little food but on the island the *pizzo* is the extortion of money for 'protection.' In the 1940s, after the liberation from Fascism, a good statistic for you to carry home to your friends, there were more murders here per head of population than in any town or city in the world."

Charley said quietly, "You don't have to talk me short, Benny, like I'm only a tourist."

At the start of the old town, where the streets darkened and narrowed and climbed to the left and fell to the right, Benny bought her a coffee and a warm roll with ham and goat's cheese. His voice was a murmur. "I will tell you one story, and perhaps from the one story you will understand. It is not the story of Navarra who was the doctor here and the parents of a twelve-year-old boy brought the hysterical child to him and told the doctor that the child had seen the killing of a man, and Navarra injected the child with a 'sedative' that killed him, and then apologized for his mistake. It is not the story of Navarra. It is not the story of Liggio who was a cattle thief before he developed the heroin trade of the mafia. And not the story of Riina who ordered the killing of the bravest of the judges and drank Champagne in celebration. Not the story of Provenzano who is called the *trattore* here, the tractor, because of the brutality of his killings. It is not the story of Ruggerio. Come."

She gulped the last of the roll. She wiped the crumbs from the front of her T-shirt. She followed him out onto the street.

"You will hear, anywhere in Sicily, the stories of Navarra and Liggio and Riina and Provenzano, maybe you can hear the story of Ruggerio. You will not be told the story of Placido Rizzotto, but that is the story that will help you to understand."

They walked down a narrow street, on cobbled stones. The balconies with wrought-iron railings pushed out from the walls above them, seeming to make a tunnel. Watched by an old man, watched by children who stopped their football game, watched by a woman who paused to rest from the weight of her shopping bags. No sun on the narrow street.

"First he had been in the army, then he was with the partisans. Then he came back to Corleone where his father was at a low level with the mafia. Placido Rizzotto returned here with opened eyes from the mainland. He became a trade-union organizer. The mafia detested the trade unions because they mobilized the *contadini,* worked against the mafia's domination of the poor. To the Church he was a communist. To the police he was a political agitator. Perhaps the mafia and the Church and the police were distracted, but Rizzotto was elected as mayor of Corleone. Do I bore you, Charley?"

They stopped. They were near to the church, a huge edifice at the front, and a bell tolled, and black dressed women hurried for the door but swiveled their heads as they went that they might better watch them. Ahead of them was a bank. A fat-bellied guard leaned against the door of the bank and his finger rested loosely in his sagging belt that took the weight of his holster, and he watched them.

"Ten o'clock at night, a summer night. A friend calls for Placido Rizzotto at his father's home, invites him to come for a walk. All the men in the town are walking in the Via Bentivegna and the Piazza Garibaldi. He was betrayed by his friend. He strolled along the street, and one moment his friend was with him and the next moment his friend was gone . . . All of the men walking that evening on the Via Bentivegna and the Piazza Garibaldi saw Liggio approach Rizzotto, saw the gun put into Rizzotto's back. All of the men, all of those who had voted for him and who had cheered his speeches, watched him led away as if he were a dog led to a ditch to be killed. Are you bored, Charley?"

The ravine was in front of them. Water tumbled from above them and fell, and the flow was broken by dark stones that had been smoothed over the centuries. Above the ravine was a fortress of decayed yellow stone built on the flat top of a straight-sided rock mass, dominating. They were alone now with the ravine and the fortress, and the watchers were behind them.

"The people went home. They emptied the streets and they locked their doors and they went to their beds. They had surrendered. And Rizzotto did not even threaten the mafia, or the Church, or the police, to all of them he was merely a nuisance. It was in 1948. Two years later his body was recovered by the fire brigade from here. His father could identify him from the clothes, and from his hair that had not been eaten by the rats. A man who had seen Rizzotto taken away said, 'He was our hero and we let him go. All we had to do, every one of us, was to pick up a single stone from the street, and we could have overwhelmed the man with the gun. We did not pick up a stone, we went home.' It was in 1948 and the culture of fear is the same today. Does my story bore you, Charley, or do you better understand?"

Her father had been three years old when Placido Rizzotto had been pitched, dead, into the ravine below. Her mother had been one year old. She had walked along the same street as the man with the pistol in his back, walked on the same pavements as the watchers had stood on, walked past the same doors through which they had hurried and which they then locked, walked past the same windows in which the lights had been extinguished. Charley Parsons, twenty-three years old, stared down into the ravine below the mountain rock on which the ruin of the fortress stood, and she thought the smell of a rotted corpse was in her nose, and she believed that at last she knew the scent of evil. Christ, yes, she understood.

"Where does Ruggerio come from?"

"From near here."

"Can I see where he comes from?"

"For what reason?"

She lied, so easily. "What you said, Ruggerio is the present. Right, I'm just a bloody tourist imposing on your day. It's what tourists do, go and visit a birth place. If you don't want to . . ."

"It's not difficult."

Each afternoon, after the quarry had closed, after the drivers of the big dumper lorries had gone and the stone-crushers had been silenced, they blasted for the next day's supply of broken rock.

The quarry was cut into the mountain across the river from San Giuseppe Jato and San Cipirello. It was where the expert tested all the explosive devices he designed.

In open ground, clear of the rock face where the dynamite charges were set, the expert and Tano had carefully parked the two cars. The car the expert had driven was an old Fiat Mirafiori. The car that Tano had driven, level with it but separated by ten meters of space, was a Mercedes, low on its wheels from the weight of the armor plate lodged in the doors. The distance between the cars had been measured with a tape, because the expert had said that in matters involving explosives detail was important.

The two explosions were finely synchronized. At the moment that the dynamite in the quarry face was detonated, the final digit of a six-figure number was pressed by Tano on his mobile telephone and the connection was made to the telephone pager set into the bomb on the backseat of the Mirafiori.

In San Giuseppe Jato and in San Cipirello, the people would have heard the explosion, what they always heard at that hour, and a reverberating echo would have masked the second explosion.

The great dust cloud from the quarry face had barely settled when the expert and Tano went forward. The Mirafiori had disintegrated, beyond recognition. The Mercedes was what interested them. The two parts of the Mercedes, and it had been sliced precisely in half, burned fiercely.

They laughed, the expert and Tano, they were bent at the waist and shouting their laughter at the quarry face from which the last of the fractured rock fell.

By the morning, before the quarry opened for work, the parts of the Fiat Mirafiori and the halves of the Mercedes would be buried under waste stone away to the side of the quarry.

"Do you have a camera?"

She started, she had been alone with her thoughts. "A camera? Why is it important?"

Snapping, and she thought now he was frightened. "Charley, I asked, do you have a camera?"

"No."

It had been brilliant country. Bigger hills than those on Dartmoor that she knew, greener than Dartmoor, but the same wilderness. They had stopped once, when she had told him to stop. She had stood beside the car, leaned against the warmth of the body of the car and gazed across a field of wild flowers to the shepherd with his flock and his dog. Something of the Bible of a child, pastoral and safe, and she had heard the symphony of the chime of bells from the sheep, and the shepherd had sung. She thought it would have been an old song, handed down from his family, a song of love. The shepherd never saw them as he sang. Benny had stood beside her, close to her. Her sort of place . . . And the town was above them, and now the nervousness played in his face.

"I don't have a camera. Why?"

"Where we go, you should not use a camera—doesn't matter."

On a winding road Benny drove toward Prizzi. He parked in a lay-by. The town stretched away from them and above them, a mosaic of yellow and ochre tiled roofs so dense that the streets were hidden.

Benny looked around him, locked the AutoBianchi. He took her arm, fingers on her elbow. He hurried her.

They were on a climbing street. The window of a *macellaio* took her eye, the thin strange cuts of meat, unfamiliar to her, and her arm was pulled.

There would not have been room for cars to pass in the road. Two terraced lines of three-story homes, wooden doors set under low arches, balconies fronting shuttered windows, plaster and paint in yellow and orange and primrose. He walked fast and she skipped to keep up with him.

"You don't stop, you don't stare." His lips barely moved as he spoke and his voice hissed as if fear caught him. "The sixth house beyond the black painted drainpipe. You have it? Don't turn your head. That is the house, the balconies one above the other, of the parents of Mario Ruggerio. It is where they live, with the brother of Mario Ruggerio, who is simple. You see it?"

He walked and he looked straight ahead. Charley saw a cat, low on its stomach, run from them.

Nothing moved in the street, but the cat. The sunlight fell on the house that had been identified for her. The door to the house was open and she heard, fleeting, a radio playing. She smelled, fleeting, the cooking of vegetables. Was that it? Was that the bloody lot? No Mercedes, no gold taps, no 9-inch cigars, no rottweilers, no Harrods curtains, bloody hell . . . She defied him. Charley stopped in front of the open door and she twisted her head to look inside, and her arm was jerked half out of the socket at the shoulder. Only the sound of the radio and the smell of the cooking. When she was three doors past the house, he loosed her hand.

"Was that quite necessary?"

"Where do you think you are? Do you think you are at Stratford-upon-Avon? Do you think the Japanese come here in buses? Are you stupid?"

"You don't have to be rude."

"I am rude because you are stupid."

He was breathing hard. His lips twitched in nervousness. He walked fast. They came to the end of the road, where more roads, identical and mean and close, veered away into shadow. Christ, where were the people? Where were the kids?

"I am sorry, Benny, I am sorry if I am stupid. Spell it out, start with the camera."

His feet, a stamped stride, clattered on the cobbles. "You see nothing here, but you are watched. There would be, of course, a police camera on the street, but that is not important. Because you do not see anybody it does not mean you are not watched. Behind doors, behind blinds, behind shutters, behind curtains are people who watch. It is the home of the family of Mario Ruggerio, and Mario Ruggerio is responsible for the deaths of many people. Such a man does not leave his family vulnerable to the vendetta of revenge. Because you do not see something it does not mean that it does not exist. If you had a camera, and took a picture of the house, it is likely that we would be followed, and the number of my car would be taken. I do not want, because you are stupid, to have those people match the number of my car with my name. To a man like Mario Ruggerio the family is the most important feature of his life, only with his family does he relax. We should not stay here."

"Where is the wife of Ruggerio?"

"Two streets from here. Why do you ask, why are there so many questions?"

"Just me, I suppose. Always talked too much."

"It would not be sensible for strangers to walk from the street of Ruggerio's parents direct to the street of Ruggerio's wife."

"I was only asking . . ."

He was walking back toward the car. Charley followed.

"In the story you told me, Placido Rizzotto was killed because he was a nuisance. Was your father a nuisance?"

"Not a threat, only a nuisance, which is enough."

"With the work you do, Benny, are you a nuisance?"

"How can I know? You know when you see the gun."

"Benny, damn you stand still. Benny, what is your dream?"

He stood, and for a moment his eyes were closed. Charley took his hand. She waited on him. He said, soft, "I see him standing, and his head is hung in shame, and the handcuffs are on his wrists, and he stands alone without the backing of his thugs and his guns and his acid barrels and his drugs. He is an old man and he is alone. Around him are the children from Sicily and Italy, from all of Europe and from America. The children make a ring around him with their joined hands and they dance in a circle around him, and they laugh at him and they reject him and they jeer at him. My dream is when the children dance around him and have no fear of him."

He took his hand from hers.

Peppino had the dollars. They had the bank.

He had not met Russians before, and he thought them quite disgusting.

Peppino had the dollars on deposit in Vienna. They owned the bank in St. Petersburg.

His first meeting with Russians was in a hotel room near the railway station in Zagreb. The two Russians wore big gold rings on their fingers, as a whore would, and bracelets of gold at their wrists. Their suits, both of them, were from Armani, which had brought the only dry smile to Peppino's face. The one smile, because he did not think they were people to laugh at, and the cut of the Armani suits did not disguise the muscle power of their shoulders and arms and stomachs and thighs. He assumed they carried firearms, and assumed also that a single blow from the gold-ringed fist of either of them would disfigure him for the rest of his life.

The deal that his brother envisaged was for $50 million to go from deposit in Vienna to their bank in St. Petersburg, and on then into investment in the oil-production industry of Kazakhstan. They owned, they boasted in guttural English, the Minister for Petroleum Extraction and Marketing in Alma Ata. His brother said that the Russians were not to be ignored, that alliances must be forged, that every effort must be made to find routes of cooperation. The cooperation would come through the investment in Kazakhstan, and in return Peppino was instructed to offer facilities to the Russians for the cleaning of their money. For himself, Peppino had only a view of money. His brother had the view of strategy. The strategy of his brother was for cast-iron agreements between La Cosa Nostra and these Russian thugs. His brother said that within five years these crude and vulgar people would have control of the biggest opium-growing area in the world and the biggest arms factories in the world, and their power could not be ignored.

They frightened Peppino.

And he was nervous also because they seemed to have no care for their personal security. It was Zagreb, and the Croatian capital was a place for scams and for racketeers, but the city offered easy access to the FBI and to the DEA. He had doubted their hotel room had been swept. He had come into the room and he had immediately turned the TV satellite rubbish up loud and he had sat himself beside the TV's loudspeaker, and they had to strain to hear him against the blast of game-show sound. Himself, he was against dealing with these people, but he would never contradict his brother.

He glanced at his watch, gestured with his hands. He apologized. He must leave for his flight out. Nothing written down, and nothing signed. He must take them on trust. He gave them a fax number in Luxembourg, and told them slowly, as if he was with imbeciles, what coded messages would be recognized. He offered them his hand, and his hand was crushed by each of them.

He stood.

One Russian said, "When you see Mario Ruggerio you should pass to him our good wishes that are sent in respect."

The second Russian said, "Mario Ruggerio is a man we learn from, we acknowledge his experience of life."

Rubbing his hand, Peppino charged away down the hotel corridor. They had spoken in deference of his brother, as if they held his brother to be a great man. What did it say, their respect, of his brother? He hurried across the foyer of the hotel and out into the street for the doorman to call him a taxi. He had thought them coarse, crude, brutal, and they were the men who offered him their admiration of his brother. He lay back in the taxi. He believed he was the messenger boy of his elder brother, coarse and crude and brutal, who owned him.

The telephone was ringing. Charley had been back an hour. The telephone was shrill. Charley was with the children in the bathroom, soaping them and trying to laugh with them. God, where was Angela to answer the phone? Charley was splashing water and making a game with the children and their shrieks did not drown the bell of the telephone. Angela had the second telephone beside her bed—the bloody pills. Charley wiped her hands on the towel. She hurried into the hall, past the closed door of Angela's bedroom.

"*Pronto.*"

"It's David Parsons. Could I speak to my daughter, Charlotte, please?"

"It's me, hello, Dad."

"Are you all right, Charley?"

"How did you get the number?"

"Directory inquiries—are you all right?"

"Didn't you get my card?"

"Just one card. We were worried."

"No cause for worry, I am very well and having a wonderful time."

"Your mother wanted me to call, you know what your mother is for worrying. Charley, there was a policeman came, from London, he wanted to know about the American. We—"

Charley snapped, "Don't talk about it."

She had heard the click on the telephone, and the sound of Angela's breathing.

". . . wanted to know—"

"You are not to call me here again. It is very inconvenient for me to take a telephone call. I am fine, and very happy. I'll try and send more postcards. I'm a big girl, Dad, if you'd forgotten, so don't call me again. Love to Mum, and to you, Dad."

She heard the breathing.

"Charley, we only wanted you to know—"

She put the phone down. Her fingers rested on the watch on her wrist, and she felt herself to be a cruel and vicious bitch. She could picture it in her mind, her father holding the telephone and hearing the purring of the dial tone, and then going into the little living room and away from the telephone on the table below the photograph of her at graduation, and then her father would have to tell her mother that their daughter had brushed him off, as a vicious and cruel little bitch would have, put him down . . . She was Axel bloody Moen's creature. She thought that, one day, she might tell her father of the dream, might tell her father of Benny's dream of dancing children and of an old man in handcuffs who suffered the humiliation of the children's contempt, one day . . .

Angela stood, sleep-devastated, pill-damaged, at the bedroom door.

"Sorry if it woke you, Angela," Charley said, and the cheerfulness was a lie. "It was my dad, I've been a bit naughty with the postcards, he was just checking I was all right."

She went back into the bathroom and took the big towels from the hook. If it were their father in the handcuffs, and their uncle, would small Mario and Francesca be dancing with the dream children? She started to rub them dry.

"It took me time to recognize him—it was the guy who picked her off the street when she was mugged."

"So, she wanted to thank him—why the blow-out?"

"She was with him all day."

"So, she's lonely, and maybe it's her free day—maybe."

"I could kick her arse, hard, with my boot. 'Vanni, she only goes to San Giuseppe Jato, and that's a poison place. Then she goes to Corleone, and that's a bad place. Where in Corleone? She only goes to the Anti-Mafia Co-ordination Group, meets up with those low life deadbeats."

"They are brave people, Axel, committed people."

"Who achieve nothing, might as well jerk off. You know where she went after that, and you could see it on the guy's face, like he was shitting himself, she went to Prizzi."

"So it's a pretty town, it's interesting."

"It's a crap place, Prizzi—there's no scenery that's good, no architecture, no history. She wasn't looking for anything good. For Christ's sake, 'Vanni, she only goes marching off down the little shit street where the big guy's parents are. Can you believe it, she walked down the street where Rosario and Agata Ruggerio live? I mean, is that clever?"

"She's got balls."

"She's got a hole in the head where her brain fell out."

"And you don't trust her?"

"To box clever? Not on this show, no, I do not."

"But, Axel, you have to trust her. That's your problem isn't it, that's the shit on your shoe? She's all you've got. The criticism is irrelevant. And you had an interesting day?"

"A great day, what I really wanted, hiking round San Giuseppe Jato and Corleone and Prizzi."

"But you were there, the chaperone."

"It's my job to be there. She was endangering herself—she could have compromised me. That is not goddam funny."

Back in Corleone, back where he had come with his grandfather and his step-grandmother when he was a teenager. Back where his grandfather had found the "opportunity" and taken the bribes and handed out the gas coupons. He had been dragged by them past the street where his grandfather had pointed out the wartime AMGOT office. He had tracked Charley past the street to which he had been taken as a teenager to meet his step-grandmother's family, and he had sweated that he might be remembered. Ridiculous to believe that he might be remembered, the features of his face recalled, but the sweat had run on his spine.

"Who is the man?"

"He dropped her off in the town. First goddam sense she'd shown, she didn't march him up to the villa. She was going nowhere but home. I went back to his place, asked around."

"Then you came running to me, like you're booked for a coronary."

"He's Benedetto Rizzo, late twenties, built like a streak of piss—he's nothing. You know, she stood in the middle of goddam Prizzi after they'd walked the Ruggerio street, and she held his hand and she looked into his face, like she was hot for him."

"Perhaps you're short of a woman, Axel."

"I don't need shit from you."

But Axel Moen had always been short of a woman. There had been women at the university, just casual . . . There had been a good woman when he was on the police in Madison, working in real estate in Stoughton, and he'd brought her flowers and wrapped chocolates, and she'd been of old Norwegian stock, and she'd made Arne Moen laugh when Axel took her up to the Door Peninsula, and it had finished the night he told her he was accepted by DEA, and going to Quantico because she said she wouldn't follow him . . . There had been a good woman, Margaret, from a publishing house on East 53rd, when he had his head buried in New York with the earphones for the wire taps, and it had taken time but he'd persuaded her to come to the weekend cabins upstate, and they'd done the long hikes and they'd loved, and it was over when he told her he was posted down to La Paz, Bolivia . . . There had been a good woman in La Paz, out of order to mess with a Confidential Informant, a sweet soul and a dedicated mind and with guts, and it was ended when he found her crucified on the back of the door at the airstrip for the *estancia* . . . There had been a good woman, Margaret again, when he had returned to New York with the bullet hole souvenir in his stomach flesh, and she liked to run her finger down the scar when they went back to the weekend cabins, but there hadn't been the love as before, and it had been trashed for all time when he'd said he was posted to Rome . . . There was a good woman in Italy, Heather, out of the Defense Attaché's office in the main building, and she was wiser than the rest and kept him at arm's length, just convenience for both of them, and they went to the parties together, kept the matchmakers at a distance by showing up at the barbecues and the functions, were seen together when they mutually needed a partner, no loving and nothing to finish . . . And there was a good woman, Charlotte Eunice Parsons . . .

"So she makes a mistake, walks down a street, isn't sensible. Maybe she knows that, maybe she won't do it again. She's lonely, she holds a man's hand to whom she has reason to be grateful. You know what I believe?"

"What?"

'Vanni laughed quietly, and whispered, "I think you are jealous of the 'streak of piss,' I think you are jealous of him."

"You are pathetic."

Axel walked out on the best friend he had in Sicily, out of the cinema.

A cinema, dark and showing an unpublicized French language film, empty, was a useful place to meet.

He took a side entrance out. It was a basic precaution, the sort of care that came naturally to him.

He was not aware that, at the front of the cinema, a man watched the builder's van that was parked half on the street and half on the pavement.

TO: Alfred Rogers, DLO, British Embassy,
Via XX Settembre, Rome.
FROM: D/S Harry Compton, SO6.

Action stations this end, going to a war footing. Big politics being played . . . To impress top brass we urgently require up-dater on MARIO RUGGERIO, inclusive of bullshit you so expert in. My last still applies. The Pepsi/peanut-butter brigade are not, repeat NOT, Need To Know. Hope this does not in-terfere with your leisure schedule. Think of Queen and Coun-try as you sacrifice your obese body.

Bestest, Harry.

11

MISS FROBISHER HANDED THE brief message to the detective sergeant.

> TO: D/S Harry Compton, SO6.
> FROM: Immigration Desk (EU entrants), Terminal Two, Heathrow Airport.
>
> BRUNO FIORI (Your ref: 179/HC/18.4.96) arrived ex Zagreb, 18.35 Monday. Regret not delayed as requested.
>
> Barnes, Dawn, Supervising Officer.

He read it five times, then telephoned the Supervising Officer—Barnes, Dawn. She had one of those chill efficient voices. Yes, Italian passport holder "Bruno Fiori" had come off last night's Zagreb flight. Yes, he had been passed through the European Union passengers' desk. Yes, there had been a request from SO6 logged, that Italian passport holder "Bruno Fiori" should be delayed—had the detective sergeant any idea of how many EU passport holders journeyed through Heathrow at that time of an evening? Yes, he had been positively identified, but the logged request for delay had only triggered with the immigration officer, a new probationer, after the passport had been returned. Yes, that officer had shut down his desk and gone through to Customs, Green Channel and Red Channel, but had failed to find Italian passport holder "Bruno Fiori" . . . "There's no requirement for that sort of talk, Mr. Compton. We do our best. If you don't like our best, then I suggest you refer the matter to the Home Office and request additional funding for Immigration (Heathrow). And a good day to you too." So that was a brilliant bloody start to Tuesday morning. Giuseppe Ruggerio back in UK, and the hope had been that if he returned he would be held first on a passport technicality, and then done over by Customs as a "random" check and held long enough for the tail to be scrambled. The brilliant bloody start to a Tuesday morning was a quality foul-up. He hammered down the corridor to his detective superintendent.

He explained.

"Shit."

He showed the communication.

"Bloody hell."

"So what do I do?" Harry Compton could play dumb insolent as well as the next. He stood in front of the boss man, with his hands folded across his groin, and the look of innocence on his face. He knew the track that the investigation had taken, that it had gone up the ladder to the commander, from the commander to the Assistant Commissioner (Special Operations). He knew the spat with the Americans had reached the stratosphere level.

"It's out of my hands."

"What's best then—that I bin it?"

"Don't smart-talk me."

"I rather need to know what I should do. We can put a full surveillance on Blake for a start, go for a full search warrant for Mr. Blake. We can shake him up."

"I'm not permitted to scratch my bloody nose on this one without authorization, not before we've heard from Rome, then I have to have you back down in Devon and a fat lot—"

"What I'm asking, do I do something or do I go back to sifting minimal scams on the good old pensioners' savings?"

Harry Compton thought the biro in the hands of his boss man might just break, big fingers twisting it in frustration. "You're a clever little chap, Harry. Put yourself where I am, ringfenced by the God Almighties, make a suggestion that's half sensible."

"Fair assumption that Fiori, Ruggerio, will go back to his good friend. I'd stake it out, and I'd sweep his paperwork—and I'd belt Alf Rogers hard, so's it hurt, and keep belting him till he delivers."

"So get on with it, and don't embarrass me. You embarrass me and you'll be back helping old ladies across the road."

He went back to his office. He phoned the car pool and the Stores section and told them what he wanted. He scrawled the message, and he was whistling because he felt good, and handed it to Miss Frobisher for transmission.

> TO: Alf Rogers, DLO, British Embassy,
> Via XX Settembre, Rome.
> FROM: Harry Compton, SO6.
>
> Relevant word in my last was "urgently." Stop squeezing your blackheads and do some WORK. Soonest, we must have up-dated biog. on MARIO RUGGERIO with assessment of links to brother GIUSEPPE. I grovel because I need ACTION. I would have thought you have a small window of opportunity for research between getting out of your pit, paying off your women, and the opening of the many bars you maintain in profit. PLEASE . . .
>
> Bestest, Harry.
> P.S. Don't know where this one's going, but it's tasty.

"Would you like to come, Angela?" No, Angela did not want to come because she had a headache and needed to stay in her room.

"Can I leave Mauro?" Yes, Angela would look after Mauro in her room because the baby was asleep.

And Charley was to be certain that small Mario and Francesca did not get cold—God, and it was 70 degrees out there, and Charley had swum off the beach at Bigbury and at Thurlestone and Outer Hope when it was bloody freezing, when her legs and body and arms were goosed. She thought it would do small Mario good, be a useful lesson to the little blighter, to be in the water and struggling because he could not swim. Small Mario was already getting to be, Charley's opinion, revolting and Sicilian, already standing in front of the mirror to check his hair, already posturing at her as if she were merely the hired help. She'd seen it that week, the difference in the child. She might just make certain that he went right under and took the sea water into his nose. It wasn't the child's fault, just the culture of the place . . . "I'll make sure they don't get cold."

So many times each day Charley had to pinch herself, gouge the nails of her fingers into herself, because then she could keep the reality with the fantasy, marry the mundane of life in the villa with the lie that was tight on her wrist. She had the towels and the swimsuits for the children in a beach bag, and in the beach bag were her own underclothes because she had already changed into her bikini, and her sun-lotion tube. She had the bright, colored water rings for the kids, and Francesca had found a toy sailing boat from last summer and small Mario had his football.

Angela's call—they would be all right? "They'll be all right, Angela. Hope your headache gets better . . ."

The gardener opened the gate for them. She didn't think he knew much about swimming. The gardener stank. She didn't think he knew much about washing. She'd get round to it one day, her bikini on the sunbed, and she'd loose the top, she'd give the old "lechie" a sight to keep the bastard awake at night. They went down the hill, and Francesca held her hand and skipped along and small Mario bounced the football like a basketball player. She wondered where he was, where Axel Moen was. Always with her, the dulled routine of minding the children and the exciting sensation of the lie. Twice she looked behind her, tried to be casual, but she didn't see him, didn't see his face nor the hanging ponytail of his hair. It would have been good to be on the beach with him, clear of the kids, on a towel on the sand with him, and in the water with him . . . They went through the piazza and the teenagers were gathered there, boys and girls, with their scooters and motorcycles, and they went past the shops that were opening again for the afternoon, scraping up the shutters, expanding the awnings. She told small Mario, sharply, that he must not bounce the ball as they crossed the road near the newspaper kiosk and close to the Saracen tower. It might have been wonderful, she thought, going through Mondello to the beach if it hadn't been for the bloody watch she wore on her wrist. And with the watch, as if to hammer her, like a replaying tape, was her voice snapping at her father, and her voice taunting the young man, Benny. It might have been perfect, going in the warm sunshine toward the gold of the beach and the blue of the sea, except that she lived the lie. The fingernails dug at the palm of her hand to kill the lie.

Across the road, they walked alongside the beach, hugging the shade of the spread pines. The tide was out and the sand was golden clean. The junk litter would come later, with the crowds, the next month and the month after when all Palermo descended on Mondello. The beach was brilliant to her, like the beaches of Thurlestone and Bigbury before the tourists came. Charley led the way down onto the sand and she kicked off her sneakers and hopped at the sudden heat on the soles of her feet, and the children laughed with her. Small Mario booted his football ahead and they ran after it, whooping and noisy, all the way to the tideline that changed the sand from pale gold to the luster of ochre. Charley was first to the football, never could kick a ball, and it skewed off to the right and careered toward a couple on a towel, and the couple were kissing, the boy under the girl. Lucky cow. She went to the ball, and the couple didn't notice her, cared not to look at her, and she picked the ball up and took it away, as if she were a prim and proper little miss. There were four boys with a transistor radio some yards behind her, and they whistled once, and Charley turned and gave them a single finger, and they jeered once. There was another couple, away toward the new town and the pier, reading magazines.

She put the bag down on the tideline.

The sea ran out into the crescent bay in front of her. Far ahead were the small boats, far beyond the small boats was a car ferry coming toward the docks at Palermo that were hidden by the scree slopes of Monte Pellegrino. From the bag she took a sheet of plastic and laid it flat on the sand, and then she laid two towels on the plastic. The sun beat on her, the strength of the sun on the sand and the water dazzled her. She wrapped her towel, the big towel, around Francesca and undressed the little girl and helped her, full of giggles, into the swimsuit, and to do the same for small Mario she had to pull faces and make a game and beat the shyness of the child. She folded their clothes and put them carefully in the bag. Francesca was puffing her breath into the plastic water-ring and small Mario dribbled the football around the towels. Charley pulled off her blouse and unbuttoned her skirt, and she did not look round to see if the boys with the transistor ogled her. The sun's force caught at the whiteness of her skin. It would have been perfect if it had not been for the lie. Francesca was pulling her hand, wanted to go to the water. Small Mario was tugging her hand, wanted to play football with her.

"A minute, darling, wait a minute. Mario, you can only learn to swim in the water, you can't learn on the beach with a football. OK, please yourself. Play football, don't learn to swim."

The lie hit her. The lie was the destruction of the world of the little boy who wanted to play football, and the lie would be agony to the little girl who wanted to learn to swim. She took the watch from her wrist, slipped it in the bag. The watch was supposed to be waterproof. The watch was the lie.

"You play football, Mario. You don't want to learn to swim, then that's fine."

There was the white ring on her wrist. It was as if she'd shed the lie. She walked with Francesca toward the sea. It was wonderful. She arched her back. The sun's warmth was on her shoulders and her stomach and her thighs. It was perfect.

He had been the day before, and the day before that, to see his *consigliere*. It was a good assumption that he would go again that day. Tano waited.

It was a good assumption that the man from Catania would come again that afternoon, as the crisis isolated him, to try to confirm the support of his *consigliere*. The home of the *consigliere* was a large house, in half a hectare of ground that was enclosed by a wall topped with broken glass set in concrete, and in a private cul-de-sac. Tano watched. Where he waited and watched he could not see the *consigliere's* home—he was on the public road, away from the turning into the cul-de-sac—but he could see with an uninterrupted view the parked car that had been taken the night before from a street in Acireale to the north, near the church of San Pietro e Paolo. If the man from Catania came in his Mercedes then he must drive past the parked car. Tano held the mobile telephone.

Tano was a careful man. He had been able to travel back across the Atlantic twelve years before because he was careful. When the net closed on his friends, colleagues, family, when the FBI sprang the trap in New Jersey, his name had not figured in the files collected around the Pizza Connection investigation. When the *squadra mobile* had mounted for the bastard Falcone the big arrest operation of the year after his return to the island, four hundred men, again his name was not included. It was natural, when it came to his offering his loyalty to one man that he should have chosen Mario Ruggerio. Mario Ruggerio was the most careful man he had worked with. With the care came Tano's loyalty.

He believed himself to be the favorite of Mario Ruggerio, and he had begun to feel in the last months, that he might, one day, succeed Mario Ruggerio—not this year, not next year, not for many years, but one day . . . He thought he was the favorite because Mario Ruggerio had entrusted to him the preparation of the bomb, the planning for the bomb and the detonation of the bomb. When this bomb was exploded he would prepare and plan and detonate the second bomb, and his position as the favorite would be confirmed, not Carmine who had the brains of a wood plank, not Franco who he thought was stupid. His future was linked inexorably with the future of Mario Ruggerio. They climbed together, him a step lower on the ladder, but it was together. He could not bear to imagine failure, slipping on the step of the ladder. Could not bear to consider the iced fury of Mario Ruggerio. But he could imagine, consider, the praise of Mario Ruggerio, the quiet half-spoken praise that brought the thrilled flush through him. Tano would do anything, *alcuna cosa,* to win the praise of Mario Ruggerio, and think nothing of what he had done. Tano had lost no sleep, not a minute of rest in his bed, after he had slit the throat from ear to ear, drawn the sharpened knife through the windpipe, of a street thief.

He saw the Mercedes.

His fist tightened its hold on his mobile telephone, his finger hovered over the button of the final digit of the number built into the telephone pager. The telephone pager was integral to the bomb of dynamite packed inside a wall of ballbearings.

He had held the scrawny legs of the man from Agrigento while Mario Ruggerio had grunted and perspired through the process of strangulation. They climbed the ladder together, and higher. He pressed the button of the final digit . . . The flash of light. The hammer crash of the explosion. The Mercedes picked up and tossed across the road, the impact collapsing the wall that the body of the Mercedes hit. The blue-gray of smoke, the flicker of the fire . . . They were at the top of the ladder.

He saw, in his mind, the pleased smile of Mario Ruggerio, and he seemed to feel the hand of Mario Ruggerio cudgel his shoulder in praise. He was the favorite . . .

The fire ripped through the body of the Mercedes.

Tano walked away.

The journalist from Berlin settled in his seat as the aircraft banked over the sea and then straightened on its course. Looking left from his window seat he could see the urban sprawl of Catania, and looking right he could see the coastline and the mountains of the toe and foot and ankle of the mainland. He reached down and took his laptop from the bag beneath his feet. He was an unhappy flier and felt more comfortable when he worked during a flight, his attention distracted from the syndromes of vertigo and claustrophobia, and it was easy to work with the laptop in the Business Class compartment that his contract guaranteed him. He was not a vain man, but it was part and parcel of his trade that the cover of the laptop should be festooned with the adhesive stickers of airlines he had flown with and cities from which he had reported. The laptop boasted of visits to Beirut and Dhahran and Hanoi and Belfast and Grozny and Sarajevo and Kabul. He started, two fingers, to type, and he was going well and his mind was diverted from the warm air turbulence until the passenger beside him spoke.

"I see you are a journalist, a journalist from Germany, and you have been in Sicily to write about the *malvagita* of our society—did you find that wickedness? It is a strange time for you to be leaving, it is peculiar that you should choose this day to leave. Myself, I am a physician, I work with children, I do not see any foreign journalists, they do not come to my surgery. I presume you have been meeting with our illustrious politicians and with our social workers and with magistrates. Are you confused? I met once with a British engineer working on a sewerage project here. The engineer said that he believed the evil in our society to be a product of imagination, a subject of discussion in the same way that the British are obsessed with discussion of the future of the weather. He told me also that in his part of Britain there was a great inland sea in which there was said to live a huge monster, a creature from pre-history, which was elusive whenever scientific examination was made of the inland sea. But the engineer said that many people desired to believe in the existence of the monster even if there was no proof that it lived. I remember, it was the monster of Loch Ness. The engineer said it did not exist in reality, and he said, his opinion, that La Cosa Nostra was similar, something that is in our imagination. If you are leaving Sicily today then you must surely follow the belief of the British engineer. I said to him, but of course he did not have the time, that he should come with me to the rotten apartment towers of Brancaccio in Palermo, where I work. He should see the children without hope who live under the heel of La Cosa Nostra, who eat when La Cosa Nostra says they should eat, whose parents work when La Cosa Nostra says they should work. And I said that he should go to Rome and Milan and taste the corruption in government and commerce that is brought by La Cosa Nostra. And he should go, I told him, to Frankfurt and London and New York and walk among the addicts of Grade A drugs and think further about La Cosa Nostra. But he said that I made a fantasy, that I saw a monster like the one in the inland sea. You leave now? It was on the car radio just before I reached the airport, a killing in Catania, a bomb. I am surprised that you are leaving at a time when there is proof of wickedness. I am sorry that I interrupt you from your important thoughts. Excuse me, forgive me . . ."

The pulse tone traveled from the antennae on Monte Gallo to the antennae on Monte Castellacio to the antennae on Monte Cuccio and on to the antennae that waited for the UHF signal. It traveled clear, sharp.

His mind was a wreckage of scrambled thoughts because, Christ, it was actually happening . . .

He had come out of the cloister and gone to a stall and bought a carton of juice and taken it to one of the solid seats on the wide and shaded balcony garden at the back of the *duomo,* where the wisteria hung in flower from high walls, where the vista reached down the valley to Palermo and the sea.

The pulse tone, carried from the CSS 900 crystal-controlled two-channel receiver and into the cordless induction earpiece, beat in Axel's skull. His hand shook, tightened on the carton, spilled the juice from the plastic straw onto his shirt and his trousers. The pulse tone hammered its coded rhythm in the confines of the bone of his skull.

It was what they taught at the camp in Laurel, Maryland. "Christ, it is actually happening." They taught the guys of the Secret Service, the bullet catcher guys, that they'd freeze, that they'd lose the power of action because, Christ, it was actually happening. When the headcase had gotten himself up close to the President, gotten his shots off, there was the photograph of one of the Secret Service guys with his arms splayed out and holding his hardware up to the skies, useless and rooted. The guy would have gone through every training simulation that could be thrown up by the Secret Service firearms instructors at the camp in Laurel, and the refreshers, and what he'd done, when the moment came, was shout, "Christ, it's actually happening."

For a moment Axel was useless and rooted.

It was the Immediate Alert code, played a second and then a third time. Shit. He was scuffling with his hands down in the bag at his feet, and the carton was on the ground and spreading juice on his trainers. He had the mobile telephone and he was belting through the numbers. He switched the goddam thing off, couldn't concentrate on the numbers. Axel needed 'Vanni Crespo. Axel needed 'Vanni Crespo because he could receive a pulse tone on the CSS 900 receiver, but didn't carry with him the electronics for location of the signal. Shit. The goddam number was engaged, was whining engaged.

Christ, it was actually happening, and he was behaving like a goddam fool, like he'd freaked. He sat still. He cleared the failed call from his telephone. 'Vanni had the back-up. They would be calling 'Vanni from the communications area, why the goddam number was engaged, they would be identifying the origin location of the pulse tone, and 'Vanni would call him and he must wait to be called. Shit. He had panicked and he felt sour with himself. He waited. He wondered where she was, how she was, and it was goddam hard to wait to be called.

He snatched the paper with the coordinates from the technician. The technician said that he'd not heard the initial signal first hand, been out of the operations area and refilling the coffee machine, but the light on the equipment had alerted him. The technician apologized for the time it had taken him to replay the tape recording of the pulse tone and then to check with the code system, but the code system was in the floor safe, and the technician had had to recall the correct combination for the lock ... 'Vanni snatched the paper from the technician and was running for the door and the corridor.

The technician shouted after him, "But it's confusing—please, listen to me. Three Immediate Alert signals, then a pause, two minutes, then Stand Down, then two Immediate Alert—"

'Vanni ran. 'Vanni didn't stop to listen.

The technician stood in the door to the operations area. He shouted a last time, "Pause one minute, then Stand-by code, and again Immediate Alert. I don't understand."

'Vanni had run faster, fourteen years younger, the length of the Via Carini toward the knot of sightseers and firemen and policemen, toward the bullet spattered cars of the general and the general's wife, of the single *ragazzo* who had guarded him. Of course, then, as he had run the dark, sunless length of the Via Carini he had known he was too late to intervene, to do anything, to be other than helpless. It was a scar on the soul of 'Vanni Crespo that he had stood, panting and helpless, beside the cars and the blood pools, too late to intervene. He did not even know what she looked like, the Codename Helen, tall, thin, fair, short, fat, dark, did not know. As he ran the length of the corridor, slower than he had run the length of the Via Carini, he prayed to his God, soundless, that he would not again be too late to intervene.

He burst, a fool stammering, into the rest room. The men of the Response Squad stared at him through the smoke haze, looked up at him from their magazines and their card games.

"Now, hurry, you bastards. Immediate Alert. We have—God, I hope we have—Ruggerio. We have a location for Mario Ruggerio. Mondello. Please move. It's Ruggerio."

There was the gathering of the weapons. There was the stampede out of the ready room. There was the thunder of boots in the corridor. There was the roar of the cars' engines.

'Vanni, in the backseat of the second car, three more behind him, yelled into his telephone, "Don't tell me what I should have done, I have priorities. I have to respond to the signal. The priority is to move. You are at the *duomo*? The piazza in front of the *duomo,* by the camera shop. Two minutes and I am there, a green Alfetta. If you are not there I don't wait."

The convoy of cars swerved through the gates of the Monreale barracks. Two boys up the road, astride motorcycles, were held back by a uniformed *carabiniere* soldier. They were not interested, there was no builder's van in the convoy. The scream of the tires hung in the afternoon air.

Not necessary, but the excitement raced in 'Vanni, forty-two years old and like a child with the anticipation of a favored present. "It's an open line, Dr. Tardelli, not secure. Our mutual interest, we have a location . . . You should clear your desk for the rest of the afternoon because I hope to bring our friend as a guest to you. Please make yourself available."

The American was running, reaching the camera shop. The second car slowed, and behind it the rest of the convoy hit their brakes. 'Vanni had the door open and he caught at Axel's arm and pulled him inside, and Axel's jerked body tangled with the cable lead that linked 'Vanni's head-set to the communications console beside the driver's knee.

"Still transmitting, confused but transmitting from Mondello. I have these hooligans, and I also have a helicopter coming . . ."

'Vanni hugged Axel.

Of the *squadra mobile* surveillance team working the Capo district, it was the turn of Giancarlo to report in person to the investigating magistrate, Dr. Rocco Tardelli. He was not even asked to sit down. He stood in the room at the Palazzo di Giustizia, and held tight in his hand was the plastic bag of vegetables he had bought along with three lemons. He explained that, in the previous twenty-four hours, the three shifts had seen nothing of Mario Ruggerio, and the man seemed hardly to hear him.

"I regret very much that as yet, *dottore,* we have no trace, but there is still time, and we have to hope that tomorrow, or the day after, is different."

He had expected a head sunk in disappointment, and an exhortation to greater vigilance, but the magistrate merely shrugged. Giancarlo believed it possible that he had interrupted the preparations for the celebration of a birthday because one of the *ragazzi* was at the table beside the draped curtains and was cleaning glasses and another of the *ragazzi,* while Giancarlo spoke, carried in two bottles of Champagne.

He believed, with his talk of failure, he intruded.

The helicopter came over her.

It came in from the sea, a thunder of noise, and Charley caught at Francesca and lifted her from the water and held her close. She could see, very clearly, the figure in the open hatch door of the helicopter, the face covered by a mask with eyeslits, the legs dangling, the machine gun that covered her. She held the child as if to protect her and she did not realize that the plastic water-ring drifted away from her, driven by the rotor blades of the helicopter. She followed the curved flight of the helicopter that was painted in a livery of midnight blue with the big white lettering, CARABINIERE, across the cabin and broken by the opened hatch, she watched the helicopter go stationary, hovering, like one of the big hawks on the cliffs near her home. She looked for the prey of the helicopter.

Oh, Christ. God, no . . .

Through the water, across the wet sand, across to the tideline and to the towels laid on the plastic sheet. Small Mario stood alone and the sand was whipped around him. The helicopter edged on, was above the esplanade and the deep foliage of the pine trees that wavered as if a gale hit them. She carried Francesca, she tried to run through the water and was stumbling and pitching. The helicopter was facing her, a predator. The water splashed around her, and once she fell and the water was in her mouth and nose and Francesca was crying out loud. She ran toward small Mario. There was a loudspeaker shouting at them but she could not hear the words above the helicopter engine. She saw the couple who kissed, the boys who had the transistor, the couple who read magazines, and they all stood and they all, as if commanded, had their hands on their heads. She did not have her watch and she did not know how long she had been with Francesca in the water, how long she had left small Mario with his football on the sand. She burst from the water. Her feet gripped the wet sand and gave her speed. She could see the men who waited in the shadow of the trees.

Beyond small Mario and the couples and the boys with the transistor that still shouted music, under the trees were men and women still as statues and children clutching them and weeping, and men in black overalls and balaclavas holding stubbed guns. She saw Axel Moen . . .

She reached small Mario. He held her wristwatch limply in his hands. The boy gazed, frightened, at the helicopter, at the men with the guns.

Charley took the watch, took it gently, from small Mario's hands. From the shadows under the pine trees, from among the men with guns, Axel Moen gazed at her.

Said quietly, as if she were back in the classroom of 2B and not wanting to drive a child to silence, "What did you do with my watch?"

Said distant and quavering, "Poppa is in England. Poppa said it was one hour behind Sicily in England. I tried to make the time where Poppa is."

"You should have asked me. I would have made it the time where Poppa is."

"I tried the buttons, I could not make it work to Poppa's time."

She put Francesca down. Charley said to the boy, "We have to go home. Please, Mario, fold up the towels."

She faced Axel Moen. She made small gestures. She reeled from the humiliation. She held the watch, she placed it on her wrist and snapped the clasp shut. She was too far from him to see the expression on his face, and the face was in shadow, but she thought that she saw his mind. She pointed to small Mario as he kneeled and dutifully folded the towels. She had failed Axel Moen and the men with guns and the men who flew the helicopter. She crossed her hands, uncrossed them, crossed them again, it was over, it was finished. She took the big towel and started to rub dry the body of Francesca, and in her bikini she was shivering. She saw Axel Moen speak to a man beside him, and the man spoke into a radio. Charley wrapped the big towel around Francesca and dressed her under the towel. The helicopter came overhead, flew out above the sea, then turned toward Monte Pellegrino and Palermo. When it was gone, when she could hear the boys' transistor again, when she had put the towel around her own body and was wriggling out of her bikini, she looked again toward the pine trees beyond the beach. They were no longer there. She shed the bikini top and the bikini bottom. She could not see the men with the guns and the balaclavas. She dragged on her pants and buttoned her skirt, and the towel fell from her as she lifted on her blouse. She could not see Axel Moen. The sun of the late afternoon caught at the skin of her arms and her shoulders, at the whiteness of her breasts . . . Hey, Charley, enough of the damn crawl. Hey, Charley, he was out there, and he was waiting, and he came running.

"Come on, Mario, time for home, time for tea. Come on."

"What was it for, the helicopter?"

Charley said, "They have to do exercises, have to do practice and training. It keeps them busy. It's something to tell your mother, that you saw the *carabinieri* on a training exercise. You won't learn to swim, you know, not by playing football."

Hey, Charley, that's power. He came running.

He put down the telephone. He sat for a moment very still.

In the room with him were Pasquale and the driver of the chase car and the one who rode in the chase car with the machine gun on his lap, and they had all been caught with the infection of his excitement. He sat for a moment with his head buried in his hands.

They knew. He did not have to tell them.

He said, "You know, when Riina was caught, when he had been brought to the barracks, when he realized that he was not in the hands of his enemies but only of the state, he wanted to be told who was in charge. It was at that moment important to him to know that he spoke to the senior man, important to his dignity. Santapaolo, when he was held, he congratulated the arresting officer that he would be on TV that night, as if he would be famous for a day. Leoluca Bagarella, when he was trapped, was said to be in a condition of shock, as if punched on the end of the nose and stunned. I wanted to know how he would be, Mario Ruggerio. For an hour I have sat here and I have allowed myself the fantasy of considering how he would be when I walked into the interrogation room to confront him. It was my hour of vanity. Pasquale, I do not think we require the glasses, and I do not think we will be drinking Champagne—would you, please, take them out because they remind me of one hour of vanity. It is hard not to believe that we snatch at stars . . . Right, I have work, you should leave me."

Pasquale carried the unused glasses through the armor-plated door of the magistrate's office, and the driver of the chase car followed him with the two bottles of Champagne.

He had not told his wife about the flowers, their rejection, but he would tell her of the bottles that were not opened and the glasses that were not dirtied. He felt an idiot because there was moist dew at his eyes. Perhaps the driver of the chase car saw the damp gleam in his eyes.

"What do we do with the champagne?" Pasquale asked briskly.

"Keep it for the funeral," the driver of the chase car said, impassive.

"What funeral?"

"His, yours, ours." There was a growled laugh from the driver of the chase car. The other men of the team were around the table in the corridor. They mocked Pasquale, as if he were an idiot for their sport.

"What sort of shit is that?"

Coolly, the driver of the chase car said, "Don't you know anything? Don't you listen to the radio? Don't you have ears? Worry less about flowers and listen more. Once, in Palermo, there was a jeweler who sold fine stones and necklaces and watches from Switzerland and he had a great fear of thieves so he protected the window of his shop with armor-plated glass. One night a car drove slowly past the shop front and half a magazine from a Kalashnikov assault rifle was fired at the window. High-velocity rounds. And the window was broken, but the car did not stop, nothing was taken. A few days later, from the same Kalashnikov, the same make of bullets, a *mafioso* who rode in his car that was fitted with armor-plated glass was shot dead. The attack on the jeweler's shop was merely to test whether the bullets of a Kalashnikov could pierce reinforced glass."

Pasquale stood holding the tray and the glasses chimed as his hands trembled. He was the object of their sport.

"If you listened to the radio. The *capo* in Catania was killed this afternoon by a bomb in a car that had been parked in a street and was detonated as he drove past. He was a rival for the supreme position sought by Ruggerio, but he was already isolated. That is what Tardelli says. Why a bomb? Why a huge explosion? Why something so public? Because that is not the way of La Cosa Nostra. Why was he not shot, or strangled, or disappeared with the *lupara bianca* into acid or into the bay or into concrete? Why a jeweler's shop?"

Pasquale shook. He thought of his wife and of his baby and of the man behind the armor-plated door who was alone with his work. They were watching him from the table, amused.

"Maybe, Pasquale, because you have his ear, because you bring him flowers, you should tell him to go back to his wife in Udine. Maybe you should request him to use his authority to have every parked car on every road in Palermo towed away. Maybe you should arrange, very quickly, for the arrest of Ruggerio. Maybe, you should resign."

"You talk shit."

They were all laughing as Pasquale stumbled away down the corridor carrying the tray of clean glasses.

"What did you expect?"

"That she wouldn't be so goddam naïve."

The argument started back at the barracks. They hadn't fought in front of the ROS men, had held back their frustration at the failure until they were clear of the squad and alone. And the attitude of the men had been so predictable to 'Vanni Crespo. Into the cars on the beachfront at Mondello, balaclavas pulled off, weapons made safe, another day and another fuck-up, and their talk in the car had been of football and the size of the breasts of the new PA to the *colonello,* and then about the next issue of boots to be given them. Another day and another fuck-up and nothing changed.

"She's an amateur."

"Of course she's an amateur. Picked up on the cheap, fast little run in and out that doesn't cost to the great DEA much. I know she's an amateur and cheap because the great DEA left it to you to run her, and you, Axel Moen, are insignificant."

"Not so goddam precious yourself. You were so naïve. The signal was a mess—Immediate Alert, Stand Down, Stand-by, Immediate Alert. Didn't you think?"

"I thought that she was an amateur. I thought she was in panic. She is not the wonderful Axel Moen, hero of the great DEA. She is a girl, she is untrained. It was reasonable to assume she'd be in panic. For the sake of Christ, Axel, think where you've put her, and what you've told her, and the job you've given her. That would make panic."

They were in a corridor. The argument had been whisper-hissed as the business of the corridor went on around them. 'Vanni took the American's shoulders in his fists and caught the material of the windcheater, and shook his shoulders.

"You make a good argument, 'Vanni, but it's flawed—she wouldn't begin to know how to panic."

But Axel Moen had let his head fall against 'Vanni's chest, and they hugged. They held each other and let the anger slip.

Axel broke the hold. "I'll see you around, some place."

"Take some food. Yes, stay close."

'Vanni called for an escort to take Axel Moen to the gate. He watched him go away down the corridor, carrying the bag with the two-channel receiver and the notes and drawings of the cloister columns of the *duomo,* watched him until he was gone through the door at the far end of the corridor. He could get away with it once, calling out the squad and not filing a report, in triplicate, on white and yellow and blue flimsies, only the once. He went, heavy-footed to his room. Ridiculous, he was a senior officer, he had been in the force for twenty years and two months, and a single failed call-out was like a wound to him. He had been one of the chosen few who had hunted, first, and closed down, second, the terrorists of the *Brigate Rosse,* the scum kids of the middle-class affluents who claimed to kill for the proletariat. He had been especially chosen as the liaison officer to Carlos Alberto dalla Chiesa. He had been nine years in the wilderness of Genoa, murders, drugs, kidnapping. He had been five years now with the *Reparto Operativo Speciale.* And he had held his pistol against the neck of Riina. How many stake-outs, how many charges in a screaming car with the firearms oil in his nose, how many surveillance operations? He thought himself a cretin because this time, among so many, the failure had wounded him. In his room he lay on his bed. It was the habit that he kept to, twenty minutes each afternoon of catnapping. He lay on his bed with a cigarette lit and with the whiskey glass on his stomach. When he had smoked the cigarette and drunk the whiskey, he would set the alarm for twenty minutes ahead and sleep. Later, in the early evening, he would make the telephone call to his daughter in Genoa and talk about her school that he had never visited and her friends that he did not know. In the late evening, with the mobile phone in his pocket and the pistol in his waist, he would drive to Trapani and bounce the arse off the woman in the back of her car. But the call would mean little and the sex would mean less because he was wounded.

He spiraled the smoke up toward the bland shade of his light, he gulped the whiskey. They came more often, now, the doubts. They came to him most afternoons when he lay on his bed with his cigarette and his whiskey, with the alarm set for twenty minutes of sleep. No doubts of ultimate victory when he had tracked the *Brigate Rosse* cells, no doubts when he had stood with controlled emotion in the congregation at the funeral of dalla Chiesa, none when he had investigated murders and trafficking and kidnapping in Genoa, and none when he had pressed the pistol down against the flesh of Riina. The doubts now were with him most afternoons. Unshared, unspoken, he doubted in ultimate victory, as if he beat against a wall and the wall did not break the force of his blows. The arm was cut, the arm grew again. The heart was knifed, the heart healed. If that was his life, fighting and not winning, then what was the point of his life?

'Vanni stubbed out his cigarette and drained his glass. He swung onto his stomach and pressed his face down into his pillow. He could not cut the sight of her. She was on the beach. She was light against the darkness of the sea. She was white skinned as the towel slipped. She was naïve and innocent, she was alone. She was being used as a weapon in a war without the prospect of ultimate victory. Mother of Christ. She was the wound that hurt him.

He was still awake when the alarm bleeped through the bare room.

It was raining hard.

There should have been back-up, there should have been support.

No support and no back-up, and so Harry Compton was dependent on a short truncheon and a pair of image-intensifier binoculars and a suction microphone linked to a tape recorder. It had been the best that Stores could supply him with, which was pitiful. About the only thing going for Harry Compton was the rain, tipping down, which meant it was unlikely that the man's wife was going to come walking round the garden with the dogs. Small mercy, because there were enough things steepling against him. With the image-intensifier binoculars he had been able to identify the heat-sensitive exterior floodlights, and the location of the bloody things meant that he had to crawl through the depths of the bloody shrubs, wet earth sliming on his stomach and thorny pyracantha clinging to the material of his overalls. He was up against the wall of the house, but couldn't bloody move, because if he moved he would be into the arc of the heat-sensitive kit. He was wet. His hands ran rainwater. With wet hands, and he couldn't use gloves because they would deny him the sure touch of his fingers, the suction microphone had become smeared and wouldn't bloody stick on the window glass. He'd had to hold the microphone in position against the glass, and stand up to do it, like a damn prune in a cereal bowl. Music on in the room, bloody pop music, and he could not filter the music from the voices of Giles Blake and Giuseppe Ruggerio. Now, that was just incredible, these two men talking after dinner business and with kids' music turned up strong. Blake's own house. Of course, they hadn't talked confidential in the hotel restaurant, but if they had music to drown them now, sure as hell they talked serious business, and he could not hear a bloody word. He was wet, he was cold, he was bloody miserable, and some time soon the bloody dogs would want putting out. He was an hour's drive from home, and at home there would be a darkened bedroom and the wife's back, cold.

There was the jewel moment. Harry Compton, wet and miserable, could have bloody well jumped and cheered. The CD, Oasis, had played out.

"... working hard at getting their different acts together. I think they'll be all right."

"You know of Roberto Calvi?"

"Yes, of course."

"They want the business?"

"Of course, and they want the commission."

"If they want the business, the commission, then they should know of Roberto Calvi. They should be told that Roberto Calvi deceived people, that he was strangled slowly."

"Do we have to have more of the same? Kids'll think I'm on monkey glands."

"Remind them to be careful. Please, something else ..."

And something else was Elton bloody John. Harry Compton would hear nothing else for forty-five minutes, maybe an hour. Within an hour, damn certain, rain or no rain, the bloody dogs would be put out into the garden. He dropped on his hands and knees from the window of the house, the nice bloody pad that went with soaping and rinsing and drying mafia money, across the flagstone path. Onto his stomach and the crawl into the landscaper's shrub bed, and caught immediately by the thorny pyracantha. His wife had planted one of the bloody things beside her little greenhouse, and he might just, next Sunday, dig the damn thing out or plaster it with weedkiller. What he'd seen of Giles Blake, and of Mrs. Giles Blake when she'd been clearing up the kitchen, luxury bloody fittings, they wouldn't do the garden because they paid for maintenance, and that was good because there was no way he could avoid smearing a trail across the earth and the mulch of the shrub bed. He went fast. He reckoned he had enough for a disclosure warrant from a judge, for a telephone intercept order from the Home Office, maybe enough for a dawn knock and handcuffs. The name of Roberto Calvi was the diamond. Rotten investments for bad people, bad people's money down the drain, strangled and left hanging from Blackfriars Bridge where the world and the world's dog could see what happened to a joker who lost bad people's money.

As he went over the wall, dropped down into the lane, Harry Compton heard the voice of the woman calling out the dogs. He loathed the sort of people who lived in that sort of house behind that sort of wall.

He himself had earned a maximum of £27,380 (inclusive of overtime) the last year. The sort of people he loathed, through scams and greed and criminality, would have clawed in a minimum of £273,800 (part-time working) the last year. He had the big thrill, like best sex, when he did the dawn call on the bastards, when he had the handcuffs open. And it would be good, best, to have the Sicilian bastard in the interview room. He reached his car.

He peeled off his overalls, kicked out of his boots. One nagging thought—what was the role of the young woman, "pressurized" by the DEA, gone as a childminder to Sicily? Where did she fit? He cut it. The young woman was altitude politics. He fed in the world of mud-smeared overalls, filth-scraped boots.

He drove home.

12

"IT DOESN'T MATTER WHAT IT says." The detective superintendent swung his chair so that he faced the window. Harry Compton held the audio cassette in his hand, then made the gesture and dropped it on the desk, onto his unread report. "I had a hell of a drenching. I crawled through the garden."

"What do you want, a medal? We are not playing at Scouts."

Harry Compton had come to work bubbling in a froth of personal satisfaction. Had left the kit, smeared in dried mud, outside the locked door of Stores section. Up to his desk in the open-plan area, first one in apart from Miss Frobisher, and she too must have realized that a jackpot had been won because he had the success gleam in his eye, and she had put the kettle on and made him a mug of her own particular coffee which was not the muck out of the vending machine in the corridor. He had listened to the tape, twice. Gone through the last Oasis track, the clean conversation, the start of the first Elton John track. He had typed his report, transcribed the tape, underlined in red the references to Roberto Calvi and then sat on his hands while the office filled and waited for his detective superintendent to get to work.

"What I am trying to say, Roberto Calvi is not a name that trips off the tongues of every pair of business people sitting down for a little chat on how to make a good buck."

"You don't cop on quick, do you?"

The detective superintendent was searching his drawer and coming up with his cigarette packet. About two days in every five, it was said, the detective superintendent tried to pack in his smoking, and the intention usually lasted about an hour or up to the first of the morning's crises. But two days out of five he could be foul tempered and sarcastic with it.

"I used to think, Harry, you were quite bright, a clever little sod. Right now I reckon you're dumb. Hear me, and I'll do it slowly. This is politics. We stumbled into something, we pushed it a bit, took it to the bosses, and they've claimed it as their own. That is politics. The politics are between us, way above me, and the Drug Enforcement Administration, way above their London man. It's good politics for us to have a stick to belt the DEA with because that's the route to trading. We make a noise, a high-level noise, we promise to make their life difficult. And to shut us up we get something in return—could be equipment, could be priority on an investigation in their backyard, could be computer access or something from their phone-tap capability, anything—that is politics. Politics are on the high ground, you and I are in the gutter. Don't make bloody faces, Harry, don't bloody sulk. While you were doing the gardening down in Surrey last night and hunting medals, the commander had the AC (SO) beating his ears for half an hour. Up above the clouds they see this as good politics and your suggestion would screw those politics, ditch the chance of trading for something in return. We play 'civilized.' Your suggestion, lift this Ruggerio man, would blow apart the DEA's insertion of that young woman—what's her bloody name?"

"Miss Charlotte Eunice Parsons. Sorry you'd forgotten."

"Can't help being clever, can you? That young woman's insertion into a mafia family is now politics."

Harry Compton flared. "She was pressured."

"She's between a rock and a hard place. She's for bartering for political advantage. She's about as irrelevant as an individual as bloody Giles Blake and bloody Ruggerio."

The cigarette smoke hung between them. The noise of the traffic below wafted through the window. He was flattened. Harry Compton reached forward and picked off the desk his report and his audiocassette.

"I'm sorry, Harry." The detective superintendent had his head down. "I was the one who flew it high, got the kite into the wind, and fucked up. You've done well, and no thanks to me. If I authorized, here, now, what you want, quite reasonably, I'd be dead in the water. Don't think I feel good."

"I doubt you do."

"Give that bugger in Rome, idle sod, another belt, then get yourself down to Devon like I told you."

"Thank you."

"I want to bury those arrogant bastards, poaching from our patch, so get me a profile on Miss Charlotte Eunice Parsons . . . and don't make waves that splash me."

"Charley? Where are you, Charley?"

She lay on the sunbed. The warmth played on her body. She lay on her back and she splayed out her legs so that the sun's heat was on her thighs. Her eyes were closed, but she could hear the scrape of the brush used by the "lechie" on a path farther down the garden. Each time that the motion of the brush was silenced she assumed that he gazed at her. She had looked in the dictionary that morning, after coming back from the school and the kindergarten, to find the word. The word was *libertino*. That was too good a word, in translation, for a lecher, foul old bastard with his peering eyes . . .

The watch was on her wrist. The watch would not leave her wrist, not when she was in the bath or the shower, not when she was in the sea. The white ring on her wrist, under the watch, would not be touched by the sun. But the rest of her body, too damn right, that would get the sun . . .

She had rung Benny that morning from a pay phone in a bar facing onto the piazza, after she had dropped the children at school and kindergarten, and heard his voice that was distant and unsure, and gushed her thanks for the day in the countryside, and resurrected the invitation for him to guide her around the *duomo* and the Quattro Canti and the Cappella Palatina and the Palazzo Sclafani. She'd bullied him and told him when she could next be in Palermo. She wanted the sun to have been on her, on all of her body except for her wrist, when she went into Palermo to see Benny. God, he wasn't much, didn't have much other than a dream, was all that was on offer.

She hadn't thought, not when she had sat on the cliff with Axel Moen, not when she had stood beside the river with Axel Moen in Rome, not on the train, not in Mondello, not in the villa, that the waiting would be so bloody hard. And it was worse now, the waiting, because she had seen the helicopter and the men with the guns, seen the response of Axel Moen to the pressing of the panic button. So bloody hard to wait. She opened her eyes, blinked at the brightness. The gardener was some fifteen paces from her and used the brush with a desultory and bored motion, and he looked away when she caught his glance. She rolled over onto her stomach. She twisted her hands over her back and unfastened the straps of the bikini top. She had never thought the waiting would be so bloody hard, maybe it would all be waiting, maybe it would never happen, maybe it was just the illusion of Axel Moen. God, it was eating at her, the waiting.

"Here, Angela. I'm here."

She pushed herself up and the bikini top fell away. Her elbows took her weight. She could not see the gardener, but away behind the bushes there was the scrape of his brush. Angela came from the patio. She saw Angela's face, distracted, and there was a tautness. Angela had seen her.

The lips pursed, the frown dug deeper. "I don't think, Charley, that is suitable."

Bloody hell, but Charley grinned. "You used to."

Snapped. "That was Civitaveccia, that was not Palermo. Please make yourself decent."

Did she want to talk about it? Was now the time to press it? Would there be tears? The lie came first. Each day she thought that Angela was more distanced from her. It was not in the interest of the lie to flush out the feelings of Angela Ruggerio, poor bitch. Charley acted the lie, the chastened girl and slipped her arms through the straps of the bikini and wriggled to fasten the clasp. Angela held a small piece of paper in her fingers, and her purse, and the fingers moved restless and wretched. It was all going to come, one day. Whether the lie was served or not, the confidences would gush and the tears would follow. Charley sat up.

She said cheerfully, "Expect you're right."

"I have a list for the shops."

"Right, I'll do it when I get the children."

"For now, Charley."

It was hell's hot out there. It was all right in the heat lying nine-tenths stripped, but it was bloody hot to be traipsing back down the hill, and in two hours she would be going to get the children. But she lived the lie.

"No problem."

Charley stood. Gently she took the list for the shopping from Angela's fidgeting fingers. A long list, a list for a meal for guests, not for a meal around the table in the kitchen where they ate when Peppino was away. She scanned it—oils, sauces, vegetables for a salad and vegetables for cooking and meat, mineral water, wine, cheese and fruit.

As if Angela pleaded with her. "You don't tell Peppino that I forgot, you don't tell him . . ."

"Of course not." She tried to smile comfort.

"Am I pathetic to you?"

"Don't be daft." She didn't want the tears, didn't want the confidences. "So how many are coming?"

"It is tomorrow the birthday of Peppino's father. It is the eighty-fourth birthday tomorrow of Peppino's father. Peppino's father and his mother. Did I tell you that Peppino's father and mother lived near to Palermo?"

Her voice was brittle, slashing. "They are peasants, they are ignorant, they are not educated, but Peppino would want them fed well, and I forgot."

"Peppino, he won't be here—"

"Back this evening, hurrying back from wherever." A sneer flickered the muscles at her mouth. "Back because it is the birthday of his father, which I forgot."

Charley interrupted briskly, "So the children, yes? You and Peppino, yes? His parents? Me?"

"Of course, you live with us, of course you are there."

Charley smiled. "That's for four, six, and me which makes seven. I'll go and get changed."

She took the list and the purse. She headed for the patio.

"For eight—it is possible that someone else comes," Angela said, from behind Charley. "But I do not think I would be told."

Charley stopped. She didn't turn. She thought that if she turned, Angela Ruggerio might see the brightness in her eyes. Charley said, "Eight, fine, I'll buy for eight. I'll just chuck on a skirt and a T-shirt."

Every time before he had ridden in the lead car, and sometimes he was given the keys to drive the lead car. But the *maresciallo* had promised that he was watched, as a probationer, and from their keen watching they would have seen his tiredness. Pasquale had been told to drive the chase car. He could not blame the tiredness on the baby, or on the soft and rhymthic snoring of his wife beside him, the tiredness was from the nightmare that had stayed with him through the night.

The route chosen by the *maresciallo* for the journey between the Palazzo di Giustizia and the Ucciardone jail took them around the sharp bends of the Piazza San Francesca di Paoli, onto Via Mariano Stabile, from Mariano Stabile a sharp left for Via Roma and then Piazza Sturzo, then straight on before the final right turn into Via della Croci, which would run them the last stretch to the gates of the Ucciardone. The route of every journey in the city was decided first by the *maresciallo*, who poured over the street maps each morning, who badgered Tardelli for his day's program and the timing of the program. The routes chosen by the *maresciallo* were not communicated to a central switchboard for fear of betrayal or interception. Now, one thing for Pasquale to drive the lead car, another thing for him to take the chase car and have his speed and cornering and acceleration and braking determined by the car in front. He was stressed. He did not have the traffic opening ahead of him in response to the blue lamp and the siren wail, he had rear brake lights and the winking indicator to guide him, and his horizon was the back of Tardelli's head, and the sun was in his eyes.

Because they had teased and mocked him, he had slept falteringly with the nightmare.

Every street they went down, every piazza they crossed, was parked up. Cars and vans and motorcycles were at the side of every street and piazza, half on the tarmacadam and half on the pavings. "Why a bomb? Why a huge explosion? Why a jeweler's shop?" All through the night, twisting and tossing in his bed beside his sleeping wife, near his sleeping baby, the nightmare had been of parked cars and parked vans and parked motorcycles. They could wait for a day or a week or a month, and they would know the inevitability that the lead car and the chase car must travel between the Palazzo di Giustizia and the Ucciardone jail, they could wait and watch a particular route and know the options for the journey were limited, and they could hold the detonator switch. And after the nightmare, after he had showered and shaved, after he had sat at the table in the kitchen while his wife fed their baby, he had seen on the television the picture of an armor-reinforced Mercedes, burned out and on its side, a death cage.

The sun was in his eyes, the tiredness was in his mind. It was the skill of a driver of a chase car that he should always anticipate the speed and cornering and acceleration and braking of the lead car. Pasquale did not see, in front of the lead car, the woman push her baby buggy out from the pavement and into the road. The junction of Via Carini and Via Archimede, parked cars and vans and motorcycles. The brake lights of the lead car blazed. At Pasquale's horizon, the head of Tardelli jerked forward. The man beside him swore, let loose his machine gun, flung his hands forward to brace himself. Pasquale stamped the brakes. Pasquale swerved as the tail of the lead car seemed to leap back at him. The sun was brilliant in his eyes.

The woman with the baby buggy was back on the pavement, arms up and shouting. The lead car was surging away. Pasquale had locked the wheels, was skidding. The siren screamed above him. He hit the lamppost. He was in shock and dazed. The woman was thrusting the baby buggy toward him, stationary against the lamppost, yelling in hysteria. The crowd was looming around him, hostile and aggressive. He threw the reverse. He clattered into something, didn't bother to look behind him. He pulled forward and nudged the crowd aside, and a man spat at his windscreen. He accelerated. Ahead was the open road. He could not see the light on the roof of the lead car, he could not hear the siren of the lead car.

Pasquale, in his tiredness, with the sun in his eyes, could have wept.

The man beside him spoke with a patronizing calmness into the radio.

"No, no, no, no ambush, no emergency, no panic. Yes, that's the problem, the idiot can't drive. The engine sounds like shit, a lamppost, we'll get there. If I have to rope the idiot up and make him pull it, we'll get there. Over, out."

He tried to go faster but the bumper bar was loosened and scraping the road. When they reached the gates of Ucciardone, as the gates were opened by the police, Pasquale could see two of the crew of the lead car and they were clapping him home, cheering their applause, laughing at him.

"I have to know more."

Desperation. "I don't know more."

"Then we do not do business."

Pleading, "I told you what I knew, everything."

"It is a disappointment to me, which means there will be a disappointment for you."

Sniveling. "Everything I knew I told you, and you promised . . ."

The magistrate scratched the scalp under his thick gray hair, and then he swung his spectacles from his face and took the arms of the spectacles, where they would fit over his ears, into his mouth. He chewed the plastic. It was his tactic. The tactic was to permit the silence to cling in the interview room. The prisoner was a criminal killer, but Tardelli, in truth, felt some slight sympathy for the wretch. The wretch had crossed over, had tried to cooperate, but with inadequate information. The next day was the tenth day, and without information of substance he would not be justified in requesting an extension of the surveillance operation. The wretch tried to barter other names, other crimes, but they were not of interest to the magistrate.

"You have to tell me more about Mario Ruggerio and the Capo district."

"I was told he used the bar. I was told he had the stomach pain. That is all."

"Not enough. Where did he stay?"

"I don't know."

"The bar is sold, new owner. The old owner, conveniently, has died. I have no one to ask but you. How often did he go?"

"I don't know."

"What did he wear?"

"I don't know."

"Who was he with?"

"I don't know."

The magistrate laid his spectacles carefully back on the table. The door opened quietly and closed quietly. He shut the file that he had studied and lifted his briefcase from the floor and placed the file in it. The youngest of his *ragazzi,* Pasquale, stood by the door. There were many approaches, differing tactics, that he employed when questioning Men of Honor. He could be stern or gentle, contemptuous or respectful. He could make them believe they were integral to an investigation or that they were irrelevant rubbish. He clicked the catch on his briefcase.

He said, uninterested, "You see my friend, when you are taken back to your cell you will have completed the program of subterfuge visits to this room. Your mother, a good and devout woman I am certain, requested that I see you, and I obliged her. Not again because I am a busy man. Let me explain to you the consequences of your lack of detailed knowledge about Mario Ruggerio and your failure to gain protection status. There will be someone, I assure you, on the landing of your cell who will know that three times you have been taken to the medical unit. There will also, I assure you, be someone in a different block, who from a high window, will have seen me arrive here three times. Someone will have seen your movements, and someone will have seen my movements. You have to hope those people do not meet, do not talk, do not compare what each has seen. But there is much talk in a place such as this, many meetings. I see that you will have a visit from your wife this afternoon, later. I suggest you talk to your wife, to the mother of your children, and tell her of our meetings, because I believe she might have the possibility of persuading you to remember more. Try hard to remember."

The prisoner was taken out.

The magistrate said, "The problem, Pasquale, is that I must deal each day with such a man. It is possible to be desensitized, to be dragged down, to lie with them in filth. You think I am vicious, Pasquale? He won't get the protection status, but after a few days for him to consider the depths of his memory, of his knowledge, I will transfer him to somewhere on the mainland where he is safer. When you lie in filth you become dirtied."

He came home from the early shift. He dumped the two plastic bags on the kitchen table. His wife ironed a skirt.

Through the kitchen's open window came the noise of the tower block, music and shouting and the crying of children and the smell of drains. One more year . . . Perhaps a small apartment by the sea on the east of the island, near Messina or Taormina or Riposto, where La Cosa

Nostra was less formidable, perhaps a bungalow with two bedrooms and a pension from the state.

She hated what he did, and she did not look up from the ironing board.

Giancarlo poured himself a glass of juice. He drank the lemon juice that she had made. He took the bags from the table and carried them to the cupboard. There were four cardboard boxes on the floor of the cupboard, one for potatoes, one for fruit, one for green vegetables and one for lemons. Another kilo of potatoes, another kilo of apples and a kilo of oranges, another cauliflower and a half kilo of spinach, and three more lemons. He looked down at the boxes, all close to being filled.

She hung the skirt on a wire hanger. She took a blouse from the washing basket.

He closed the door of the cupboard.

"It is finished. From tomorrow you do your own shopping."

Giancarlo took his pistol from the shoulder holster under his lightweight jacket, and cleared it and took out the magazine. She went on with the ironing. He went to their bedroom to rest. After tomorrow there would be no more lemons for the cardboard box in the kitchen cupboard, and no more potatoes nor green vegetables nor fruit. He had been too long in the job of surveillance to feel a sense of failure.

Franco drove. It was an old Fiat 127, a model that was no longer in production. The bodywork was rusted, but the engine beneath a layer of oil and grime left for casual police inspection, was finely tuned and capable of reaching a speed of 170 kilometers per hour. It was the right car to bring a humble and elderly priest from a country village to a home in mourning. Nothing was left to chance, everything had been prepared with care, the movement of the humble and elderly priest was the responsibility of Franco. Franco, with a day's stubble on his face and wearing a poorly fitting coat and a tie that was not quite straight against the collar of a shirt that was a centimeter too tight, drove slowly because Mario Ruggerio did not like to be thrown around in a fast car. The radio set in the dash between the knees of Franco and the priest did not play the music and talk of the RAI stations but was tuned to the extremity of the VHF band to receive warnings of military road blocks from the two cars that traveled ahead and warnings from the car behind of any possible suspicion of a police tail.

The sun was down now over the mountains to the west. The lights of Catania merged with the dusk.

The responsibility of moving Mario Ruggerio to the home, in mourning, of the man from Catania brought rare pride to Franco. There would be police, not in uniform, on the pavement outside the apartment block. There would be hastily rigged cameras, positioned by men dressed in the overalls of the telephone company or the electricity company, covering the front and the rear of the apartment block. The number of the Fiat 127 and its paint coloring would be noted, of course, but by the morning the car would have been resprayed and the registration plates would have been changed. A humble and elderly priest, from the country, would not be harassed by the police, not questioned and or body searched, in the aftermath of death. The pride of Franco came from his belief that the responsibility given him provided an indication, clear as mountain water, that he was now the favorite of Mario Ruggerio—not Carmine, who was an arrogant idiot, not Tano who was a toad and blown out with self-importance. He believed that more responsibility would be given him until he stood at the right shoulder of Mario Ruggerio, undisputed as the *consigliere* to Mario Ruggerio. The radio stayed silent. No military road blocks on the approach to the apartment block and no tail. The bastards would be relying on the surveillance teams on the street and the remote cameras. He drove along the street, and when he started to change down through his gears he nudged Mario Ruggerio, respectfully, and pointed to the ashtray. The humble and elderly priest stubbed out a cigarillo, coughed hard, spat into a handkerchief. He pulled up smoothly in front of the main entrance to the apartment block, where the streetlights were brightest. When he was out of the car, when he would be seen by the surveillance men and by the cameras, Franco seemed to examine a scrap of paper, as if directions had been written on it, as if he were a stranger to the city, as if he merely brought a humble and elderly priest from a village in the country.

Two young men stood in the shadow near to the door, and there would have been two more across the street, and two more down the street, and they would have cameras. The priest walked with the help of a hospital stick, one that had a reinforcing clamp for the upper arm, and Franco walked with him as if ready to take his other arm should the priest stumble. The priest murmured a greeting, perhaps a blessing, to the policemen as he passed them, and they ignored him. The priest walked hesitantly over the marble floor of the hallway to the block as if such luxury were not a part of his life in the village. They took the elevator. The face of Mario Ruggerio was impassive. Franco could not read his thoughts. The man was magnificent. The man had such authority. Small, old, and such presence. The empire of the man extended across the width of the island, the length of Europe, the ocean, and Franco was his favorite. It was typical of the magnificence of the man that he came to the front door of the apartment and rang the bell for admittance to the home of a slaughtered rival.

The door was opened.

Franco carried a pistol strapped to his shin. He felt a winnowing of fear.

The apartment was crowded with the supporters of the dead rival and the family. A moment's gesture, Mario Ruggerio's hand on Franco's arm, a grip that was steel-hard, the order that he should stay back, and he was passed the hospital stick. Mario Ruggerio, murderer, now *capo di tutti capi* because a rival had been removed, went forward and the supporters and rivals backed off and made an aisle for him. Franco saw that none dared catch his eye, none had the courage or the stupidity to denounce him. Franco followed, into the living room and he waited by the door as Mario Ruggerio approached the widow, black-clothed, sitting, eyes reddened. The widow rose to greet him. He took the widow's hands and held them in his own, he spoke the words of sincere sympathy. He brought respect. He declined the offer of alcohol from the son of the dead man, a juice would be most welcome. He gave dignity. Gravely, Mario Ruggerio, watched by Franco, thanked the son of the dead man for the juice. His presence was accepted because he brought respect, gave dignity, to a dead man. Franco understood. The power of Mario Ruggerio, dressed as a humble and elderly priest, over La Cosa Nostra was absolute.

For more than an hour Mario Ruggerio talked with the widow and the widow's son and the widow's family. When he left, he hobbled on his hospital stick past the policemen on surveillance duty, past the cameras.

With two cars in front and one behind, Franco who was swollen with pride, drove him back to Palermo through the night's darkness.

She looked the prisoner straight in the eye, and when he dropped his head, she reached forward and lifted his chin so that he must look at her.

She was the daughter of the *capo* of the Kalsa district of the city. Her brothers followed in the footsteps of her father.

Across the table, in a low voice so that she would not be heard by the guards and by the other prisoners and their families, she spat at him her message.

"I will tell my children, not your children, my children, that they no longer have a father. I will tell them that they should forget their father. To me, to my children, you are dead. You listened to your mother, always to your mother, so now your mother can wipe your arse for you, but not me and not my children. If I am offered protection, then I will refuse it. What you intend will bring shame on you and on me and on your children. It now disgusts me that I lay with you and made children for you. You swore the same oath as my father, the same oath as my brothers, and you betray the oath. I tell you your future, from the time that I leave here, from the time that I meet with my father and my brothers. Wherever they put you, look to see if anyone is behind you when you stand on steep steps. When you approach any group, consider which man carries the knife, when you lie at night and hear a footstep, consider whether the rope is brought for your throat. When you eat then consider whether the poison is in your food. That is your future. Not my future, not the future of my children, who have no father. To me, to them, you do not exist, never existed."

She let his chin fall. The tears flowed on his cheeks. With poise, without looking back, she walked to the door.

"What I am saying, Bill—you secure at your end?"

"Secure. Go."

"I'm saying there is regular shit stirring at this end."

"Am I dumb, Ray? What's your end to do with it?"

"This show, Codename Helen, the baggage your guy came for."

"That's our problem."

"My problem, too. I got mugged by one of the local people here. Quote, 'Taken it upon yourselves, you arrogant bloody people, to pressurize and then send a small-town girl to Palermo for some bloody operation you've dreamed up. Who've you cleared it with?,' end quote. Bill, that's why it's my problem."

"Where's that going to lead?"

"Why I'm sweating on it, don't know. I've been in this city, Bill, three years. In three years you get to know the way people work. Here they work devious. The old lion is losing his sight, got flea scrapes, yellow teeth, but he still thinks he hunts with the best of the pride. I'm accused of getting hold of his tail and twisting it. He's angry, and he's quiet, which means he's thinking devious."

"You're away ahead of me, Ray."

"I thought you should know, they may try to fuck us about."

"Aren't we all going in the same direction?"

"Wouldn't that be nice? What I'm getting to, it would raise a powerful shit-smell if anything happened, unpleasant, to Codename Helen, to your bit of baggage, like I might be run out of town, like it would go all the way to the top floor. I'll stay close. Goodnight, Bill. I just have a bad feeling."

He put down the telephone. He switched off the scrambler, then dialed again. He told his wife that he was about through for the evening, and he gave her the name and address of the restaurant in the Fulham Road where he'd meet her. He was clearing his desk when he realized that Dwight Smythe was still at his desk outside, and it was always necessary when the secure scrambler was used, to speak that bit louder.

"Did you hear that, Dwight?"

"Sorry, but it would have been difficult not to."

"What are you thinking?"

"Same as I told you first time, same as you ignored. The plan was crazy. When a crazy plan gets disseminated, goes to the top, when the big guys have to guarantee a crazy plan, they run for cover. You're out on your own, Ray, but I expect you thought of that."

She lay on her bed and she turned the pages of her book.

"If that's everything, Angela, I'll get on with the children's baths," Charley had said. "I think you've done wonders."

"Thank you for your help," Angela had said.

And Charley had gone into the living room where Peppino, home an hour before and jacket off and whiskey in his hand and tie loosened, sat and where the children played with the presents that had been brought them. There was a battery-powered car that *piccolo* Mario raced across the tiled floor, and a doll that Francesca had stripped and then dressed again. For Angela there was a silk headscarf, and for Charley there was a box of lace handkerchiefs. She had left Angela in the kitchen with the pasta ready to go into a saucepan and the sauce already mixed, the meat thin-sliced and in the refrigerator, the vegetables washed, the fruit in a bowl and the cheese on the wood block. The wine was chilled and the mineral water. Beyond Peppino and the children, in the dining alcove, the table had been laid by Charley for eight people.

"Come on, Mario and Francesca, bath time, come on," Charley had said.

"So soon, so early?" Peppino had asked.

Charley had glanced down at the watch on her wrist. "Think I'd better be getting on because then I'll need a shower and time to change. I thought I'd wear what you—"

And Peppino had said, so casual, "I don't think you need to be with us, Charley. I understand Angela told you that it is my father's birthday—family talk, Sicilian talk. I think that for you it would be very tedious, very boring for you."

"Don't worry about me, I'll just sit—"

And Peppino had said, "My father and mother are from the country here, Charley. I think it would be difficult for you to understand their dialect. They would not be at ease with a stranger—not a stranger to us but to them—so it is better that you do not sit with us tonight. Angela will put the children to bed."

"Of course, Peppino. I quite understand . . ."

Into the dining alcove, to the table, and Charley had stripped a laid place and removed a chair. Seven places left, and seven chairs. She had gone into the kitchen and told Angela, without comment, that Peppino thought she would be bored by dinner with his parents. She had watched Angela, and seen the woman's face stiffen, and she had wondered whether Angela would stride from the kitchen and into the living room and make an issue of Charley at dinner. Angela had nodded, as if she did not have the will to fight. She had bathed the children, dressed them in their best clothes and brought them back to Peppino. She had made herself a sandwich in the kitchen. She had gone to her room.

She tried to read. She lay on her bed, dressed, and she turned the pages and learned nothing from them. She listened. A car came. She heard the murmur of voices and the happy shouting of the children. She heard footsteps in the corridor, beyond her door, which she had left an inch ajar. She heard the sounds of the kitchen.

She tried to read . . .

For Christ's sake, Charley . . .

She turned the page back because she was absorbing nothing of what she read.

For Christ's sake, Charley, it is just a job of work.

She put the book on the table beside her bed.

For Christ's sake, Charley, the job of work is playing the lie.

She pushed herself up off the bed. She straightened her hair.

It was what she had come for, traveled for, it was why she had left the bungalow and the class of 2B. She took a big breath. She put a smile on her face. She walked out of her room and she went first toward the kitchen and she saw the dirtied plates of the pasta and meat courses, and there was another plate beside the cooker that had a saucepan lid put on it as if to keep the plate warm. She went along the corridor toward the voices in the dining alcove beyond the living room. She came into the living room and the smile was fixed hard on her face. Only the children bubbled laughter at the table and played with the car and the doll, but the talking died. The chair at the head of the table was empty. She kicked away the quaver in her voice, spoke boldly.

Charley asked Angela if she could help by putting the children to bed.

Angela and Peppino sat opposite each other, then the children, then the two old people. There was a smear of annoyance on Peppino's face,

and the expression of Angela was pain. At the end of the table, either side
of the empty place and the empty chair, were the parents of Peppino. The
old man wore a poor-fitting suit, but good cloth, and his collar and tie
drooped from a thin neck. The old woman wore black, with white sparse
hair gathered in a bun. Charley had seen their house, she had walked past
the open door of their house, she had heard the radio playing in their
house and smelled the cooking in their house.

Peppino said, "That will not be necessary, Angela will see the children
to bed. Thank you for the offer. Goodnight, Charley."

He did not introduce her. The eyes of the old man were on her, bright
in his aged and lined face. The old woman looked at her, disapproving,
then started again to peel the skin from an apple.

Charley smiled. "Right, I just wondered. It will be good to get an early
night."

She went back to her room. She again left the door an inch ajar. She
sat on the bed. Her fingers rested on the face of her wristwatch. She wondered where he was, whether Axel Moen listened. Plain to her that she
was not welcome and there was the empty chair and there was the food
kept warm on the plate. The rhythm of the codes played in her mind.
Where was he? Did he listen? Her finger edged toward the button on
the watch on her wrist.

She made the signal. She paused. She made the signal again. Where was
he? Would he have heard it? She pressed the button, the same rhythm.

The excitement ran in her. It was her power . . .

She went to the bathroom, washed and peed, and back in her room she
undressed. The pulse tone she had sent, three times, was her power . . .

For a moment she held the bear close to her, as if the bear should share
the excitement that was hers because of the power. She switched off the
bedside light. She lay in the darkness. Trying to stay awake, hearing sounds
in the kitchen, hearing the flushing of the lavatory, hearing the children
going with Angela to their rooms, hearing the indistinct murmur of the
voices. Trying to stay awake, and drifting, with the finger resting on the
button of her wristwatch, and drifting further, as if the excitement exhausted her. When she drifted, she dreamed. When she came through from
each dream, sporadic, she jerked herself awake and killed each dream and
looked at the fluorescent face of her watch. Ten o'clock coming, and
eleven, and midnight, and the dreams were harder to kill, and she drifted
faster, further.

She dreamed of the young man in the newspaper photograph with the
throat cut and the blood spread, and of the story that Benny had told,
and of the helicopter.

She dreamed of the shadow in the doorway, and of her door closing.

She dreamed of the hovering helicopter and the men in balaclavas, and of the soft-shoe shuffle in the corridor, and of Axel Moen standing under the trees beyond the beach sand . . . Charlie slept.

"What time is it?"

"It's thirty minutes on from when you last asked."

"What the hell's she at?"

"You want me to go to the door, wake the house, request to speak to her, then ask her?"

"She sent the Stand-by."

"She sent the Stand-by. She has not sent Immediate Alert, nor has she sent Stand Down."

"It is seven hours since she sent Stand-by."

"Correct, Axel, because it is now three o'clock, which is half an hour after we last had this discussion."

"Don't understand it."

"What I understand, Axel, I am quite pleased that I did not call out the heroes of the *carabinieri*. Overtime, the need for a report, I am very pleased."

"I'll kick her butt."

"She will be very bruised. You said that half an hour ago, and an hour ago."

"But, it is just goddam unprofessional."

"Exactly, Axel, because she is not a professional."

They sat in the car. The last of the discos had long closed, the piazza bars had shut, the kids on the motorcycles and the scooters had roared away into the night. Mondello was emptied. The street where they were parked, off the piazza and a block from the shoreline, was deserted. Axel took a Lucky Strike from the packet and swore under his breath and passed the packet to 'Vanni and 'Vanni took the last cigarette from the packet. The match flashed in the interior of the car.

"That sort of settles it, doesn't it? I mean, I'm not goddam sitting here without cigarettes."

Axel crushed the empty packet. He dropped it on the floor beside 'Vanni's finished packet and beside the squashed wrapping of the pizzas they'd eaten. They smoked. They eked out their cigarettes until their fingers burned. They dropped their cigarettes through the open windows.

"What do you think?"

"I think, Axel, that we go to bed. You are angry?"

"I'll kick the butt off her."

"I think—you know what I think? I think, and you will not love me."

247

'Vannie grinned wide. "I think you care, and I think you are very frightened for her."

"I'll kick her so's my foot hurts."

There was only the night duty officer as company for Harry Compton.

In a mood of stubborn anger he had telephoned Rome, and been told by Alf Rogers that the report was coming, but late that night, and he said that he would wait on.

There was a phrase the commander liked to use, something about the primary work of SO6 being "putting faces to illegality," a phrase recited to visiting politicians and bureaucrats. In front of the detective sergeant, on his desk, was the source of that stubborn anger. A camera at Heathrow had put a face to illegality. Italian passport holder Bruno Fiori, seven hours earlier had passed through Terminal Two, Heathrow. The photograph, taken by a camera on a high wall bracket, showed him presenting the Italian passport at the emigration desk, and the order that the holder of that passport should not be delayed, not be quizzed, not be made aware of any investigation, had been most specific. The bastard had gone through, without let or hindrance, to his flight. The photograph showed a smoothly handsome man, well dressed, relaxed, and the bastard should have been in the interrogation rooms or in a cell.

A bell rang. The bell was piping and sharp. The night duty officer was pushing up from his chair, but Harry Compton waved him down and back to his newspaper. He hurried through to Miss Frobisher's office, abandoned and left pristine for the morning.

The message churned from the printer. He read . . .

TO: Harry Compton, SO6.
FROM: Alfred Rogers, DLO, British Embassy, Via XX Settembre, Rome.
SUBJECT: MARIO RUGGERIO.

DOB: 19/8/1934.
POB: Prizzi, western Sicily.

PARENTS: Rosario b. 1912 (still living) and Agata b. 1913 (still living). Their other children—Salvatore b. 1936 (imprisoned), Carmelo b. 1937 (mentally subnormal), Cristoforo b. 1939 (murdered 1981), Maria b. 1945, Giuseppe b. 1954 (see below).

FAMILY: Married Michela Bianchini (from LCN Trapani family) 1975. Salvatore (s) b. 1980, Domenica (d) b. 1982. Living now in Prizzi.

DESCRIPTION: Height 1.61 meters. Weight (est.) 83 kilos. Blue eyes. No surgical scars known of. Believed of heavy and powerful build (no photograph for 20+ years, no positive sighting in that period). Not known whether dark brown hair now grayed or dyed, also nk whether wears spectacles routinely.

He carried the sheets of paper back to his desk.

"Like a mug of coffee, squire? Just making one for myself." The night duty officer was folding away his newspaper.

"No, thank you."

BIOGRAPHY: Formal education, elementary school, Prizzi, 1939–43. Traveled with his father—contraband lorry driver. 1951—convicted of attempted murder, Court of Assizes, Palermo (victim alleged to have denied him "sufficient respect"). In Ucciardone prison alleged to have strangled two fellow prisoners, no witnesses, no evidence. Released 1960, having become sworn Man of Honor. Not arrested since. Charged *in absentia* with murder, narco trafficking, much else. Believed FBI/DEA have sufficient evidence for indictment in USA. An ally of Corleonesi (Riina, Provenzano, etc.), but thought to have maintained independence. In power struggle (post-Corleonesi arrests) indications that RUGGERIO is responsible for disappearance of Agrigento *capo* and most recent murder of Catania *capo*.

"You all right, squire? Sure you won't have a coffee? There's a sandwich here, missus always makes enough for a bloody tea party."

"No, thank you."

"Just asking. Only you look like someone's grabbed your goolies and given them a god-almighty twist. Didn't mean to interrupt . . ."

ASSESSMENT: Extraordinarily secretive, reputation of taking extreme care of his personal security, no successful wire taps, no documentation found. Has also tightened overall security of "families" in LCN under his control, introduced cellular system, hence no recent information provided against him by the *pentito* (super–grass) program. Seen by Italian authorities as ruthless killer.

SCO report: "Ignorant but he has intuition and intelligence, his actions are most hard to predict."

Squadra mobile report: "Violent, aggressive, vindictive, with above-average shrewdness and determination."

DIA report: "He has power over life and death, an incredible personal presence, and a streak of violent sadism, BUT (my emphasis, AR) he is reduced to a miserable condition because he cannot move openly, cannot live with his family openly. He is submerged in the terror of assassination, exists in an atmosphere of tension and fear, hence violent paranoia."

Magistrate Rocco Tardelli (investigating Ruggerio) in a recent report to Min. of Justice: "[Ruggerio] is a supreme strategist, believes future of LCN is in international dealings, acting as broker for cartels, Triads, Yakuza, Russian mafia. His reputation goes ahead of him, he is seen as combining experience with shrewdness. If he achieves domination of LCN, he will seek to direct the enormous power of that organization beyond Italian frontiers."

At a time when the effort of the Italian state against LCN is losing impetus, it would seem that Ruggerio has taken control.

(See attached for GIUSEPPE RUGGERIO.)

Alfred Rogers, DLO, Rome.

He had thought once that the young woman, in the graduation photograph on the wall above the telephone, was not his concern. He felt a keen sense of shame. He locked the report in the wall safe.

"I think I'll push off then, I'm about wrapped up."

"Best place, squire, in bed with the missus. They don't thank you here for playing all conscientious. Don't mind me asking—you seen a ghost or something? Sorry, sorry, just my little joke . . ."

13

"You will be late, Charley. Can that not wait?" Angela shouted from the kitchen door.

She was hurrying along the back path, past the gas tank and the rubbish bins, to the washing-line. Her bras and knickers and T-shirts and jeans dripped in her hands. The washing-line was behind the villa. Beyond the washing-line was the rear wall to the property. Recessed into the wall was a strong wooden door with a padlock fastening it shut. The wall was too high for her to see over, but above the wall was the coarse scree and rock-sheer slope of the cliff.

"Won't be a second, Angela—won't be a minute."

She grabbed a fistful of pegs from the plastic bag hanging from the washing-line.

She was pegging the clothes to the line. She saw the bastard. Hey, "lechie," *libertino,* getting a thrill from watching bras and knickers hung out? Want to get your dirty hands on them? He stood beside the barrow and when she challenged him with her gaze, he started to scratch with his broom at the path to the door in the wall. He bent. The old hand, weathered and bony and dirty, reached down to the ground beside the path and he picked something up, and threw it into the barrow. She saw it. She saw the crushed end of a cigarillo on the top of the leaves in the barrow. The line of clothes was complete. She stopped, she considered, then she ran back to the villa.

Angela had the children ready on the front patio, and the pram with baby Mauro, and the shopping list for the day.

"Don't bother to wash up last night's dishes, Angela, I'll do that when

I'm back. And it's all right for me to get a bit of culture into the system this afternoon? I'll see you. Come on, kids."

When she'd woken, Peppino was already up and sitting in the living room with work papers. When she'd gone into the kitchen to get the kids breakfast and to warm the milk for the baby, the sink had been filled with the dirtied dishes topped by saucepans and Angela had been making coffee. Not possible for her to examine the padded seat of the chair at the end of the dining table, not possible for her to check the number of plates used, nor the number of knives and forks. She thought herself pretty damn clever to have offered to wash the dishes. Right, pretty damn clever that she had noticed the "lechie" pick up a cigarillo end at the back of the villa near the door in the wall. He smoked cigarettes, foul Italian ones, and Angela didn't smoke cigarillos and Peppino didn't smoke cigarillos, and the old man from last night would hardly have been sent out through the kitchen and past the gas tank and the rubbish bins for a sharp puff. And there was the jumbled memory of her dream.

Not pretty damn clever that she had slept . . . shit . . . had failed to stay awake.

Her mind was compartments. One compartment was walking down the hill and easing the pram around the dog dirt and the street rubbish and the road holes, taking the children to school and kindergarten, having the purse and the shopping list. A separate compartment was the lie and the watch on her wrist, and dirty plates in a sink, and a chair, and a cigarillo end . . . She dropped small Mario at school and walked Francesca to the kindergarten door. She was in the piazza, a hand resting casually on the pram's handle, and there was the blast of a horn. She was studying the shopping list. She swung round. Peppino waved to her and then powered away in his big car. She waved back. If she were pretty damn clever, clever enough to arouse suspicion, then would it be Peppino who strangled her, knifed her, beat her and then took his dinner? She bought the milk and fresh bread rolls. She was going to the fruit stall.

"Keep walking, down to the sea, don't turn."

A cold and harsh voice. God, and the bloody voice was without bloody mercy. She stiffened her back, like she was trying to show defiance, but she did as she was told and she walked down to the main road, waited for the lights, never turned, pushed the pram across the road. She leaned against the rail. The baby was waking and she rocked the pram gently.

"If you can't cope with it, then you should say so, and you should quit."

"That is bloody unfair."

The growled voice, the sharp accent, rasped behind her. "If you can't handle it then go. Go home."

She stared out over the water. The small fleet of fishing boats was putting out to sea, riding the swell. The wind freshened on her face. "I'm doing what I can."

"You want the list? Item, you give your communications to a goddam child to play with. He plays, we scramble. We had a helicopter up, we had a full team out—you fouled up."

"It won't happen again."

"Won't happen if you quit. Item, you send Stand-by last night. I am sitting with company, holed up in a car till half after three this morning. I have a heavy team on Ready till half after three. Did you forget to send Stand Down?"

"I am doing my best."

"If your best isn't better, then you should go home."

"I am sorry."

"Goddam should be. Why didn't you send the Stand Down?"

She heaved the breath into her lungs. The wind whipped her hair. She said, small voice. "I thought he might come. It was a little family party for Giuseppe's father's birthday. I wasn't included. I was told it would be 'tedious' for me. I tried to stay awake in my room, I tried. I went to sleep."

"That is pathetic."

"I did my damn best . . ."

"Did he come?"

"Does he smoke cigarillos?"

"How the hell should I know?"

"Then I don't know if he came."

"Think about going home if you can't do the job."

She turned. She broke the rule he had made. She faced Axel Moen. She saw the coldness in the eyes of Axel Moen, and the contempt lined at the mouth of Axel Moen, and the anger cut in the frown of Axel Moen. She wanted to touch him, and she wanted him to hold her . . . She turned away from him. There would be a storm because the wind was rising.

He said, hacking the words, "If you can't handle it, then you should walk out."

She was watching the fishing fleet, diminishing, riding the wave crests. She went to buy the fresh fruit.

Back at the villa, Charley found that Angela had finished washing the plates and cutlery from the previous night, and they had been put away in the cupboards, and the upholstered chair in the dining room had been brushed with the other chairs and she could not see whether it had been sat on.

————

"The conclusion?"

Giancarlo stood with the others of the team, all of them except for those who had done the last night shift. It was not routine for the *squadra mobile* surveillance unit to meet with an investigating magistrate who tasked them at the beginning of an operation and at the end of an operation, but it was the requirement of this small and sad man. The small and sad man sat on his desk, his legs a little too short for his feet to reach the floor, and his arms were hunched across his chest. Giancarlo thought, a ridiculous thought and inappropriate, that the magistrate had in his eyes the dull tiredness of death, that the dimmed room had the gloom of a *cella dei condannati a morte*. They had nothing to say and nothing to report, but he had insisted on seeing them.

There was no conclusion. No sighting of Ruggerio, no trace of Ruggerio. But it had been three teams of only three men, and a labyrinth such as the Capo would swallow a hundred men. It had been a gesture, but the gesture was a token.

"Thank you for your endeavor." The endeavor was to walk and to stand and to look at faces and to try to match the faces of old men to a photograph. The photograph was twenty years old. Some computer-enhancements of photographs were good, some were useless. They might have seen him, might have stood beside him. "Thank you for your commitment."

"For nothing . . ." The leader of the unit gazed, embarrassed, at the floor.

And Giancarlo held the present behind his buttocks. That moment he wondered how often there was laughter in this room. Like a mortuary, this room, like a place of black weeds and hushed voices. A place for a man who was condemned . . . Did the poor bastard, small and sad, condemned it was said, ever get to laugh? The men on the door outside, condemned with him it was said, they didn't seem fun creatures who would make the poor bastard laugh. Giancarlo was the oldest on the team, the most experienced, the one who gave no respect to any man, and he had been chosen to offer the gift to the small and sad man, to make him laugh.

"As an appreciation of working for you, *dottore* . . ."

Giancarlo handed the parcel, wrapped in shiny paper and bound with gift tape, to the magistrate. They watched as his nervous fingers unbound the tape and unwrapped the paper.

Lemons cascaded on the desk, lemons bounced, lemons fell to the floor, lemons rolled on the carpet.

He understood. A quick smile slipped to his mouth. He knew their work, knew the difficulty of going into the Capo district day after day and finding a process that enabled them to blend with the crowds in the alleyways. He slipped off the desk and came to Giancarlo and pecked a kiss on each of the man's cheeks, and Giancarlo thought it was the kiss of a condemned man.

When it was the time for exercise, when the bells clamored and the keys scraped in the doors' locks, the prisoner stayed on the bunk bed.

The men with whom he shared the cell went on their way for exercise in the yard below. A *carceriere* saw him sitting hunched on the lower bunk and asked the prisoner why he was not going to exercise and was told that he had a headcold.

When the landing of the block was quiet, as it would be for thirty minutes, the prisoner stood. It surprised him that his hands did not shake as he unbuckled his belt. Holding his belt, he scrambled up onto the upper bunk. He could see now, through the squat window, through the bars, the panorama of Palermo. The window of the cell was open. A hard wind came on his face. Through the bars he could see the mountains above Palermo. In the mountains was the home of his mother, in the city was the home of his wife and his children. As he hooked the buckle of his belt around a bar at the window he heard only the howl of the wind.

His wife had told him that he was dead. The magistrate had told him he would die by the push, or by the knife thrust, or by poison.

He pulled the belt hard and tested that it was held strong by the bar.

Suicidio was a crime against the oath he had taken many years before. When a man took his own life he lost his dignity and his respect, and that was a crime against the oath.

The prisoner wound the end of the belt around his throat and knotted it. There was not an adequate drop from the top bunk bed, nor was the belt long enough, for him to break his neck when his slid his weight clear. He would strangle himself to death.

He had nothing more to tell the magistrate, nothing more to tell of Mario Ruggerio.

He mouthed a prayer, and he tried to find in his mind the faces of his children.

He was suspended, kicking, choking, writhing, and below the cell window men walked the monotonous circles of exercise.

"So this is home?"

"This is Cinisi and it is my home."

"Quite a nice-looking little place, a lot of character," Charley said brightly. She looked up the main street, the Corso Vittorio Emanuele. At the end of the street was a granite mountain face, and above the rim of the mountain there was a clear azure sky in which cloud puffs raced in the wind. Against the gray rock face, dominating the street below, was the church that had been built with sharp and angular lines.

"My father, before they killed him, called Cinisi a *mafiopoli,*" Benny said. He held the door of his car open for her. She thought it a nice-looking place and the character was in the smart terraces of houses that flanked the main street. The windows of most of the houses were masked with shutters, but there were potted plants on the balconies and the paint was fresh on the houses' walls, white and ochre, and the main street was swept clean in front of the houses. Set in the paving between the houses and the street were flowering cherry trees, and under the trees was a scattering of pink blossom.

"I can't see anything, Benny, can't feel it. Maybe I could not see much in Corleone, maybe I could feel something in Prizzi, but not here. There doesn't seem to be anything to touch."

"Look to the mountain," Benny said.

Charley wore her best skirt, which she had bought with Peppino's money, and her best blouse. She stood with the sun and the wind on her thighs and shins. The force of the wind tunneled down the main street. She stood boldly with her feet a little apart, as if to brace herself. There was scrub on the lower slope of the mountain, where the fall was less severe, but higher on the rock wall nothing grew. The mountain was a harsh presence above the main street.

"It's a mountain, it's rock, it's useless."

He touched her arm, a small gesture as if to direct her attention, and there was a softness in his voice. "You are wrong, Charley. Of course you are wrong, because you do not live here, you do not know. They own the mountain, they own the rock, they own the quarries. Did you not come on the plane to Palermo?"

"Came by train," Charley said. Axel Moen had told her that the vulnerable time for an agent was the sea change between overt and covert, the journey from safety to danger, told her it was good to take time on the journey to reflect on the sea change. Charley lied. "I thought it was wonderful to come by train, sort of romantic, on a train through the night and crossing a continent."

"Because they own the mountain and the rock and the quarries, they wanted the airport for Palermo built here. The runways are two kilometers from here. There is too much wind and the mountain is too close, but that was not important because they owned the mountain, the rock, the quarry. Cinisi was a place of farms and vines and olive trees, but they turned the *contadini* off their land, and the stone made the base for the runways, the stone could be a base for the concrete, and they came to own the airport. They own everything that you see, Charley, every person."

They were outside a smart house. There were recently fitted hardwood surrounds to the windows and a heavy hardwood door with a polished brass knocker.

"Is your mother inside?"

"Yes."

She said with mischief, "And waiting for your washing?"

"Yes."

"Can she wait a little longer for your washing?"

"Of course—what do you want?"

"I want to see where they killed your father, where you were in the car when they killed him."

Perhaps she had startled him. His lips narrowed and his eyes glinted and his cheeks were taut. He walked away from her. She followed him. Benny went past small groups of old men who stood in the sun and let the wind grab at their jackets and they did not meet his eyes and he did not look at them. A woman with shopping stopped as he came close to her and then in ostentation she turned her back on him to stare into the window of an *alimentari*. As he went by them, three boys who gossiped and sat astride their scooters revved their engines so that the black exhaust fumes carpeted his face. Charley followed. He stopped, as if challenging her, pointed to a *gelateria,* every sort of ice-cream, every flavor, and she shook her head. At the top of the Corso Vittorio Emanuele was the piazza of Cinisi. A priest came from the church and saw Benny and looked away and hurried on, his robe driven by the wind against the width of his hips. There were more men in the piazza, more boys idle and squatting on their motorcycles. She was making him live the moment again, and she wondered if he hated her.

He talked her through the chronology of a death, as if he were a tourist guide in the *duomo* or at the Quattro Canti or at the Palazzo Sclafani. He pointed to the street beside the church.

"It was done there. I had been late at the school for instruction in the violin. My father had collected me on his way back from Terrasini, he came for me because it was raining, and they would have known which afternoon I stayed at the school for music, and they would have known that if it were raining he would collect me. It was not important to them that I was in the car, that I was ten years old. That afternoon it was convenient for them to kill my father . . ."

There was a bar on the corner of the piazza. The wind gusted the wrapping of a cigarette packet past the closed door to the bar. It had been seventeen, eighteen years before—of course, there was nothing to see. A narrow street leading into a pretty piazza under the shadow of the church of San Silvestro, a killing zone.

"What had he done? What had your father done?" She knew that she would take him to bed, that day or that night.

"He told the *contadini* that they should not give up their land. He said that they would be robbed if they agreed to sell their land. He said that they were farmers and they should continue to harvest the olives and the oranges and to grow maize. He said that if they sold their land and the airport was built they would never work again because the jobs made by the airport would go to people from Palermo, who were not *contadini*. He said to the people that the success of the airport would be a triumph for the *mafiosi,* and a disaster for the *contadini*. He was only a shopkeeper, but he was an honest man, his honesty was respected. There was a time when people began to listen to him. My father called a meeting of all the people in the town and the peasants who had the olives and the oranges and the maize. The meeting was to be here, where we stand. My father was going to tell the people that they should oppose the building of the airport. The meeting was for that evening."

"So they killed him, to silence him." She would lie with him on a bed, that day or that night.

"Because he obstructed them, and because he made fun of them. The night before, I had heard my father in the bedroom practice the speech he would make. He had many jokes to tell about them. The family in Cinisi at that time, destroyed now, replaced, was the family of Badalamenti. He spoke of the 'Corso Badalamenti' where they lived and of the leader of the family as 'Geronimo Badalamenti.' He had jokes to tell about the wealth that would come from the airport when they had stolen the land from the *contadini,* about the Badalamenti family eating from silver plates and taking baths with hot water from gold taps. He was a threat to them because he would laugh at them, and have the people laugh with him."

"What happened? Tell me what happened?" On a bed she would take the clothes from his body, that day or that night.

"How is it important to you? Why do you wish to know?"

"Please, tell me."

The sneer was at his face, and the wind caught at the fineness of his hair. "You are a nanny for a rich family. You take your money for minding small children, for doing the work of their mother. Why—"

"See, touch, feel, so that I can understand."

"Am I an amusement to you?"

"No, I promise. Help me to understand." She would take the clothes from his body and kneel over his body and kiss his body, that day or that night.

"A car crossed the piazza and it stopped in front of my father's car. He did not recognize the people in the car because he shouted at them. Did they not know where they were going? It was late in the afternoon, the light was going because of the rain. Already in the piazza the preparations had been made, there was the sound equipment for my father, there was a place for him to speak from. He shouted at the people in the car because he thought he would be late for the meeting. There was another car that came behind us, it drove into us. I saw one man only. The man had a small machine-gun and he came from the front toward us and he threw a small cigar from his mouth and he raised his machine-gun. There were more men, with guns, but I did not see them because my father pushed me down in the seat. He tried to protect me. If he had been alone, I think he would have attempted to run, but I was with him and he would not have left me. There were eighteen shots fired, thirteen of the shots hit my father. The priest who came, who was there first, before the *carabinieri* and the ambulance, the priest said that it was a *miracolo* that the child was not hit. I think credit was given to the killers of my father because I was not hit. I can remember still the weight of his body on me, and I can remember still the warmth of his blood on me. Someone brought my mother. She came, and the body of my father was lifted off me. My mother took me home."

"It happened here?"

"Where you stand is where the car stopped to block my father. Do you wish to learn more?"

"So that I may understand . . ." She would kiss his body and put his hands on her body and find his love, that day or that night.

"Two days later there was the funeral for my father. Where we stand now I walked then with my mother and the whole length of the Corso and the width of the piazza was lined with the people of Cinisi, and the church was filled. There were eight thousand people then living in Cinisi and around the town, and three thousand came to my father's funeral, and the priest denounced the barbarity of the *mafiosi*. It was a fraud, it meant nothing. It was a spectacle, like a traveling theater on a festival day. The airport was built on the land stolen from the *contadini*. The people who had filled the church, stood on the Corso and in the piazza, were bent to the will of the Badalamenti family. There was a short investigation but the *carabinieri* told my mother that guilt could not be proved. They own the town, they own the airport, they own the lives of everybody here."

"Why, Benny, do they not kill you?"

His head hung. She thought she had slashed at his pride. He looked away from her and he murmured in bitterness, "When opposition is ineffective, they do not notice it. When opposition is only an irritation, they ignore it. When opposition is threatening, they kill it. Do you seek to humiliate me because I am alive, because my father is dead?"

"Let's get your washing home," Charley said.

They walked back down the Corso Vittorio Emanuele. She took his hand and led him, set the pace for him. It was useful for her to be able to touch warm blood and feel the weight of a father's body and to see the shock in a child's face . . .

She should think about going home, Axel Moen had said. She should think about going home if she could not do the job, Axel Moen had said . . . He did not speak, they reached the car, he lifted a filled pillowcase from the floor at the back of the car. The gale, funneled down the main street, beat on them. He rang the bell at the door.

She was introduced.

She played the part of the innocent.

She was offered juice and a slice of rich cake.

She was the nanny to a rich family from Palermo, and she was ignorant.

She talked, innocent and ignorant, with Benny's mother. The mother had darting sparrow's movements and bright cobra's eyes. Charley thought the woman must have quite extraordinary courage. She had trained, since her loss, as an accountant. She could live anywhere on the island, work anywhere in Sicily or on the mainland, but she had chosen to stay. She wore a bright scarlet skirt and a grass-green blouse, as if it would have been a defeat to take to widow's black. The courage of the woman, Charley thought, would come from facing each day the people of the town who had stood aside when her man was butchered, and from facing each day the people who had filled the church and lined the Corso for her man's burial. Charley ate her cake and drank her juice, sucked in the strength of the woman. The courage of the woman was in walking, each day, up the Corso past the home of the people who had ordered her man's killing, and seeing their families in the bars, and standing with them in the shops, and knowing that they slept well at night.

If she were not to quit, go home, walk away, she needed that courage.

She waited for the woman to clear away the glasses and the plates. She waited for the woman to take the pillowcase to the washing-machine in the kitchen.

Charley reached for Benny's hand. The hand was limp. She controlled him. She led him to the staircase of cleaned and polished wood. She heard the churning motion of the washing machine. The door to the bathroom was open. The door to the principal bedroom, the woman's room, was open. She led Benny through the door that had been shut, into his room. It was cool in the room because the shutters were closed and the sunlight came in zebra lines, filtered, onto the single bed, onto the skin rug on the floor, onto the picture above the bed. The picture was from a newspaper. A car was isolated in an empty street. The body of a man was beside the car. A woman stood near to the car and held a small child against her. Giving space to the body and the woman and the child was a crowd of onlookers. Charley fed from the photograph, as she had eaten the cake and drunk the juice. She must draw strength from the woman and the child.

She took the jacket from his shoulders and he made no move to help her.

She kneeled and slipped the shoes from his feet, and the socks.

She took the tie from his throat and the shirt from his chest and loosed the trousers at his waist. She stripped the man bare and she saw the tremble of his knees and the smooth flatness of his stomach, and she saw the heave of his chest below the hair mat. She thought he pleaded to her. She heard, from below, the rattle of the plates being rinsed and the clatter of the glasses.

He lay on the bed. She squatted over him. She kissed the mouth and the throat and the chest and the stomach of Benny, drank the juice of his sweat. She made lines with the nails of her fingers on his skin and tangled his hairs. Only when the moaning was in his throat, as the wind moaned in the cables outside the shuttered window, did he reach for her. He tore at the buttons of the blouse and at the clasp of her bra and at the waist of her skirt. She had control of him. She put the rubber over him, as she had known she would.

Charley rode the man.

Not the lecturer from college on the carpet, not the guy from the picket line in the caravan, not the schoolteacher who had lifted her, bruised, bleeding, scarred, from the pavement.

Charley held his head and her fingers, frantic, searched for the ponytail of blond hair that was held tight with an elastic band. Charley pounded her fingers into the pale face with the day of stubble beard on it. Charley pulled the arms around her, muscled and powerful. He drove at her, hard in her, as if he were trying to buck her from him.

She murmured the name of the man . . .

"Axel . . . fuck me . . . Axel . . ."

He came, he was sagging, he was spent.

She crawled off him. He tried to kiss her, to hug her, to hold her, but she pushed him back and down onto the bed. She took the rubber off him. She walked, cruel and vicious bitch, from the bedroom to the bathroom and she flushed the rubber down the lavatory. She sat on the seat. She wondered where he was and whether he had watched her. Her fingers rested on the nakedness of her arm, on the coldness of the watch on her wrist. She came back into the room. He lay on the bed and his arm was across his face so that he should not see her.

Charley started to dress.

"Who killed your father?"

"My father is mine. He is not your business."

She was dressing fast, snatching at the crumpled heap of clothes. "Is it good to be so ineffective that one is unnoticed? Who killed him?"

"When a man from Catania is to be killed they bring in an assassin from Trapani, when a man from Agrigento is to be killed they find a man in Palermo." He hissed the explanation. "It is an exchange of favors, a barter of services. When a man from Cinisi is to be killed—"

"They bring a killer from Prizzi? Is it good to be only an irritation and ignored?"

"What is it to you?" His arm was off his face. He pushed himself up on the bed. She thought he had a fear of her.

"I'll take the bus back," Charley said. "I'll go on the bus because your mother won't have had time to dry your washing and iron it. You're safe from Mario Ruggerio, Benny, because he won't even have noticed you."

Carmine brought the minister to the apartment.

The apartment was at Cefalu and the business of the minister was at Milazzo, which was nearly 150 kilometers to the east. Carmine had been given, by Mario Ruggerio, responsibility for bringing the politician from the oil refinery at Milazzo to the holiday apartment at Cefalu. It was a serious and important responsibility. The minister was now in charge of the budget for Industry, but Mario Ruggerio had told Carmine that the minister was a rising star and eyed Finance. A half year before the minister had sent a signal, in a speech in Florence he had spoken of the glory of a united Italy and the duty of all Italians to support their fellow citizens of Sicily. Mario Ruggerio had read the code of the signal: government funds should continue, as before, to cascade onto the island, and the supply of government money, trillions of *lire,* were the lifeblood of La Cosa Nostra. A month before, the minister had sent a second signal; on a late-night television program broadcast by a private channel, he had warned of the excesses of the judiciary in Palermo in their use of *pentiti* as trial witnesses. Two signals, two coded messages that the minister was ready to do business with Mario Ruggerio. A contact through an intermediary at a Masonic meeting in Rome, and now Carmine had the responsibility of bringing the minister in secrecy from Milazzo to Cefalu. Not simple, not for an arrogant shit like Tano, not for a fool who had air in his brain like Franco, to bring a minister from Milazzo to Cefalu. The responsibility was entrusted to Carmine because he had the intelligence to arrange the security necessary for the meeting. The minister had toured the oil refinery with his guides and his guards, had worn the hard hat, had walked alongside the kilometers of pipelines, had stood in the control areas with the technical directors and his guards, and had pleaded a headache from the fumes of the refinery. The minister had taken refuge in his hotel room. The guards of the minister of Industry, not a prime target, were relaxed. They had been called, at Carmine's direction, to the end of the hotel corridor for refreshment. In the few moments when the distraction of the guards was total, the minister had been brought from his room, through the door on which the *"Non Disturbare"* sign hung, and out onto the fire escape.

Carmine drove the car from Milazzo to Cefalu. He had given the minister a flat cap to wear, and the minister had a scarf half across his mouth. The beauty of Carmine's plan, the guards in the hotel would never admit to loss of control of their subject, they would never confess that the minister had been given an opportunity to leave his hotel room unseen.

He took the car into the parking area under the apartment block. He parked beside the Citroën BX, the only other car there. The tourists, they would be Germans, had not yet come to Cefalu to scorch themselves on the beach and to wander in the Piazza del Duomo.

The minister, at the base of the concrete steps, hesitated, but Carmine smiled reassurance. The stupid bastard was already hooked, the stupid bastard had nowhere to go but up the concrete steps. He led. They climbed. The minister panted. Three raps at the door of the second-floor apartment.

The door was opened. The damp of the winter had been at the wood of the door, warped it, and it whined as it was opened.

The small body of Mario Ruggerio was framed in the door, and his head ducked as if in respect to the minister's rank, and the smile on his face was of gratitude that a man of such importance had made such the journey to visit him. He wore baggy trousers that were hoisted with a peasant's braces to the fullness of his stomach, and the old gray jacket that was his favorite, and he took the minister's hands and held them in welcome. And the old worn face of the peasant brushed a kiss to each side of the minister's cheeks. He gestured with his hand, humbly, that the minister should come into the apartment.

Carmine was not a party to the meeting. He closed the door. Carmine waited.

He assumed that by the next morning a bank draft for, perhaps, a million American dollars would have been transferred to an account in Vienna or in Panama or to the Caymans or to Gibraltar. Mario Ruggerio said, always said, that there was a price for every man, and perhaps the price for a minister of the state was a million American dollars. And Mario Ruggerio would know because he had already found out the price for judges and for policemen and for a cardinal and for . . . It was the power of Mario Ruggerio, Carmine was under the protection of that power, that he could own those at the very heart of the state. There was so much that could be bought with a million American dollars,—the blocking of investigations, the opening of contract opportunities, recommendations and introductions abroad. He stood outside the door and basked in the glory of the power of Mario Ruggerio. One day, at some time, when Mario Ruggerio tired of the glory of power, stepped aside, then it would be Carmine who replaced him . . .

An hour later Carmine led the minister back down the concrete steps. Three hours later, when refreshments were again offered to the guards, the minister climbed the fire escape of the hotel in Milazzo. Four hours later, the minister appeared at his door and called to his guards that the headache from the oil refinery fumes was gone.

The telephone rang.

It shrilled through the darkened apartment. In the kitchen the *ragazzi* of the magistrate had their own telephone and their own radio. They pretended an indifference each time the telephone rang, talked louder among themselves, took a greater interest in their card game. They pretended they did not listen, after the telephone call, for the quiet scrape of Tardelli's feet coming from his room to the kitchen. Pasquale felt the new mood of the protection team. The joke, sad, sick, had been against him, but he recognized now that the joke affected all of them. He had been the sole target of the joke—"Why a jeweler's shop?"—but it claimed them all. Less talk, raucous, of the last two days of overtime and screwing women and holidays. More talk, somber, of the last two days of greater speed in the cars, less predictable routes, more weapons training. Each time the telephone rang they waited for the scrape of Tardelli's feet coming from his room to the kitchen, stiffened, pretended, listened. Pasquale suffered each night the dream of a parked car or a parked van or a parked motorcycle exploding in fire as they passed, and he knew the bomb would be reinforced with ballbearings and detonated via the link between a mobile

264

phone and a telephone pager. He knew it, they all knew it, because the *maresciallo* had told them what he had heard from Forensics. He knew, they all knew, and the *maresciallo* did not need to tell them, that there was no protection against the bomb in the parked car or van or on the pannier of a motorcycle. They waited, they listened, as they did each time the telephone rang in the apartment.

He came, scraping his feet, to the kitchen door. There was a grayness to the color of his cheeks, his fingers moved fidgeting in a clasp across his stomach. With his eyes he apologized.

"I have to go out."

The *maresciallo* said breezily, "Of course, *dottore*—the Palazzo, the Palace of Poison?"

"There is a church beside the prison . . ."

"On the Piazza Ucciardone, *dottore* . . . ? When would you like to go?"

"Please, I would like to go now."

"Then we go, now—no problem."

"He took his life. The man I played a game with, made fear for, to help his memory, he hanged himself in his cell."

He was gone, shuffling through the hallway for his coat. The *maresciallo* rapped out a route to the Piazza Ucciardone, a route past the close-packed parked cars and vans and motorcycles with panniers. They lifted their vests off the floor, they took the machine-guns from the table and the draining board beside the sink and the work surface beside the cooker. The radio carried the message, staccato, to the troops in the street below the apartment. They took him out. They hurried him down the staircase, with the two drivers stampeding ahead so that the engines of the cars would have been started before he hit the pavement. They ran across the pavement, into the last light of the afternoon, and the gale scorched grit into their faces. Pasquale was front passenger in the chase car, and the *maresciallo* was behind him. Sirens on. Lights on. At the end of the street, as the soldier held up the traffic, they swerved onto the main road and past the lines of parked cars and vans and motorcycles. They went faster than usual, as if it were necessary now always for them to go faster than the time taken by a man to react and press the last digit on a mobile telephone linked to a pager.

"Pasquale. What are you, Pasquale?"

The voice of the *maresciallo* whispered in his ear. His eyes were on the traffic ahead, and on the line of parked cars, vans, motorcycles they hurtled past. He held the machine gun hard against his chest.

"What are you, Pasquale?"

"I don't understand."

"You want me to tell you what you are, Pasquale? You are a stupid and pathetic cretin. You do not have a magazine loaded."

His hands were rigid on the stock and trigger guard of the machine-gun. He looked down. He had not loaded a magazine, thirty-two rounds, into it. He bent and laid the machine-gun on the floor between his feet. He took his pistol from the shoulder hardness. The cars swerved, screamed, cornered.

The journalist from Berlin was settled comfortably in his chair. The embassy was a little piece of home for him. There was a strong beer from the Rhineland on the table beside him. To be back in Rome again was to have returned to Europe, to have left that Arab world of half-truths, coded statements and conceit. He had telephoned his editor for more checks to be sent him and they would arrive in the morning at the American Express. He had won a few more days . . . As a veteran of so many wars, he was reluctant to make the last leg home and have it said in the office, by younger ankle-snapping colleagues, that he had failed. In truth, so far his journey in search of the mafia was a failure, but he believed that a few more days in Rome, distanced from this war that he could not sense or smell, would supply him with the copy for his article. There was a counselor at the embassy who liaised for the *Bundeskriminalamt* with the Italian agencies. He wrote a sharp shorthand note of what he was told.

". . . We had the opinion, five, six years ago that the collapse of the Christian Democrat machine, and those of the communists and socialists would remove from the mafia the protection they had enjoyed for forty years. We thought then that for Italy a new era of clean politics was coming. We were wrong. There was the businessman's Government that followed. Far from attacking the mafia this Government took a most dangerous line. Anti-mafia magistrates in Palermo were denounced as self-seekers and opportunists, the *pentiti* program was condemned for making bad law. There was a small window of opportunity to strike against the mafia after the killing of Falcone and Borsellino, when the public, in outrage, demonstrated against criminality, but the opportunity was not grasped. I believe it now lost. What I hear, it is increasingly difficult to persuade prosecutors and magistrates to travel to Sicily, there is on-going and debilitating rivalry between the many agencies, there is incompetence and inefficiency. The Italians forever plead with us to make greater efforts against a common enemy, but—hear me—look at the construction of the businessman's Government. There was a Fascist appointed to the Interior Ministry, there are men with proven criminal associations introduced to the peripheries of power. Would we wish for such people to have cooperation given them? Should they be granted access to BKA files? Only because the Sicilian mafia pushes drugs and dirty money into Germany, do we have an interest in the matter of organized crime in Italy. The British, the Americans, the French, we are all the same. We are obliged to be interested as long as the Italians demonstrate their unwillingness to tackle their own problem. But, Sicily is a sewer of morality, and our interest achieves nothing. Do I disappoint you?"

There were two women in the church, in black, kneeling, several rows of seats ahead of him.

He had taken a place near the back of the church on Piazza Ucciardone, and at the far end of the seats from the aisle.

He kneeled. He could hear the traffic outside and he could hear the beat of the wind against the upper windows of the church. In his mind, in silence, his knees cold on the floor tiles, he prayed for the soul of the man who had hanged himself . . .

It was what he had chosen. It was the fifteenth year since he had chosen to come with his wife and children to Palermo, brought by ambition and the belief of career advancement. It was the fourth year since he had chosen to stay in Palermo, in the comfort of his obsession, after his wife had left with the children. Huddled on his knees, he prayed for the spirit of a wretch. To come to church, to pray, he must have an armed guard at the door to the priest's room, he must have a *maresciallo* sitting with a machine-gun three rows behind him, he must have a young guard with a sullen and chastised face standing at the door of the church with a pistol in his hand, he must have two armed guards on the outer steps of the church. There was no more ambition. The ambition was dried out, a cloth left on the line in the sun. The ambition had been overwhelmed by the assassination of his character, by the drip of the poison, by the scheming stabs at his back in the Palazzo di Giustizia. He was left only with the obsession of duty . . . for what? The obsession hanged a man by the throat until his windpipe was crushed . . . for what? The obsession brought the risk of death, high probability, to five wonderful men who were his *ragazzi* . . . for what? The obsession brought him closer, each day, to the flower-covered coffin that would be filled with what they could find of his body . . . for what?

The priest watched him. The priest was often in the prison across the piazza. The priest knew him. The priest did not come to him and offer comfort.

If he sent the message, if he cut the obsession from his mind, then on offer would be a bank account abroad and a position of respect in Udine and the return to his family and the last years of his life lived in safety. To send the message would be so easy. Within a few hours a message would reach the small man, the elderly man, whose photograph had been aged twenty years by a computer . . .

He pushed himself up from his knees. He faced the altar and he made the sign of the cross. He turned. The magistrate, Rocco Tardelli, saw the face of the youngest of the *ragazzi*. To reject the obsession would be to betray Pasquale who had come with his wife's flowers and who had crashed the chase car and who had forgotten a magazine for his machine-gun, to betray all of them who rode with him, gave their lives to him. Each day the weight, the burden, he thought was heavier. Back to his office where the obsession ruled him, back to the files and the computer screen, back to the aged photograph.

He laughed out loud.

His laughter cracked the quiet of the church, and the women who prayed turned and glowered at the source of the noise, and the priest by the altar scowled hostility at him. He laughed because he remembered the long-haired American who had introduced into Palermo "an agent of small importance." There was a manic peal to his laughter. If "an agent of small importance" should lead to Ruggerio, succeed where his obsession failed . . . He bowed his head.

"It is a difficult life, *maresciallo,* for us all. I apologize for my unseemly behavior."

They closed around him as he walked out of the church and hurried him the few paces to his armor-plated car.

". . . It's Bill Hammond . . . Yes, Rome . . . Not too bad. Hey, Lou, when did you get to Personnel? That's a good number, yes? . . . Lou, this is not official, I'm looking for guidance. No names, OK? . . . Something we're doing down here, I can't talk detail, it might, might, get unstuck. One of my people, he's put a heck of a time into it. If it gets unstuck I'd want some candy for him. What you got going, foreign placement? . . . What sort of guy? . . . No, not a high-flier, not like you, Lou. He's a field man, not a computer guy, one of those people that scratch in the dirt. The sort who's going nowhere but that we wouldn't want to lose, you with me? If it gets unstuck I wouldn't want a bear with a thorn in its ass round my patch, and I'd want to see him right . . . Lagos? Is that all you got, Lagos in Nigeria? . . . Yes, we could dress Lagos up. Yes, I could make it sound like San Diego. Be kind to me, Lou, don't fill the Lagos slot till you've heard back from me. It's just that too many people have gotten involved, and they're sort of squeamish people . . . Yes, we could have lunch when I'm next over, that would be good . . ."

It was dusk when Harry Compton drove down the lane. He saw the light, bright in the porch of the bungalow, but it was not his intention to visit David and Flora Parsons. He stopped halfway down the hill at the outer gate to the farmyard. They had nothing they would willingly offer him about their daughter that he did not already know. The obvious way was rarely the best way. When a child was missing it was from the neighbors that detectives learned whether the disappearance was "domestic" or a genuine abduction. When a company had gone crooked it was the competitors who most often dished the serious filth.

He ignored the dog snapping at the back of his trouser legs.

He rapped on the back door of the farmhouse.

Daniel Bent, aged sixty-nine, farmer . . . "What's she done? If you've come from London there's something she's done. Don't expect you to tell me. You want to know what I think of her? Write this down. She's a stuck-up little bitch. When she came here with her parents, they're all right but just feeble, you could see from the first day that she didn't think we were good enough. Doesn't say anything, of course not, but it's in her feckin' manner. She's superior. Look at her, butter wouldn't melt in her, but under the skin she's a right little superior madam, and hard as feckin' nails. That's not what you expected to hear, is it?"

He went on down the lane.

He rang the bell of a pretty cottage where the honeysuckle rambler was greening.

Fanny Carthew, aged eighty-one, artist . . . "I don't like to speak ill of people, particularly young people, but it would be difficult for me to speak well of her. You'll think I'm rather old-fashioned. You sometimes find the unpleasant trait of pushiness in that class of girl. You see, she's manipulative. She looks for self-advancement through people she can manipulate. It's not my business as to what trouble she's in, why a policeman has come all the way from London, but I doubt you'd want lies from me . . . She seeks to control people. If she perceives someone to be useful to her, then she is their friend, if she decides they are no longer useful to her then they are ignored. Quite a few of us offered a little hand of friendship when she came four years ago, but we've now been outgrown, we don't matter. 'Determined' would be the nice description, but I'd prefer to call her ruthless. Well, I've said it. Two years ago my daughter came down with her boy, Gavin, a very quiet boy and academic. The Parsons girl took him onto the cliffs and then she persuaded him to climb down, sort of taunted him. Well, it was all right for her, she knows the place, but my daughter lives in Hampstead, very few cliffs. He managed to get back up the cliffs, but he was quite traumatized, quite affected. Normally he wouldn't have done anything so idiotic, but she'd taunted him. What I mean, there's a rather soft exterior but underneath there is something quite distastefully tough."

He knocked.

The shouted response told him the door was not locked, he should come on inside.

Zachary Jones, aged fifty-three, disabled . . ."Can't stand her. She'll look at you, all sweetness, but the eyes are the giveaway, she's reckoning your importance to her. If you don't measure up, then you're ditched. I thought she might be company for me. I'm not much, but I've good stories to tell, I can get a giggle out of people. She used to come here, drink a beer and smoke a fag, and her pompous goddam father would have burst blood vessels if he'd known—Even used my toothpaste to clean her breath. Hasn't the time of day for me now. So she's in trouble or you wouldn't be here. Bloody good. No tears from me. I'll not deny it, she's a pretty little face—what she's short of is a pretty little mind. It's like she's trying to capture people all the time, capture and milk them and when they're dry she walks away. I'd not trust her as far as I could throw her."

The light from the porch of the bungalow shone across half the lane.

There was a fresh spit in the air, and the sea crashed in the dusk on the shingle. He went in shadow past the creaking "Vacancies" sign.

Daphne Farson (Mrs.), aged forty-seven, bed-and-breakfast . . ."You stay out in the kitchen, Bert, this is none of your business . . . My Bert thinks the sun shines out of Miss Parsons's bum, he'll hear nothing against her, but he's stupid. I thought I liked her once. I gave her work the first summer she was here, helping with the beds and cleaning up in the season. It was good pocket money for a schoolgirl. Doesn't speak to me now, like I'm beneath her, because she's been to college and had an education. I haven't an education, but I know kids. She went to college but she didn't have any friends, no one ever came to see her in the holidays. My nephew's been to college, Bert's brother's boy, his home's like a damn dormitory in the holidays. She can't make friends because she's so bloody, excuse the French, superior. Tell you what I think, I think she sets herself targets, and if you can't help her reach the targets, then you don't exist. She's a very hard young woman. If you weren't strong with her, then she'd destroy you . . . Bert, put the kettle on, and there's cake in the tin."

He saw a clergyman and an odd-job gardener and a crab fisherman and the District Nurse and a retired librarian.

He built a picture of Charlotte Eunice Parsons.

He had not heard a good word said of her. Some had hacked her with a meat cleaver and some had stabbed her with a stiletto.

He sat in his car halfway up the lane. With his pencil torch he leafed through the pages of his notebook. Harry Compton was not a psychologist, nor was he an expert in the science of personality, but he thought he knew her better for what he had been told. He wrote in his notebook, and she was in his mind.

CONCLUSION: A very strong-willed and focused young woman. DEA most fortunate to have unearthed her. The danger, she will push to the end, she will hazard herself to reach her target (whatever that may be). She will not have the necessary background to assess fully the hazard of a covert operation(?) in Sicily. Because of her quite obvious determination to succeed, I fear for her safety.

14

SHE RANG THE BELL.

She hadn't telephoned ahead, hadn't called to be certain he would be in his apartment. Charley kept her finger on the button. She could hear the shrill baying of the bell behind the door. There was no response, no shout from Benny that he was coming, no slither of footsteps from behind the door. She had her finger a long time on the bell and she swore under her breath.

When the door beside Benny's scraped open, bolts drawn back and locks turned, she took her finger from the bell button. The couple coming through the door beside Benny's were elderly and dressed for Sunday. The man wore a suit and the woman wore black with a dark-gray headscarf over her hair. They eyed her, they seemed to indicate to her that it was not appropriate to make so great a noise on a Sunday morning, then looked away. It was Palermo. They did not ask if they could be of help, they did not tell her if they knew where Benny was. It was Palermo, and they minded their own affairs, did not involve themselves. The man in his suit performed the ritual of locking the door behind him, two keys. Not easy to gauge their wealth. His suit was poor and his watch looked ordinary and his shirt was well washed. Her dress and coat were tired and the scarf on her hair was frayed at the hems and her brooch was very simple. It was Palermo, they made a fortress of their home, guarded their possessions, however meager, and they hurried to commune with their God and carried their Bibles and their prayer-books. Her finger was off the bell's button, the couple were going slow and unsure, down the formal staircase, and again Charley cursed. She cursed Benny for not being there when she came for him. She had not considered that he might not be there, and waiting.

A Sunday morning . . . Peppino going with Angela and the children to Mass, not to the church nearest the villa in Mondello, but to their regular church beside the Giardino Inglese. She had begged a lift, she had said that she would wander in Palermo and made a joke that Sunday morning was the safest morning to be alone on the streets. She had left them, as they had mingled outside their church with the *professionistici* and the wives in their finery and the children in their smart best. Now she cursed Benny Rizzo because he was not in his apartment, not available to her. Perhaps he had gone to his mother, perhaps he had gone to deliver a photocopier, perhaps he had gone to a talk-shop meeting. She felt raw annoyance, and she stamped her way down the staircase and out into the sunshine. She could not see him, and she wondered if he was there, and if Axel Moen watched her.

Sunday morning . . . She walked aimlessly. She was on the pavement of the Via del Libertà. The heat was rising. The sun was bright. The street was taped off as the long-distance runners prepared for their race. They were slapping their bodies, or jogging nervously at the thought of pain, and some were checking that they had brought the silver foil to wrap around themselves after the exhaustion and dehydration of the run. The pavements were her own. A few responded to the tolling church bells and hurried past her. She went by shuttered restaurants and darkened shops, past the strident monuments of cavalier men posturing on rampant horses, past the deserted market of the Borgo Vecchio with the empty, skeletal frames of the stalls. She had no map with her, she did not know where she was going. She passed the shadowed alleyways that led into an old quarter, and the modern blocks of the new buildings on the harbor front, and she saw the towering hulks of the waiting car ferries. She was so alone. She had not considered that Benny would not be there, waiting, available. She stared at the prison, the ochre walls in which weeds grew, the guards with the rifles on the walkway above the wall, at the high, small windows from which underpants and socks hung to dry, at the patroling military truck in which the soldiers carried rifles, where Peppino would be taken and where Angela would go with small Mario and Francesca and the baby at visiting times. She had needed him, needed Benny, and she despised him.

Sunday morning . . . Charley walked without purpose. She went by cats that glowered at her then ripped at the rubbish bags, past packs of dogs that slunk from her. She lingered outside the Teatro Massimo where the walls were boarded against the vandals and the weather, where pigeon dirt and vehicle fumes had stained the walls in equal measure. She stood under the trees beside the derelict building and she looked at the horses that were harnessed to the *carrozzi,* and she thought of the picket line of decent people at Brightlingsea and of how they would have responded to the dismal horses hooked to the empty tourist carriages. There was a lovely roan-and-white horse with its head down in passive acceptance. She was at the Quattro Canti. It was where Benny should have brought her. Shit, it wasn't much. Shit, all the fuss in the guidebook. Shit, the statues were grimed, fume-polluted, crumbling. So alone, so miserable, so lost . . . She swore again because he was not with her, was not available.

She was on Via Mariano Stabile. The church was a red-stone building. She heard the singing of the hymn, familiar. She did not go to church at home, nor did her father and nor did her mother. The red of the church was so out of place in the gray and ochre of Palermo. She did not go to church at home because there she was never alone and miserable and lost. She crossed the street to the church. She stood outside the opened iron gates. It was so bloody unfair that she was alone and miserable and lost.

The words were faint, feeble. A reedy chorus.

> Then sings my soul, my savior come to me,
> How great Thou art, how great Thou art.

She was drawn to the door. She walked into the gray light of the church, broken only where the sun was against the many-colored glass of the window. The door slammed shut behind her and faces turned to notice her, then looked away. She stood at the back. She saw the plaques remembering the long-dead. The organ rose in a crescendo, not matched by the scattered voices.

> Then I shall bow in humble adoration, and then pro-
>   claim,
> My God, how great Thou art . . .
> Then sings my soul, my savior come to me,
> How great Thou art, how great Thou art.

It was the end of the service. A woman came and spoke to her, in piping English. Was she new to Palermo? Had she mistaken the time of Sunday worship? She was most welcome whether or not she could sing, but could she sing? Would she like coffee? Charley hoped so much to be wanted, loved, and she said she would like coffee. She went with other ladies, dressed as they would be for church in Exeter or Plymouth or Kingsbridge, up into the living room of the clergyman's apartment be-

side the church. She wanted so much to please and to be welcomed . . .
She was told that they were the remnants of a great English society that
had been based in Palermo, they were the nannies who had married Sicilians and stayed, they were the artists who had fallen for the light over
the mountains and on the sea and stayed, they had come to teach the English language and stayed . . . She was a toy plaything exciting because she
was new. She fled. They wanted her name and her telephone number and
her address. She could not lie to them. They wanted to know whether
she would sing with the choir, whether she would come to the barn-
dance evening, whether she could help with the flowers. If she stayed she
would lie. She left them bewildered, confused, she fled out into the bright
sun of the street.

Alone, miserable, lost, she went to the bus stop on the Via del Libertà
that would take her back to the villa at Mondello, and she cursed Benny
for not being available.

In the car, beside her husband, Angela had withdrawn into the web of
her mind.

She wore a fine dress of respectful green, chosen by her husband, and
a coat of fox pelts, chosen by her husband. She wore discreet jewelry at
her throat and round her wrists and on her fingers, chosen by her husband. Her husband liked the coat of fox pelts and she wore it as if it were
a badge of submission. The air conditioner blew cool air over her. Her
face was hidden from him by the dark glasses, chosen by her husband,
that protected her eyes from the sun's glare that glittered up from the road.
The children were in the back of the car, and the baby was corraled in
the special seat and they were quiet, subdued, as if they caught her mood.
In the web of her mind were cascading thoughts . . .

She loathed Sicily. After Mass they had been to an apartment along
the Via della Libertà, near their own apartment in the Giardino Inglese
and they had drunk aperitifs of Cinzano and nibbled at canapés, and her
husband had murmured that their host was useful as a contact in business, and deference was shown her by the other wives . . . She had magnificence around her, status, ever more lavish presents brought from
abroad . . . She loathed the half-truths of the people and the double-talk
of their coded whispers. She was a prisoner . . . She had asked, quietly,
if they could go to their own apartment in the Guardino Inglese, just
to visit, not important, to collect clothes and more toys, and her husband had dismissed the suggestion. She had wondered if his woman was
there . . . She could not leave him. Her upbringing, her schooling, her
rearing all served to prevent her leaving her husband. Her upbringing

275

was the influence of her father, Catholic conservative and working in the diplomatic section of the Vatican. Her schooling was the work of nuns. Her rearing was the effort of her mother to whom divorce was unthinkable and separation was disaster and marriage was for the extent of life. No court in Sicily would give her custody of the children if she left . . . If her husband recognized her unhappiness, driving the fast route to Mondello, if he cared for her unhappiness, he gave no sign to her. Only once had the mask cracked on his face, the morning he had been called down to the EUR to meet with the magistrate and the investigators of the *Servizio Centrale Operativo*, only that one morning had the bastard man crumpled—and he had come back, and he had laughed off the ignorance of the magistrate, and the matter was never talked of again. She did not know the detail of his involvement, she was the Sicilian wife kept quiet and beautiful under the weight of presents. She believed now that her husband's involvement was total, and she could not leave. The wife of Leoluca Bagarella had tried to leave, and it was said that she was dead, it was said in the *Giornale di Sicilia* that her way out was to have taken her life . . . He stroked her hand, a small and unimportant gesture to him, as if he patted the paw of a prized pedigree dog, and he smiled in his confidence . . . Angela detested her husband. If it were not for the brother, the stumbling fat little snail of a man, then her husband would be nothing more than another criminal on the streets of the island she loathed. It made her sick, physically sick, when the rough hands of the brother touched the smooth skin of her *piccolo* Mario, when he slipped through a back door early in the morning or late in the night and touched her son and played on the floor with her son . . .

Angela smiled at her husband, and he could not see her eyes.

The tail was on 'Vanni Crespo.

Before, the tail had been successful only sporadically, but Carmine had directed more men, more *picciotti,* to the tail.

The tail could now report each day on the pattern of the life of 'Vanni Crespo. They knew the clothes he would wear, casual or formal or the builder's overalls. They knew the cars he would use, the Alfetta, the Fiat 127, the builder's van. By trial, by error, Carmine had dictated what resources were necessary to cover the movements of 'Vanni Crespo. Each end of the main road leading from the *carabinieri* barracks at Monreale was watched that Sunday morning by a car and by two youths on motorcycles.

The previous evening, it had been reported to Carmine, 'Vanni Crespo had driven the builder's van to meet with a woman in a lay-by on the road between Trapani and Erice, and the previous afternoon he had used the Fiat 127 and called on the home of a colleague living in Alto-fonte, and the previous morning he had been in the Alfetta to the barracks at Bagheria.

Carmine had learned the patience of Mario Ruggerio. Each time he met with the men who drove the cars and the *picciotti* with the motorcycles, he repeated the description—weight near to 80 kilos, height near to 185 centimeters, fair skin, gold hair—of the American man taken to see the magistrate, Tardelli.

Two cars, three motorcycles, changing position as they went, followed the Fiat 127 from the barracks at Monreale down the fast road, Route 186, toward Palermo.

"I said to him, "It is a sad game to play when there is no trust," I said that to him."

"He told you that it was not personal."

"I suggested to him that he had put 'an agent of small importance' close to Mario Ruggerio."

"Which he did not care to confirm."

"I remarked to him that I would not wish it to lie on my conscience, the danger to that agent, unless the life of the agent was held to be of no importance."

"He did not debate semantics with you," 'Vanni said. "May I tell you, *dottore,* what he asked me when we came out of your place in the Palazzo? He asked why you pissed on him. I said you were anxious that you might not have a free hole in your diary for his funeral and for his agent's funeral. They're earnest people, the Americans, he found it difficult to register the humor of what I said."

" 'Vanni, please, I need help."

They were alone in the sunless room of the apartment. Out in the kitchen a radio played, and there were the distant voices of his *ragazzi.* He had apologized sincerely for interfering with the Sunday plans of the *carabiniere* officer, but that was the day in the week when he conducted his business within the confinement of the office in his apartment. He did not go to Mass on Sundays, did not take the bread and the wine of Communion, did not think it right to go to a church with his guards and their guns. He would go to church only for funerals and for occasional moments of stressed reflection when he could judge that a church would be emptied, but not on Sunday mornings. His wife would be in church for the Mass in Udine with his children, and he could tell himself that he did not care what man now stood and sat and kneeled beside his wife.

"How may I help, *dottore?*"

"I grasp at straws. Mario Ruggerio has taken, with blood, the supreme position."

"I read the digests from Intelligence."

"Each new man, when he takes the supreme position, must demonstrate to the families that he has strength."

"I know the history."

"To demonstrate that strength he must attack the state, show that he has no fear of the state. It is now, 'Vanni, a time of extreme danger." The *carabiniere* officer, without asking permission, had lit a cigarette, and the smoke from the cigarette watered his eyes. "It is possible that I am the target, possible, that will demonstrate the strength, but there are many others." The *carabiniere* officer was shifting in his seat, awkward, dragging at his cigarette. "I take you into areas of confidence, 'Vanni, as I hope you will take me into your confidence. This morning I go to the Chief Prosecutor, by whom I will be criticized and taunted, with great politeness, concerning my efforts to capture Mario Ruggerio. I had a wretch who wished for the status of *pentito.* On the limited information he provided I was given meager resources for a surveillance of the Capo district, a failure. I urged the wretch to give me more information, played on the psychology of his fear, and he hanged himself, a failure. I have spoken in the last hours with the DIA and with the *squadra mobile* and they have nothing for me, more failure. All around me is the murmur of sneering laughter."

"What do you want of me?"

"You run an agent of small importance, you collaborate with the American, you thought last week that the agent was close. We had Champagne iced, and we waited . . . It was a blow to my stomach. Please, give me hope, more than a floating straw, 'Vanni, share with me the detail of your agent."

"You embarrass me, *dottore,* but the gift is not mine to give."

The *carabiniere* officer jackknifed to his feet. The magistrate saw the turmoil that he had made, and the officer bit at his lip. It was the true moment, and he recognized it clearly, of his isolation.

"Of course. Thank you, on a Sunday, for your time."

Within fifteen minutes of the departure of the *carabiniere* officer, 'Vanni Crespo, his friend who would not share with him, Rocco Tardelli was on the move. The *ragazzi* were quiet around him, moodily silent in the cars. They read the signs of the isolation of a man. The signs were across the inside pages of the newspaper. The newspaper wrote that a prisoner in the Ucciardone gaol had three times met with Magistrate Tardelli, and wrote that the prisoner had been told by his wife that she rejected his collaboration, and wrote that the prisoner in the Ucciardone gaol had hanged himself, wrote that there should be restrictions on the activities of ambitious magistrates.

They crossed the city . . .

The Chief Prosecutor had glanced sharply at his watch, as if to indicate that he had guests to welcome shortly. He had given no indication that Rocco Tardelli should join his guests for lunch.

"You are an impediment, Rocco. You make a bad image. You disturb the equilibrium. You make a problem for me. You fight a crusade, you bully your colleagues, you demand resources. Your crusade, your bullying, your resources, where do they take us? They take us to a prisoner, harassed and threatened, driven to take his own life. Where do we go now? From which direction comes the next tragic disaster? I recommend, as a true friend, Rocco, that you should consider your position most carefully. You should consider your position and your future."

He could go so easily. He could pass his files to a colleague, he could turn his back on the sniggered laughter and the poisoned barbs, he could be off the island by the evening car ferry or by the early-afternoon flight. He could win the smiles and relief and thanks of his *ragazzi*. He could go so easily. "What do you say, Rocco? What would be the best for all of us?" The smile beamed on his face as if to reassure him. "Is it not time, that new horizons beckoned you?"

He felt old and tired and frightened. The bell rang. The guests had come with flowers and with presents. Old, tired, frightened, and dressed in the clothes he wore for Sundays because he did not go to Mass and did not entertain. His Sunday clothes were crumpled trousers and a shirt that should have been washed and shoes that should have been polished. After he had been hustled through the door, down the flight of stairs, across the pavement and into his armor-protected car, after they had driven past the parked cars and vans and motorcycles, after they had come back to his home, he would eat alone in his room. That would be his Sunday, and the next Sunday, isolated . . . He had needed to know the detail, hold the comfort of it, of the agent in place . . .

He murmured, as he went to the door, "I don't quit."

Benny held the spray can.

The door was closed. The shutters were across the windows.

The radio played inside.

He aimed. He squirted the spray can. His hand shook. The paint of the spray can was a brilliant red. The red was the color of blood. The blood from the wounds of his father, the blood that had seeped and spilled on him. The word was forming on the door beside the black drainpipe. A dog barked at him. What she had said beat in his mind as the red paint formed the word . . . "Is it good to be so ineffective that one is unnoticed?" She made the strength for him as if she stood beside him, goaded him. "Is it good to be only an irritation and ignored?" Goaded him because he was ineffective and an irritation and he helped with a newsletter and went to meetings and gummed envelopes. It was for his father. The word, dripping with the scarlet of blood, was on the door of the home of Rosario and Agata Ruggerio. It was a madness.

ASSASSINO.

For the love of Charley, for the nakedness of Charley over him, the word "murderer" was in blood, his father's blood, on the door of the parents of Mario Ruggerio. The word was sprayed crudely.

The madness was done.

Benny dropped the can.

He stood in the narrow street, and he heard the sharp whistle behind him. A man watched him, and in the shadow under the peak of his cap the man held his fingers to his lips and whistled. The dog had come and taken the can in its mouth and the spray ran from its mouth as if its jaws bled, as his father had bled. He looked a last time at the work of his madness. He started to walk away. He should have run, but she would not have run. He should have charged, but she would not have, as if her nakedness that covered him gave him her protection. He heard the man whistle again, and he turned, twisted to look behind him, and the man pointed to him . . . She was not there, with him, guarding him . . . When he started to run there were men already across the narrow road ahead of him. When he stopped, when the fear locked his legs, when he turned, there were men already across the narrow road behind him. She had driven him to the point of madness. The men closed on him, coming from ahead of him and from behind him . . . She was not there . . . He ran back down the road and past the bloodred paint. Turned, ran again, turned, and stumbled.

Benny fell.

He lay on the ground and waited for the men to reach him.

Mario Ruggerio had been early to Mass, mingling with the worshipers at a church on the Via Marqueda, swimming with the crowds. Most Sundays he used a different church, but the one on the Via Marqueda was the favorite among many, a great and gloomy vault of a building. He had laid a 10,000 *lire* note in the collection tray, nothing ostentatious, because the church was patronized by the unemployed and the destitute and the jobbing workers of the Capo district and of Via Bari and Via Trabia and Via Rossini, and he matched their best but shabby clothes. He would not have casually missed the celebration of Mass early on a Sunday morning, the Mass was important to him. There were few regrets in the life of Mario Ruggerio, but it was a continuing frustration to him that he could not sit and stand and kneel beside his wife, Michela, at the Mass, nor be with his children, Salvatore and Domenica. He assumed they were followed, watched. Whether he was in the church on the Via Marqueda, another humble and elderly man searching for a path closer to his God, or in any of the other churches that he used, he always thought hard at that time of his family.

It was now the middle of the day. The restaurants on the Via Volturno and the Via Cavour waited for the families to come, the bars on the Via Roma and the Corso Tukory were filled with talking men. The traffic clogged the streets, the pavements bustled with movement. Before the afternoon, before the time for sleeping came, it was good for Mario Ruggerio to be on the move.

In a bar Tano told him of the movement patterns of the magistrate, Rocco Tardelli. Twelve men, he was told, now logged the routes used by the magistrate for his journeys from the apartment to the Palazzo di Giustizia, from the apartment to the Ucciardone prison, from the Palazzo to the Ucciardone prison, and the reverse routes. He listened, he asked few questions. Tano told him that there were only three streets that the two-car convoy could use when it left the apartment and when it returned to the apartment. Tano gave the information. He coughed on his cigarillo, he swilled the dregs of the coffee, he gave the instruction that the bomb should be prepared, he said where it should be placed.

He moved on busily.

In the Piazza Castelnuovo, among the crowds gathered to watch the end of the fifteen-kilometer race, under the blare of the loudspeakers, he met with a businessman. The businessman had never been convicted of criminal association, was not subject to investigation. The businessman told him that an investment broker from Paris had driven his car the previous Thursday to the sand dunes of the Pas de Calais and there hooked a length of rubber tubing to the exhaust and run the tube into the car and had been found dead the previous Friday. The investment broker had recommended the placing of $1 million in the construction of the tunnel beneath La Manica, and the tunnel between the English coast and the French coast had lost Mario Ruggerio that $1 million of investment. He listened without comment.

As he moved he was shadowed by three young men who stood back and apart from him.

In the Piazza Virgilio, sitting on a bench in the sunshine, an old man who talked with an old friend, he met with the cousin of a man from Prizzi. He had known the man from Prizzi all of his life. He had known the cousin as a youth, but the cousin now lived in Hamburg and had made the long journey specifically for twenty minutes of conversation on a bench in the warmth of the sun. With the cousin of the man from Prizzi he discussed, in close detail, the investment opportunities in the proposed construction of a business park in Leipzig, and the tax breaks that were possible, and afterward he talked of the similar opportunities in the housing market at Dresden. He pledged, for investment in Leipzig and investment in Dresden, a minimum of $5 million. He noted the deference of the cousin of the man from Prizzi, as if it were known that he was now the power of La Cosa Nostra.

On his way again, walking fast, his escort ahead of him and behind him. He was to take a late lunch at an apartment on the Via Terrasanta with the physician who advised him on the remedy for the rheumatism in his hip, but before his lunch he had to meet with the *consigliere* from Messina for an explanation of that family's future options and their investment cooperation and the percentages of profit . . . and he was due also to meet with Carmine on the matter of a *carabiniere* officer and an American . . . and with a chemist from Amsterdam who promised facilities for the manufacture of the new range of benzodiazapines and barbiturates . . . and with Franco to confirm the detail of the *pellegrinaggio* to the grave of his brother, Cristoforo, the annual pilgrimage with his parents. It was his Sunday, the same every Sunday when the streets and parks and piazzas were crowded, it was his *terra-terra* routine, down-to-earth and basic, the rhythm of his life on the day the city rested.

He waited for the traffic lights on the junction to change. The cars swept by him, and down the column of cars was a bus. He lit another cigarillo.

When he was not tasked for duty, Giancarlo always came on a Sunday with his wife into Palermo. He met with the leader of his team, and the leader's wife, for the regal pomp and majesty of the celebration of Mass at the *duomo,* and then the four ate an early lunch in a *ristorante* on the Via Vittorio Emanuele, and the men tried not to talk of work and the women elbowed them viciously when they failed in their intention, and there was laughter, and after the early lunch they went home to sleep through the afternoon.

When he came into the center of Palermo on a Sunday, Giancarlo always took his wife on the bus—too many cars, too few parking places.

The bus was full. He and his wife stood, and they gripped tight the back of a seat. The bus pitched them when the driver braked, threw them when the driver accelerated. In the morning the leader of the team had told him, while they walked between the *duomo* and the *ristorante,* they started a new assignment on the Piazza Kalsa. Just that morsel of information . . . Maybe he would be in a car, maybe in a closed van, maybe, God willing, in a building with the video camera and the binoculars and a good chair—maybe there would be no market where they were staked out, and no lemons. The bus stopped sharply. He lurched into his wife. The driver had tried to beat the traffic lights, but had not squeezed through.

Giancarlo, standing in the aisle of the bus, looking over the shoulder of the driver, saw the family cross the road and the children held balloons that bounced on lengths of string. When their own kids had been that age, little hooligans, he grinned, they had loved to carry balloons . . .

Giancarlo saw the man.

The kids with the balloons were in front of the man. A couple with a pram were behind the man. A woman in a fur coat and carrying a posy of flowers was beside the man.

Giancarlo saw an old man. The man had turned to face the bus, as if to satisfy himself that it had indeed stopped. Giancarlo saw an old man, a pudgy and weathered face below a flat cap, a jowled chin and throat above a rough cloth jacket.

Giancarlo saw an old man crossing a road at his leisure. The face of the old man leapt in Giancarlo's mind. There was a face in front of the bus. There was a face in a photograph that had been computer-enhanced, aged from twenty years before.

The face was gone behind the shoulder of the driver. Giancarlo squirmed to see past the shoulder. He saw the face of the man a last time, and the man was smiling down at one of the children holding a balloon. Giancarlo matched the face, smiling, with the face, smiling at a wedding reception, of the photograph.

His wife abandoned. Other passengers pushed aside. The driver shouted at. The ID card, shoved into the driver's face. The doors slowly hissing open. The man, reaching the far pavement . . .

Giancarlo jumped from the bus. He cannoned into a couple, in love, hand in hand. He did not look back at his wife, at the shock on her face. The lights changed. The bus pulled forward. Giancarlo ran behind the bus. The horns of the following cars blasted anger at him, brakes squealed. The man was walking away on the far pavement. Giancarlo had no telephone. The leader of the *squadra mobile* surveillance team carried a mobile telephone at all times, but mobile telephones were expensive, a rationed item. His personal radio was on the charger at the Questura, he was off duty, and his pistol was locked behind the armory door in the Questura. There was a telephone pager on his belt, which only carried incoming messages. He ran forward, reached the far pavement. Because of the anger of the horns, and the brakes' screams, because of the abuse shouted at him through open windows, Giancarlo was for a critical moment of time a center of attention.

In that moment of time, the man stood and faced a shop window.

Giancarlo, among his own, was venerated for experience and professionalism. For the teaching of surveillance tactics to new recruits to the teams he was often used. If a young recruit had run across a street, through traffic, become the target of horns and insults, become a center of attention, then Giancarlo would patiently have explained the error of the young recruit. He would have talked to the young recruit about the requirement to merge and blend. He did not know whether he had shown out, whether he was busted, and he did not see the *picciotto,* a swarthy and heavy-set youth, who protected the back of Mario Ruggerio. In the flush of excitement, experience and professionalism gone, he had displayed the rashness of a young recruit. He stood stock-still. He watched the back of the old man move on, a slow walk, up the Via Sammartino and then turn into the Via Turrisi Colonna. He did not know whether he had shown out.

There was a bar.

Giancarlo ran into the bar. There was a payphone on the counter. A woman talked on the payphone.

Maybe she talked with her sister in Agrigento, maybe with her mother in Misilmeri, maybe with her daughter in Partinico . . . Giancarlo snatched the telephone. He terminated her call. She howled her protest at him and he flapped his ID in her face. He was scrabbling in his pocket for a token for the telephone. He was bawling at her for silence, and he fed the *gettone* and dialed his control. He did not see the swarthy and heavy-set youth sidle across the bar toward him. Again, for a critical moment of time, Giancarlo made himself the center of attention. The bar's customers, the men, the women, the staff, the matriarch at the cash till, sided with the wronged woman. The screaming was in his ears. With his body he tried to block their hands from reaching the telephone.

His control answered.

His name, his location, the name of his target.

The pain caught him. The pain was in Giancarlo's back and then seeping to his stomach. He said again his name and his location and the name of his target. The questions from his control beat at him, but his concentration and ability to respond to the questions were destroyed by the pain. Which way was the target going? What was the target wearing? Was the target alone? Was the target in a vehicle or on foot? He said again his name and his location and the name of his target, and his voice was weaker and the pain was more acute. He dropped the phone, and the phone swung loose on its reinforced cable. He turned. He looked into the eyes of a swarthy and heavy-set youth.

Giancarlo swayed. The pain forced his eyes shut. He reached for the source of the pain in his back. He found the hardness of the knife's handle, and the wetness. When his knees gave, when he could no longer see the swarthy and heavy-set youth, when the telephone swung beyond his reach, when the screaming burst from grotesquely blurred mouths around him, Giancarlo realized, puzzled, that he could no longer remember the questions that control had asked of him.

The pain was a spasm through his body.

A square had been made.

The bar was at the center of the square. The north of the square was the Via Giacomo Cusmano, the south was the Via Principe di Villafranca, the west was the Via Dante, and the east was the gardens of the Villa Trabia.

A hundred men with guns, with flak vests, quartered the square. They were from the DIA, and there were two sections of the ROS, and there was the stand-by team of the *Guardia di Finanze*, and there were men from the *squadra mobile*. The cordon around the square was given to the military, Jeeps at street corners, soldiers with NATO rifles. They did not know what the man, Giancarlo's target, looked like, they did not know how he was dressed, they did not know in which direction he had gone, they did not know whether he walked or whether he went by car.

The bar was emptied but for the owner and the matriarch who guarded her cash till.

The body was on the floor. In the back of the body was a short-bladed, double-edged knife. The owner of the bar, facing a wall, his wrists handcuffed in the small of his back, had seen nothing. Perhaps the customers had seen something? The matriarch had seen nothing. The customers were all strangers to her and she knew none of them.

A car brought the wife of Giancarlo to the bar, and a young priest had run from the church on Via Terrasanta. The photographers from the newspapers and the cameramen from the RAI crowded the pavement.

The *maresciallo* elbowed a way through for the magistrate and Pasquale bullocked him into the bar, into the crush that circled the body. There were some who had come from family gatherings and wore their suits, some had come from the tennis courts, some from their seats in the football stadium, some from their sleep. Beside their shoes and sneakers and sandals was the body and the blood. The magistrate saw the face, bleak, of 'Vanni Crespo, and pushed toward him.

"It was shit luck," 'Vanni Crespo said. "We were so close . . ."

The tail had watched the car of 'Vanni Crespo, the *carabiniere* Alfetta car, from the barracks at Monreale to the bar on Via Sammartino. The tail was locked on 'Vanni Crespo.

"He brought me lemons, 'Vanni. I had fish for my meal on Friday. They are not supposed to do my shopping, my boys, but they prefer to do it than to take me to the market, so they break the rule, they bought fresh mullet for me. He had brought me lemons and made a joke of it. I had one of his lemons with my mullet. He was the best of men."

"It was shit luck," 'Vanni growled. "He was on the bus with his wife. He saw Ruggerio. He got off the bus. He ran through the traffic. That's the decision. You wait and you lose the target. You run and you alert the target. You've ten seconds, five seconds, to make the decision and you live by it and you die by it."

"The lemon was most sharp in the taste."

"He would have shown out when he ran. Ruggerio would have had a back marker. He had to go to the bar for communication. The back marker would have followed him. You need the luck and all you get is the shit."

"There are six more of his lemons in my kitchen . . . Do you believe in luck, 'Vanni?"

He saw the tears well at the eyes of the magistrate. He took out his handkerchief. He did not care who saw him. In the crowd in the bar, he wiped the running tears from the magistrate's face. "I believe in nothing."

"Do you believe your agent of small importance will be lucky?"

He remembered her, as he had seen her, the last look back from the side of the road before he had dropped down into the car. The last look, across the pavement, and between the trees, and across the sand, and she had stood against the brightness of the sea, and the sun had caught the white of her body skin as her towel had slipped. In the bar, with the corpse, with the soft whimpering of the widow, with the crowd, with the smell of cigarettes and cold coffee, he remembered her.

"I am sorry, *dottore,* I cannot share with you because it is not my gift."

He drove a way through the crowd in the bar, pushed through the crowd on the pavement and the street. A good man had had ten seconds, five seconds, to make a decision and the result of the decision was a mistake, and the result of a mistake was to lie dead on the dirty floor of a bar that was lit by flashlights. He went to his car, walked leaden in the dusk light.

The tail followed the Alfetta driven by 'Vanni Crespo. The tail was delayed by the military cordon around the square of streets after the Alfetta had been waved through, but it was of no consequence. The tail was linked by radio to a second car and to motorcyclists who waited outside the cordon. As if a chain held the tail to the Alfetta car . . .

When he had heard the explosion of the car horns, and then heard the insults shouted, Mario Ruggerio had paused in front of a shop window. He had appeared to study the contents of the shop window. An old practice, one that his father would have known, was to use a shop window as a mirror. He had seen a man come at desperate speed through the traffic lanes, and then reach the pavement and stop. The man, stopped, had stared up the street toward him. If the man had had a radio he would already have used it, if the man had had a mobile telephone he would not have run through the traffic lanes, if the man had carried a firearm he would not have stopped. In the reflections of the window he had seen the *picciotto,* a good boy, behind the man. He had known he was recognized and he had known the man panicked. He had realized it was a chance recognition and not a part of a comprehensive surveillance. He had made a small gesture, a single movement of his index finger, a cutting motion. He had walked away. He had turned the corner . . .

It was two hours later. Mario Ruggerio sat in the darkened room on the first floor in the Capo district. His feet ached, his lungs heaved, the ashtray was filled with the stubbed ends of his cigarillos. The two *picciotti* who had been ahead of him on the Via Sammartino had made a brutal pace for him, up to the Piazza Lolli, one pocketing the cap he had been wearing, across the Via Vito la Mancia, one taking his jacket and folding it on his arm so that the material could not be seen, past the Mercato delle Pulci, hurrying him along as if he were an old uncle out with two impatient nephews. He had slipped away from them behind the *duomo*. Even when he gasped for breath, when exhaustion bled him and he swayed on his feet, he would not have considered allowing the *picciotti* to take him to his safe house. The sweat ran on his face and on his back and on his stomach. He smoked. He held the photograph of the child he loved.

Charley sat on the patio.

The sun had gone down and only a feeble layer of light fell on the seascape ahead of her. The family had gone down to the town. She had lost the loneliness that had hurt her in Palermo. She felt, sitting in the comfortable chair on the patio, a supreme confidence. The villa was her place. The family would be walking on the esplanade, under the trees, patroling like the caged bears she had seen in zoos, where they would be seen . . . It was the time of waiting. She was in control, she felt her power. The power was the watch on her wrist. She sat with her legs apart, and the cool of the evening air made feather strokes on her thighs. She was at the center of the world of Axel Moen and the people who directed Axel Moen. She had power over Giuseppe Ruggerio and over the brother. As she watched the last of the sunlight flee the smooth surface of the sea. Because of her control and her power it would be her story that would be told, the story of Codename Helen.

In the gray light, on the patio, an arrogance tripped in Charley's mind.

The tail was locked on 'Vanni Crespo. Three bars in Monreale. The tail watched him drink alone in a bar near the *duomo,* in a second bar near the empty market stands, in a third bar high in the old town. The tail watched and followed where 'Vanni Crespo led.

Through the window of the *pizzeria* he saw 'Vanni. 'Vanni was going slowly, confused. He was lit by a street lamp and his face was flushed, and his hair hung on his forehead in careless strands, and he lurched to a stop beside the window and was struggling to find the cigarette packet in his pocket. Axel turned away. There was nowhere in the *pizzeria* for him to hide. He turned away and hoped that his face was not seen, but he heard the whip of the door opening and then the slam of it shutting and he heard the shuffle of the feet and then the scrape of the chair opposite him.

'Vanni sat in front of Axel, and he swayed on the chair before his elbows thudded down on the table.

"I find the American hero . . ."

"You pissed up or something?"

"I find the American hero who comes to Sicily to achieve what we cannot."

"You're drunk."

"We Italians are pathetic, we cannot wipe our own arses, but the American hero comes to do it for us."

"Go fuck yourself."

"You know what happened today, because we had shit luck, what happened . . . ?"

"We don't break procedure," Axel hissed across the table.

Two young men, carrying their crash helmets, were at the counter of the *pizzeria* and asking for the list of sauces.

The hand in which Axel held his fork was gripped in 'Vanni's fists. "We had surveillance people in the Capo, that's a shit place, to target the bastard. The surveillance was called off, nothing seen . . . One of the team, on a bus, sees the bastard. Off duty, no communications. We are pathetic Italians, we do not have the money to give out, sweets and chocolates, mobile telephones. Not carrying his personal radio, off duty, no sidearm. He tries to use the telephone in a bar. The bastard would have had a guy behind him, back marker. The message was incomplete, that's the shit luck. No profile and no description, no clothes, before he was stabbed to death. The bastard's gone. It's cold."

At the bar the boys with the crash helmets studied the list of pizza sauces.

"Get the hell out of here."

"He was in our hand. We snatched. We lost him. Isn't that shit luck?"

"Go and sleep with your woman."

"I drink, I don't weep. The man was dead on the floor with the crap and the cigarettes and the spit and his blood. Tardelli came down, he wept, he doesn't drink. He asked me—"

"Get some water down you, some aspirin, get to your bed."

"He's isolated, he's got the stink of failure. He has nothing, nothing to hope for. He begged . . ."

The boys with the crash helmets had seen nothing on the list of sauces that they wanted. They pushed their way out of the door, into the street.

"What did he beg?"

"Offer him something to hold to. I said it was not my gift to give. His mind is blocked, too much work, too tired, he cannot see the obvious, not followed the line of the family, as we have. He wanted me to share with him the detail of your agent."

"Bullshit."

"Your agent of small importance. He wanted the crumbs off your table. 'All I want is someone to hold my arm and walk with me.' But that's the usual sort of shit talk in Palermo when a man is isolated, that's not the talk to impress an American hero."

"I don't share."

"With Italians? Of course not. I tell you, Axel, what I saw. I saw a body on the floor, I saw the blood, I saw the fucking crowd of people. I saw her, I saw Codename Helen, I saw her body and her blood. I drink, I don't weep. Enjoy your meal."

The fists released Axel's hand that held the fork. The table rocked as 'Vanni levered himself to his feet. Axel watched him go . . . He did not see her on the floor of the bar, but she was clear in his mind and she was hanging from the nails on the back of the door of the hut at the *estancia* airstrip . . . He pushed the plate away from him. He lit a cigarette and he dropped the match on the plate, into the pizza sauce.

The tail learned the name of the woman who owned the house, and late into the night the tail watched the light burn in the upper room.

"What are my options, Ray? What do I chew on?"

The voice boomed back, metallic, from the speaker. Dwight Smythe leaned over the Country Chief's desk and twisted the volume dial. The Country Chief was scribbling headlines.

"Could you wait out, Herb? Could you let me have a minute?"

"Have two—I fancy it's better we get this right, now."

It had been a bad bloody Monday for Ray. He had been called, two hours' notice, to New Scotland Yard for late-morning coffee with biscuits and a hard-going session. He had sat with Dwight, he had been faced by the commander (SO6) and the Assistant Commissioner (SO) and the detective superintendent who was a cat with cream, and there'd been a young guy there who'd not spoken. He'd had a heavy time and they'd done their work on Mario Ruggerio (worse than the worst) and they'd a profile on Charlotte Parsons (Codename Helen). He'd broken, he'd said he needed to talk to Headquarters, and back at the embassy he'd sat on his hands waiting for Herb to show up in his office from the beltway drag into Washington. It had to be Herb he spoke to, because it was Herb who had authorized the operation.

"Got it together . . . I'm not happy, Herb. I feel I'm pushing in over Bill's space."

"Forget Bill, he'll do as he's damn well told. I get the feeling this isn't a time for standing on ceremony. Hell, I've fourteen situations going in Colombia, I've eight in Peru. I've situations running in Bangkok, Moscow, Jamaica. I'm not getting an ulcer for one situation in Sicily. I want the options."

Again Ray paused. What they hated, the big men in Washington who'd made it to the floor with the pile carpets and the drinks cabinets and access to God, was getting bounced for a decision early on a Monday morning. It was a time when his own career could go down the drain, and his hopes of ever getting his feet on that carpet and his hands on the cabinet keys, but he reckoned there wasn't room for evasion. He plunged.

"At high grade level, the British have *Angst*. They say, and I quote, 'It is intolerable that a young woman should have been pressurized by the DEA, entrapped, and then persuaded to travel to Sicily as the central part of an American sponsored anti-mafia operation,' end quote. That's, my opinion, not the core of their hand-wringing. What's right up their nose, quote, 'All DEA activities inside the UK are governed by procedures of liaison and we were not informed, prior to your inveigling Miss Parsons, of your intention to recruit her,' end quote. And most important, they have the shits on this one. They see her dead, they see the *paparazzi* crawling over her, they see an almighty inquest on what an untrained innocent was doing there in a role central to an investigation, they see the blame hammering on their door . . ."

"I asked, what are the options?"

"Two, Herb. You can tell them to go jump, tell them they are small guys running small shows and suggest they stick to softball in the park."

"We do good business with the Brits. My second option?"

"You can withdraw your sanction, Herb, close it down, you can pull her out. You can wind it up."

"Ray, we've known each other a long time, too goddam long. I am not interested in the sensitivities of Bill Hammond. The plan isn't Bill's anyway. The plan belongs to that guy Axel Moen, and I do not care whether I massage his ego or whether I kick him. Which side of the fence are you falling? I want it straight."

He glanced up at the loudspeaker on the wall, beside the Green Ice operation photograph. Herb, front row, smiling, was always the bastard who turned up late and took the credit, and hacked off early to avoid the blame. Dwight Smythe, opposite him, made the quick gesture, a finger across the throat. He spoke into the microphone, he felt dirty.

"What I want to say, Herb, I don't give a fuck for the susceptibilities of the British. They'll complain for a week, and after a week they'll be good as gold and looking for a candy hand-out. Myself, I'd ignore them."

"I hear you. Right, thanks, I'll call Bill Hammond and tell him."

"Sorry, Herb, I'm not through. This kid is on a limb, this kid has no covert training. She's been given the glamor treatment. She should never have been asked to go. I can take newspaper flak, I can handle an inquiry if she ends up dead. But I don't think, I'd want that at my door. It's a precious thing, my self respect. But, of course, Herb, if it goes sour, then it's on your desk that it lands because you authorized it."

He thought he had rolled a hand-grenade across a pile carpet and the grenade might just bounce against the imitation antique of a drinks cabinet and it might just come to rest against a desk on a high floor of Headquarters. He winked, grim, at Dwight Smythe.

The voice boomed, "Kill it."

"I think that's a good decision, Herb."

There was rain falling on the garden of the square that the embassy faced onto. The square was a goddam morgue, and the daffodils were flattened by the rainfall, and the crocus blooms were crushed. Dwight Smythe drove, and held his peace. Ray reflected. He had bled his conscience over the telephone link. Maybe he was too old and too tired, too fucked-up, for the job. Maybe he had gone too soft for the work. If the work mattered, sure as Christ it mattered, then maybe it was worth hauling any kid, any innocent, off the street, then maybe pressure was justified, if the work mattered . . . Axel Moen had been in his office, Axel Moen had treated Dwight Smythe like he was just the hired hand, Axel Moen hadn't gone hiding behind conscience, Axel Moen was a cold bastard, Axel Moen would believe the work mattered . . . They crossed central London and Dwight Smythe parked up outside the main doors of New Scotland Yard and threw the keys in an arc to a constable . . . Maybe he should feel comfortable because his back was protected, and Herb's back was safe, and the men waiting for them upstairs in the building could feel good because their backs were covered, and maybe he'd be offered a drink because all the big guys were protected and safe and covered, and in this fucking awful world that was what mattered. If it had been for the kid, the innocent, if it had been for protecting and saving and covering the kid, then he could have felt good, but it wasn't . . . They came out of the elevator and stamped along the corridor behind the constable escorting them. It was a bad bloody Monday.

"I talked with Washington. Washington say we abort."

The AC (SO) said, "Not next week, not next month. We'll send our own man."

The commander (SO6) said, "The operation will be terminated immediately. For verification, you understand."

The detective superintendent said, "We'd like to be certain there's a degree of urgency. So we know you haven't welshed."

He was introduced to Harry Compton, who hadn't spoken, who had the thick file. He said that since it was a DEA operation into which there was now British input, gagged on "intrusion," he would send his administrative officer, Dwight Smythe, to accompany Compton, gagged on "hold his hand."

The AC (SO) said, "Very satisfactory, good cooperation."

The commander (SO6) asked, "Not too early for a drop of the hard stuff, eh, Ray, and you, Mr. Smythe? Ice, water?"

"Are you into this story, Mr. Compton? Scotch, yes, stiff."

"I am."

"You've evaluated Charlotte Parsons, this innocent?"

He had intended to sneer, never could do it well, was a poor hand at sarcasm.

"Yes, I have. Your people chose well. I'd rate her as brilliant. Stubborn, tough. That's why I fear for her safety. What I've heard and learned, she is the type who will cling in there. And, sir, when you have a very strong personality placed in such position as she is, I would also fear for the safety of those around her."

"Would you now? A hell of a shame she's coming home, don't you think, gentlemen? A shame we all needed to get our snouts in the trough . . ."

15

AROUND HIM WERE THE SMELLS. He was blindfolded. He could see nothing, not even strips of faint light at the bottom of the cloth over his eyes nor at the top. The cloth had been wound tight round his head at least three times and on top of the cloth was a broad, sticky tape. He did not know how many hours, how many days and nights, he had been there.

The smells cloyed at Benny's nose, they hung in his nostrils. They were the smells of the animals and of his own body. The smells were of the excreta and the urine and the filthy hair coats of animals, and of the shit in his trousers and the piss that was raw-warm on his legs, and the sweat at his armpits and his groin that came from the fear.

His arms had been wrenched behind him when they had dragged him from the vehicle and brought him to the byre. Any movement that he tried to make carried fierce pain because his arms had been looped round a post of coarse wood and his wrists had been lashed tight, and if he tried to move, the sockets of his shoulders seemed about to break. He did not know how many hours he had been there, but he believed that when he next heard men's voices they would have come to kill him. He did not want to hear them come, hear a car reach the barn, hear the voices, because then they would have come to kill him. But, in his fear, Benny strained for the slightest sound. There were the heavy clumsy movements of the animals in the byre, jostling each other, and there was the grunting of their breathing, and there was the heavy chewing as they ate. Sometimes they touched him, great creatures that seemed in the blackness of his imagination to tower over him, but it was always with gentleness.

Sometimes they nuzzled at his face, hot breath, and sometimes they licked the hands that were lashed tight behind the post, slobbering tongues. Because he waited for the car to come, and the voices, he heard every movement of the animals around him. He did not know how many hours it was since the muscles of his stomach had broken and he had messed in his trousers, but the slime was now cold. It was more recently that the piss had burst from his bladder, and his thighs were still wet. It was because of the girl.

The animals heard the car before Benny did. The animals bellowed, great voices booming in the byre. He heard the car. It was because of the girl, and he hated the girl for what she had made him do. The car pulled to a stop and he heard the tires on loose stones. He would, if it had not been for the girl, in the afternoon of tomorrow or yesterday—he had lost track of time—have driven after school to Corleone and collected the photocopier and driven it back to San Giuseppe Jato, and would have known that he was involved and caring and playing a part, but the girl had destroyed him. The girl had made him tell the story of his father, and his father had not carried a photocopier back from Corleone to San Giuseppe Jato, his father had fought them, and the girl had made him tell his father's story. He heard a padlock unfastened. It had been the fault of the girl. The hysteria rose in him and he tried to push himself farther back against the post. It was his father who had the blame. He heard the door scrape open. He heard a coughed spit and the smack of a hand on the body of an animal and the sounds of the stampede of the feet of the beasts as if a way was cleared to him. Benny wanted to shout, to plead with them, tell them that it was the fault of the girl, that the blame was with his father. He had no voice.

His hands were pulled back from the post and the pain riveted in his shoulders. He felt at his wrist the sharp nick of a knife blade, then the twine that had bound him to the post was loosened. He was pulled upright. They laughed. Three separate shouts of laughter, growled and shrill and quiet, and he stood and they would have seen the stain on the front of his trousers and the damp weight in the seat of his trousers. He was led, stumbling, over the fodder floor of the byre.

There was sun on his face, on his cheeks, below the blindfold. He heard birdsong. His feet caught on the stones. Without warning, the hair of his head was caught and his skull was pushed down, but his scalp caught against a metal edge. He was forced low into the trunk of a vehicle, and there was the slam of the top closing on him. He was crushed, fetal, the way he had lain as a child in his parents' bed, between his mother and his father. The vehicle bumped away and his body was pierced by what he thought was a jack, but it might have been a heavy wrench-spanner. They were taking him away to kill him. The petrol stank in his nose, and the fumes of the exhaust. They would not hear him when he shouted that it was the fault of the girl, that his father should be blamed. He hated the girl. He rejected his father. He was so frightened. He could go into the drum of acid, he could go into the concrete, he could go into the dark depths of the gully where the crows did not feed and where Placido Rizzotto had been thrown. No one knew where to search for him. He had not told his mother that he was going to Prizzi, nor his friends in Palermo, nor the man who owned the photocopier in San Giuseppe Jato, nor the women who wrote the newsletter in Corleone. The vehicle was on tarmacadam and speeding. He wept, and the tears clogged his eyes beneath the cloth blindfold. On his side, squirming in the trunk of the car, choking on the fumes, he screamed for their mercy, but he could not be heard. He wondered if they all shouted for mercy before they went into the drum of acid or the concrete or the gully, if they all rejected their fathers and their girls. The vehicle stopped sharply, and the piss was running warm on his thighs again.

The air was on his face. There were the sounds of other cars and of a motorcycle speeding past, and a dog barked and radios played.

"Please . . . forgive me . . . please . . ." He heard the croak of his own voice.

He was pulled from the trunk of the vehicle. The piss dribbled hot on his legs. Hands gripped his arms. He was led down a slight slope and his feet were on old cobbles. He could not break free, could not run, he was broken. The arms jerked him back and stopped him. The tape was dragged from the cloth. The cloth was unwound from his face.

ASSASSINO.

The word was in paint on the door. The door was beside a black drainpipe. In front of the door was a plastic bucket of steaming water, and an old brush with stiff bristles floated among the suds of the water. He took the brush from the water and he started to scrub at the word he had written in paint. The dog that had taken the spray can came and sniffed at him and snarled. Children came and shrieked laughter and held their noses because he stank. As if the house behind the door was empty, there was no sound from inside, no radio, no movement. The girl had destroyed him. He scrubbed at the painted word until his fingers ached and his arms ached and his shoulders ached, until he had removed the trace of his protest. The girl had made him tell the story of his father. He scrubbed until the door was clean, as if the word had never been written. He was broken.

He straightened. The last of the water had been used, the bucket was empty. He placed the brush in the bucket and put the bucket on the step of the door. The road was in shadow and deserted. The children had gone, and the dog, and the men who had brought him. On the cobbles behind him was his wallet, pegged down with a stone. There was no trace of the word, as there was no trace of his life. He walked away. His car was where he had left it.

Later he would return to his apartment in Palermo, and before he had stripped his clothes and washed his body he would tear the posters from the walls.

"I should apologize, yes? I should ask you to forgive me?"

Charley held the plastic tub of washed, wet clothes. Angela pegged the clothes methodically to the line. It was inevitable. The only surprise to Charley, it had been so long coming. Angela did not look at her and she spoke in a flattened monotone.

"When I told Peppino that I wanted you here, I thought if you came it would be different. I thought it would be the same as it was in Rome. But this is not Rome, it is Palermo. Palermo is not our home, as was Rome. Do I make a confusion for you? You are not an idiot, Charley, you can recognize that we have changed. Why have we changed? Palermo is the true home of Peppino, Palermo is the place for the peasants, it is the place of the family. I knew nothing, in Rome, of the truth of Peppino, I lived my own life and I was happy, and you came and you were a part of that happiness. Do you look around, Charley, and do you wonder what is now different?"

Charley passed the children's clothes and the pegs. She stayed silent, she could offer no comfort. To offer comfort was to endanger herself.

"We were comfortable in Rome, we had a wonderful apartment, we had the good life. You saw it and you went away. Four years later you come back—what do you find? We are a new generation of Sicilians, we live like the princes of the Bourbons, the caliphs of the Moors, the nobility of the Normans. An apartment that is a palace, a villa, money so that it ceases to have meaning, jewels, cars from the latest production, always the goddam presents. Do you ask, Charley, alone in your room, where it comes from? Do you ask how it is that Peppino, a businessman in Rome and ordinary, is now in Sicily a businessman of the superstratum? I would ask, if I were you. But you see, Charley, in Sicily there is the web of the *famiglia*—I have every material possession I could want, perhaps I seem ungrateful, and I have the family of Peppino . . ."

The voice drove on, breaking off when a garment slipped from the line because a peg did not hold it. She lived the lie, she had the watch on her wrist, she had the access and she waited for the opportunity. She kept her silence.

"...Do you know, Charley, that while you were in the city on Sunday, when Peppino and I and the children were at Mass, that men came into our home, my home, and they swept it with electronic devices to see that we were not listened to, to see that the police had not placed listening devices in our home, my home? Every second Sunday they come. Why? Have you heard Peppino talk here about confidential business? Never. It is not for industrial sabotage, it is for police microphones. Peppino must be certain that conversations concerning the *famiglia* are not listened to. Put it together, Charley, the wealth and the family, the affluence and the family. Where does the wealth come from? From the family ..."

In front of Charley was the strong wooden gate set in the high fence. Beside Charley was the path from which the gardener had picked up the crushed tip of a cigarillo. She held Peppino's shirts and the damp ran on her arms. She played her part, the innocent home-help, played the lie.

"...He is a grotesque sham. My Peppino is a creature created by his family. He fulfills a need for the family. What would he be if the need did not exist? A criminal? An extortionist? A killer? Do I upset you, Charley? There are enough of those in the family, they have no need for more. They need the sham that is *rispettabilità,* you understand me, Charley? They have the wealth, the family, but they need the sham of respectability. I am a part of the sham, I am from the pedigree of the Vatican, I give respectability. He is a criminal, my husband and my children's father, as his family. Why I am so alone, Charley, so isolated here, so devastated here, why I need you, Charley. He is controlled by his brother, has the criminal guilt of his brother ..."

Her voice died, as if in sudden submission. For a moment she looked behind Charley, then at the pegs and washing on the line. Charley thought, like she's trapped, like she has no escape. Charley turned. The gardener pushed the wheelbarrow, on the path round the villa, toward them. She passed Angela the last of Peppino's shirts.

Back in the kitchen the baby was crying. The confessional was finished. Angela, in her kitchen, made the baby's feed, brittle, sharp movements.

Harry Compton and Dwight Smythe met at Heathrow. Each had made his own way west out of the capital, each would have said that there was no requirement to share transport. They met at check-in. If there was mutual respect, they hid it. The detective sergeant of SO6 and the office administrator from the DEA, were brusque in their greetings, showed a minimum of courtesy. Harry Compton would have said that he, alone, was perfectly capable of extracting Miss Charlotte Parsons. Dwight Smythe would have said that he, alone, was perfectly capable of aborting Axel Moen. They went through Departure, showed no sign of being colleagues who traveled together, they went their separate ways in Duty-Free and the Briton bought Scotch and the American bought Jack Daniel's. They sat on the bench and read newspapers. Each was an intrusion into the world of the other. They were called for take-off.

Cautiously, Pasquale knocked at the door. The call came. He carried the mug of hot coffee into the room, and he went to the magistrate's desk and put the coffee mug down beside the computer's screen.

"Thank you, that is very kind. Very considerate of you. How goes it, Pasquale?"

He grimaced. "This morning the *maresciallo* wrote his assessment of me."

"He read it back to you?"

"That is the regulation, I am entitled to know." He had come to work at five and then the bedroom door of the magistrate had been open, and the door of the living room had been closed and the light had shone under that door. He saw the wan tiredness on the face of the magistrate.

"It is good coffee. Thank you. What did he write of you? If you do not wish to . . ."

Pasquale said, "That I was unsuitable, that I was inefficient, that my enthusiasm did not compensate for my mistakes, that I tried to make a friend of you, that I crashed a car, that I was late for duty, that I had forgotten to load a magazine—"

"You are very young, you have a baby, you have a wife, you have a life in front of you. Is it for the best?"

He said simply, "It's what I want to do. But the *maresciallo* says I endanger you and my colleagues by my incompetence."

"Do you wish my intervention?"

"I would be ashamed if, through your intervention, I held my job."

"So each of us, Pasquale, each of us has a bad day."

Such sadness on the magistrate's face, and no attempt to hide it. He bled for the man. He could not ask the magistrate to intervene for him, could not call that card. More than anything in his police career he wished to succeed in this work. To turn his back on the magistrate, Rocco Tardelli, to return to the uniform, would be humiliation. He hesitated. He was a humble policeman, without rank and without seniority, and he wanted to say something that was of comfort to this older and troubled man. He did not know what he could say. He hesitated, then started for the door.

"Pasquale, please—sometimes it needs a younger mind, sometimes it needs the freshness. I have no lead, I have nothing, I have to begin again. Please. Where does Ruggerio go? What must Ruggerio have?"

He blurted, "A dentist?"

"How many dentists in Palermo? How many more dentists in Catania and Agrigento and Messina and Trapani? Has he dentures? Does he need a dentist? I cannot have every dentist on the island watched for the one day a year when he is visited by Mario Ruggerio."

"An optician?"

"I do not know that he wears spectacles and, again, if he does, how many opticians on the island are available to Mario Ruggerio? Help me, with a young mind."

Pasquale furrowed his forehead, considered. "You have investigated the family?"

"I ask for a young mind, not the obvious. The family is the beginning, the middle, the end. We have a camera at his father's house. I should not tell you. And I should not tell you, we have a camera and we have audio close to the house of his wife. His brother, a brute, in prison in Asinara—you do me great damage if you repeat what I say—we have audio in his cell. His other brother is handicapped and we forget him. His sister, we forget her, alcoholism. Please, my boy, give us credit for the obvious."

The apology was on his lips . . . He stared, amazed. A shock wave seemed to Pasquale to flow across the magistrate's face. Tardelli jerked out of his chair, slipped, was on the carpet. Pasquale was rooted. He crawled on his hands and knees to the bedroom wardrobe that was so strange in a living and working area. He dragged it open. Files cascaded on him. Closed files and opened files, files held with tape and files bound with string. Pasquale watched. He groped among the files, scanned the titles of the files, pulled more files from the wardrobe. He whistled an aria as the heap of files grew. Papers scattered and he swept them clear, and they were buried by more files. He found one. He ripped the tape from it. No longer whistling, he now cooed like a dove. The papers fluttered from his hands. He shouted, a noise of exaltation. He held two sheets of paper.

"There was a brother, Pasquale, I interviewed him myself. Four years ago, in Rome, I interviewed him. A banker. So plausible, the link with the criminality of the family cut. I accepted it. No surveillance, no telephone intercept. I buried the memory. The memory was lost under blankets of information, new strata of information, further leaves of information. My mind lost him. I am ashamed . . . It is the place to look, isn't it, Pasquale, where you have forgotten to look, where there is no connection?"

He stood. His face, to Pasquale, was ripped by a sort of manic happiness.

He hugged Pasquale.

At the desk he snatched for the telephone. He dialed. He waited and the aria climbed to a peak.

"Gianni? Tardelli, the 'walking corpse' of Palermo. Gianni, four years ago, in EUR, I met with Giuseppe Ruggerio. Yes, no connection. What of him now? Gianni, call me."

There were two and a quarter hours between the arrival of the London flight and the departure of the Palermo flight. There was no ceremony. They sat in Bill Hammond's car, Dwight Smythe in the front with the Country Chief and Harry Compton in the back. Bill Hammond had brought coffee from a kiosk.

"It's a sad damned day . . ."

"What we're saying in London, Mr. Hammond, it should never have gone this far," Harry Compton said, sparring. "We are also saying that if there had been correct consultation at the start, then there would never have been this difficulty. I don't think anyone's enjoying it."

"As you eloquently put it, Bill, it is a 'sad damned day' because the plan was irresponsible from the kick-off," Dwight Smythe said, sullen. "We are left with dog shit on our shoes."

It was a new world for Harry Compton. He had never before been overseas for SO6. All pretty structured back in London. A good pattern of seniority to lean against back in London. He sat in the car and held the coffee, had a single sip and thought it gritty. Perhaps, he had thought, when the two of them were together on the flight, beside each other, they could defrost the chill of the inter-organization spat, and they hadn't. They'd worn their badges, different armies, in cold hostility. Perhaps, he had thought, they'd be given the good treatment when they landed at Rome, and given a good meal and a good briefing and a dose of civilization, and he was uncomfortable in a car out on the edge of a bloody parking area.

"Did I hear you right? Dog shit?"

"That's what I said," Dwight Smythe intoned.

"And you, what did you call it? A 'difficulty'?"

"That's our opinion," Harry Compton said.

"I wasn't happy, I had cold feet. Hear me through—the plan was brilliant. It's the sort of plan that comes along off the rainbow, and it just stands a chance. It stands a chance because Axel Moen is one hell of a fine operator. He's not you, Smythe, not you, Compton, not a blow-in, not a smart-ass who comes in on the big bird and thinks he knows the fucking game. Axel Moen is top of the tree. What does he get for being top of the tree? He gets a posting to a shit place like Lagos, and a bastard like me dresses Lagos up as a good slot."

Harry Compton said, "I don't think obscenities help. Our priority is to get Charlotte Parsons. . . ."

"Where'd they dig you up from? A creche? A nursery? Training school? You don't ever name names. She's a code, she's Codename Helen. You don't throw names in Sicily. You work in Sicily, you have to be big, not a fucking ant. It's a sad damned day when people like you—and you, Smythe—get to interfere."

"Has your agent been told, that we are bringing Codename Helen home?"

A bitter smile crossed the Country Chief's face. "You are a funny man, Compton, you make me laugh. You think I'm doing the crap work for you. I messaged him to meet you. You tell him his plan was shit and made a 'difficulty.' Tell him yourself."

He thought he was followed, but he was unsure of it. He thought he was followed as he left the *duomo* in Monreale. As Axel walked away from the cloister he saw, on the other side of the street, a man of middle age and wire-thin build take off his cap and slip it into the hip pocket of his trousers, and a hundred meters farther on, at the edge of the piazza, the man wore another cap of a different color and a different material. A hundred meters farther on, by the stalls that sold fish and meat, vegetables and fruit and flowers, the man had gazed into a shop window, studying women's clothes, and Axel had passed by him, and he had not seen him again. He could not be certain that he was followed. Maybe the man, forty something, with the wire-thin build, had bought a new cap and was dissatisfied with it and put his old cap back on, and maybe he looked at women's underwear because that gave him a jerk-off thrill or because his wife's birthday was coming up, or maybe he followed the procedures of foot surveillance. Axel breathed hard. In La Paz he had been followed, once, and he had hit the numbers of his mobile and called out the cavalry and two streets later he had walked on a wide pavement that was suddenly crawling with his own guys and with the Bolivian task force people, and the tail had flaked away. He had no cavalry in Monreale. His training was in surveillance, not in counter-measure tactics. He breathed hard, deep. He assumed, if he was indeed followed, that they would use the technique of the "floating box." There would be men ahead of him, men behind him, men on the same side of the street and men on the opposite side of the street. But it was early in the afternoon, and the siesta hours had not started, and the pavements were full. If he ran, suddenly, tried to break out of the box, then he told them, put it up in neon lights, that he knew he was followed. His mind ratcheted, going fast, considering how he should act . . . His problem, on the busy streets, he could not identify the operators or the command operator of the floating box. He walked faster and slower, he lingered in front of shops and in front of stalls, he passed a *tabaccaio,* then turned sharply to retrace his steps and went inside and bought a throwaway lighter, and he could not confirm that he was the centerpiece of a floating box, nor confirm that his strained imagination merely goaded him. He walked on. He did not know. He made a long loop, and he came back to the garden terrace at the back of the *duomo.* He sat on a bench. From the terrace, among the flowers climbing on walls and under the wide shade of the trees, he could look down onto Palermo and the sea, where she had been. Axel did not know if he was watched . . .

"It is the thirteenth."

"No, the ninth."

"I do not wish to dispute with you, Mama, but it is the thirteenth."

"You told me, it was fifteen years ago, that it was the ninth, it is what a mother remembers."

"Mama, I promise you, it is the thirteenth."

His father said, growl of the peasant's *dialetto,* "Last year you said it was the eleventh, the year before it was the fourteenth, the year before that it was—"

"Papa, I assure you, you are mistaken."

"No, Mario, it is you that are mistaken. Each year you make a different number and argue with your mother."

At the start of the viaduct, where it climbed on columns of concrete to cross the river valley and carry the *autostrada,* No. 186, from Monreale by the high route over the mountains to Partinico, the car was parked on the hard shoulder. Each year they made the argument because each year Mario Ruggerio forgot the number he had given in 1981. The problem, for Mario Ruggerio, he did not know in which column of concrete was the body of his brother.

Franco was at the wheel of the parked car and had his head down in a newspaper. Franco would not dare to snigger at the ritual dispute over which column of concrete carried the body of Cristoforo. There was a second car parked farther back, and a third car stopped at the far end of the viaduct, near the sixtieth column or the sixty-first.

His mother held the lavish bunch of flowers. He could not tell his mother that he hazarded his security each year when he came to the viaduct and then argued over which column of concrete held Cristoforo's body. He could not lash his mother with his tongue because his mother had no fear of him. He could not tell his mother that he did not know in which column of concrete . . . His father always sided with his mother, as if his father wished to cut him to size. Did they want him to blow up the viaduct, drop it, then dynamite each column of concrete, then break each column with pneumatic drills? Did they need to know so badly in which column was his brother, Cristoforo?

"I think you are correct, Mama. It is the ninth."

His mother bobbed her head, satisfied. He loved two people in the world. He loved his small nephew who was named after him, and he loved his mother, loved them more than his own wife and his own children. And he could not spend the day standing in public view on the viaduct and arguing. His father would not let the matter go. His father had three reasons, he accepted, to be in a foul temper.

"You were wrong then, Mario? You accept that you were wrong?"

"Yes, Papa. I was wrong."

"Cristoforo is in the ninth column?"

"The ninth, Papa."

The first reason for the foul temper of his father. A young man, the son of a nuisance enemy, had daubed paint on the door of his father's house. The young man could not be adequately punished because the door of the house in Prizzi was covered by an unmanned police camera. If the young man disappeared or was found adequately punished then the *carabinieri* and the *squadra mobile* would be swarming through the home of Rosario and Agata Ruggerio and stressing them. The matter was dealt with, the camera would show the act, and the camera would show the contrition. The film from the camera was taken, a poor secret, each fourth night for examination. His father had wanted, personally, to slit the throat of the young man.

The second reason for the temper. The pilgrimage to the viaduct had been delayed for twenty-four hours, missing the exact anniversary of the entombment in concrete, because it had been necessary for Mario Ruggerio to review his security after the close call in the Via Sammartino, and that he would not discuss with his father. His father no longer understood, at eighty-four years of age, his son's life.

The third reason for the temper. It had been a long journey for his parents. He could not guarantee that they were not under surveillance.

A bus to Caltanisetta, from the crowded market in Caltanisetta to the rail station, escorted by Carmine. The slow train to Palermo. Picked up by himself and Franco at the *Stazione Centrale* in Palermo and driven to the viaduct.

He walked back to the start of the viaduct. He counted. He strode toward his parents and the parked car. It was beneath his dignity to rush. He came to the ninth column of concrete. His brother had worked for the Corleonesi of Riina. His brother had been killed by the men of Inzerillo, and Inzerillo was dead from armor-piercing bullets, tested on a jewelery-shop window, in his car. The men who had acted on the orders of Inzerillo were in the bay, once the food for crabs. He had been told the same month, by the Corleonesi of Riina, that they had heard his brother was buried in wet concrete during the construction of the viaduct. The Corleonesi had killed Inzerillo. Mario Ruggerio, with his own hands, with rests to regain his strength, had strangled the four men who had taken Inzerillo's orders. He had only the word of the Corleonesi that Cristoforo's body was in one of the viaduct's columns of concrete. In truth, the cadaver of Cristoforo could be anywhere . . . It would distress his mother, whom he loved, should he raise a doubt about the ultimate resting place of her favorite son.

"Here, Mama, the ninth column . . ."

He looked over the edge of the parapet, leaned forward so that he could see the great weather stained column of concrete. He had thought, and never said so to his father and mother, that his brother had been an idiot to have associated with the Corleonesi of Riina.

His father grumbled, "But there are two columns, one for each side. Is it the ninth column on the left, or the ninth column on the right?"

"On the right, Papa, the ninth column on the right."

His mother held the flowers over the parapet. They had cost 50,000 *lire* at the stall beside the entrance to the *Stazione Centrale*. He held his mother's arm. She crossed herself. She let the flowers slip from her hand, and they fell far down past the column of concrete and broke apart, scattered, when they hit the rocks of the riverbank.

He still held his mother's arm, to propel her back to the car where Franco waited. His father trailed behind, refusing to be hurried. The ritual was done. He opened the door for his mother and Franco had the engine running. He helped his father into the car after his mother. It would be bad for the dignity of Mario Ruggerio to scurry but he went fast to the front passenger door of the car. They powered away. He turned to his mother. It was a question that would not have been appropriate while they mourned the dead Cristoforo.

"Have you had notification of when Salvatore is brought to Ucciardone for the court? When does he come? I would wish you to take a personal message from me to Salvatore . . ."

" 'Gianni, I would not have called you if it were not important . . . It is not good enough, my friend, please . . . Please do not just tell me that he no longer lives on the Collina Fleming. Where does he live? Another place in Rome, in Milan, in Frankfurt or Zurich, where? I think, 'Gianni, I have not much time, how could you understand because you are not in Palermo? I know, I know, we said there was no connection . . . I know, I know, he attacked because he was persecuted without cause for the blood relationship. I am blundering in darkness, 'Gianni, I look for any light however faint. Please, where now is Giuseppe Ruggerio?"

Axel sat in his room.

He heard the widow, the Signora Nasello, moving on the floor below, and he heard her television. The smell of her cooking came into his room.

Axel sat on the bed in his room.

It was a long time since he had felt true fear, but the memory stayed clean. It was back to his fifteenth year, when he had been with his grandfather out on the water of Eagle Harbor, out from Ephraim and toward the distant shape of Chambers Island, and the storm had come fast out of the mist. Gone after the muskie with his grandfather, trolling big spoons from an open boat. The landmass of the Peninsula State Park, and the lighthouse on the Eagle Bluff, had disappeared, so quick. No sight of land, the white wave caps above gray, cold water . . . The boat pitching, the bilges filled, the spray coming into the boat, the engine failing. He had felt, in his fifteenth year, a true fear then. His grandfather had spent thirty minutes, seemed an eternity, working at the outboard with the cowling off, and had regained the power. Cold, soaked, frightened, his grandfather had brought him back to the jetty at Ephraim, and not re-marked on it . . . He had not felt fear in La Paz, not when they had hit the firefight on the *estancia* airstrip. He had not felt fear when he had been called in by the big guys in Washington and told, serious and heavy, that a video of him arriving at the Grand Jury hearing to testify had been picked up in a house search down in Colombia's city of Cali . . .

Axel sat on the bed in his room and, with a handkerchief he wiped each moving part of his dismantled pistol.

He felt the fear because he was alone. The guys in La Paz, the guys in New York, the guys at Headquarters and the guys on the Via Sardegna would have, he reckoned, bet money that Axel Moen didn't know true fear—they would have bet their shirts and their salaries. The bastards didn't know . . . Couldn't call 'Vanni, he had bad-mouthed 'Vanni. Couldn't call 'Vanni to tell him that he understood the story of the general who wanted the comfort of having his arm held because he had pissed all over that story. Couldn't call 'Vanni to tell him that he might be under surveillance, and might not, couldn't, tell him that he had shit fear because a middle-aged man on the far side of the street had changed caps and then stood in a window and eyed ladies' clothes. He was too goddam proud to be laughed at, as 'Vanni would have laughed at him. The fear held him . . .

When he had reassembled the pistol he cleared the magazines and let the bullet shells lie on the coverlet of the bed, and then he began carefully to reload the magazines.

She would have understood. If she had been beside him, sitting with him on the bed, he could have told her. He could have said, slow, to her, that he apologized for the bullshit he had given her about being strong. He could have said that it was the tactic to use smart talk to toughen her, and he could have held her hand and talked to her of his fear. He could have kissed her forehead and her eyes and talked about his fear and his loneliness. She'd know the agony of fear. She would be in the villa, and maybe sitting on her bed, and maybe her fingers ran on the face of the watch against the skin of her wrist. The world seemed to him, to Axel, to close around him, as the darkness had closed on him when he had come back from the terrace behind the *duomo,* when he had made all the clever moves that the instructors predicted would be used by a target under surveillance in a floating box, when he had failed to confirm the tail . . . He saw her face. She was in the garden behind the bungalow, and on the cliff near to her home. She was by the river in Rome. She was on the pavement in Palermo and bleeding. She was on the beach and dressing. He saw the frightened bravery on her face. He wanted to be sick. He felt, never before, that he despised himself. She should not have been asked . . . She might be on the patio in the darkness or in her room, alone. She might be with the family, living the lie. She would have the fear, as he had the fear. He shivered.

He reloaded the pistol with the filled magazine, and he pocketed the other magazines. The guys would be at the airport. He could not be at the airport as he had been instructed, because, maybe, he had a tail on him. He thought he knew why they came.

"Is this the way you normally do business?"
"Don't bad mouth me."
"Your man said we'd be met."

"I heard it, like you heard it."

"Well, where's the welcoming delegation. Where is he?"

"I don't know."

And Dwight Smythe, again, looked around him. It had been the last flight of the evening into Punta Raisi airport from Rome. The passengers had gone, gone with their baggage. Policemen watched them, and check-in girls, and porters. They stood in the middle of the Arrivals hall. Harry Compton wouldn't have admitted it, not willingly, wild horses to drag it from him, but he was frightened. Because he was actually frightened, he sneered at the American.

Dwight Smythe, honest, said, "It's kind of threatening, isn't it? It's just an airport, it's just like any other goddam airport, but you feel sort of sick in the gut. I mean, it's a place you've heard about, read about, seen on the TV, and you're here and your greeter doesn't show and you're kind of scared . . . When I was at Quantico, where we train, years back, there was a professor who talked to us, Public Affairs, he said, 'Down there it's a war of survival, as it has been through history, a bad place to be on the losing side, it's a war to the death.' I just push paper, don't aim to get onto the battleground, it's why I'm scared."

"Thanks."

"One more thing, but it's worth saying. You gave your evaluation of that kid—'brilliant, stubborn, tough'—but that doesn't justify what was asked of her. This war's going nowhere, it can't be won. Sending her was a gesture, and that's not right, gestures are lousy. You scared?"

He hesitated. He nodded.

Harry Compton was frightened because he had spent six hours the previous evening, gone on until the street outside the SO6 office was quiet, in their library. He had gutted what they had in their library, the files that were headlined "Mafia/Sicily," and then he had driven over to New Scotland Yard and kicked the doziness out of the night duty man in Organized Crime (International) and read more. He had taken in the statistics of product, volume, profit of La Cosa Nostra—and the figures of homicide, bombings, extortion cases—and the photographs of the Most Wanted—and the assessments and intelligence digests.

The night duty man must have warmed to him, had seemed pleased to talk, to break the boredom of the empty hours. The night duty man had coughed through a life story. Northern Ireland as liaison with the local force for Anti-Terrorist, a stress created breakdown and shipped out to a desk job, handling informers, the twilight people in the Provo ranks who were turned, had built the stress running "players" with a future of torture, and then a bullet in the skull had bred the breakdown. "They get dependent on you, you're not supposed to but you get involved with them, you put them in place and you use them and you manipulate them, they lead bloody boring lives and they're there for one moment in time that matters, you've put them there for that one moment, if they can't handle the one moment of something that's important then they're dead."

He thought he was sharp, he hoped to make the grade through night study for the business management degree, and he had realized when he had finished with the files that he was going into water where he would be out of his depth . . . Christ, miserable Miss Mavis inquisitive Finch, counter clerk in the bank on the Fulham Road who had filed the disclosure report on the cash deposit of Giles bloody Blake, had pitched him in . . . He'd gone back home to Fliss, some god-awful hour, and she'd sulked and said it was her mother's anniversary he'd be missing . . .

Dwight Smythe grinned. "Maybe we get to share a room tonight, maybe we leave the light on . . ."

The American tried again on the mobile telephone. It was the fourth time since they had landed that he had tapped the numbers for Axel Moen's telephone, the fourth time the call had not been answered.

"So what's to do?"

Dwight Smythe flashed his teeth. "Ride into town, get that big room with the bright light, and wait. You got anything else to suggest?"

They took a taxi into Palermo.

The journalist from Berlin waved his bank note for 20,000 *lire* at the steward. He thought the bar of La Stampa Estera to be the most dismal drinking hole that he knew, a heavy and darkened room and company to match. But they should know, the journalists who worked the Rome beat, the reality of the strength of La Cosa Nostra. He bought his second round of drinks, and none of those he entertained had complained and demanded the right to buy. They drank what he bought, and he believed they mocked him. He was not proud of himself for coming to such a place and seeking the input of fellow trade hacks, but his story was littered, so far, with cavities and loose ends. He needed their assessments. Was the corruption in central government so widespread? Was there indeed a third tier of bankers and politicians, generals and secret servicemen, who protected the principals of the organization? Was a victory in Sicily possible? What was the lifestyle of the *capo di tutti capi* and how did he evade arrest? They mocked him, and they drank the Scotch he bought and the beers.

A magazine writer from Rotterdam said, "Never go down there, a played-out story. Go to Sicily, and all you end with is confusion. What my people are interested in is the Tower at Pisa, after the last earthquake, whether it's going to fall on a bus load of our tourists."

A freelance writer from Lisbon said, "I can't get a word in the paper about Sicily. Haven't been down there for nine months. It's expensive. Anyway the food in Palermo is revolting. Nothing changes. It is the most tedious story in Europe. Now the Brazilian who is playing for Juventus, the striker, that is a page lead . . ."

An agency lady from Paris said, "The mafia? The mafia make my people go to sleep. If I want anything in the paper, and I have to want it because I am paid by the line, then I write about fashion and I write about the new gearbox in the Ferrari."

A super-stringer on retainer to a London daily said, "Nobody is interested, nobody cares, Sicily might be another planet. It is where they make an art form of deception, an industry of misinformation. Do you think they will use your story? I doubt it, I think you chase ghosts."

An Italian woman under contract to nine evening newspapers in Japan said, "There is no interest because the mafia story is not about real people. The judges, the policemen, the criminals, they are the characters of a cartoon strip. People we can understand, people we can believe in, they do not exist in Sicily . . ."

The telephone rang. They listened. When the telephone was on secure, and the voice strength was diminished, then the magistrate always shouted. It was past midnight, it was quiet in the kitchen. In deference to the magistrate's request they did not play the radio in the kitchen late at night. If they played the radio late at night then the cow from the next apartment, with the common wall, would come in the morning and rail against the magistrate that she could not sleep. It was as if the *ragazzi* believed their man had sufficient problems without adding the cow's complaints. They listened.

"... I do not believe it, 'Gianni . . . How is that possible? Why was I not told? We all have a work load, 'Gianni, we are all buried under a work load . . . Yes, I have it, I have written it. Of course, I am grateful . . . I told you, I look for any light, I do not know where I will find the light . . ."

There was a time of silence and then they heard the shuffle of his feet.

He came to the kitchen door. He wore his slippers and a robe over his pajamas. There was a gray tiredness in his face, and his hair hung clumsily on his forehead. The *maresciallo* snapped his fingers at Pasquale.

Pasquale asked, *"Dottore,* would you like juice, or coffee, or tea?"

The shaken head. Pasquale wondered if the magistrate had taken a pill. He had gone to his bedroom a good hour before. He could have taken a pill, he could have been deep in sleep. There were four of them round the table with their newspapers and their cards and the filled ashtray.

"Nothing, thank you. *Maresciallo,* please, I ask a favor of you. It is only a request because what I ask is outside the remit of your duties. What I ask is forbidden, you would be within your rights to tell me that what I ask is not possible."

Pasquale watched the face of the *maresciallo,* and the face was impassive and gave no answer. They were not permitted to shop for the magistrate, and they did. They were not permitted to cook for him, nor to clean the apartment.

"It is always the family, correct? I follow the family of Ruggerio and always it leads me into darkness. There has been a member of his family that I have missed—my own fault, I cannot justify my error: his youngest brother. The error is with me because, four years ago, I interviewed this brother in Rome. The youngest brother is Giuseppe Ruggerio, a businessman, he attacked me with what I believed to be justification. Was it his fault that his eldest brother was a *mafioso?* What more could he do than leave Sicily, make his own life away from the island? Was I not guilty of persecution? I believed him, erased him from my memory. I can make excuses. I can justify why I let the trail slip from me. But, the reality, I am humiliated. Now, I am told—I grovel because it was my error—The youngest brother is in Palermo. I have his address. I want confirmation that he is here. I ask you, *maresciallo,* to go and confirm for me that Giuseppe Ruggerio now lives in Palermo. It is always the family. Please . . ."

It was forbidden that the *ragazzi* should shop, cook, clean for the man they protected. A more serious offense, to take active part in an investigation. Grim faced, the *maresciallo* reached out and took a scrap of paper from the magistrate. Pasquale saw an address written in pencil on the scrap of paper. They faced the same danger as the man. Because they rode with him and walked with him they were as exposed to risk as he was. Pasquale understood why the *maresciallo* took the scrap of paper and lifted his coat from the draining board, and checked his pistol and went out of the kitchen. They walked with death, together.

16

THE GREAT WOODEN HORSE FIG-
ure was being towed by men in modern dress into a farmyard, and the
men carried firearms and were swarthy-faced, hard-weather faced, and
from the pockets of their trousers and their jackets and their anoraks spilled
American dollar bills, and there were dollar bills in the mud and ignored,
and they started to search the interior of the wooden horse figure, clam-
bered into the hatch door in the horse figure's belly, and she was far to
the back of the interior, and the torches of the men found her, and she
screamed, and he heard the sirens . . .

The first sirens of the day had woken Harry Compton.

He'd slept rotten. Not the fault of the bed in the hotel room that he'd
tossed half the night. He'd tossed, he'd put the light back on in the small
hours and he'd tried to win some sleep by reading the file he had accu-
mulated on Charlotte Parsons, Codename Helen, and he'd dreamed.

He thought he might have slept a little over three hours. He had thrust
himself out of the bed and walked over the scattered bedclothes, and gone
to the window and pushed back the shutters. He had seen the two cars
powering along the street with the lights on the roofs and the sirens blasting. He'd seen the guns, he'd seen the guards, he had seen the slumped
figure in the back of the lead car.

They'd met for breakfast.

At home, Fliss left him alone for breakfast. If she sat with him they argued. He took his breakfast alone in the kitchen at home, a snatched apple
and a piece of toasted bread smeared with honey and coffee. The American didn't seem to want to talk, which suited Harry Compton. The Amer-

ican had eggs and sausage and bacon cooked to extinction. They'd talk after breakfast, that seemed to be the deal. It was the American's problem that they hadn't been met, for the American to sort out, and for the American to argue that the mission of Codename Helen was dead in the water, aborted . . . There were mostly tourists in the breakfast room. There were couples from Britain and Germany and they wore bright clothes that were ridiculous for their age and their eyes were on their food and their guidebooks. Breakfast would be inclusive, so they were eating big, like the American, and they were gutting the guidebooks so that they would seem intelligent each time they were dumped off the bus and marched to the next antiquity. He was contemptuous of tourists because his mortgage was £67,000, monthly repayments hovering at £350 a month, and if the baby came then they would need a bigger place, bigger mortgage, bigger monthly drain. Most summers he went with Fliss for two weeks to her aunt's cottage in the Lakes, and most summers after a week there he was yearning to get back to SO6 work. Harry Compton had told his wife that he'd be gone forty-eight hours, that he wouldn't be getting to see anything . . . He chewed on the bread roll, not fresh that morning, and the coffee was cold . . .

The man came from behind him.

The hand of the man brushed across the table and bounced the small basket that contained the bread rolls.

He had his back to the entrance of the breakfast room, hadn't seen the man come.

The hand was tanned and it had fair hairs growing on it. The hand scooped up Dwight Smythe's room key from beside the basket of bread rolls.

He was half out of his chair, the protest was in his throat, and he saw the American's face, impassive except that the big lips moved nervously.

"Leave it, Harry," the American growled, water on shingle. Dwight Smythe, no fuss, laid down his fork and rested his hand loose on Harry Compton's arm.

He subsided back onto his chair. The man walked on, slipped the key to Dwight Smythe's room into his trouser pocket. The man was dressed casually, a check shirt and jeans, and he carried a plastic bag that was weighted, and the top of a sketch pad protruded from the top of the bag. The man wore a long ponytail of fair hair, held close to his neck by a red plastic band. He was, to Harry Compton, like a drop-out, like a druggie. The man went to the end of the breakfast room and he was looking around him as if for a friend, as if to find someone he was due to meet. The man turned, the man had failed to find his friend, and he came back past them. Harry Compton saw the man's face. He saw drawn lines, as if the man were scarred with anxiety. He saw the man's waist and the bulge below where the shirt was tucked into the trouser belt. The man was gone past him.

"I think we'll have fresh coffee," Dwight Smythe said, and his tongue brushed on his lips. "This coffee's cold shit."

Dwight Smythe called the girl, and it was ten minutes before the coffee came, and while they waited for the coffee the American ate two rolls of bread with jam on them, and he didn't talk . . . He was a detective sergeant, headhunted for an élite unit, he was supposed to have the qualities of a policeman and an accountant and a lawyer, and he reckoned that he knew nothing . . . They drank most of the second pot of coffee, and Dwight Smythe wiped the crumbs off his face . . . He wasn't firearms-trained, he had never carried a weapon more lethal than his truncheon, he knew nothing . . .

They went out of the breakfast room and crossed the hotel lobby. The British tourists were loading noisily into their bus, and the Germans were crowding round their courier. They walked up the wide staircase, and then down the corridor. There was only a chambermaid in the corridor with her trolley of clean sheets, clean towels, soaps and shampoos. Harry Compton realized that he had glanced her over, as if a chambermaid could be a threat. The *"Non Disturbare"* sign was on Dwight Smythe's door. He thought there would be a fight, but the fight was the American's problem. The chambermaid was in a room down the corridor. The American knocked lightly on his own door. The accent, American, was a murmur—the door was not fastened.

The man sat on Dwight Smythe's unmade bed. On the crumpled pillow was an ashtray. The man smoked his second cigarette, looked up as they came in, his hand had been over the bulge in his waist and now dropped away. The strain was stamped on the man's face. It was the American's problem, the American's job to do the dirty talk.

"Hi, Axel, good to see you."

"Sorry, for last night."

"Not a problem. Axel, this is Harry Compton, out of London, a detective in the—"

Axel jerked across the bed and his body upset the ashtray and spilled the cigarette debris over the pillow, and he reached for the TV control and flicked buttons until he found loud rock, and he raised the volume.

Dwight Smythe said, soft, "We were sent together, there's been high grade crap between London and Washington."

The cigarette went to the mouth, the hand snaked forward. The murmur stayed with the voice as if, Harry Compton thought, the shit had been kicked out of him, "I'm Axel Moen, happy to meet you, Harry. Sorry I didn't make the airport."

"Didn't matter, we had a good ride in," Harry Compton said awkwardly. Not his problem, it was for the American to dish the shit.

"Axel, I'm not carrying good news," Dwight Smythe blurted, "I'm sorry, I'm only the goddam messenger."

"What's the message?"

"Let me say this. When we met in London, when we traveled, we may not have hit it. I might have sparked you. Maybe I thought you arrogant, maybe you thought me fourth grade. That's past, gone."

"Spit it."

Dwight Smythe scratched at the short curled hair of his scalp, like he was buying time. "It's not easy, not for me and not for Harry . . . Up on high, Washington and London—Axel, they've killed it."

Harry Compton waited for the fight back, waited for the anger to jut the chin, waited for the tirade about big men being short of balls.

"They're aborting. They've gone cold. They're frightened. They want your Codename: Helen shipped out. They want her home."

He saw Axel Moen's shoulders drop, as if the tension drained.

"They want her removed, immediately, from the field of danger. It's why I'm here, why Harry's here."

He saw the light flicker back in Axel Moen's eyes, like a lamp hit them where before there had been darkness.

Axel Moen said, conversational, "That's good thinking, it's right thinking, it's what I was getting to think myself. You see, not certain, but I think I am followed."

He saw the slight smile break on Axel Moen's mouth, like ice was fractured.

Axel Moen said, "They'd be too good for you to know it. It's what I think, that I am followed. I think they have a tail on me. Don't have the moment how, where, they made the link. It's why I didn't come to the airport to meet you. It's why I didn't plug in the phone when you were calling. If they can put the tail they can put the bug. If there is a tail then I have to believe they are here, outside, and waiting on me. When you think you have a tail then you get sort of neurotic, because it can't be confirmed and it can't be denied. You know what I do each morning? I go out where she is, I watch her, I see her take the kids to school. I'm not close up, you understand. I'm two hundred meters away, three hundred, but I see her. I see her take the kids to school and I see her do the shopping. Sometimes, when she comes into the city, I follow her, I see where she goes and who she meets. I'm there, I'm a goddam shadow . . . You see, she's alone, it's like she's in a pit with them . . . I didn't go last night, and

I didn't go this morning. Maybe they've seen me near her, maybe I'm providing a pattern for them. Maybe, if I'm there each day, I give them a chance to see the pattern . . . I'm cut off from her, I can't watch her, I can't protect her."

He saw the shrug of Axel Moen, like a dream had died. The music played loud.

Harry Compton said, boorish, "My instructions are to terminate this operation, to bring her home immediately."

The cigarette was stubbed into the ashtray. The man had taken a pad from his pocket and he wrote briskly on it. Harry Compton waited. He had thought the man would fight and the man had crumpled. He had recognized the stress of Axel Moen and he saw now only a spent relief. The single sheet of paper was torn from the pad and passed to him. Axel Moen lifted the bedside telephone and dialed. He read the message again. He understood. He took the telephone from Axel Moen. He shivered, as if he crossed a chasm.

"Hello, hello . . . I am afraid that I do not speak Italian . . . I do apologize for the intrusion . . . I am the chaplain to the Anglican church on Via Mariano Stabile, just out from England for a few weeks. Miss Charlotte Parsons came to our service last Sunday . . . Oh, she's out at the moment, is she? Please, could you pass a message to her? I wanted her to know that we have an escorted tour this afternoon of the cathedral, with a guide. She seemed so interested in church history in Palermo. Three o'clock we are meeting outside the cathedral. We would be so delighted to see her if her duties permit it. Thank you so much . . ."

When the *maresciallo* had returned to the apartment he had not disturbed the magistrate. He allowed the poor bastard to sleep. He had crossed the hall of the apartment, walking on his toes, and he had heard the dull snoring of the magistrate. His report on the residence in the Giardino Inglese would wait. He should have gone off duty, should have gone home to catnap for a few hours. He stayed on. He sat quiet in the kitchen, nursing the cold coffee, when the day shift arrived. They were all quiet men when they came, the driver of the chase car, the passenger for the chase car, Pasquale, all subdued.

They were making the breakfast, heating the bread rolls when the alarm bleeped in the bedroom. It was good that he had slept, the poor bastard, and the *marescialllo* wondered if he had taken another pill. He had not yet shaved when he came to the kitchen door. He was a figure of wreckage.

"I spoke, as you requested, with the *portiere,* who declined to be co-operative. I made a call. My friend on night duty at the Questura gave

me what I needed . . . The *portiere* had a conviction at the assizes in Caltanisetta, many years back but a conviction for theft. If it were known
that the *portiere* of such a building had a conviction then he would lose
his job . . . now, he was cooperative. Giuseppe Ruggerio is a banker, he
is a man of ostentatious wealth. He has the apartment, and he has a villa
for the summer on the coast. His family—his wife and his children, a foreign girl who helps the *signora* with the children—are at the villa. The
villa is at Mondello. Sometimes Giuseppe Ruggerio is at the villa, sometimes at the Giardino Inglese. At the moment he is in Mondello, I have
the address of the villa. *Dottore,* I have to tell you that I was not kind to
the *portiere.* He made the wise decision to be more cooperative. Three
weeks ago, perhaps a little longer, Giuseppe Ruggerio took his family away
for a weekend and men used the apartment. He knows that because there
was a rubbish bag left out for him to clear, and he saw that there were
many cigarettes in the rubbish, and the waste from food and bottles, but
the *portiere* was sensible, he saw none of the men. It is the classic indication, *dottore,* as you will know better than I, of the use of the apartment
as a *covo.* That is all I have to report." The *maresciallo* shrugged, as if it were
nothing that he reported, and he saw the frail smile break on the magistrate's mouth, like there was light, small and faint light.

The magistrate shuffled away, scraping his slippers on the floor of the
hallway. At the table they ate the bread rolls and drank the coffee, and
read the newspapers. He kept his secret, but the eyes of Pasquale were
never off him. He heard the voice of the magistrate, from the office, across
the hallway, into the kitchen.

The *maresciallo* chewed on his bread . . . Was the captain, 'Vanni Crespo available to take a call?

He drank the coffee . . . When was it expected that the captain, 'Vanni
Crespo, would return?

He glanced over the headlines of the newspaper . . . Would the captain, 'Vanni Crespo, meet with Dr. Rocco Tardelli at five o'clock that afternoon at the *posto di polizia* at Mondello?

All the time that he ate, drank, read, he kept his secret and avoided the
eyes of the young man, Pasquale. His name was called. He heard the reedy
voice of the magistrate. He was a dour and hard man, he was not popular with those who worked for him and nor did he seek popularity. He
surrounded himself, picked the team, with men of a similar black-
humored resignation. They were unique in the service, they were aloof
from the other teams of *ragazzi,* they guarded the magistrate who was
the "walking corpse." He could make an error of selection and when he
knew his error then it was rectified. He heard his name called and with
a studied slowness he finished his mouthful and drank another gulp of

the coffee and folded his newspaper. He went to the office in the living room, and he closed the door after him. He loved the man, he loved Rocco Tardelli as if they were family, he loved the poor bastard who sat at his desk in old pajamas and a frayed dressing gown. He thought he had brought the glimmer of light to the magistrate.

"You called, *dottore?*" Said in complaint.

"I have asked 'Vanni Crespo of the ROS to meet me this afternoon in Mondello. I want to see it for myself, the villa of Giuseppe Ruggerio."

"To go to Mondello is to take an unnecessary risk."

"I have to go, please, I have to see. I believe I have missed an opportunity, I believe the opportunity was there for me, I believe I have no one to blame but myself."

"Then we go to Mondello," the *maresciallo* said without kindness. "We take the unnecessary risk."

It was not in his way to show kindness to the man he loved.

"Thank you."

He said brusquely, *"Dottore,* the matter of the boy. I filed my assessment on the boy. I have the answer to my recommendation, that he should be dismissed. You could, if you wish, intervene on his behalf, you could countermand the order."

For a moment the magistrate tapped a pencil on the surface of his desk. "If he is inefficient then he endangers us, if he endangers us, he should be got rid of. I will work here until we go to Mondello."

Charley trudged up the hill, carried the day's shopping . . . Her mother would, that morning of the week, be going with her father to the supermarket in Kingsbridge, walking down the same aisles, groping for the same boring packaged food, grumbling at the cost, like she sleepwalked. The bell would be ringing in the playground for her 2B class to come back inside and, that morning of the week it would be painting, followed by reading, followed by arithmetic. Danny Bent would be walking his cattle from the milking parlor up the lane to the 15-acre field, and Fanny Carthew would be dusting her pictures and thinking she had talent, and Zach Jones would already be settled at his window and would be polishing his binoculars for another day of prying into strangers' lives, and Mrs. Farson would be on her doorstep complaining to anyone who'd the inclination to listen that the Tourist Board did nothing for her and the County Council was mean with grants. The bird would be on the cliff perch, that morning and every morning of the week, high over the sea. She missed the bird, she missed only the killer peregrine hawk . . . She rang the bell at the gate. The "lechie" admitted her. She walked up the path to the villa, and halfway up the path she stopped, and she pointed imperiously to dead leaves at the path for the "lechie" bastard to clear.

Angela was in the kitchen. Peppino had gone to work. The baby slept in the carrycot on the kitchen table.

"There was a call for you."

"For me? Who?"

"You did not tell me you had been to church last Sunday."

"Sorry, no, I didn't."

"It is not necessary, Charley, to apologize because you went to church. They rang for you."

"For me? Why?"

"The priest rang, the chaplain. You told them you were interested in the history of Palermo."

"Did I?"

"You must have, because they rang to say there was an escorted tour of the cathedral this afternoon—they hoped you would come. Three o'clock."

She didn't think. Charley said, "Can't, not then. The children have to be picked up."

She saw the puzzled frown of Angela, the confusion. There was no make-up on Angela's face, she did not use cosmetics until the evening, until Peppino came home. Without make-up, Angela's face was easier to read because the worry lines and the frown lines were sharper. The talk, the confessional, beside the drying frame had not been referred to again, as if it had never happened. Angela stared at her.

"I think you should go. I will do the children. It is good that you should make friends here, Charley. When you came to Rome you were a child, you were from school. You have come back, you are a woman, you have a job. I worry for you, Charley. I say, and I do not understand why does a young woman come back here, leave her home and leave her job, to do the work of a child? Why? You have eyes, you have ears and senses, you know what sort of family we are. We are not a house of happiness. Each day, every day you are here, I wait for you to come to me to say that you wish to go home. Why are you here? What have we to offer you, Charley?"

Charley tried to laugh, "Right, culture beckons. God, I'll have to catch up on the guidebook. It's very kind of you, Angela, to get the children."

She went into the bedrooms. It was an escape, making the beds. He had said that she should never relax, never be complacent with her security. When she had finished the bed in small Mario's room she sat on it, and she held tight at her wrist so that her fist enveloped the watch . . . At the end of the service in the Anglican church on Mariano Stabile, the chaplain had listed the forthcoming activities of the parish—a jumble sale, a bring and buy sale, choir practice, an outing to the Valle dei Templi at Agrigento—but no mention of a visit with a guide to the cathedral in Palermo. She understood. She took the broom and began, methodically, to sweep the floor of small Mario's room.

The wind came off the sea. The hot air of the wind blew hard through the coils of the razor wire topping the walls, and it howled in the watchtowers, and it eddied over the compound where the helicopter waited. Salvatore Ruggerio, in prison uniform, was handcuffed to a *carabiniere* soldier before the barred gate to the compound was unlocked. Under the terms of Article 41 ll (1992) he was subject to "harsh prison regime." He must wear uniform for the flight, he must be handcuffed at all times. He had made a droll joke as the handcuff was snapped on his wrist. Did they think he was going to run away? Did they think that over the sea he would open the hatch door and jump? Did they think he intended to jump into the sea and then walk away over the sea? They had all laughed with him, the *carabinieri* and the prison staff, because it was always wise to laugh at the humor of a "harsh regime" prisoner. The safety of themselves, of their families, could not be guaranteed if they made an enemy of a "harsh regime" prisoner such as Salvatore Ruggerio. And he joked more with them. He said to them that, for certain, the judges would find him innocent of the charges laid against him, murder and extortion and intimidation, and that he was confident of release. Other charges of which he had been convicted, murder and extortion and intimidation, would be set aside. He would be disappointed not to meet with them again. They had all laughed at his joke . . . He walked slowly, his own pace, across the compound, and the young *carabiniere* handcuffed to him did not hurry the brother of Mario Ruggerio. He was pasty, pale-faced from eight years in the cells. A prison official walked behind him, carrying his small suitcase that held his clothes for the court appearance. He was already sentenced to life imprisonment, when he was tried again in the bunker of the Ucciardone he could expect only further life sentences. As was right for a man of his age, he was helped up into the military helicopter. The handcuff on his wrist was now shackled to the iron frame of the cot seat. He listened with indifference as the loader recited the emergency landing procedures, and the procedures if they splashed down over water. Ear baffles were carefully slipped onto his head. They would fly from the island prison of Asinara, across Sardinia to the airforce base at Cagliari, refuel there, then take the long haul of three hundred kilometers over the sea to Palermo, and he would sleep.

They had come from the garage. In the garage was the car taken from outside an apartment block in Sciacca. The car was now fitted with new registration plates, and the bomb was laid on the backseat of the car and was covered by a rug.

They had come from the garage, and they stood on the junction of the narrow Via Delle Croci, where it was crossed by the Via Ventura. It was important to Mario Ruggerio that he should see the place for himself. He walked round the delivery van that kept the space on the Via delle Croci.

He saw it for himself, and was satisfied. Tano told him, with detail, that most times when the magistrate came away from the Ucciardone he was driven up the Via delle Croci. He passed no comment. Standing at the back of the van he could look down the street to the walls of the prison . . . His opinion, there would be a week of ferocious denunciation, a week of demonstrations in the streets, a week of politicians queuing to enter television studios, and then the silence would fall. For a week, he could live with the clamor . . . His opinion, a signal would be sent through Sicily and Italy, and the signal would be read by his people in Germany and France, the signal would reach New York and London, and the signal would travel to Cali and Medellín and to Tokyo and to Hong Kong, to Moscow and Grozny. It was necessary that it was understood, by means of the signal, that a new power ruled in Palermo.

He asked Franco where should be the celebration for his family—in Palermo, in the country, in a hotel or a restaurant or a villa . . . ?

The telephone bleeped in the inside pocket of Carmine's jacket.

He said, dry, "It'll be the death of you, that thing, as it has been the death of many."

Carmine listened. The call was a few seconds in length and coded. The city was divided into numbered squares for the code, and principal buildings or landmarks inside the squares had been allocated separate numbers, and the name of the American in the code was a single letter of the alphabet.

"Or the life of me, or the life of you," Carmine said.

Now Mario Ruggerio checked again with Tano as to the hour in the night when the delivery van would be driven away and replaced among the parked vehicles by the car in the garage that had been taken from Sciacca.

Carmine hurried, in the few seconds' length of the coded call he had heard the urgency of the tail. He waddled, his short and thick legs striding quickly, toward where his car was parked.

In the garden outside the sweat had run on him. Inside the cathedral it seemed to freeze on his back. Dwight had followed the Englishman through the low arched door, and maybe six times in the last five minutes he had glanced down at his watch. They stood at the back and the Englishman leafed through the pages of a guidebook he'd bought, as if to hold the cover it was necessary to do the tourist thing.

He could see Axel Moen. He had been there before them. Dwight Smythe could see the back of Axel Moen and there was light on his hair that fell below his shoulder line. There was a tremor in the Englishman's voice, like he was frightened, like they both were . . .

"Do you know, this pile was started by an Englishman. He was archbishop here. He was Gualtiero Offamiglio, which is Walter of the Mill. Do you know, he started putting this lot together exactly 810 years ago? Think on it, I mean, what sort of journey was it from England to here, 810 years ago? Forget the building, just getting here was incredible—"

"Can you leave it?"

"I was only saying that it was—"

"I was saying, cut the shit."

He was supposed to push paper and balance a budget and keep the leave charts tidy. He wasn't supposed to stand with the sweat freezing on his back and on his gut to watch an agent meet with an informer. Dwight Smythe liked church, but he liked church that was simple. He went with his wife each Sunday to a Baptist place up in London's Highgate, where the middle-classes of the Anglo-African community came, where they sang loud to lift a low roof. The cathedral wasn't his place. The Baptist church that he knew was a place of safety and light—and, hell, here it was danger, it was gray darkness. He watched Axel Moen's back. Up ahead of Axel Moen, where the light pierced from high windows and made a many colored tapestry of cones, was a group of tourists. Farther ahead of Axel Moen, young unseen voices, was a choir practicing.

The Englishman whispered, "I think that's her." He made a small gesture. Dwight Smythe followed the line of the pointed finger. There was a young woman walking slowly down the central aisle. At times the light shafted down on her and lit the fairness of her hair in green and blue and red and white, but mostly her hair was in gray gloom. She went down the aisle slowly and looked around her. He thought she played a part, did it well, a foreigner in the aisle of the cathedral and looking around her with awe, like there wasn't danger in the place. She wore a white blouse that was cut away on her shoulders. Her shoulders were red from the sun, as if they had already been burned and not yet been tanned. She wore old faded jeans. She was going down the aisle toward where Axel Moen sat. He would not have seen her yet.

"You know that's her?"

"There was a picture in her home. I saw the picture." There was a hoarseness in the Englishman's voice. "How's she going to be when she gets told?"

"Get her out tonight?"

"Too right, straight on the freedom bird."

"Is she stupid?"

"Not what I hear."

"If she's not stupid she might just kiss you when she hears it's finished."

They watched. She went down the aisle. She went past the line of wooden seats on which Axel Moen sat. She was good. She did not give a sign of recognizing him, but she would have seen the pony-tail of hair on his shoulders. She faced the altar and genuflected and crossed herself, and then she slipped into the row of chairs in front of Axel Moen. Maybe he said something to her, but she gave no sign of it. She sat for a full minute on her chair, as if in contemplation. He wondered what was the future of Axel Moen. Could be the slot they'd made in Lagos, and it could be there was no future—could be that he was headed for that place in Wisconsin and hooking trebles into small fish . . . She stood. She went forward and she tagged with the tourist group. She was goddam good.

The *maresciallo* was bent over the street map, the map was spread over the table. Under the map were the used plates from their lunch, and their cups and their guns. The chase car driver lay on the floor beside the cooker and slept, and the passenger of the chase car sat on a hard chair and his head was on his chest and his eyes were closed. Pasquale studied the manual of the Beretta, tried to learn each working part, and the words and the diagrams seemed to bounce back from the tiredness of his mind.

His eyes never left the map. There was a cruel coldness in the abrupt voice of the *maresciallo*. "I regret, Pasquale, as a result of your assessment, you are not considered suitable for this work."

The boy was staring at him, gaping mouth, in shock. "Why? . . . Why?"

"For the most obvious of reasons, inefficiency."

The boy was peering at him, blinking his eyes fast. "When? When do I leave?"

"There is a replacement tomorrow. You go when the replacement is available."

The boy was trying to hold back tears. "Did Dr. Tardelli not speak for me?"

"It was Dr. Tardelli who said you were not fitted for the work."

He might have punched the boy Pasquale, might have kicked the boy. The *maresciallo* wrote from the map the name of each street they would use on the journey to Mondello.

Carmine was in the traffic on the Corso Vittorio Emanuele, jammed. The city was closing down for the siesta. The tail called him again on his mobile and gave him the code digits and the code letter. Carmine was in the traffic, locked.

Axel went forward. A full five minutes he had left her with the group around the guide. He had waited until the guide was criticizing a woman for wanting to take flash photographs. In the moment of distraction he went forward and he took her arm, where it was narrow at the elbow below the sleeve of her blouse and he squeezed her arm, and she didn't turn. He stood behind Charley.

The tourists were German. The guide spoke in German.

"There is still, as you see, enough of the original Norman carving to impress—it is the shame of the building that too much of the craftsmen's work of the twelfth century was destroyed by the barbarians of the Gothic period . . ."

Axel murmured into her hair. "We speak Italian, these people won't understand Italian."

"OK."

They moved with the group. ". . . Both the portals that you see and the doors are from the fifteenth century. In the desecration of the interior it is remarkable they survived. The building is a hybrid, each generation and each imperial conqueror came with his own desire for immortality, and achieved only historic vandalism." The tourists tittered.

"I don't mess with you, kid. I don't play with you. I always gave it to you straight."

"What do you need to say?"

"It's not easy, what I've to say . . . I respect you . . ."

"Say it, what you want to say."

There was an advance-course instructor at Quantico. He didn't get the rookies, he worked with the guys who operated in danger. The instructor was said to be, on the use of agents, super-Grade A, shit-hot. Axel Moen had done the week's course before he'd shipped down to La Paz. The instructor said that when you handled agents, then you lost your moral virginity. The instructor said that an agent was an item without human value, the agent was just a means to an end, the agent was a coded cipher, the agent was never a person . . . An agent had died, crucified on the back of a door . . . An agent stood in the dark shadow of the cathedral of Palermo . . . Christ, the goddam instructor at Quantico would never have run an agent himself, never felt the dependency and the trust, and never known the dirtiness.

Axel said it quick. "It's over, finished, it's killed. The big cats say it's wound up. It's the time, their order, to abort."

No expression in her voice, a calmness. "It's in place, it's happening, just have to be patient."

"Not me, not at my level. You've been brilliant. The fat cats want you gone. They want you on the flight out."

"Why?"

"It should never have happened. You were pressured. Shouldn't have been asked, shouldn't have traveled."

"Not an answer."

"Put straight, the risk to your safety is too great, the danger to your person."

"And I've been through three levels of hell for nothing?"

"It's not your fault, there's no blame attached to you. The opposite . . . It is finished because the fat cats made an order, but anyway it is not sustainable. I have watched you each day, I follow you, I'm a shadow to you. Not anymore, I am under surveillance, I think I have a tail. As much as them, I am the danger to you."

"Then fuck off away."

She'd turned. She looked into his face. He saw a blazed anger.

Axel said, soft, "At the main door there's an Afro-American, and there's an English guy. You go to them, they'll take you home."

As if she despised him, "And you?"

"I'm shipping out. I don't make the rules. I'm just a servant of government." She hurt him. He could not think when he had been worse hurt. Like she stripped him, like she laughed at him. She seemed to him, as if in contempt of him, to be listening to the guide . . . The guide was talking about the tomb of Roger II, crowned in A.D. 1130, buried at Cefalu, followed by William the Bad who was succeeded by William the Good who funded Walter of the Mill to build the heap, who brought back the remains of Roger II . . . She listened, she ignored him. She left him dead.

"The guys at the door, get on over to them."

She had the sweet smile. It was the mischief smile in the photograph at her home, and what he had seen on the cliff where she had taken him, it was the smile that the instructor on the agent course at Quantico would have warned against. It was the smile that he loved.

325

"Listen for when I call. If you've quit, give the gear to someone else who'll listen. Make sure that somebody listens, if you've quit."

She was away from him. She intruded into the heart of the group, she was beside the guide.

The helicopter arced over the city. Salvatore had woken. The new blocks of Palermo were laid out in a geometric shape below him, and the old districts made puzzle patterns. He did not believe it was within the power of his brother that he would ever again walk on the new streets and in the old districts. The old days, the days before Riina, the days when Luciano Liggio controlled the Court of Appeal and could achieve the quashing of sentences, were finished. Escape was against the ethic of La Cosa Nostra, to attempt to escape was to betray a man's dignity. The helicopter banked. He wondered where in the new streets and the old districts was his brother. It was said in the jail at Asinara that his brother was now *capo di tutti capi,* and he had noted the new deference that was shown him by men who had previously groveled to his fellow prisoners, Riina and Bagarella and Santapaola. He did not love his brother, but if his brother held the supreme power, then life in Asinara would be more easy. He saw the old ochre walls of Ucciardone prison climb to meet him.

Carmine came into the cathedral. He had left the car double-parked. He had run, hard as he could, the last two hundred meters. The tail was by the wall in shadow. He squinted the length of the aisle. He saw the tourist group, he saw a girl who was younger than the other women of the group, he saw the guide, he saw the group moving farther away from him, he saw the long fair hair of the American. The girl left the group, and he saw the radiance in her face and he thought it was like so many of the bitches who had found their God . . . The American with the long hair was talking urgently to a tourist. The tourist had a camera and binoculars. He saw the American stand beside the tourist and talk with him.

"Is that the contact?"

And the tail admitted, stammered, that perhaps it was the contact, but he had had to come out to call, he could not call from inside the cathedral building. They watched the American.

The last thing she heard, when she split from the group of tourists, was Axel's voice. Axel was speaking harsh conversational German. She thought that he talked in German, had chosen one of the group to speak with, in case he was followed, in case he had been watched, as if to draw a tail from her. She learned. She walked up the aisle toward the low set door through which the sunshine pierced the gloom. They were at the door—God, they were so bloody obvious—the black American and the Englishman. The black American took half a stride toward her but the Englishman caught his arm. She looked through them, she went past them.

What she had wanted, more than anything she had ever wanted, was to be held and loved by Axel Moen . . . and the bastard walked out on her. She was alone. It would be a fantasy for her, to be held and loved by the bastard, have the buttons undone and the zip pulled down by the bastard, only a dream. The bastard . . .

The sun hit Charley's face. Just a little bit of a girl, was she? Could be given the big talk, could she? Could be pitched in, could she? Change of plan. Could be aborted, could she? The brightness of the sun burst on her eyes. Charley walked. The anger consumed her. The target of the anger was Axel Moen who quit on her, and the African American and the Englishman who looked scared fit to piss . . .

Charley walked fast down the Corso Vittorio Emanuele.

They were pathetic.

She strode down the Via Marqueda and over the Piazza Verdi and onto the Via Ruggero Settima. She was going to the room of Benny Rizzo. She would use him because he was available. Going to his room to unbutton and unzip, use him as a substitute because he was available. She went into the street behind the Piazza Castelnuovo, and past the closed gates of the school where he taught. She pushed her way into the building and she scrambled fast up the stairs. At the landing, outside his door, were two black plastic rubbish bags, filled. She pressed the bell. She heard no sound from inside. She kept her finger on the bell. She needed him. He did not have a death threat because he was ineffective. He was not killed as his father had been because he was not noticed. The bell shrilled behind the door.

"He is not here."

An old woman came up the stairs. It was the woman she had seen going to church.

"Not back from school?"

"Not coming back, gone." The woman put down her shopping bags and was searching her handbag for the key to her door.

"What do you mean?"

"Did he not tell you?" The slyness was on face. "Not tell you that he was taking the ferry for Naples? You do not believe me?"

The old woman bent and her claw nails tore at the tops of the black plastic bags. The rubbish was revealed, the pamphlets and the sheets from the photocopier, and the books. Charley saw the poster, crumpled, a pool of blood on the street and the slogan caption *"Basta!"*. She was alone ... She heard the laughter of the old woman ... It would be her story, hers alone, that would be told ... She ran back down the stairs.

They drove into the yard at the back of the police station. The magistrate looked around the cars parked in the yard. The boy, Pasquale, had driven badly, and the *maresciallo* had cursed him. He looked for the familiar face. The boy had been told, and the boy would believe he was betrayed, the boy would not understand that he was saved. For one more day only the boy would have to travel past the endless ranks of parked cars and parked vans and parked motorcycles. He did not expect to be thanked by the boy because the boy would never be told that he was saved. At the far end of the yard was a butcher's delivery vehicle. He saw 'Vanni. 'Vanni jumped out of the vehicle and came quickly across the yard. He was dressed as a butcher. He stank as a butcher. 'Vanni slipped down into the car, beside the magistrate.

"Thank you for coming, 'Vanni, I talk while we go."

"Whatever, please ..."

Out on the street, and the chase car had dropped back, and the light was off the roof, they went slowly. Perhaps the boy had forgotten how to drive as a normal motorist, but they burst a junction when they should have given way, and twice the boy missed his gears, and the curse of the *maresciallo* was in the boy's ear. Maybe, one day, the kind and good boy, Pasquale, would understand what had been done for him ... They traveled on the road round the crescent of the beach.

"One may be intelligent, and at the same time display stupidity. One can see everything, and at the same time be blind. One can be supreme in complicated analysis, and at the same time lose the obvious. I hunt Mario Ruggerio, and I have been stupid, blind, I have missed the obvious. The family will be the core of his life."

They came to the old town, and they passed the Saracen tower.

"To strangers and rivals he will display a psychopathic cruelty, but for his family he will have only a sickening sentimentality ... Four years ago, in Rome, I met with his youngest brother. His brother was Giuseppe, he was a bright and alert businessman, a credit to the enterprise of the modern Italian—don't laugh, I checked, he actually paid his taxes in full. It was impossible to believe that he came from the same peasant stock as his eldest brother."

The *maresciallo* gave the whispered directions to the boy. They turned toward the hill over Mondello, went slowly up a narrow and cobbled street.

"He attacked me, he criticized me for calling him to an interview at the SCO building. He said that he should not have been persecuted for his blood relationship. I apologized. I forgot him. The memory of him died in an unread file, forgotten. This morning I hear that he returned three years ago to Palermo. I hear that he lives in great affluence. He has a home that is a palace in the Giardino Inglese, he has a villa here."

They wove a way round a gaping hole where electricity men worked, they went past the high walls and the big gates and the leaping dogs.

"He is connected in business with the wealthiest of the city, he is frequently abroad, he is a success. I could go to my peers, 'Vanni, I could again request resources for surveillance, I could beg and plead for resources, and I would again be criticized for the persecution of an innocent. I can come to you, 'Vanni, I can talk of an old friendship."

The *maresciallo* turned. His finger came fast from its resting place on the safety of his machine-gun, and pointed to the gates of the villa. There was wire on the top of the gates, and there was shattered glass set into the top of the wall beside the gates. Again the sharp hissed whisper of the *maresciallo* and the boy braked the car. Through bushes, between trees, over the gate and the wall was the roof of the villa and the upper windows.

"I can ask for the team of the *Reparto Operativo Speciale* to move on this villa, no connection with me. I can ask it of you . . . Never have we found the banker of Mario Ruggerio, never have we known the link of Mario Ruggerio to the international situation. I think, perhaps, it was under my feet, beneath my eyes . . . You will do it for me?"

"No."

"For friendship, 'Vanni, for the trust we have in each other."

"No, I cannot."

"Search it, turn it over, hunt for a notebook or a deposit book, an address book. I am in darkness. Please."

He caught the collar of the butcher's coat, and 'Vanni would not look into his face. 'Vanni stared at the floor of the car. He said dully, "I cannot—I would compromise an operation."

"What operation?"

The *maresciallo* had heard the footfall first. He was twisted in his seat. He held the machine-gun just below the level of the door's window.

"I told you that it was not my gift to give . . ."

The boy heard the footfall and his hands were rigid on the wheel and the gearstick.

". . . I am sorry, I cannot share it."

Tardelli turned. She walked past the car. She did not look into the car. She wore a cut-away blouse low on her shoulders and clean jeans. Her head was high, and her chin was out, and she walked with a brisk purpose. He saw the strength in her face and the boldness of her walk. She went to the gate ahead of them and she reached up to the bell. He saw no fear in her. She scratched at her back, removing an irritation. There was no weight to her, no size to her. She was "an agent of small importance." He slapped Pasquale, the boy, on the shoulder, and made the gesture. He looked away from her. As the gate opened, as a servant stood aside for her, the car powered away.

"You know why we do not win, 'Vanni? You knew, and you did not mark it for me, you did not share. We cannot win when we fight harder against each other than we fight against them."

He slumped back in his seat. The darkness was around him.

In the evening Salvatore received the visit of his mother.

She came alone and she told him that his father suffered that day from the problem with his chest. He thought her more frail than when he had last seen her, but it was two years since she had been declared well enough to make the long journey to Asinara. He could not kiss his mother because he was a prisoner subject to a harsh regime, there was a screen of thick glass between them. He asked about the health of his father and the health of his brother, Carmelo, and the health of his sister. He did not speak the name of his elder brother into the microphone that linked them, nor did he speak the name of his youngest brother. He told his mother that his own health was satisfactory. He showed no emotion, no misery— to have complained or to have wept would be to show a loss of dignity in the presence of the prison officials. From her handbag his mother took a handkerchief. She blew her nose into the handkerchief. She held the handkerchief, and her crabbed old fingers unwound the single sheet of cigarette paper. The cigarette paper was, for a short moment, revealed in the palm of her hand, close to the glass screen. He read the message. His mother crumpled the paper into her handkerchief, put her handkerchief back into her handbag. He told his mother that he hoped she would be able to visit him again soon, and that then his father might be well enough to come with her. Salvatore had been nine years old when he had first come to the damp and dark visiting rooms of the Ucciardone to see his father. He had been sixteen years old when he had first come with his mother to the same rooms to see his elder brother. He had been nineteen years old when his mother had first come to visit him. He understood the workings of the prison, as if it were a home to him. After the termination of the visit, as he was escorted back to his cell, Salvatore Ruggerio requested a meeting with the governor. He walked with dignity to his cell, and men stood aside for him, and men ducked their heads in respect to him. At each step of the iron staircase, at each pace on the stone landings, he felt the power of his brother that settled on him. At his cell door he repeated the request, that he should meet with the governor. The door of the cell was locked behind him. He stood heavily on his bed. He could see between the bars of the cell. He looked at the lights of the city, and he remembered the message from his brother that had been shown him.

17

A DELIVERY VAN WAS MOVED. IN ITS place, on the junction of the Via delle Croci and the Via Ventura, a car was parked. In the back of the car, hidden beneath a tartan rug, was a wooden tea chest.

The city woke, the city shimmered. The pall of the night mist hung on the city and would disintegrate under the climbing sun. The pollution haze would come to the city choking from the exhaust fumes of cars. Another day had started in the cruel history of the city . . .

Salvatore, the brother of Mario Ruggerio, stood respectfully in front of the governor of the Ucciardone prison and said, that day, he must speak in private with the magistrate, Dottore Rocco Tardelli.

Through that cruel history, the Palermitans had learned when catastrophe would strike. Nothing tangible to place a hand on, nothing to see with their eyes, but a sense that was personal to the people of that city allowed them to know when catastrophe was close . . .

The men of Mario Ruggerio were in place. Tano watched the parked car and the mobile telephone was in his hand. Franco sat in the warmth of the sunshine on a bench and held an opened newspaper and observed the soldiers who protected the apartment and the two cars parked against the curb. Carmine leaned against the door of the bar where he had clear sight of the entrance gates used by magistrates when they came to the Ucciardone prison.

. . . The men of the city hurried to their work, or they lounged on the street corners and they waited. The women of the city washed the nightclothes or went early to the market and were anxious to be home where they could wait. There was a quiet about the city as there always was when a man was isolated, had been through history when disaster edged near . . .

Using an old razor so that he would not risk cutting his jowled throat, Mario Ruggerio shaved carefully at the basin of the small room on the first floor of the Capo district and, as of habit, washed in cold water.

. . . The normality of the city was a superficial thing. Deep in their hearts, deep in their veins, deep in their minds, the people of the city knew that catastrophe was close, disaster was near, and they waited. It was a city of killing and violent death, as it had been since the time of the Romans and the Vandals, through the time of the Normans and Moors and the Spanish, over the time of the Fascists, now in the time of La Cosa Nostra. A shivering excitement that morning held the city in thrall . . .

The governor of the Ucciardone prison relayed the message of Salvatore Ruggerio that he requested a visit, that day, from the magistrate, Dottore Rocco Tardelli.

. . . The people of the city did not know the place nor the time nor the target, but the instinct of history was with them, and the inevitability. They understood when a servant of the state was ridiculed, isolated. They waited . . .

The boy, Pasquale, took the bus to work on the last day that he would act as bodyguard to the "walking corpse."

. . . The fascination with death, the majesty of murder, gripped the lifeblood of the city. A stranger would not have seen it. But the people of the city knew and watched, waited . . .

"So what do we have?"

"We have the same as last night," Harry Compton said.

"Can we recapitulate? Can you fly it by me again?"

Harry Compton thought Dwight Smythe talked like a bureaucrat, like they were at a meeting high up in his embassy, or on the fifth floor of SO6. All bureaucrats liked to "recapitulate," gave them time to think. His feet were still sore because the shoes he'd brought were too lightweight for the pounding of pavements and cobbles he'd put in the evening before. He felt an irritation. He stood by the window, and Dwight Smythe was on the bed, and they hadn't yet taken their breakfast.

"He has a box tail on him. It's professional. If I hadn't done it myself, I wouldn't have seen it. The one place that a box tail can be seen is from far behind. You have to be behind the back marker, that's the only place you get a chance to see it. There were four men on the box and there was a control in charge. They're not using radios which makes the professionalism more critical—it's hand signs. He acted like he wasn't certain of the tail, and he was governed by not showing out, which is right. He took them a hell of a dance, we walked half round the city and back again. He did running, he did stopping, he did sitting. He had the box on him for four hours, till he gave up, till he went to his car. They had their own wheels, I saw that. Your man, after four hours . . . who wouldn't? He looked broken up to me, but I told you that last night."

"He's not taking his calls." Dwight Smythe had a notebook open on the bed. "I called three times last night."

"You told me."

"I called twice this morning. Our people in Rome, they talk about a guy called 'Vanni Crespo, can't reach him."

"And you told me that last night."

"I can't abide sneering, and I didn't sleep last night, so cut it out. She was with me all last night, that kid. Christ, there's nothing to her . . ."

Harry Compton said, sincere, "What I thought, I'd never seen anyone look so vulnerable. You saw the body language, I saw it—she told him to go jump. In her position, God, that is big talk."

"Went past us, like we didn't exist. I don't know what to do."

Harry Compton said, "Nothing you can do—because it is a total and complete and comprehensive fuck-up."

"You've a helpful way with words."

"She's a bitch."

"She's an obstinate goddam bitch."

"She's gone out of control."

"You lose control of an agent and you're walking in shit."

"What are we supposed to do?"

"I am ordered out," Axel Moen said.

"What am I supposed to do?"

"She's yours, you're welcome."

"You taking it bad?"

"What the fuck do you think?"

'Vanni said, "I think, Mr. American, that you have broken a primary rule."

"Don't patronize me."

"There is a primary rule in the handling of undercover operatives."

"You want your teeth down your throat?"

"The primary rule is that you do not have emotional involvement."

"I don't tell you again."

"You don't go soft on an agent, the primary rule—you pick them up and you drop them, it is a throwaway society. You don't get to be gentle with agents."

Axel hit his friend. With a closed fist he hit 'Vanni Crespo. He hit him a little to the right of the mouth and he split 'Vanni Crespo's lip. He covered his face with his left, like he'd been taught as a kid in the gymnasium at Ephraim, and he hit his friend again, and 'Vanni Crespo tried to smother him. He kicked hard, like he'd learned as a kid in the school yard at Ephraim, and his friend went down. He fell on his friend, and he was raining the blows on 'Vanni Crespo's face. He was held, he sobbed, he was hugged. He lay on the rock-strewn ground under the orange trees and 'Vanni Crespo, his friend, held him. He shook, convulsed, in the arms of 'Vanni Crespo.

'Vanni Crespo said, "It was deserved. I have the guilt, I began it. I had the letter, I opened the letter, I brought the letter to you. I first saw the chance. You hit me, you kick me, that is nothing, I should burn for what I did . . ."

Muffled words, words said against the cloth of 'Vanni Crespo's shirt. "It's an act, so hard, so tough, playing at manipulating innocents—it's a fucking show."

"I went last night with Tardelli. He is desperate, he is alone, he pleads for someone to take his arm. He has found Giuseppe Ruggerio. He saw her. He wanted the villa searched for anything that linked it with Mario Ruggerio. I rejected him, I said it would compromise an operation that I could not share with him. He saw her, your Charley, and he understood. I isolated him, and he did not complain—and for that, too, I should burn . . ."

"Do I have the right to ask you to forgive me?"

'Vanni held him. He thought his breath would still smell from the whiskey he had put down the night before. He thought his body would still smell from the sweat he had made with the woman from Trapani in the back of her car the night before.

"It is what they do to us. It is what happens to us when we fight a war against filth. It is how we become when we go down into the gutter to hunt them. When you fight and you do not believe that you can win . . ."

"Are you going to walk away, 'Vanni, as I am?"

"If I could, but I cannot. She is as much mine as she is yours. Not while she is still in place."

'Vanni stood. His friend reached down into the plastic bag and took out the sketch pad. For a moment 'Vanni saw the drawings of the cloister columns, and then Axel's hands were ripping the images into small shreds of paper. 'Vanni watched the destruction of Axel Moen's cover. His friend had climbed from the bathroom window of the little apartment, and over the slates, and had lost the tail, and had needed him through the night, and he had been with his woman. His friend had sat in the orange grove, in the valley below Monreale, through the whole of the night, his friend had needed him and not called him, and he had been making sweat with his woman . . . He thought of Axel Moen, alone in the orange grove through the night hours, and holding the pistol, and waiting for the dawn before calling him, he thought of the misery of his friend. He took the plastic bag from his friend. He pulled his friend to his feet. They walked between the orange trees. The fruit was ripening. They left the torn pages of the sketch pad behind them. It was a place of quiet and beauty, where Axel Moen had waited through the night. They went toward the cars. The men at the cars wore the deep blue coats of the ROS team that bulged over their vests and the skintight balaclavas that were slashed at their mouths and their eyes.

"You'll keep her safe?"

"If I don't then I should burn."

Charley made the children ready for school and kindergarten.

That day, nothing said, nothing to guide her, an atmosphere of savage tension held the villa. She knew the atmosphere well. When her parents scrapped, when she was been a child, they fought out of earshot so that their precious daughter would not learn the cause of the argument. She didn't know whether the atmosphere was important or whether it was trivial. When her parents rowed, out of her hearing, it was always something of mind-bending unimportance at the heart of the dispute—where they would go in the car the following Sunday, what they would be eating for supper, what shade of wallpaper was right for the spare bedroom. At home, the precious daughter thought the fighting was pitiful, and kept her distance. It was only an atmosphere, they had kept the cause of the argument from her.

She dressed the children. She washed their faces. The children were sullen with her. Peppino was on the patio with work papers and the baby was beside him and sleeping in the pram, and Angela was in the kitchen. She collected the books from the children's rooms for their schoolbags.

She went into the kitchen. She told Angela that she was ready to go to school. She made a smile for her face and acted dumb ignorance as though she had not sensed an atmosphere, and Angela nodded distantly like the children and the school were irrelevant to her.

There was no criticism. "Angela, sorry . . . there's no shopping list." It was said in innocence.

"I forgot the shopping list? I am guilty of forgetting the shopping list?"

There was a cold mocking savagery from Angela. "Can't you do the shopping for yourself? You live with us, you eat with us. Is it beyond you to decide what we should eat for lunch?"

And Charley smiled again with sweetness. Wasted because Angela's back was to her. "I think I know what we need. I'll see you."

The children hadn't kissed their mother. Francesca was sniveling. Small Mario, crossing the hall, kicked viciously at his new toy car and cannoned it over the marble flooring. Charley wondered whether it would work again, and she thought the car cost more than she was paid for a week's work—spoiled little bastard. She took Francesca's hand. She didn't care that the child held back and sniveled. She yanked Francesca after her, and small Mario trailed after them. It would take more than the bloody children sniveling and sulking to destroy Charley's sense of calm. Again and again it had played in her mind, the taunting of Axel Moen. Like it was her anthem. "Listen for when I call. If you've quit, give the gear to someone else who'll listen. Make sure that somebody listens, if you've quit." Like it was her chorus.

She came onto the patio. "Just off to school," Charley said brightly. "I'll take the baby."

Peppino looked up from his papers, balance sheets and projection graphs and account statements. "Did Angela tell you about this evening?"

"Didn't say anything about this evening."

"We are out this evening. We will be taking Francesca and Mario. Please, this evening you will look after Mauro?"

"No problem."

She walked down the path to the gate. The "lechie" bastard opened it for her. She thought it strange that Angela had not said the family were out that evening. She walked toward the town. She wondered if Axel Moen had already quit, and she wondered who watched her. So calm, because it was now her story, alone, that was played.

The *maresciallo* had been called by the magistrate. They had spoken in his office.

He came back into the kitchen.

They watched the *maresciallo* as he took the street map from the table. Dark eyes that were somber, without luster, never left him as he studied the web patterns of the street map.

At the sink, Pasquale rinsed the coffee cups and the plates on which they had eaten bread. There was no liquid soap to put in the bowl. They had finished the liquid soap the evening before and none of them had written on the list that was fastened on a magnetic clip to the refrigerator door that it needed replacing. Pasquale did not remark on the absence of liquid soap. It would be the last time that he should wash, as the junior member of the team, the cups and plates and the knives and spoons, and they could find for themselves that the liquid soap was finished. He had told his wife, in the night before, when their baby slept, summoned the courage, and she had stood behind him and nursed his head. He had held the bottle of beer in his fists, and with a quiet flatness he had told her that he was rejected, and she had nursed his head against the breasts that suckled their baby. He'd thought she'd wanted to cry in happiness, and she had said nothing. He had held the beer, not drunk from the bottle, and he had told her that he had been betrayed by the magistrate to whom she had sent flowers. He'd thought she'd wanted to kiss him in welling relief, and she had not.

He was already isolated from the team. He was not a part of the team of the older *ragazzi* that morning. They did not share with him the gaunt black humor that was their own. Nor did they laugh at him. It was not necessary for Pasquale to wash the cups and plates and the knives and spoons, and because they now ignored him they would not have told him to do the job.

The *maresciallo* said they were going to the Ucciardone prison, and he told them what route they would be using, and Pasquale laid the washed cups and plates and the knives and spoons in neat piles on the draining board beside the sink. He hated them all, he hated the *maresciallo* who rejected him, and the magistrate who betrayed him, and the older men who ignored him. He hated them. A cup slid from the draining board and, frantic, Pasquale tried to catch it. It fell to the floor, and the handle broke clear and the cup was cracked and a chip came free. The *maresciallo* seemed not to see and went on with the intoning of the route they would use, and the men at the table did not look at him. He kneeled on the linoleum floor and picked up the pieces of the cup and put them in the rubbish bin under the sink. He was rejected and betrayed and ignored.

He stood by the sink. He interrupted the litany of the names of the streets and the piazzas. "When is he coming?"

He saw the dagger glance of the *maresciallo*. "Is who coming?"

"When is my replacement coming?"

"He is coming today."

"When, do I not have the right to know?"

"When he is available, that is when you are replaced. I apologize, I do not know when, today, he is available."

The magistrate stood in the doorway. He held a briefcase across his stomach and his overcoat was draped loose on his shoulders. For a moment he was ignored by the *maresciallo*.

The route was detailed, which streets they would travel on, through which piazzas. So difficult for Pasquale to hate the man who stood at the kitchen door, but the man had not spoken for him and that was betrayal. There was such tiredness in the face of the man, there was no light in the eyes of the man. He caught the dulled eyes, and the man looked away. The route was confirmed. There was the clatter of the guns being armed. The vests were thrown on. There was the thud of the feet down the staircase, and they passed a woman who climbed the staircase and carried a shopping bag from a boutique and bright flowers and she gave them the glance of contempt.

They were in the sunshine on the pavement. The soldiers had their rifles readied.

The convoy pulled away. The sirens wailed, the tires screamed on the corner. They went into the streets where there were, close packed on either side, parked cars and parked vans and parked motorcycles. It was the day when Pasquale's replacement would be available. The *maresciallo* drove, and Pasquale was beside him with the machine gun tight in his hands.

The prison was a part of the antiquity of Palermo.

The prison was a place of pain, torture, death, from the history of Palermo.

The walls of the Ucciardone prison, built by the Bourbons to impose their rule, were now covered with weeds in pretty flower, and the mortar crumbled in the joints between the stones. At the base of the walls the military trucks passed in continuous patrol, at the top of the walls the armed guards gazed down listless on the exercise yards. Beyond the exercise yards, spread out from the central building like the arms of an octopus were the cell blocks. The cell blocks had failed to break the resistance of La Cosa Nostra. The Men of Honor had been sent to the cell blocks by the officials of the king, and the officials of the fascist Duce, and by the officials of the democratic state—and the officials through history had failed to break the spirit of La Cosa Nostra. It was the place of the Men of Honor, where they ruled and where they tortured and where they killed.

The cell blocks, that day, sweated under the brilliance of the sun.

There was a quiet, that day, in the Ucciardone prison, and word seeped along the corridors, and up iron staircases and through locked doors, that Salvatore Ruggerio had requested a meeting with Rocco Tardelli, the magistrate who hunted his brother.

The men in the cell blocks waited.

———

The aircraft lifted. The journalist from Berlin sat rigid in his seat, and the aircraft banked over the beach at Ostia, and climbed and turned again, and headed north. He thought he returned to the track toward civilization ... Champagne, yes, he would appreciate a glass of champagne. He thanked the Lufthansa girl ... He could not remember when he had last felt such relief at the completion of an assignment. There were no headwinds, no turbulence pockets, it was a steady flight, and he tried to relax. The problem, his difficulty, and it was a wound to his pride, he did not believe in the story he had written, it was his failure. When the champagne had been brought to him, he pulled down the table flap and laid his briefcase on it. He took his copy from the briefcase. He read back the story he carried home.

"There is the appearance of war on the island of Sicily. There are military road blocks, there are armed men guarding politicians and law enforcement officials, there is talk of war. But, if there is combat, your correspondent has not found it.

"I remain unconvinced of the reality of conflict. It is possible there is only a delusion of war. My area of confusion, I could find no battle lines and there is a complete absence of the traditional no-man's-land. There are military commanders and police chiefs who talk a good war, but I could not find, nor touch, nor feel their alleged enemy.

"Your correspondent has reported from many of the world's darker corners. In Saigon I met with General William Westmoreland; in Hanoi I was privileged to meet General Vo Nguyen Giap. I saw Saddam Hussein in Baghdad and General Norman Schwartzkopf in Riyadh. Yassir Arafat and George Habbash in Beirut. I drank coffee with the secessionist leader, in his Grozny bunker, as he was shelled by Russian tanks.

"Where is the enemy in Sicily? Does he exist? Is he a figment of Sicilian imagination as they display their island trait of demanding uniqueness? The commander of La Cosa Nostra in Sicily, if indeed such a person exists, does not give news conferences or television interviews nor does he issue war bulletins. For three weeks I have chased shadows. I remain in confusion.

"What is said: from this humble, poverty-ridden island are spewed the most sinister criminals of our time ..."

He read no more. He returned his copy to the briefcase. He sipped his Champagne.

They sat across a table.

"You are well, *signore?*"

"I am well. And you, *dottore,* you are well?"

"I thank you for your inquiry. Yes, I am well."

The magistrate pushed across the table a packet of cigarettes. Salvatore Ruggerio, in Asinara and Ucciardone, would have as many cigarettes as he cared to smoke, but it was a gesture. The magistrate kept in his jacket pocket a packet of cigarettes, opened, with three taken out. To have passed Salvatore Ruggerio a full packet, unopened, would have offended his dignity, would have implied that he was short of cigarettes. It was necessary to maintain the dignity of the man. Salvatore Ruggerio lit a cigarette, and the smoke wafted over the table, and he pushed the packet back toward the magistrate.

"Your mother and father, they are well?"

It was a fascination to the magistrate, the calm politeness of these men. He was never aggressive with them, and he tried hard not to be arrogant toward them. They craved respect and he gave it them. And he made a rule, always, of asking a question to which he knew the answer. He knew that, for their age, the parents of Salvatore Ruggerio were well.

"I saw my mother last night, she seemed well."

They were alone in the room. The *maresciallo* would be immediately outside the door with an officer of the prison staff. There were microphones built into the legs of the table, and their conversation would be recorded. Because he did not know the answer, he did not ask Salvatore Ruggerio why the meeting had been requested.

"And in two days you go on trial again?"

"They pluck fantasies from the skies. They bring new charges. What can a poor man do, *dottore*, an innocent man? They use old lies from the disgraced *pentiti* to persecute an old and poor and innocent man."

There were some who threatened him. Sometimes he was warned. Did he take his guard to the toilet with him? He should. Was he concerned for his health? He should be. Some had their friends and families send him funeral wreaths and photographs of coffins. He did not expect to be threatened by a man of the stature of Salvatore Ruggerio because to issue a threat would be beneath the dignity of a man who gave himself such importance. It was often his thought, why did such gifted men need to pursue criminality in order to find that craved dignity?

"Have you been recently to Prizzi, *dottore?*"

"Not recently."

"You have not had the opportunity to see my parents' home?"

"I have not."

"It is the humble home of old people who live in poverty."

He did not know yet where the road of their conversation would lead. He shifted in his seat. It was hard for him, but he should not show impatience. He squirmed on his chair, and he felt the tickle of hair on his neck. His hair was too long, should have been trimmed, but it was a military operation to take him to a hairdresser, and the *maresciallo* would not permit a *parrucchiere* to be given access to the apartment. There was a woman in the offices of the *squadra mobile* who came occasionally to cut his hair, and then it was crudely done . . . He believed it valuable to talk with the brother of Mario Ruggerio. The body language was important, and the attitude. There were morsels to be gathered.

The magistrate had, between the time he had received the message from the governor and the departure for the prison, gutted the files he held on Mario Ruggerio and the family of Mario Ruggerio. He knew the material by heart, but he had again dug into the files. The father of Mario and Salvatore Ruggerio was a millionaire in American dollars, the man was crippled by rheumatism from his prison days and could afford the best treatment available on the island. The father of Salvatore and of Mario Ruggerio was neither humble nor living his last days in poverty. The magistrate had no need to score a cheap and small point.

"There are many in Prizzi who are humble and who live in poverty. It is the value of the family that is more important than material possessions."

"I think you speak the truth, *dottore.*" The smile played on Salvatore's face. "They tell me, *dottore,* that you are not blessed with a loving family."

It was a barb. Always, inside the tracks of extreme politeness, they would try to ridicule him. The smile was obsequious. Probably they knew to the hour when his wife had left. Probably they knew the identity of the man with whom his wife slept. Probably they knew which schools his children attended.

"We cannot choose our family, and the circumstances of the family. It must be, *signore,* a source of disappointment to your parents that Giuseppe does not live close to them." He played a card, he sparred.

No expression. Salvatore stubbed the cigarette. "In a flock there is always one sheep that looks for a greener field. The other sheep forget. *Dottore,* I have a small request."

"Please."

"My parents are old."

"Yes."

"My father has rheumatism. My mother is frail. The journey to Asinara is long and expensive. They are old, they live without money. Should I not receive freedom . . . It would be a most charitable gesture to them should I be transferred from Asinara to Palermo. It would bring a small joy to the last years of their lives."

It would be a decision of the Justice Ministry. It was not in the power of the magistrate. There was a sub-committee. Salvatore Ruggerio, a "harsh regime" prisoner, a murderer with sentences of life imprisonment that were accumulating, would know the procedures.

"If you, *dottore* were to speak on my behalf—for my parents ..."

"I will see what is possible."

The brother of Mario Ruggerio stood. He bobbed his head in respect. He went to the door. He turned at the door and looked at the magistrate and his face was impassive. He was gone through the door. He would be taken back to his cell.

The magistrate sat alone at the table. He did not understand. He had not known what would be asked of him, nor whether a warning threat would be offered him. It was ridiculous that Salvatore Ruggerio had requested a meeting to ask for a prison transfer, and he had come like an obedient dog. Perhaps the *maresciallo,* with his keen and suspicious nose, would have comprehended why he had been called to a meeting with no content. He did not have the nose of the *maresciallo.* He did not understand.

There was a football game alongside the parked cars in the yard. One goal was the piled coats of the *ragazzi* of Tardelli and the second goal was the piled coats of the men who guarded the governor of Ucciardone. It was a lunatic game, as if the *ragazzi* of Tardelli had a fever for victory. Alongside the parked cars, close to the bunker building, beneath the old walls of Ucciardone, the *ragazzi* of Tardelli tripped and elbowed and kicked their way to a victory, as if nothing else was of importance to them. Pasquale was not a part of the game. Pasquale was not given the bouncing and careering ball. Pasquale was an onlooker to the game.

There was a shout from the gate. The game stopped. The ball ran free.

A man walked from the gate toward the cars and the piled coats. He had a thin and pinched face. He had sparse gray hair. He had bent shoulders above a body that was without fat. The others of Tardelli's *ragazzi* went to him. He carried a small bag, and a dried smile cracked his face. The driver of the chase car embraced him. The passenger of the chase car thumped his shoulder. Pasquale watched the greeting given his replacement. Pasquale was ignored. He heard the man say that he had been able to come earlier than he had expected, so he had come. He was from the team that guarded the mayor, and the mayor had flown to Rome. Pasquale thought the circle was again joined, as it had not been when he was a part of the team. The *maresciallo* stood in the outer door to the yard and the replacement came to him and held up his hand for the *maresciallo* to smack with his own, as if an old and dear friendship was renewed.

"Am I needed? Am I wanted?" Pasquale felt the depth of humiliation.

The *maresciallo* looked over the shoulder of the replacement. "I think the cars are full. Take a bus, Pasquale, to the Questura and they will find you something to do."

Pasquale bit at his lip. He went to the lead car and he took from the floor his machine-gun, with the magazines, and his vest. He gave them to the replacement. He was not thanked. The replacement to the team would have been told that there was a boy who was inefficient, whose inefficiency endangered them all. The replacement had a hard face. There was no fear in the face. Pasquale wondered whether the replacement had a wife, had children, wondered whether the replacement had volunteered to travel with the "walking corpse."

He walked away. Behind him was laughter, as if an old story was told from old times.

He went out through the gates of the yard. He walked past the policemen and the soldiers who guarded the gates. He walked under the walls of the Ucciardone prison. He saw a heavy built man with slicked oiled hair leaning against the door of the bar on the far side of the street who talked into a mobile telephone.

He turned into the Via delle Croci. He passed a young woman. She wore a shapeless gray skirt. She stood with her mother. She waved a handkerchief. She shouted at the wall and at the cell block behind the wall. He wondered if it were her lover or her husband or her brother who was held in the cell block. He passed a cat that gnawed at bones from a rubbish bag. He passed a woman who was bent under the weight of her shopping bags, and two businessmen who walked arm in arm and who both talked and did not listen to the other. He passed the flower stall. He heard, away behind him, the starting of the siren wail. He walked on the pavement of the Via delle Croci, beside the tight line of parked cars and vans and motorcycles.

He did not turn. He did not wish to see the car of the magistrate and the chase car. He could not shut out from his mind the sirens' call.

He heard, behind him, the scream of the tires as the cars turned into the Via delle Croci.

He passed a man. The man had the face of a peasant from the fields, the clothes of a businessman from the office. The man tapped the numbers of a mobile telephone.

The cars came from behind Pasquale.

The replacement was in the passenger seat of the magistrate's car, was in Pasquale's seat, there was the back of the *maresciallo's* head, there was the screen at the back window, there was the chase car, and he saw the tension on the old, worn faces of the driver and the passenger. He saw the cars accelerating away from him and they would have seen him on the pavement, all of the bastards would have seen him, and there had been no wave, no kindness.

Pasquale saw the flash.

In the moment after the flash there was the flying debris.

Pasquale saw the flying debris break against the magistrate's car and toss it.

The magistrate's car was lifted. It was thrown clear across the road and over the parked cars and vans and motorcycles, over the pavement. The magistrate's car hammered into a wall.

There was the thunder roar and the spurting dust cloud, and then the crash of the debris landing and the fall of glass in shards. The chase car was stopped in the center of the road and then the dust cloud claimed it.

He had no telephone. His mind was a flywheel. He must telephone.

He had passed a man with a telephone.

He turned. There was no man with a peasant's face, with the clothes of the office.

He understood. The pistol was in the holster strapped across his chest. He had walked past the man who had detonated the bomb. He had seen the man, he had had the power to stop the man, and the man was gone. He shook. The whimper was in his throat. The silence was around him. He wanted to howl to the world his acknowledgment of failure. His body trembled.

Pasquale walked forward.

He went by the chase car and he heard the screaming of the driver into the car's radio.

He stepped over the debris of the disintegrated car. He walked past the magistrate's car that rested, shattered, upside down, and he did not look to see the magistrate, nor did he look for the body of the *maresciallo,* nor did he look for the face of the replacement. He went by the fire and the smoke. He was not a part of it, he did not belong to the team. He thought he knew why he had been dismissed from the team. The tears streamed on the face of Pasquale. He walked toward his home. He walked briskly, did not bother to wipe the tears from his cheeks, did not bother to stop for apologies when he cannoned into an old dumpy man who stopped to light a cigarillo. He hurried to his wife and to his baby because he knew why he had been dismissed from the team.

Some saw the white heat of the flash, and some heard the thunder roar of the detonation, and some saw the smoke climb above the rooftops of the city, and some heard of the killing when the lunchtime programs of the RAI were interrupted.

The city learned of the bomb.

There would be, in the city, a manifestation of shock and a wailing of despair, and there would be, also, a charge of raw excitement. The excitement would, as through the history of the city, overwhelm the sensations of shock and despair.

The city knew the story. A man had been ridiculed and isolated and destroyed. The story was written through the history of Palermo.

At the newspaper stand, where the Via delle Croci met the Piazza Crispi, Mario Ruggerio had stood with Franco. He had watched. He had seen the blue lights and he had heard the sirens. He had seen the flash of light and he had heard the thunder roar. He had watched until the gray-yellow dust cloud had masked the street. He had made no comment. He had gone on his way. On the Via Constantino Nigra, a young man who wept had buffeted against him and hurried on. They came in a cavalcade of noise past him, the fire engines and the ambulances and the cars of the *carabinieri* and the *squadra mobile* and the *vigili urbani* and the *polizia municipale,* and if he noticed them he gave no clue of it to Franco. Franco told him of the arrangements made for that evening, for celebration . . . Near to the Villa Trabia, he looked for a bench that was empty and he sat upon it. He sent Franco to get him a coffee from the stall.

His power was absolute. His authority was confirmed. He was the new *capo di tutti capi.* Across the continents of the world, that night, a thousand million people would see on their television screens the evidence of his power and of his authority . . .

Tano came. He told Tano that he was pleased. He smiled at Tano and he gripped Tano's hand, and he saw the pleasure ripple over Tano's face.

Carmine came and whispered congratulations in his ear. Carmine told him that the American was now hidden at the barracks in Monreale. He felt the flush of invincibility. He gave his instructions.

Franco and Tano and Carmine were around the short and pasty-faced old man who sat in the heat of the sun. He gave them his opinion. There would be a week of denunciation and of demosntrations in the street, there would be a month of demands for more powerful legislation against the organization, and normality would return. They competed to agree with him.

He said he was tired. He said that he wished to rest before the celebrations of the evening. He should be refreshed for the evening when he would receive the congratulations of his family, when he gathered his family, his strength, around him. He believed himself invulnerable.

346

"Get him out tonight."

"Put him on the plane this evening."

'Vanni said, "We have to clear his apartment, get his things. We can have him ready for the late flight."

Axel slept. He lay on the bed in the barracks room, and above him was the portrait of the general, and beside him was the photograph of the teenage girl. He was sprawled on the bed. They moved around him, and they drank 'Vanni Crespo's whiskey.

"Like, sure as hell, to go with him, but I can't," Dwight said.

"She's not your responsibility, she's mine. It's me that has to stay," Harry Compton said.

"You just joined the game late. It's our show. I stay."

"No way I move out, not while she's here."

"Then he goes alone on the flight."

"He doesn't go with me."

'Vanni Crespo refilled the glasses.

Axel slept as if he had found peace. His breathing was monotonous regular. He slept still, like he did not dream, like the weight was shed. There was youth again on his face . . .

Dwight Smythe said, soft, "You'd be kind of frightened to wake him."

Harry Compton said, "When I saw the tail on him, and saw him try to wriggle off the tail, then I bled for him."

"But he's a dinosaur, his time's gone. These things should be done with computers."

"Shouldn't be done with people, not real people like that girl."

"It got out of hand."

"It was your crowd—"

'Vanni snapped. "It is not the time to argue. In the Via delle Croci they are searching for pieces. They look for pieces of bodies. It is necessary to have pieces of bodies to put into coffins. But then they are only Italian bodies. No other foreigner that I have known has tried harder to help us. No other foreigner has realized more the need for cooperation. But you come and you argue and you criticize. You interfere. Now you are frightened because now you understand the responsibility you have prized from Axel Moen."

Axel slept.

"She doesn't come."

"If she doesn't come, then I don't."

The argument hissed through the villa.

"It is for the family. You have to come."

"She comes or I don't."

Charley sat in the living room and she watched the television. It was live from the Via delle Croci, shaking images. The argument was on the patio and in the kitchen and in the bedroom. Angela would walk away, from the patio or from the kitchen or from the bedroom, and cross the living room, and then Peppino would follow her, and the argument would resume when they believed they were beyond her hearing. She listened to the argument, merged with the frantic commentary of the television.

"She cannot come—you know she cannot come."

"Then the children don't come."

"The children have to come, it is the family."

"I don't and the children don't."

There was no weeping from Angela. Angela had been sitting in front of the television with Peppino when Charley had come back from the town with the shopping. Charley had first, before she had understood, tried to tell Angela what she had bought, but Angela had waved at the screen . . . She remembered the afternoon they had sat, in shock, in front of the screen in the apartment in Rome, the death of the magistrate Borsellino, then Peppino had come into the living room and made a re-mark about what clothes the children should wear that evening, and the argument was born. Angela was cold, in control, brittle-voiced. When she walked away from him, back to the patio, to the kitchen, to their bed-room, Peppino followed. Charley thought that Angela had chosen the ground for war with care.

"You will go yourself. Alone, you will go to your family."

"You have to be there, the children have to be there."

"And what would he say? If I am not there, and my children are not there, what would he say?"

"It is a gathering of the whole family."

"Are you afraid of him? Are you afraid of what he would say?"

She sat in front of the television. *Piccolo* Mario kneeled on the floor and, a miracle of God, the battery-powered car still worked. Francesca, on her lap, made a family of her dolls. The images of the television were sometimes soft-focus, sometimes zooming to close-up scenes, sometimes in wild and uncontrolled panning. There was nothing new for the tele-vision cameras. The scene was the same. There was the broken car, up-side down, there was the following car stopped in the center of the street, there was the wreckage of cars parked at the side of the street, and there was the milling mass of uniformed men . . . She thought Angela must hate her husband, sincere hatred, to taunt him so to his face.

"It is not her place, to be with my family."

"Then I don't go, and the children don't go, and you have to find the courage to tell him that you cannot discipline your wife ... and what will he tell you? Knock her about a bit, Peppino. Give her your hand, Peppino, across her face. Are you frightened of her, Peppino? She comes, I come, my children come, and then that creature can touch our son."

"Why?"

"It is a normal family party, Peppino, yes? Just an ordinary family party?" Her voice was rising. The sarcasm was rampant, as if she knew that she was heard. "Of course, in respect of Rocco Tardelli, many normal and ordinary family parties tonight would be postponed. It is natural that a *bambinaia* should accompany the children to a normal and ordinary family party ... and it would give me someone to talk with so that I do not vomit at the table."

He came to the door.

Charley watched the television.

Peppino said, "Charley, Angela would like you to accompany us this evening to a family gathering. Please, you will come?"

"You sure?"

"Quite sure."

"I'd be delighted." She did not, at that moment, know why Angela Ruggerio had chosen to make her part of a battleground in war. Her fingers brushed against the watch on her wrist. She wondered if he had gone yet, if he had quit. She wondered who would listen to her call.

"Thank you."

18

Tʜᴇʏ ʜᴀᴅ sʜᴀᴋᴇɴ ʜɪᴍ.

He had been far away. He had been with his grandfather. He had been with his grandfather to pick cherries, and there was the warmth of summer on him, and he had taken the cherries to his grandmother. He had sat on the broad scrubbed kitchen table, and his grandmother had put the cherries, two fistfuls for each, into a row of big bottles, with a half cup of sugar that he measured out for each, and a fifth of vodka for each. The Norse people of the Door Peninsula called it Cherry Bounce, and when Christmas came he would be allowed a small drink. They had shaken him to wake him. He was a child, he would be allowed only enough of the brew to cover the bottom of the glass. In the kitchen, on the range, was the "boil." The smell of the boil was in his nose. The boil was white fish with potatoes, with carrots and onions, sometimes with cabbage.

He woke, but his eyes stayed closed, and there was the murmur of the voices around him, and it was 'Vanni's voice that led.

"To understand his commitment you have to know what drives him. He doesn't drink, God help him, so it wasn't alcohol talk, what he told me once . . . He was dumped as a kid, when his mother died, when her parents found him impossible and his father was traveling for work. He was dumped on his father's parents. It would have been a trauma, and they had to become the rock that he could hang to, they were God and they were safety to him. They took him to Sicily when he was seventeen years old. They brought him here. His grandfather had been in the Allied Military Government. His grandfather had gone home in 1945 and brought a Sicilian peasant girl with him for his new wife. I use a word that's often spo-

ken in Sicily, *isolato.* His step-grandmother was isolated in that close little
Norwegian community. It would have been a fiercely lonely childhood.
They came back here to see relations, to see his grandfather's office, where
he'd been a paramount king round the Corleone and Prizzi area. He told
me, they were at the airport, they were getting the flight out, his grandfather made the confession. He was a teenager, he wasn't a priest in the box,
he was a kid. The confession was corruption. His grandfather had been
bought, he was paid for petrol coupons, for food coupons, for lorry per-
mits. What was at home, back in Wisconsin, the farm, the land, the home,
the orchards, was from corrupt money. All that he believed in, hung to, was
corrupt. He went looking for another rock. The new rock was DEA, but
it could have been FBI or Secret Service or Customs. He went looking
for a rock that he wouldn't be washed off. For most men, for me, it is a
rotten job and a fun job. I work the hours and I drink and I screw. For him
it is a rock. If he were to lose that rock, to slip from it, then I do not think
he could survive. He told me, and I understood the obsession. I understand
more. When he was told to quit, walk out on his agent in place, abandon
his agent, you'd have thought he would kick and that he would fight. He
did not, he accepted the verdict of the rock. There is nothing else in his
world. You say there is a posting to Lagos waiting for him—a seriously awful
place—but you will hear no complaint from him, he will go, that is the
way he stays with the rock. Everything I know of him, it is very sad."

"More like it's obscene," Dwight Smythe said.

"You don't mind me saying so, but obsessionalists, crusaders, they're
juveniles, they don't have a place anymore," Harry Compton said.

"If that's what you want to believe ..."

His shoulder was shaken. Axel Moen opened his eyes. The lying bastards, Dwight Smythe and Harry Compton were all warmth and concern. Yes, he'd slept well. He thought that the warmth and the concern
were shit.

He went to the basin and sluiced cold water on his face and on his
hands and his arms. He thought 'Vanni Crespo tried to be gentle and sincere. 'Vanni told him that, while he had slept, the magistrate had been
killed. A bomb had killed him. The magistrate with whom he had not
shared Codename Helen was dead. He took a cup of water and swilled
it in his mouth and spat it out. He looked around him a last time, his eyes
soaked in the bare room, and he knew that he would never see his friend's
room again.

Time to quit.

They went down the corridor and out of the living quarters of the
barracks.

They stopped at the communications room, waited in the corridor.

He saw 'Vanni Crespo lean over the technician, and smack his hand with emphasis on the work table, and in front of the technician was the second of the CSS 900 two-channel receivers. He thought of her. He thought of his love for her. The Englishman carried his own receiver, and he would have no love for her.

They went out into the falling sunshine of the late afternoon, to the cars.

She broke the rule. The rule had been set by Axel Moen. Axel Moen had quit.

"Angela, why—?"

"Why what?"

"Why did you make an issue—?"

"An issue of what?"

"Angela, why did you insist—?"

The rule set by Axel Moen was that she should never question, never pester, never persist. They stood beside the washing-line and Charley held the washed clothes that would hang on the frame overnight, and the pegs and passed them to Angela.

"Insist on what?"

"Angela, why did you demand that I come with you tonight?"

"I have small children."

"Yes."

"I have a nanny."

"Yes."

"I have a family occasion to attend and my husband would like our children to be with us. If the children are with us then so, too, should be their nanny."

"Yes."

The strain was off the face of Angela Ruggerio. Her smile was sweetness. To Charley, there was a strength in the face of Angela Ruggerio. But the smile of sweetness was not open. The smile was enigmatic, the smile was a fraud.

"You confuse me, Charley."

"I'm sorry, I don't mean to."

"In pain, Charley, in depression, I asked Peppino to bring you back to me. Everything that I ask for is given me by Peppino. But you have no life here, you have no happiness, you are a servant. But you do not complain. That is my confusion."

"It was just an opportunity, you know, the right chance at the right time."

"I took a telephone call for you. The caller said he was the chaplain of the Anglican church. You were later coming back than I thought. And you had to take the bus into Palermo, and then you would have had a long walk to the cathedral. I was worried, Charley, that you would be late for the start of the tour."

"No, no, I was there in time."

"Because we offer you so little, I thought it was good for you to have friends. In the book I found the telephone number of the Anglican church. I wanted to be certain they would wait for you. I spoke to the chaplain, to tell him that you were coming, that they should wait for you. I am glad, Charley, that you were not late for the tour."

She had broken the rule. She had pushed, pestered, persisted. With the broken rule came the broken cover. She passed the last of the shirts from the basket and the pegs to hang it from. She could not read the face of Angela Ruggerio. They walked back to the kitchen.

The army colonel said that a new brigade of troops would be in Palermo within forty-eight hours, probably a paratroop unit.

"To do what? To direct the traffic?" It would be the Chief Prosecutor's last post before retirement. He had cracked a mold with his appointment. Before he had taken the post it had been given, for many years, to an outsider. It had been his great pride, that he, a Palermitan, had won the appointment.

The *squadra mobile* colonel said that four new teams of trained surveillance officers would be transferred from the mainland within the week.

"Excellent. Then we will know which dogs foul which pavements." He felt a great weariness, an engulfing impatience, and a dripping flow of shame. He had shown no love for Rocco Tardelli and less support. He had laughed behind his hand at the man, and sneered at the man.

The deputy mayor said that the Minister of Justice would come himself to the funeral, and had telephoned his instructions that all resources should be diverted to this investigation.

"More resources. What generosity. We may have more flowers and a bigger choir in the cathedral." The Chief Prosecutor threw down his pen at the papers in front of him. "And we have to do something. It is required of us that we do something."

The Deputy Mayor said that, in an hour, he would make a televised statement, a strong denunciation.

"Which will have a quite extraordinary impact upon the Men of Honor. Perhaps they will fart when they see you."

The colonel of the *squadra mobile* said that every possible associate of Mario Ruggerio would, that night, be watched.

"But we don't know who are his associates. If we had known he would have been incarcerated this year, last year, ten years ago."

The army colonel said that each soldier under his command in Palermo was out now on patrol in every quarter of the city.

"Your soldiers are ignorant and untrained conscripts, and we cannot even tell them what is the appearance of Mario Ruggerio. Probably they would stop the cars and help him across the street."

"I think you take a very negative attitude," the deputy mayor said.

He had come to this meeting, down the great corridor on the third floor of the Palazzo di Giustizia, the place they called the Palace of Poisons. He had passed the office of Rocco Tardelli. He had recognized the guard. The guard was dust-covered and his face was blood-smeared. He thought the guard had the look of a woman who will not leave the mortuary where a stillborn baby lies. From behind the door was the sound of the violation of the office of Rocco Tardelli. He had come to the meeting and he had heard the gestures that would be made.

"Do you know what happens at this moment? Do you know the reality of what happens? In the apartment of my dead colleague and in the office of my dead colleague, there are now artisans working with oxyacetyline cutters so that the personal safes at his home, at his work place, may be opened. For each safe he kept only one set of keys and the keys were on his person and his person is in bits. We have not found his keys in the Via delle Croci. He had only one set of keys because he did not trust those with whom he worked. He employed no secretary, no aide, no staff. He did not trust us. That is the kernel of my problem, that a brave man could not trust his colleagues. Maybe in one of his safes will be his description of an avenue of inquiry that he did not share because he had no trust. And Mario Ruggerio will laugh at our gestures and celebrate and walk in freedom. Yes, my attitude is negative."

From a distance, the tail watched the house and the closed street and the parked cars and the *carabinieri* with their guns and flak vests and balaclava masks. The arrival at the house was reported.

"How long have we got?" Harry Compton fidgeted his fingers.

"Enough time," the Italian said.

In London, of course, there were police undercover men and women. They'd be undercover in Vice or Organized Crime or with Drugs Squad.

Harry Compton didn't know any of them. They'd have the full back-up. They'd have a chief superintendent wetting his smalls for them each night. They'd have support. He stood in the apartment.

The man seemed to have no interest in the packing of his few effects. The bag was packed by the Italian and the Afro-American. The man, Axel Moen, had let them in, like he didn't care that they trampled through his life, and he'd gone to the table against the wall on the far side of the room from the window. The light came badly from the small ceiling bulb, and he sat in shadow and wrote. Harry Compton stood by the door beside the big policeman who wore the anorak of the *carabinieri,* who held the machine-gun. He watched, he was an intruder present at the end of a dream and he was responsible for the waking.

The Italian collected the books on archaeology, Roman and Greek and Carthaginian antiquities, and the Afro-American took the clothes from the wardrobe and the chest and folded them and laid them with precision in the bag, and the man sat in shadow and wrote busily on a big notepad.

The man hadn't spoken as they had driven from the barracks to the narrow street. They'd brought three cars, and they'd blocked off the street ahead of the house and before it. Harry Compton, stretching his mind, could not imagine what it would be like to live undercover, without back-up. The bag was packed, was zipped shut. The room was stripped of the presence of Axel Moen. The Afro-American was about to speak, probably he'd something asinine on his tongue about planes not waiting, but the Italian had touched his arm. Axel Moen, sitting in the shadow of the room, wrote his letter, and the Italian guarded his last rites as a vixen would have protected a cub.

They'd get him out, Harry Compton thought, get him on the flight, get shot of the responsibility for him and then he would make his pitch for the girl. There was fierce argument in the street below. There was a hammering cacophony of horns because the street was blocked by three cars and by armed men. Harry Compton's pitch about the girl would be that they should drive from the airport to the villa, wherever it was, and lift the girl out. If she wanted to go screaming, then she could go that way, if she wanted to go kicking, then she could kick, if she needed to be handcuffed, if she needed a straitjacket, then he would oblige, if she argued, the way he felt, he'd tape her mouth. He could recognize the symptoms of fear. He was so bloody aggressive. They should get the man on the flight, they should get the girl out of the villa, they should close down on the place and turn their backs to it, fuck the hell out of it and go. The aggression came from the fear. The fear came from the growing dusk falling on the street, the guns that guarded them. And the man kept on with his writing, like there wasn't a hurry, like the flight would wait. She'd kill him, Fliss would, if he came back without a present for her, and she wouldn't understand, and he wouldn't tell her why he hadn't gone shopping, why he hadn't even bought anything for Miss Frobisher, wouldn't tell her of his fear . . .

The notepaper, three sheets, was folded. There was shouting on the stairs, a woman's voice, shrill. The man, Axel Moen, in his own time, took an envelope from the drawer of the table, and put the sheets of notepaper into the envelope. He slipped his hand into the breast pocket of his shirt and lifted out a small gold wristwatch, a woman's watch, and placed it in the envelope with the sheets of notepaper. He licked the flap of the envelope and fastened it down. He wrote a name on the envelope, and there wasn't the light for Harry Compton to read the name, and he gave the envelope to Dwight Smythe.

They went out through the door. They had stripped the room and taken the identity from it. The dream was gone. Harry Compton had killed the dream . . . The woman was at the bottom of the stairs and she shouted her abuse at the policeman who barred her, at them as they came down. He caught the drift. She screamed at them in a *patois* of English and Italian. She had taken a spy into her house. What would happen to her? They had endangered her. The whole street knew a spy had lived in her house. Who would protect her? She was not answered. She spat in the face of Axel Moen.

The car doors slammed. They pulled away into the dusk. The dream was dead.

From a distance, the tail watched as the men came out of the house. A description was given of the long-haired American. It was reported that he carried a travel bag.

Charley asked, "What should I wear?"

Peppino lounged on the big chair in the living room. His papers were around him. He looked up and at the first moment there was annoyance at the distraction, and then the slow grin came to his face.

"Whatever makes you feel good."

She was in control. She felt no fear. The darkness gathered outside the living-room windows and she saw the shadow shape of the gardener pass.

"I'd want to wear the right thing—wouldn't want to get it wrong."

"If you would like it, I will come and help you choose what you should wear."

"Good."

She had the power over him. He stood. He glanced furtively toward the kitchen. Angela was in the kitchen with the children and their coloring books and their crayons. She had the power over them all. The power flushed in her . . . Axel Moen would have sworn at her, and warned her . . . The power was a narcotic in her. She led him into her room. He followed. He waited at the door. She drew the curtains of the window and then she crouched down at her chest of drawers and took out the blouse that he had paid for, and the drawer was left open and he would be able to see her neatly folded underwear . . . She did not care that Angela knew the lie, and she did not care that Axel Moen would have sworn and warned . . . She faced him, and she held the blouse of royal blue across her chest so that he could see the line of it and the cut of it, and swiveled with it and then tossed it on the bed. She sought control. She went to the wardrobe, and he drifted toward her. She heard the brush of his feet, coming closer to her. She took the skirt of bottle-green from the clip hanger in the wardrobe and she held it across her hips and stomach and thighs. She felt the warmth of his breath on the skin at her shoulders and she knew the scent of him. His fingers touched her and groped under her arms and toward her breasts. She demanded control. She lifted him, she collapsed him.

"Sorry, Peppino, it's 'curse' time—bad luck."

The tail was a motorcycle and a car. The motorcycle was ahead and the car followed. The pillion passenger on the motorcycle used a mobile phone to report that the convoy had taken the route to the Punta Raisi airport.

They took the ring road west of the city. At the junction with the *autostrada,* the convoy was flagged down for a road block. They had to slow for the driver of the lead car to wave his ID at the soldiers and to point back to the two following cars. They slowed enough for Axel to see the illuminated turning to Mondello. He was sandwiched between 'Vanni Crespo and the Englishman, and the Englishman had the plastic bag between his feet. Dwight Smythe was in front, beside the driver. There was no talk in the car, so they heard each transmission on the radio between the driver of the lead car and their driver and the driver of the chase car. They accelerated through the road block, away from the sign to Mondello and into the long tunnel. Axel wondered where she was, what she did . . . He thought of her on the cliffs at her home, and he thought of her pushing the pram toward the Saracen tower, and he thought of her mocking him in the cathedral when the bright lights from the high windows had coned on her head . . . They'd said they were going to get her once he was on the flight, and 'Vanni hadn't bothered to argue it. They were going to get her and they were going to ship out with her, and 'Vanni had let it ride. He'd be in his own bed, in Rome, that night and it would be behind him, just as La Paz was behind him. Shit . . .

The car rocked and swerved. The convoy cut inside a dawdling vehicle. Axel knew why the van went slowly at that place, over the viaduct of the *autostrada*. People went slowly over there because it was Capaci, and it was where the bomb had taken Falcone's life, went cautiously as if to remember and to stare. Axel saw, a flash moment, a weathered and disintegrating wreath on the guard rail of the viaduct. In a year's time there would be a wreath, rain-swept and sun-baked, in the Via delle Croci, and people would go past it slowly, and nothing would have fucking changed. As soon as they had moved him on, because the plan was killed, they were going to lift her out, and nothing would have fucking changed. There was the evening, there was still the evening before they went for her, and the old disciplines caught Axel Moen. He reached up into his ear, he prized into his ear with his fingernail. He took out the inductor earpiece. He wiped it on his handkerchief. He passed it to the Englishman. He couldn't remember the Englishman's name, and he had learned enough to know that the Englishman had killed his plan, had come snouting and interfering into his plan.

"What do I do with that?"

"You put it in your head, and you listen. If you don't want to put it in your head, then you shouldn't have come. It's owed her."

He reached down, into the dark space between the Englishman's feet, and he felt with his fingers. He knew it well enough to find the switch from touch. He saw the glow of the light. The guy, reluctant, put it in his ear, and grimaced.

" 'Vanni'll tell you the codes."

The Englishman bridled. "I thought it was finished . . ."

"When the lady stops singing, when you have her on board, then it's finished."

He wriggled in his seat, and then he was thrown against the Englishman, and the convoy careered past a slow-going lorry. He could see the guide lights of the airport runway over the driver's shoulder. He contorted himself and he slipped the harness of the holster from his chest, he didn't make a comment, he gave the holster with the Beretta 9mm pistol to 'Vanni. 'Vanni checked it and aimed it down between his shoes and

cleared the bullet out of the breach, and he gave 'Vanni the spare magazine. The cars went fast into the airport.

It was not the way of La Cosa Nostra to make a killing without the most
thorough and careful preparation, but Carmine did not have the opportunity for thorough and careful preparation.

In the hierarchy of La Cosa Nostra, where the confidences were exchanged, it was boasted that a *mafioso* under the control of Mario Ruggerio had never been arrested at a killing ground, but Carmine acted on
the direct instruction of the *capo di tutti capi* and must improvise.

He wore his best suit, from Paris, because he was invited that evening
to a celebration of the family. Beside the door to departures he met with
the tail. Through the glass doors he saw them. They were at the check-
in desk. Through the glass he saw the back of the target's head, the long
hair caught tight with an elastic band, and he saw the men with him, and
the guns.

He squirmed. He did not know how it was possible to obey the instruction given him by Mario Ruggerio.

She had toweled the children from their bath, now Charley dressed them.

Angela had chosen the clothes they should wear, then gone to her
bedroom.

A floral dress for Francesca, and a long brushing of her jet-colored hair,
and a ribbon to go in her hair. A white shirt and a silk child's tie for small
Mario and black trousers that Charley had ironed, and a comb run
through his slicked hair, and lace-up shoes that Charley had polished. She
played firm with the children, so that they laughed, and she won them
over as she could, no sniveling and no sulking, and she told them how
angry she would be, breathing fire, real fire, if they dirtied their clothes
before they left the villa. She bathed the baby, tickled the baby in the bath
so that it gurgled happiness, and she dried the baby and powdered its body,
and buttoned on the nappy, and dressed the baby in a romper suit of
burgundy-red.

Charley showered.

When she came out of the shower she took her towel and she dried
the watch on her wrist, over which the water had cascaded.

She went back down the corridor to her room and she wore only her
dressing gown. She passed Peppino and she dropped her eyes, and she
thought she saw the bulge of him, and she had believed she had control
of him. She sprayed herself with lotion. She dressed. The blouse of royal-

blue and the short skirt of bottle-green. She stroked the brush on her hair.

She went into the kitchen.

Angela was beautiful. Angela wore a hugging dress of turquoise and the jewelry flashed at her throat. Angela was packing a shopping bag with spare nappies for the baby and a filled bottle . . . She remembered the old people who had come to dinner, Peppino's parents, peasants. Charley thought that Angela made herself beautiful so that she stood apart from those people, the peasants, so that she was separated from the brother . . . And there were books for Francesca and small Mario in the shopping bag.

Angela looked up, saw her. "You are lovely."

"Thank you."

"Very young, very explosive, very vital."

"If you say so."

"But, you spoil it . . ."

"I do? How?"

"You wear that watch. You are so feminine, so *gamine,* but the watch is for a workman or a diver under the sea or a soldier."

"It's the only one I've got," Charley said.

"You want a watch? I have four watches, four of Peppino's presents. I will find you—"

"Doesn't matter, but thank you."

"It is so vulgar, you have to have another watch."

Charley blurted, "It was a gift, from someone I admired. I do not want to wear another watch."

She felt the weight of the watch on her wrist, clumsy and awkward, dulled steel on her skin. Angela's eyes danced brightly in front of her, but her face was a mask.

"I only try to be helpful, Charley. You wear what you want to wear."

"I need to get some lipstick on. Excuse me."

She was going to the door of the kitchen.

Angela said, conversational, "It is a very bad day for all of us, Charley. It is the day when a good man was murdered. He would have made a mistake. Of course, I do not know what was his mistake. Maybe he made the mistake of trying to work alone. Maybe he made the mistake of trying to swim against the currents in the sea. Maybe he made the mistake of trying to push too hard . . . With your complexion, Charley, I think a pink, quite soft, would be nice, for your mouth . . . It is most dangerous, as the poor man found, to make mistakes here."

She said that she had a pink lipstick, crushed pink, quite soft. She made a play at smiling. She felt the sinking dead weight in her stomach. She went back into her bedroom. She sat on the bed and she scratched in her mind for the code call, sat so still until she was certain of it. Her finger was on the button of the watch on her wrist. She wondered who would listen if Axel had quit. She wondered how quickly he would come, come running as Axel had come. She'd find him, one day, afterward, she'd find him and he would give her back her own watch, the gold watch that was her father's present to her, but she would never wear that watch. She would find Axel Moen, somewhere, and he could give her back the gold watch. She would not wear it. She would wear, until the day she died, God help her, the watch of vulgar dulled steel that was cold on her wrist.

She pressed the button. She made the signal.

His legs jerked up.

It was as if a shock charged through his body. The shock was the bleeping pattern of the tone call in Harry Compton's ear. Because the inductor was deep in his ear the pattern of the call seemed to ring in every recess of his skull.

He gulped. He was struggling for concentration. There was a call, simultaneous, for the last passengers for the flight to Milan. The sounds merged . . . They were through into departures. They'd gone through the passport check. 'Vanni Crespo's ID had taken them all through, and the balaclava brigade were behind them. The shops and the bar were on the wrong side of the door, and they were scattered on benches. There were two empty seats between Harry Compton and Axel Moen who sat close to the Italian, and Dwight Smythe was away from them and by the glass floor-to-ceiling windows looking out onto the apron.

"The call—the call went," he stammered.

The Italian jacknifed off the bench and came to him.

"What was the call?"

He was supposed to be a trained operative. He reckoned himself among the best and among the brightest of the young intake into SO6. He reckoned himself shit hot on close-up surveillance and the art of gutting a balance sheet. He squeezed his eyes shut and he tried to find the concentration. He could have said when the flight would leave for Milan, what gate it would board through, and the time it would arrive at Milan . . .

"I'm trying—"

"What was the signal?"

The Italian was close to him, spurting garlic breath and whiskey breath and cigarette breath at him. Harry Compton jabbered, "I'm sorry, I didn't get the pattern, there was so much other . . ."

Dwight Smythe had sidled close and stood awkward, like he didn't know how he should intervene, what he should say. Axel Moen was blank-faced, staring at the ceiling. The Italian had his hands locked onto Harry Compton's head and his fingernail was digging into Harry Compton's ear. The Italian, with his nail, was gouging the damn thing from the ear. It came again.

Harry Compton flung his head back and he pushed the Italian away, and he had the palm of his hand over his ear, and his head sank down between his knees. He heard the second transmission of the signal. He described the rhythm, gave the pattern of the tone call, the pauses, the short blasts and the long blasts that cried inside his skull. The Italian crouched beside him.

"It's Stand-by alert. Holy Mother, she sends the Stand-by alert," 'Vanni Crespo murmured.

Another bleeping between them, and 'Vanni was scrabbling in his pocket.

Axel Moen said, total calmness, "Today he has killed the man who investigated him. He has eliminated a threat to him. Perhaps it is the time of the crowning, the anointing with goddam oil. Perhaps it is the time he gathers his court, his goddam family . . ."

'Vanni Crespo had the mobile phone out of his pocket, had killed the bleep, pressed it at his ear, listened.

". . . If she is going away from the villa, if she is going outside the radius of transmission pickup, if she doesn't know where she is being taken, then she is instructed to send a Stand-by alert. She is instructed to give us time to get there, to Mondello, because to tail her we have to track her."

'Vanni cut his call. "It's from the villa—communications says it's from the villa. We may have very little time."

"I'm with you," Dwight Smythe said. "She is my responsibility."

"Fuck you," Harry Compton hissed. "My orders are to bring her home. If her neck's on the bloody line, I'm there."

"If she calls, I answer. I get to ride with you." Deliberately, Axel Moen pushed up from his seat.

Dwight Smythe snapped, "No way."

Harry Compton snarled, "You're off the pulse, friend."

"It's mine. She doesn't know your fucking names. She calls for me."

"We don't have time," 'Vanni Crespo pleaded. "You argue, you goddam women, you screw her up."

"You don't exist to her, nothing to her."

Harry Compton stood full square in front of Axel Moen. It was the moment he wondered if he would be hit, kicked. "You go nowhere, we don't need you."

Dwight Smythe found courage, jabbed at Axel Moen's chest so that he pitched back into his seat. "Your rock is DEA, you obey orders, otherwise you get washed off the rock."

"I'm obligated, I owe her."

'Vanni Crespo said, soft, "It is only the Stand-by. I promise, if it is Immediate, then I'll be there, I'll care for her like she's mine. Trust me."

Axel Moen sat quite still. He was composed, and he locked his fingers and flexed them.

Dwight Smythe hissed, "You're identified, you've no place with this now."

Harry Compton whipped, "You're just a liability to her, and always have been since you first walked in on her."

Axel Moen dropped his head. The fire was doused.

'Vanni Crespo said, fast, "I need the guys, I can't leave the guys with you. I'm trying to think on my fucking feet. I pulled rank to get the guys. If I leave them, then I have to call up, I have to explain, I have to start telling some bastard about an operation . . . 'Who authorized it? Who do you report to? Wait out, I have to check . . .' I don't have the time."

"It's a public place," Axel Moen said. "I'm comfortable. I sit here, I wait, I get on the plane. So get the hell out."

'Vanni Crespo held Axel's face in his hands. He kissed both his cheeks. Harry Compton nodded at him—he'd understand orders. Dwight Smythe shrugged—he'd appreciate responsibilities.

They were gone. It was eighty-five seconds from the first call. It was sixty-one seconds from the second call. They went out of Departures. Harry Compton looked back once, through the glass, at the back of the head of the man, at the pony-tail of his hair. He thought the man belonged to yesterday, and he hurried to catch the Italian.

Out in the night darkness, they ran toward the cars.

Peppino had the engine started and Angela was beside him and smoothing her dress straight so that she would not crease it. Charley was fastening the harness belts for the children. The gardener, at the bottom of the drive, was scraping open the gates.

She did not know who would be there, whether they would be there. And she did not know if anyone listened . . .

"I'm sorry, I've forgotten something."

No play at hiding his irritation, Peppino snapped, "Please, Charley, already we are late."

"I won't be a second. Can I have the keys, please?"

Angela said, "I am sure it is something important—yes, Charley—or you would not ask."

She was given the keys. She ran back onto the patio and she unlocked the front door. She was out of their sight. She could do it there ... Christ, but she had to bring something back to the car ... She scurried for her room. She pulled open a drawer. On the top of the clothes in the drawer was a small handkerchief. She snatched it up. She stood, and she breathed hard.

She remembered. Not Immediate Alert, and not Stand Down. She remembered the code. She did not know where they listened, or if anyone listened. Her finger wavered again on the button. She pressed hard, drove the back of the watch down on her wrist so that it hurt her. She made the pattern of the code for Stand-by.

She breathed again, deep, to swallow the trembling in her arms. She switched off the light and she locked the patio door behind her, and she went to the car. She was barely into the car when Peppino drove away. She sagged down into the seat and maneuvered the carrycot onto her lap. They drove out through the opened gates. She did not try to look out of the back window to see if they were followed, if anyone had listened. She reached forward and passed the keys of the villa to Peppino. They came out of the narrow street that led to the piazza and swung onto the road that ran along the beach. They passed the Saracen tower ...

"Well, Charley," Peppino asked, cutting, "what had you forgotten?"

She said, felt the feebleness of it, "I'd forgotten my handkerchief."

There was the tinkle of Angela's laughter. "You see, I was right. I said that it would be something important."

"Herb? It's Bill Hammond ... Yes, I'm in the office, I'm in Rome. Herb, would you go to secure ... You OK now? ... The Codename Helen thing, they've just gone to Stand-by ... Yes, it's a hell of scene down there today. He was a good guy, Tardelli, he was the best guy. They don't deserve people like that down there. They hung him out to dry—but that's history ... We got the Stand-by, that's the one below Immediate. I thought you'd want to know ... What? Come again? ... Yes, the procedure's in place. If they get the fat cat, then I send the wings down from Naples, I throw my weight on the extradition business, we go fast track—that's *if* ... Yes, yes, Axel Moen is obeying the order you issued. He's at the airport, Palermo, waiting on his flight ... No, no, didn't seem sore, sounded fine. Dwight and some English jerk with a crowd of Italians are out on the hunt ... I'm kind of excited, Herb, and I wanted to share it . . . Yes, of course, I'll stay in touch. What you got, meetings all afternoon? You Washington people, Herb, you don't strain yourselves— that's meant as a joke . . . You'll hear the moment after I hear, but right now it sounds good . . . Herb, when I call next I may not be on secure. I'm going out to the airport to meet Axel off his flight . . ."

19

No flash overtakings, no hammering on the horn when he was behind a lorry. Peppino drove with caution. He had the power in the big car to go fast. No blinking of the headlights when he was behind a tractor. Peppino didn't talk. Charley thought she read him.

There were soldiers at a checkpoint on the ring road, and more soldiers and another checkpoint at the cramped little town of Altofonte, and after they had weaved through the narrowed streets and bumped on the rough cobbles and then climbed there was a third checkpoint. Each time, as he was waved down by the flashing torch, Peppino lowered the window and produced his documents and was a study in politeness. Each time at the checkpoints she saw the young soldiers and their guns and their drab and ill-fitting uniforms. They made a show of checking the papers and they shone lights around the interior of the car, over Angela's face and the children's and over Charley as she held the carrycot on her lap. She reckoned most of them were not from the island, strangers, as she was. She thought that Peppino drove steadily so that he could be certain he did not attract attention, and he was gracious in his courtesy to the soldiers each time he was gestured forward.

After the third checkpoint, Charley turned and looked back through the rear window and she could see the lights of cars that followed them away, and far in the distance and far below were the patterns of lights that were the city. Peppino had the radio on. The RAI station played solemn music, German classical music, and she thought it would be a mark of sympathy for the magistrate who had been killed. She did not know whether they were followed, and she did not know who might follow. She could not press the button, send the tone signals for the Stand-by alert because she feared that a transmission would interfere with the radio in the car. She must take it on trust that they followed, that someone was close by.

She held the carrycot tightly and the hand of Francesca was on her elbow and gripped it.

She remembered the road.

It was the road along which Benny had driven her. They skirted the lit homes of Piana degli Albanesi where, Benny had told her, a Greek itinerant population had settled five hundred years before. So much going on in her mind but she remembered that bloody useless, bloody irrelevant, morsel of information. The headlights of Peppino's car, and the lights of the cars behind him, wafted on the road bends across tended, rich fields and found the same opaque-colored flowers and the same horses. He meant nothing to her, he had been used, he had been available. She thought that now he would be sitting alone in his small room and writing tracts for his pamphlets, or he would be at a meeting and spewing words. He meant nothing to her because he was ineffective. She sat in the back of the car with the children and she thought that Benny Rizzo was a loser. It was she, Codename Helen, who held the power. They climbed. A few times, not often, the rock outcrops were close enough to the road for her to see the harshness of them. It was what she had come for, it was where she wished to be, it was her story. Once, a car passed them, swerved by them at speed, and she saw the backs of the heads of men in the car . . . She took it on trust that she was followed, that there were men close by, men who would listen.

And Angela knew. Angela who was silent and who sat upright and so still and who gazed unmoving into the cones of glare thrown forward by the headlights, she knew . . . Charley saw the sign for Corleone and the car slowed and the lights caught at a flock of goats that meandered in the road. And Axel Moen had told her that if she aroused serious suspicion then she would be killed—and the men who killed her, afterward, would eat their meal and think nothing of it. She felt the strength flow in her.

At the airport of Punta Raisi . . .

In a door that should have been locked, a key turned.

Along a corridor that should have been lit, a light was switched off.

Outside the door of Departures, in shadow, an officer of the Guardia di Finanze passed his ID card to a man, and was promised that his co-operation would not be forgotten.

In the cockpit of an aircraft, fueled and waiting for passengers to board, a technician reported a malfunction in the avionics and called for a delay of the flight until the fault was repaired.

Axel Moen sat alone, apart from the other passengers, and waited.

One car was up ahead, and one car was close behind the target, and the third car held back.

Harry Compton thought they did it well. It was his training and he didn't find a fault. Three times now the car up ahead of the target and the car tailing the target had exchanged positions. He was in the car that held back. It was plenty of miles since he had last seen, clearly, the target car, been close enough to read the registration, and it was plenty of minutes since he had last seen the tail lights of the target car. 'Vanni Crespo was in the front passenger seat and he had a cable earpiece hooked in, and Harry Compton was in the back with the American.

So calm in the car, unreal.

It was like an exercise, like routine. It was the quiet in the car that unnerved him. They said, back home, he thought it was on his assessment file, that he was good at stress handling. Christ, true shit, he had never known hard stress. Easier if the radio had been blasting, if there had been static howl and frantic shouts, but 'Vanni Crespo had the earpiece hooked in and he would whisper to the driver and sometimes they'd slow and sometimes they'd accelerate, but he was not a part of it and it was unreal. The American shivered beside him. The American had the stress bad. It was the American who pulled Harry Compton back from reckoning that it was all unreal.

There had been nothing, no signal, coming into his head, hitting the curves of his skull. Each kilometer or so, regular as a church clock, 'Vanni Crespo turned and looked back at him and queried with his eyes, and each kilometer he shook his head. Nothing, no signal, and each kilometer or so the American cursed, because he had the stress bad. Must have been another kilometer gone, because 'Vanni Crespo turned and he shook his head again and the American cursed. He laid his hand on the American's and felt the shiver.

"You reckon it's a bum?" the American murmured.

"She's there, she's followed, can't say that—"

"She's not called you up?"

"She's not."

"Why wouldn't she?"

"Don't know, maybe it's not possible. How the hell do I know?"

"I reckon it's a bum."

"If that's what you want to think . . ."

"What I want is a piss."

"Not in my pocket."

There was always one of them, Harry Compton thought, sure as hell there was always one man in a surveillance job or on a tail job who had the stress bad and who needed to jabber. They had only been in position three minutes, all sweating and all tensed up and all on the adrenaline edge, when the gates to the villa drive had been opened and the big car had pulled out. He'd seen her then, in the light thrown by a streetlamp, sat in the back of the big car and looking straight ahead, and he'd seen her chin jutted out like it was set in a way of defiance. His eyes had lingered on her for three, four seconds. He'd thought she'd looked, no lie, just bloody magnificent. There had been a woman in the front, just seen the flash of her, classily dressed. There had been the man driving. It was his talent to be sharp on recognition and the profile of the head had registered, the sighting such a damn long time ago in the hotel restaurant on Portman Square . . . He had seen the woman and the man who drove, but it was the jutting chin of the girl that captured him. They'd made it by three minutes, and the stress had built from that time.

"God, I'd give a heap of my pension for a piss."

Most cruel was the silence in his ear. The inductor piece was a poor fit. All the time he was aware of the pressure of its presence. Harry Compton waited for it to bleep, was dominated by it, and there was only silence. He could not help but think of her, what 'Vanni Crespo had said about her. So boring, her life, so tedious. Her life in the villa, behind the big gates he had seen opened, was a routine of dressing kids, feeding kids, walking kids to school, reading to kids, cleaning kids' rooms, washing kids, putting kids to bed, and waiting . . . He might just, if he ever was posted to an undercover course, stand up, tell the instructor that he talked bullshit, and talk about the miracle of an untrained operative who had survived boredom and tedium.

"Where's this?" There was the hiss in Dwight Smythe's voice.

They were into a queue of cars. There was a road block up ahead and beyond the road block were the lights of a town that fell the length of a hillside.

'Vanni Crespo turned. His face was screwed in concentration, as if the radios were going from the two cars ahead. "It is Corleone."

"What does that mean, 'Vanni?" Harry Compton asked. "What does it tell you?"

"It is their snake pit, it is where they come from. It is where they kill, it is where they are comfortable. It is a time—"

Dwight Smythe shuddered. "I'd give more than all my pension for a piss."

"Would you please be quiet? You distract me. Understand, it is a time and a place of maximum danger to her when she goes with them into their snake pit . . ."

They drove through the lit town.

It was where she had walked with Benny Rizzo.

They drove beside the piazza and then up the narrowing main street. The shops were closed, and the bars were empty and the market had been dismantled for the night. She remembered what Benny Rizzo had told her. Corleone was the place of Navarra and Liggio and Riina, and now it was the place of Mario Ruggerio. They drove where she had walked, and where a trade unionist had walked, but then a gun had been in the trade unionist's back, but then the men of the town had hurried to their homes and locked their doors and shuttered their windows. They drove past the same doors and the same shuttered windows, and past the church, and over the bridge beneath which the torrent of the river fell into a gorge, and it was where the body of the trade unionist had been dumped so deep that the crows would not find it . . . "He was our hero and we let him go. All we had to do, every one of us, was to pick up a single stone from the street, and we could have overwhelmed the man with the gun. We did not pick up a stone, we went home" . . . She felt the weight of her arrogance. It was as if she thought that she alone could pick up the stone from the street. Axel Moen had taught her the arrogance . . . The boy, *piccolo* Mario, was excited, and his father quietened him and told him that the journey was nearly complete. The road climbed out of the town.

There was a junction, there was a road sign to Prizzi, there was the turning to a hotel.

A coach was parked outside the hotel. It was an English touring coach. The coach came from Oxford and had TV and a lavatory at the back. Some of the tourists were still in the coach, wan and tired and beaten faces peering and blinking at the windows as the headlights of Peppino's car caught them. Some of the tourists, those with fight in them, were with the courier and the driver at the steps of the hotel, and the argument raged. Charley heard the protest of the tourists and the shrugged answers of the manager who held the high ground at the top of the steps and who guarded his front door.

"Why can't you help us?"

The hotel was closed.

"We are only looking for a simple meal. Surely . . . ?"

The hotel's dining room was closed.

"It's not our fault, is it, that in this godforsaken place we had a puncture?"

They must find another hotel.

"Is this the way you treat tourists to Sicily, feeding money into your damned economy—show them the door?"

The hotel was closed for a private function.

"Where is there another hotel where we might, just, find a degree of hospitality?"

There were many hotels in Palermo.

It was, for Charley, the confirmation. The hotel was closed for a private function. Peppino had opened the door for his wife, studied manners. Small Mario was out of the car and running, and Francesca was chasing him. Charley lifted the carrycot from the car and the bag. The tourists were sullen and bad tempered and they stamped away with their courier toward the coach in the shadow of the car park. She was the donkey. Charley trailed after the family with the weight of the carrycot and the bag. She was the dog's body, and there was the weight of the watch on her wrist. She did not look round, she did not turn to see whether there were car lights back down the hill. The manager ducked his head in respect to Angela and shook Peppino's hand warmly and he tousled the hair of small Mario and pinched the cheek of Francesca. He ignored the young woman, the donkey, who struggled up the steps with the carrycot and the bag. He'd bloody learn. They'd all bloody learn, before the night was finished . . . He ignored Charley but he made a remark about the baby in the carrycot, spoke of the beauty of the sleeping baby.

They went through the lobby of the hotel.

There were three men in the lobby, young and wearing good suits, with neatly cut hair, and they had their hands held across their groins. They watched. They did not move forward, they did not come to help her, they watched her. There was no receptionist at the desk in the lobby. Charley saw the precise lines of room keys, perhaps fifty keys. The hotel, of course, was closed for a private party . . . She was the horse made of wood, she was trundled through the gates on rollers, she was Codename Helen, she was the point of access . . . The manager ushered Angela and Peppino and the children, oiling respect, across the lobby toward the dining room door. He knocked. An older man opened the door and there was a smile of welcome. It came very sharp to her, to Charley, the thought of what Axel Moen had said. The older man had a hard and bitter face that the smile did not mask, and the smile had gone and the older man had seen her. "If you arouse serious suspicion they will kill you and then eat their dinner, and think nothing of it . . ." She listened.

"Who is she?"

"She is, Franco, the *bambinaia* of our children."

She heard the exchange between Peppino and the man, anger meeting hostility.

"I was not told she was coming."

"It is a party for the family, perhaps why you were not told."

"I am responsible. There is no place laid for her."

"Then, make a place for her. She was cleared. She has been investigated to the satisfaction of my brother."

Her thoughts were a fast jumble. In the street, knocked down. In the photograph, a boy dead beside a motorcycle. Her bag snatched from her. A boy from the tower blocks dead and with his mother grieving over him. Her handbag returned by Peppino. She stood, she waited, she played the dumb innocence of ignorance. The man, Franco, gazed at her, then stood aside and she followed the family into the dining room.

It was a long and narrow room. There was a single table in the center of the room. There were fifteen places laid at the table, the best glasses and the best crockery and the best cutlery, and there were flowers. At the side of the room was a long buffet table with hot plates and with mixed salads.

She stood inside the door. She had no place there. She was there because Angela had made the battleground for her. Angela knew . . . What depth of viciousness, what pit of vengeance, what total hatred. Angela knew . . . Angela walked the length of the table, serene, a queen. Charley put the carrycot on the floor and she kneeled beside it, and she could see Angela walk toward the family at the far end of the dining room. She understood why Angela had dressed her best, why she had worn her most precious jewelry. The family were peasants. Angela brushed the cheek of her mother-in-law with her lips, the barest gesture. She let her father-in-law peck at her face, only once. There was the grinning Carmelo, big and awkward and constrained in an old suit, and she held his hands and made a show of kissing him. There was the sister, gaunt and with her dress hanging on bony shoulders. Another woman stood behind the parents of Mario Ruggerio, and Angela went to her and held her momentarily, and the woman had a teenage boy and a teenage girl with her. The woman's eyes flitted nervously and she tugged at the waist of her dress as if not comfortable in it and the teenage boy had a sullen face and the girl was dumpy with puppy fat. Charley watched. She busied herself at the carrycot, and she watched as Angela greeted each of them. And she saw that each of them gestured toward her or glanced at her, as if they queried her presence, as if they checked who she was.

Peppino was beside her.

Peppino asked, considerate, "You have everything you need?"

"I'll have to heat the baby's bottle. Evening feed."

"You will amuse the children if they are bored?"

"They seem pretty excited," Charley said.

"It is a family party, Charley."

"You won't notice me."

"Would you like a drink, anything?"

Charley grimaced. "Not while I'm working. Don't worry about me, just have a lovely evening."

They did notice her. They noticed her as if she were a wasp at a tea table, as if she were a mosquito in a bedroom. They noticed her and they asked. The man, Franco, looked at her and his eyes had the coldness of suspicion. She made the baby comfortable. She did not know where they were, nor if they listened . . .

The voice was from behind him.

"*Signore,* I do apologize for disturbing you . . ."

He turned, reflex. The card, for a moment, was held in the palm of a hand. He saw the flash of the photograph on the card, he read the words in heavy print "*Guardia di Finanze,*" and he saw the emblem.

"There is a telephone call for you. I was asked to be discreet. You should take the call in a place of privacy. Please, could you follow me?"

He pushed himself up. He trailed after the man. The man was heavily built with wet, sleeked black hair and a waddling walk. Axel Moen was led to a door in the shadowed extremity of the departure lounge. On the door was a "No Entry" sign. The loudspeakers were calling the flight for Rome.

"I am sure it will only take a moment—you will not miss your flight."

The man smiled. His hand was on the door, and he stood aside so that Axel Moen would go first. He opened the door. The darkness gaped at Axel Moen, and the weight of the man bullocked him through and into the corridor. The door slammed behind him, the blackness was around him. The startled shout, "Oh, Christ, shit," spinning, clawing at the man. The blow hit him. He sagged. He fought for his life. He had no weapon, not a pistol and not knife and not a baton. In the darkness, blows and kicks hammering him, hands and fists dragging on him, he thought there were four men. To protect his life, biting, scratching, kneeing . . . There was a gag in his mouth, pulled tighter, and he could not scream. No help would come, no light would flood the darkness of the corridor. Alone,

Axel Moen fought dirty for his life, and there were four of them who tried to take it, precious, from him.

Dwight Smythe urinated noisily into a scrub bush.

Harry Compton bit at his lip.

'Vanni Crespo had the guys around him. Took Harry Compton back to his youth, when he played sports, when the team came together before the first whistle and the arms were around the shoulders and they hugged for strength, took him too far back. Like 'Vanni Crespo was the captain of a team and talked the final tactics . . . They were parked down the road from the hotel, difficult to be certain in the darkness but he reckoned they were a clear four hundred meters from the lights of the hotel. Dwight Smythe blundered to Harry Compton's side and was pulling up the zipper.

"What do we do?"

Harry Compton snapped, "We close our bloody mouths. We wait till we're told what to do."

"Where is she?"

"We'll be told."

"Ever thought of taking up medicine? It's a wonderful bedside manner you have."

Harry Compton watched. The men broke from 'Vanni Crespo. Going for the first whistle of the game, lining up the positions . . . checking radios, arming the weapons, sliding the masks down over their faces, loading the gas canisters into satchels. They were off the road, up a track and round a corner from the road, and the town of Corleone was below them, and the hotel was above them. He needed to say it . . . There were six men who had broken from the huddle with 'Vanni Crespo, and two had flaked away into the darkness toward the hotel on the left of the road, and two had waited for the headlights of a car to pass and then crossed the empty road to go toward the hotel on the right of it, and the last two had gone to one of the cars and eased the doors silently open and sat inside, and there was the glow of their cigarettes . . . He needed to say it, as if to clean himself.

"There's something, 'Vanni, that I have to tell."

"Is it important?"

"Not important to anyone but me."

"Can it keep?"

"What I have to say . . . I am a boring little fucker. I am a small town policeman. I am out of my depth. I interfered, and I did not know what I was putting my nose into. I thought I was clever, I thought it right at the time, and I blew the smooth running of your operation out of the water. I thought she was pressured, an innocent, and I started a ball going down a hill. When I realized the stakes, when I learned about her, then it was too late to stop the ball going down the hill. I feel a guilt. I apologize."

He couldn't see, in the darkness, 'Vanni Crespo's face. He heard the voice, cold with dislike. "Don't apologize to me. Keep it for him. He backed off rather than argue with you. To argue was to lose time. You thought of your status, he thought of his agent. Go find Axel Moen after this and make your apologies."

She had been to the buffet.

She had held the plates for small Mario and for Francesca, and let them choose, and put the squid and the salad and the shrimps and the salami slices and the olives on their plates. She had gone back to the table, and she had cut the squid pieces smaller and knifed through the salad for small Mario, lazy little bastard. She had cut everything on the plate of Francesca. She had poured water from the bottle for the children.

She had the last place at the table.

At the far end of the table, at the head of the table, was the empty chair.

On the far side of the table, at the far end, was the woman with the nervous eyes who was not comfortable in her dress. Charley had not been introduced, not to any of them, but then she was only the donkey. Next to the empty chair was a place of honor—she would be his wife. She had broad, working hands, her stomach bulged in the dress. She toyed with the squid and she picked up the prawns with her fingers, did not shell them, crunched them in her mouth.

Then Agata Ruggerio, the matriarch of the family, who scowled, and Charley thought her complaint was that she was dispossessed from the chair taken by the wife, frowned because she would not sit beside her eldest son. Then Peppino who talked dutifully with his mother.

Next on that side was the sister. When the wine was passed round, pointedly it was carried past the sister. Her face was yellowed, her fingers shook and food fell from her fork. An empty chair was beside the sister, Maria. Then the teenage boy with the sullen face, then Francesca. The boy made a remark to her and Charley pretended that she did not understand. The remark was in the dialect of the Sicilian countryside. She knew he wanted the oil for the salad passed to him, but she pretended that she did not understand him. She let small Mario, next to her, pass the brat the oil. She wondered what was his life and what would be his future, the teenage boy who was the son of her target. She wondered whether he was already addicted to the power of his father, or whether he could walk away from that power and make a different life. She wondered if he would ever hold hands with children and dance around his father . . .

Beyond small Mario, on Charley's side of the table, was the teenage girl, self-conscious with her weight but scooping food into her mouth, then an empty place, then Franco . . . Franco watched her. Each move she made was watched by Franco. He had small fine hands with pared nails. She would have shivered if the hands of Franco had touched her . . . Next was Carmelo, the simple brother, who lived with his aging parents, and then there was Angela . . . Angela was politeness. Angela was beautiful. Angela was the crowned queen. Angela played a part as much as Charley played a part. Angela asked after Rosario's health, talked with the old *contadino* beside her as if his health mattered to her, and talked about the rabbits that he bred as if his rabbits were important to her. Next to Rosario, at the head of the table was the empty chair . . . She had gained access, she was the little dog's body, she had power over all of them . . .

"Are you not going to eat, Charley?"

She was far away. She had won the access, had taken the power, she was with Axel Moen on the cliff and by the river and in the cathedral . . .

"What? Sorry . . ."

Small Mario pulled a face at her, like she was a cretin. "Are you not going to eat?"

Franco watched her. His gaze lanced her. Too wrapped in her own thoughts. To think of Axel Moen was a mistake, to make a mistake was to invite suspicion. She stood. There was a murmur of conversation along the length of the table. She went to the buffet counter. God, how long, how bloody long . . . ? She must eat, not to eat was to make a mistake. There was a ripple of applause behind her. She did not turn. She smelled the tang of the smoke from a small cigar. There was a shout of congratulation behind her, and the hammering of cutlery on the table. She did not turn. There was a growl from an old throat, Rosario's throat, of pleasure. She put squid on her plate and salad and sliced ham. She turned to go back to her chair. The plate shook in her hand. She could not control the shake of her hand. Her plate clattered down onto the table, and he looked at her, as if then he noticed her.

He was at the far end of the table.

He was bent over his mother. His opened fist rested on his mother's shoulder, and he looked down the length of the table to her. For a moment there was a frown. She saw Peppino's lips move, did not hear what he said, what Peppino explained. Charley sat. There was another man, and she heard the name Tano used by Franco, and there was a sour spark between them. At the buffet counter, behind her, was the presence of Tano, and the lotion scent of his body. The plate of food was in front of her, and she did not dare to eat because she did not think she would be able to control her knife and her fork. He left his mother and he went to his wife. There was a grim sadness in the wife's face, and a steadfastness, and she offered her cheek to him. He kissed his wife's cheek. He went to the teenage girl and to the teenage boy and they kissed him with formality, as if they kissed a stranger. He went to his place at the head of the table, and in the silence Tano laid a filled plate in front of him. He looked around him. The silence cut the room. Tano filled his glass. He drank from the glass, he banged the glass down onto the table. He shouted . . .

"*Piccolo* Mario—come to your uncle."

The big smile played on his face. The room exploded with laughter. The little boy catapulted from his chair and ran the length of the table and jumped onto Mario Ruggerio's lap. He started to eat, spearing his food with his fork, fondling the child. Tano spoke to Franco, pointed to her, and Franco shrugged and gestured toward Peppino. She saw the brittle smile on Angela's face as her child was touched. The talk bayed around her.

There was a magnetism about the eyes of the man.

She thought the presence of the man was all in the eyes.

They were wide, deep-set eyes that were clear blue in coloring. There was a tiredness in the bulged flesh under the eyes, but the eyes glistened with alert life.

The eyes roved over the table. The eyes caught Charley. If she had had her knife in her hand she would have dropped it. She was a pheasant in a car's lights. She was a mouse that a stoat closed on. When the eyes caught hers, Charley looked away.

He terrified her.

Such a small man, except for the eyes. Such an ordinary man, except for the eyes . . .

The baby cried.

He wore a well-cut suit and a white shirt and a simple tie of deep green.

The baby's scream grew.

Eating, he made a play of one handed boxing with small Mario, and the child squealed in happiness, and there was soft sentiment at the mouth of Mario Ruggerio, not in the darting eyes . . .

The baby howled.

Charley did not know whether she could stand, whether she could walk. The fear held her. Angela looked at her, flicked her fingers and pointed to the carrycot. Peppino looked at her, savage, and gestured to the baby. She pushed herself up. She steadied herself against the table . . .

She did not know whether they listened, whether they were close by . . .
He was so small and he was so ordinary and his face was pasty, dull, and
the hands that played with the child were roughened. She staggered to
the carrycot. She kneeled. She lifted out the baby. She held the baby. She
picked up the bag with the baby's feed. She went, sleep-walked, toward
the door to the kitchen.

"Please . . ."

She stopped.

The voice was tires on gravel. "Please may I see my nephew?"

He whispered in the little boy's ear. Small Mario slipped from his knee.
The boy had the sulky look of a rejected lap-dog.

The voice was waves on shingle. "Please bring my nephew to me."

She walked toward him. She was dazed. The steps were automatic, ro-
botic. His eyes never left her. She trembled as she moved closer to him.
She went past Francesca and past the teenage girl, past the empty chair,
past Maria and Peppino and Agata Ruggerio. She held the baby tight
against her body, and the baby was quiet. His eyes never wavered from
hers, she was mesmerized by his eyes, clear blue. She was close to him.
She smelled the stale scent of the cigars. He held out his arms, and she
went past his wife. He reached out with his arms. The big hands brushed
against her arms and he took the baby Mauro. He smiled. There was a
titter of appreciation around the table. He smiled an aged gentleness. The
softness came to the old face, the lines of his face cracked in pleasure. What
she noticed, he held the baby but his eyes never left hers.

"And you are the English *bambinaia?* You are Carlotta?"

"They call me Charley, that's my English name."

"You are very welcome at our small celebration. We are not used in
our family to a person such as yourself, but Angela brings to our family
new horizons. Angela is the first of our family to have required a *bambinaia*. But we are humble people and my mother did not have the money
for someone to come into the midst of her home to look after her children. My wife, she has reared our son and our daughter, she has been able
to do that without paid help in her house. But Peppino is a great success
and we are all proud of his success. We measure the degree of his success
that he can afford a *bambinaia* to help Angela with her children."

The head of the baby was thrown back and the baby screamed piercing.

"Why does the baby cry?"

"For his feed, it's the time for his feed," Charley said. The big hand, so
carefully, brushed the fine hair on the baby's head. Charley did not dare
to look at Angela. The broad fingers made little loving patterns on the
baby's scalp.

"Then you should do your work, you should feed my nephew."

She saw the power of the hands and the fingers. They held the baby and passed the baby back to Charley. The eyes gazed into her face, as if they stripped her, as if they searched for the lie. If she could have run, she would have. She was stunned. She walked dreaming toward the push doors of the kitchen. He had killed the father of Benny Rizzo, and he had sat *piccolo* Mario on his knee. He had climbed to power and killed a man from Agrigento, and he had played the sweet uncle with *piccolo* Mario. He had had her attacked and robbed so that her bag could be searched and he had killed the thief, and he had reached with loving arms for the baby Mauro . . . She backed into the push doors of the kitchen . . . He had bombed a car that morning and killed a magistrate and two of the magistrate's bodyguards, and he had brushed his fingers on the soft hair of baby Mauro . . . She stood inside the kitchen, she gasped for breath . . . He was an evil, heartless bastard, Axel Moen had said it. He had fought for power with the delicacy of rats in a bucket, Axel Moen had said it. He sat a child on his knee and he stroked the hair of a baby . . . Where the fuck was Axel Moen? . . . Until the men stood, she had thought the kitchen was empty. They were by the outer door of the kitchen, and one had been on a stool and one had been on a chair. She walked toward them.

"Hold the baby, please," Charley said. "And would you, please, heat a saucepan of water?"

They were young, they were dressed in suits of charcoal-gray. They were neat and scrubbed clean. She put down the bag on the far side of the central shining-steel work area. She walked boldly—Christ, it was a lie—round the work area. One, smaller and shorter and more powerful, hesitated and then clattered his machine pistol down on his chair, and he had the awkwardness of a man who does not hold babies. She went to him, she gave him the baby Mauro to hold. She faced the second man.

"A saucepan of water, please, heated. It is for his nephew." The second man slid a pistol into his trousers' waist and looked around him, looked for a saucepan.

She went back to the bag. No staff, of course. The food prepared, the food left, no witnesses to the gathering of the Ruggerio family. She understood why it was possible for Angela to have demanded her presence, nothing of substance would be said in front of Carmelo who was simple and Maria who was an alcoholic. The shorter man cooed at the baby, the second man searched cupboards for a saucepan. She slipped to her knees. She put the baby's bottle on the work surface, where they would see it. She had regained the calm. The pattern of the code was in her mind. She heard water surge into a saucepan. The one who held the baby was coming closer to her, as if to watch her. Her hands were in the bag. She felt the button on the watch on her wrist. She made the rhythm of the call.

She heard the second man put the saucepan down on a burner, and the shorter man was closer to her. There was laughter behind her, through the push doors. She made the call again, of the pulse tone for Immediate Alert. The shorter man looked over the top of the work surface, and Charley lifted a clean nappy from the bag . . .

She did not know if anyone listened, if anyone was near.

"You are certain?"

"The first time was three long tones, three short tones, that's—"

"That's Immediate Alert."

"Repeated, three long, three short—"

"Then we go."

They ran to the cars. For a moment 'Vanni Crespo was bent at the window and talking urgently to the hooded *carabinieri* men, then he split from them. He was breathing hard. He turned the ignition, stamped the clutch and then the accelerator.

'Vanni Crespo drove smoothly. He was up against the bumper of the other car, no lights. Harry Compton was beside him. He felt a desperate and sickening loneliness. He had made his confession and tried to purge himself, and he had failed. The vomit was in his throat. She was the girl with the mischief in her face, the girl who posed in her graduation gear. 'Vanni Crespo had said she was in the snake pit. He was passed a pistol, Axel Moen's gun. He could have said, truth, that he was not firearms trained. He could have said, honest, that it would be catastrophe if he were involved in a shooting in Sicily. He took it. The American whimpered behind him . . . There would be two men going through the kitchen and two men going through the ground-floor fire exit, co-ordinated on 'Vanni Crespo's radio, and they would go through the front bloody door . . . There was truth, honesty, in the American's whimper. So frightened, but he had responsibility for her, he had to go through the front door, and he couldn't chicken out of the responsibility.

They drove up the road toward the hotel, no lights.

'Vanni Crespo murmured. "Don't look at her. Don't acknowledge her, or you kill her . . . if we are not already too slow."

Harry Compton was sick over his trousers, over the pistol.

With her backside, Charley forced the push doors open. The baby was quiet. She held the baby against her. There had been an empty chair, and the chair was now taken. He had wet, sleeked black hair, and she thought the man had just washed, and the fatness of his face was flushed, and the eye that she could see was reddened and closed. He held a handkerchief to the cheek that she could not see. The doors swung shut behind her. Angela looked at her, and the wife and Maria and Franco, brief glances. Mario Ruggerio held court. They were absorbed by his story. She did not understand the story because she had not heard the start of it, but the laughter rippled as if on cue when he paused, when he coughed on the smoke of his cigar, when he spat phlegm into his napkin. Rosario and Agata, Carmelo and Franco and Peppino did not look at her, but hung on the story of Mario Ruggerio. She walked quietly behind them, the length of the table. The man with the sleeked hair, the man who had come late, stared at her. The eyes of the man with the sleeked hair followed her, and he swiveled his head, and there was first the puzzlement, and then the confusion, and then—Charley saw it—the dawning of the recognition. He scraped his chair back on the tiled floor, he rose from his chair. He went, rolling on his hips, past Maria and Peppino, past Agata and the wife . . .

Charley was laying the baby in the carrycot.

The story of Mario Ruggerio was at a peak. They were rapt. His evening, his gathering, his celebration for the family. And his eyes flashed anger and she thought the man with the sleeked hair wilted. But the interruption was made, the story was destroyed. The eyes of Mario Ruggerio, that had glistened like warmed milk when the child had sat on his knee and when the baby was held on his lap, blazed. She saw the shiver of the man.

"Yes, Carmine? What, Carmine?"

His hand, gripping the handkerchief, came away from his cheek. His cheek was a web of weeping nail lines, scratches. The handkerchief, bloodred on white, jabbed at her. The fist that held the handkerchief pointed to her. He stammered, "In the cathedral, when the American was in the cathedral, she was there . . . I saw her . . . She was in the cathedral, she was close to the American . . . I saw her . . ."

It was a little moment of death. She heard the denunciation. It was a moment of serious suspicion. They had not yet finished their meal. They had eaten the salad and fish buffet. They had taken the pasta from the hot plates. There was meat on the hot plates and there were fruit bowls. Axel Moen had said they would kill her, and then eat their meal, and think nothing of it. He gazed the length of the table at her and his eyes, clear blue, squinted at her, and she saw the suspicion growing.

"Come here." A rasped command. "Come."

Only the children did not understand. She walked slowly past the faces, she saw in the faces hostility and hatred. Angela looked straight ahead, Angela alone was impassive. She walked toward him. She would say that the American had spoken to her, yes. She would say that she had joined a tour of the cathedral and that the American had been beside her, yes. She would say that the American had pestered her, yes . . .

They would know she lied. She would not be able to hold the lie against the clear blue eyes.

She walked past the meat in the dishes on the hot plates and past the bowls of fruit. She was drawn to him. She could not help herself but go to him, moth to a light. His hand reached for her. He took her wrist. The strength of his hand closed over her wrist and the watch of dull steel.

She would not be able to maintain the lie.

The two men in the lobby were covered by guns. The manager stood and faced the wall and held his hands high.

"Do we come with you?" the American murmured.

"It is not necessary," 'Vanni said.

He had the report on his radio from the kitchen area, two men disarmed. In the car park was a driver lying on the tarmacadam with his wrists handcuffed behind his back. He would go himself, it was his own business. He would have taken Axel Moen . . . He felt, then, a great tiredness, there was no elation and there was no pride. He took his ID from his pocket and slipped his pistol into his belt. He pushed open the door to the dining room.

He heard her voice, strong. "There was an American, yes, pestering me, yes, I told him to get lost, yes . . ."

He walked briskly alongside the table and he held up his ID card.

There would be no resistance, not from the family gathering, because to resist was to throw away the dignity that was most precious. It was a good likeness, the computer enhanced photograph of Mario Ruggerio was close to the reality of the man who now let slip the wrist of the young woman . . . They were all the same when they were confronted. They were all passive. If the bastard had swung from his chair and dived toward the kitchen door, then it would have made for a moment of excitement. None of the bastards did, ever. He was so ordinary, old and weary and ordinary. That night in Palermo there were seven thousand troops deployed to find him, five thousand policemen hunted him, the agents of the ROS and the DIA and the *Guardia di Finanze* and the *squadra mobile* searched for him, and he was so fucking ordinary. He would crave respect, he would want to go with his dignity, as all of the bastards did. No handcuffs, because he should not be humiliated in the presence of his family. No guns, because he should not be humiliated in the sight of the children. He had let slip the young woman's hand and she backed away from him. He would ask for a moment of time with his wife and his children, and 'Vanni would give it him. In the car park, out of sight of those he loved, he would offer his wrists for the handcuffs, as all the bastards did.

Just an ordinary old man, a peasant, and he peered up at the ID card held in front of him, and satisfied himself.

'Vanni did not look at the young woman. To recognize her would be to kill her.

"Herb, it's Bill Hammond here. I'm not on secure. Herb, we scored. We got the fat cat, the kid took us to him. Actually, it was you that scored, Herb, because you authorized it . . . Nice of you to say that, Herb. No, I'm at the airport. Too right, I'll be getting straight down to the Justice people, get them out of bed, bet your life, get them off the nest . . . Yes, Dwight was right there, on the ground, it was him that called me, he was integral to the liaison, he did well . . . No, that's my problem, Axel Moen's not with me . . . I don't know what the fuck's happened, but he didn't get the flight . . . You ever been here, Herb? You ever tried to raise sense out of Palermo when the last flight's gone? . . . OK, he's a big boy, but I just don't understand why he wasn't on the flight . . . That's right, Herb, it was his kid that pulled it."

EPILOGUE

SHE SAW, AS SHE RODE HER scooter down the slope of the lane, the Jeep that was parked outside the bungalow.

They'd all have seen it, and the curtains would have twitched, and they'd have peered through half-open doors. At least, now, they didn't have the detectives to talk about, at least the detectives and their guns had gone from the bungalow's garage. The light was slipping. The clocks would change the next weekend, and then she would be riding home in total darkness. She was home later than usual because the last night's gale had blown the golden autumn leaves onto the lane and that morning's rain had greased the leaves, and the scooter wasn't stable when the lane was coated with wet leaves. She'd gone slowly. She turned off the lane and into the driveway in front of the closed garage doors—the detectives had made their base in the garage for the three months that they had guarded the bungalow, but they had been gone five weeks and the garage had been returned to her father for his car—she took off her helmet and shook her hair free, and lifted out of the panniers the schoolbooks that she would mark that evening. She remembered him. The big, black-skinned American had been in the lobby of the hotel as she had left with Angela and the children, but that was a long time ago, and it was autumn now.

He slammed his door shut, and he came toward her, and he held an envelope in his hand.

"Miss Parsons? I'm Dwight Smythe, from the embassy."

She said that she knew who he was.

"This is kind of embarrassing. You know, when you mislay something, it's sort of upsetting. You've a lot on your mind. It went into a drawer, meant to deal with it, didn't. I go back to Washington tomorrow and I was turning out my desk, and I found it. Well . . ."

What had he found?

He bit at his lip. He handed her the envelope. Her name was written on it. She tore it open and the watch fell from it. She had wondered where the watch was, why it had not been returned, and she had told her father when she came home that she had lost the gold watch. He shifted, one foot to the other. The watch had stopped, but it was more than six months since he had taken it from her wrist. She put it on. She had to stretch the strap of it so that it would fit high on her wrist above the big watch.

"He gave it me. I was to pass it to you. I feel pretty inadequate . . ."

She took the letter from the envelope. The gulls were screaming down on the stone beach. She read.

Dear Miss Parsons,

I take the chance, late, to express my feelings on what you have given us.

I don't have much time and in a few minutes I am being taken to the airport to quit on you, and I am afraid that even in better times I am a poor correspondent.

I have never had the chance to tell you how very sincerely I admired your response to my request for help. I don't apologize for that request.

"It's unfortunate that you weren't told. I guess the idea was that you should be left alone. It was for your own safety. The decision was made up high that we shouldn't talk with you, bad enough for you having police here. I hear they've been called off. I can't justify it, you not being told, but the decision was to let you get back to your life."

What was unfortunate?

He seemed to her to squirm. He wore a good coat, a city man's coat, and it would not be the cold that made him shiver. She had never asked questions, she had come home, she had argued for her job and won the argument. She had never talked, not even to her mother, of the Palermo spring. She had never spoken, not a single word, to the detectives who had come each night to her father's garage.

"We were at the airport when your first call came through. We left him there. I mean, it wasn't our problem. You were the problem. He was the second priority, after you."

Where was he now? What was his posting?
She read on.

> That I was brutish and rude to you, that I was a bully
> to you, is not anything that I am sorry for. In my judg-
> ment it was necessary to give you strength for the ordeal
> of living a lie with that family. That the strength you
> showed, the courage, went to waste is a matter of deep
> personal disappointment to me, you deserved better of us.

"He never made the flight. What we found out afterwards, a guy spoke
to him at the airport. He was through in Departures. There was another
passenger, heard something about a telephone call for him. He followed
this guy out of Departures, going to take his call. He's not been seen again.
I wouldn't want you to think that we haven't tried. We have moved
mountains to get a lead on what happened to him. He went off the face
of the earth. We all feel bad about it. In the Administration we take pride
that we look after our people. It's the way, down in Sicily, people disappear like they never existed, and you run into silence like it's a wall."

Evidence—hadn't there been evidence to show the fate of Axel Moen?

> You should know, because in a short time you will be
> safe and at home, the reality of what was asked of you.
> The Drug Enforcement Administration competes for
> federal funding. It was considered necessary to register a
> high-profile success in Washington, that way the funding
> goes up. The budget rules. Out of success comes further
> funding. In that respect, you were used, but that is the way
> of the world. If it had been possible to capture Mario
> Ruggerio, fly him to the States, indict him, convict him,
> lock him away, then the DEA's budget would have ben-
> efited. I don't apologize.

"What we know, there was a hell of a fight in a closed corridor at the
airport. Two jerks were picked up in a routine road block late that night,
they'd hired a taxi from the airport to a hospital when they were lifted.
One had pretty severe testicular damage and the other was hemorrhag-
ing bad in the stomach. Then there was the affiliate of Ruggerio who
came late to the meal, had the closed eye and the face scratches. They
were all focused on. They look at the floor or the ceiling, they don't talk.
We think he fought to survive, and he lost. There was a *carabiniere* officer,

the one who reached you, the one who worked with him, who took it hard and personal. He bounced them round the cells a bit, more than he should have, but the silence held. About a month ago they transferred the officer out, went up north, and the thing sort of lost steam. We just don't know."

What had happened to Mario Ruggerio?

> Nor do I apologize for using you, someone who has no professional training. I don't want to preach, and most certainly I do not wish to sound like a crusader. This is not work that can be sustained by salaries. The matter of organized crime is too important to the survival of our societies. The prosecution of organized crime cannot be left only to paid agencies. The people have to stand their corner. Simple people, people off the street, people who live next door, they have to stand and they have to be counted. People like you, Miss Parsons.

"It didn't work out as we'd hoped. You should have been told, of course you should. I don't suppose it made the papers here, but then it's kind of routine, isn't it? It was because a magistrate had been killed, the Italians wanted to hang onto him. We pushed for the extradition but our charges weren't in the same league as the murder of a magistrate. We let it drop. It was a good result for us, we were only short of the cream . . . The one downside, the Italians couldn't indict the brother, the banker. He had to walk free. You win some and you lose some. Actually the Brits lost as well, I heard afterwards—the brother had a money-washing scam at this end, but they couldn't produce evidence that would have satisfied a court. Because Ruggerio's brother walked free the decision was taken to cut off contact with you. We did something quite clever. My suggestion, actually. We had a word slipped into their net that one of the affiliates was the leakage point, just dropped the word, and that jerk had an accident in jail, fell down some steps, fell a long way. It seems there are ways down there that messages can be sent. When a guy of the status of Ruggerio is lifted there's going to be a hell of a serious inquest in the organization, and when the answer to the inquest shows up then the organization goes looking for blood. We had the word sent that the affiliate, and we named him, had given the *carabinieri* the location where Ruggerio would be. It wasn't playing clean, but we don't lose sleep over that, it had a purpose. It was making a shield for you because we felt responsible."

Would he go on searching for Axel Moen?

> I have to tell you, and it is the one area that hurts me,
> in itself the capture of Mario Ruggerio would make only
> a small difference in this war. If we had taken him, then
> he would have been replaced. If we had locked him up,
> then another would have filled his shoes. But it is neces-
> sary to fight them. If the simple people don't fight them
> then they have won. If they win, we have betrayed a gen-
> eration not yet born.

"Not me—I'm not in that sort of scene. I'm going back to Washington for budget analysis. We have a powerful amount of computer soft-
ware going in and my new job is to oversee the costings. No disrespect,
but that's the way forward. What you were asked to do was just Stone
Age, it's computers that are going to bury these people. Sorry, Moen isn't
forgotten, it's that fewer work hours are devoted to it. He treated you
badly. You should put him out of your mind. We ran a study on the operation, of course. He may be in concrete, he may have gone into acid
and been flushed down a sewer, he may have been weighted down and
gone into the bay, but he knew what he had gotten himself into. He knew
the dangers. But, he had no call to involve you, that was wrong. There's
a tighter rein on Rome now. You know how it all started? Of course, you
don't. You should know. Last December, the week before Christmas, there
was a traffic accident in Palermo, a minor shunt. A uniformed low-grade
cop took the details. Held up in the queue behind the shunt was a *carabiniere* officer, an undercover man. The shunt involved a Seven series
BMW—it's always amusing when a big BMW gets a shunt. The officer
listened, and he heard the name of Giuseppe Ruggerio, and he knew that
name. It was that much of a chance. He dug, he made the link with the
name. Hear me, there's a bagful of agencies that would have been interested to know that Giuseppe Ruggerio was living in Palermo, but he
didn't share. He went his own way, he came to us, to Axel Moen. The
carabiniere officer should have shared you, and did not. We should have
shared you, and did not. You were just part of a selfish little game, you
were a figure that was moved across a board. It shouldn't have been asked
of you. Maybe you don't want to hear that, it's not your problem. What
you *should* think, it was a good result."

Would he leave her? Would he, please, get the fuck out?

> That's heavy sort of writing, Miss Parsons, but it is what I
> believe. I thank you for your courage. I value what you gave

me, more than you can understand. I wish you well in your future.

May your God watch over you.

Faithfully,
Axel Moen

"I appreciate you feel sore, us losing your letter. That's a very pretty watch. You should trash the other one, put it all behind you. You got the check?"

The check had reached her, had been cleared, was in her account.

"You shouldn't take offense at the time it took. You were very patient. The problem with any sort of money order that comes out of federal funds—well, you know how things are. Has to go through a jungle of committees, and there's a joker on each of them who wants to have his say. If it's not impertinent, what are you going to do with the money?"

She was starting next week at Edinburgh University. She was joining the law school. The teaching was just to fill in the time, relief work. She had chosen Edinburgh because it was about as far from the south Devon coast as she could get. The course was for four years, commercial law. It was not impertinent of him to ask—she thought that a course in commercial law would open doors for her, provide good opportunities. Would he, please, pass her thanks to the committees who had authorized the payment to her?

"That's if you don't mind my saying so, a very positive step. I don't think there's anything more. Good evening, miss."

She watched him drive into the distance and the lights of the Jeep speared up the hill of the lane.

She left her schoolbooks on the front door step, under the porch.

She rode her scooter away from the bungalow. She took the coast route. The night was close around her.

She went to the place above the cliffs. She could not see in the darkness if the peregrine perched on its rock. She heard the crash of the waves below her . . . He had come back to her. The children made a circle and held hands and they danced around an old man with clear blue eyes. He was with her. The children danced faster and the old man spun with them until he fell. She had no more need for the power he had given her, nor for the story he had made for her, nor for the lie he had fashioned for her. He watched her and he willed her to do it. Charley took the watch from her wrist, felt the cold weight of it . . .

He was there, he listened, he waited.

She threw the watch, with her love, into the night, into the emptiness beyond the cliff, into the void above the sea.